A Winter's Wish for the Tram Girls

Lynn Johnson left school with no qualifications. With determination and hard work, she ended her career as a Human Resources Manager with a large County Council. Born and raised in Stoke-on-Trent, she now lives in Orkney with her husband and six cats. Lynn is a member of the Romantic Novelists Association.

Also by Lynn Johnson

The Potteries Girls

The Girl from the Workhouse
Wartime with the Tram Girls
The Potteries Girls on the Home Front
A New Day at Paradise Pottery
Heartache For The Tram Girls
A Winter's Wish for the Tram Girls

LYNN JOHNSON

A Winter's Wish *for the* Tram Girls

canelo
HERA

First published in the United Kingdom in 2026 by

Hera Books, an imprint of
Canelo Digital Publishing Limited,
20 Vauxhall Bridge Road,
London SW1V 2SA
United Kingdom

A Penguin Random House Company
The authorised representative in the EEA is Dorling Kindersley Verlag GmbH. Arnulfstr. 124, 80636 Munich, Germany

A CIP catalogue record for this book is available from the British Library.

ISBN 978 1 83598 116 0

This book is a work of fiction. Names, characters, businesses, organizations, places and events are either the product of the author's imagination or are used fictitiously. Any resemblance to actual persons, living or dead, events or locales is entirely coincidental.

Cover design by Diane Meacham

Cover images © Shutterstock, Gordon Crabb

Printed and bound in Great Britain by Clays Ltd, Elcograf S.p.A.

Look for more great books at
www.herabooks.com | www.dk.com

1

MIX
Paper
FSC™ C018179

To all those who have fought for the rights of women, and to Michael for being part of my dream.

Part One

Chapter One

June 1920

Alice let herself into Holmorton Lodge and stood for a moment in the hallway. After the noise of the wedding guests celebrating in the North Stafford Hotel and the tram journey, the silence was welcome. She took off her coat and hung it on the stand beside the front door and trudged into the sitting room.

She had left the celebrations in Stoke, a distance of some four and a half miles away, to make sure everything was ready for the few special guests who were invited back to the house at nine o'clock. As it was, she needn't have bothered. The house was as tidy as it could be. Patty Goodwin, the girl Connie had taken on to help Alice in the month before the wedding, had done a grand job, and Alice couldn't have been more pleased.

She wandered into the dining room where Patty was laying cloths over the wedding supper on the large oak table. Patty looked up and grinned.

'Hiya Alice. Did it all go to plan? Is Miss Connie wed?'

'Oh, yes. Mind you, there are things that even Connie can't control.'

'What d'yer mean?' Patty frowned. 'What couldn't Miss Connie control?'

'How about her friend Ginnie going into labour?'

Patty's eyes bulged. 'Oh my word. When did she do that?'

'At the end of the church service. Uncle James rushed Ginnie and Sam home, and the baby arrived at three o'clock. Ginnie wasn't due until next week, but it looks like he decided he'd waited long enough. Connie and Robert went to see them before going on to the function to greet the rest of their guests.'

Patty laughed. 'Poor Ginnie. She was looking forward to the wedding an' all. At least she didn't miss it. Anyway, I didn't expect yer back yet but am glad to see yer. I was worried about what I might do without yer.'

'I thought you might need help. It felt wrong to leave you here by yourself to get it all laid out. Besides, I felt a little out of it, to be honest. Connie invited a lot of guests and was busy with them – and Robert, of course. So, I came away thinking I'd be more useful here. You seem to have it all under control.'

'Yes, am all but finished now. We'll be ready as soon as they come through the door.'

Alice smiled at the anxious-looking Patty. At fourteen, Patty was eight years younger. What a shame she was temporary. They would work well together, Alice was sure.

It was another hour before the guests arrived, giving time for Alice and Patty to rest. Once the knocker on the front door sounded, the two walked into the hall to greet them and make them comfortable. Connie's mother, Agatha Copeland, and her brother, Uncle James, entered first, followed by Connie and Robert, Stephen and Jean Adams, Betty Dean and Duncan Kennedy, all showing signs of merriment, but not drunk. Connie looked to have enjoyed chatting about old times when they were clippies with the Potteries Tramway Company, otherwise known as the PTC, during the war.

Alice congratulated Betty on her engagement, which had been announced during the evening. Betty's face flushed. What a pity Ginnie wasn't able to be here. She hadn't been a clippie but the next best thing – a personal friend of Connie's.

'Be careful with my fur, young lady. If there's any damage you'll have to pay for it.'

The voice was loud, and a bright-faced Patty nodded and scurried from the room. Alice didn't know the guest concerned, but she knew her behaviour left much to be desired, even if she was a toff.

Alice kept an eye on Patty throughout the evening, but nothing further happened. She looked happy enough. Alice decided to speak to Connie about it in the morning, not wanting to disrupt anything just now.

As the clock ticked, Alice wanted to make up a bed for Patty in one of the attic rooms, but the girl was quite willing to make her way home on her own.

'Jackfield Street's only a couple of streets away. Dunner worry about me. I'll be home in two shakes of a lamb's tail.'

Alice took another bottle of champagne into the garden room to be greeted by a loud voice.

'Alice, my dear, could you get my bed ready? I'm so tired. My brother will be retiring soon after all his running about today, so make sure his room is ready too.'

'Of course, Mrs Copeland.'

–

Soon, Alice heard people in the hall saying their farewells. The front door closed and she could just make out the sound of Robert and Connie talking. She tidied herself and went to the hall. It was deserted. Connie and Robert seemed to have made a prompt start to their married life, but Alice felt they could have said goodnight to her. She felt cast aside on this important day in Connie's life.

Alice remained working until one o'clock in the morning, with a last check that all the downstairs windows and doors were locked and the gas lights turned off. It had been a nineteen-hour day, and there was no doubt more to come tomorrow and Monday. She climbed the stairs up to her room, her eyes almost closing. She'd hoped to spend more time at the wedding, but it was a little naïve to think this would happen. She wasn't family. She was just an employee and was bound to see less of Connie now that she was married.

–

A bleary-eyed Alice rose from her bed at seven o'clock the next morning. She had been too tired to sleep.

Alice put the kettle on, as Patty was due to arrive at half past. She went over everything that still needed to be done before the new Mr and Mrs Caldwell were due to depart to spend two weeks in Llandudno. Alice had helped Connie to pack after Connie arrived home from the office last Friday, so there were only last-minute toiletries and personal effects to be added.

When Connie arrived downstairs she was smiling.

Alice looked up and bid her good morning. 'Did you get a good night's sleep?'

'As well as could be expected.'

'Will Mr Caldwell be joining you for breakfast?'

'I should think so.' Connie gave Alice a wink and they both burst into laughter leaving Alice with a bright red face.

Connie buttered her toast and drank her coffee. 'Oh, Mother says she might stay with Uncle James for two weeks, Alice. She will let you know when she will be returning. She said it might be boring staying here with only you for company.'

She must have seen the shocked look on Alice's face because she rushed on. 'I think she meant that Uncle James would take her out in his motor car and provide company for her.'

Alice thought she knew very well what Agatha's views were – she didn't want to remain at Holmorton Lodge with only a servant or two for company. Agatha was happy to associate with people like her when she had to, when no one else would be aware of it. It should have come as no surprise, but it did. She had thought more of Agatha than that.

'Alice, dear?'

Connie's voice cut across Alice's thoughts. 'Yes, Connie?'

'I believe you should get some extra help in. There's far too much work for you to do single-handed as well as being cook. You look dreadfully tired.'

That Connie noticed surprised Alice. She had been so caught up with recent events. Perhaps this was to be a new start for each of them. She glanced around. There was no sign of Patty, so she could talk freely, although she lowered her voice just to be sure, not wanting to raise Patty's expectations.

'I believe Patty has done very well since coming to us. Would you mind if I asked her if she wanted the job on a more permanent basis?'

'Patty? Oh, you mean the girl who comes in to help you. Isn't she a little young?'

'Oh, no. She's fourteen and a good worker. Nothing's too much trouble.'

'She would have to live in. Would her parents allow that?'

'Patty comes from a large family, and it's a tight squeeze for a couple with five children in a smallish house. Also, it means that I won't be on my own while you're away. I'm sure she could start immediately. I could call to see her mother to be certain.'

Connie looked doubtful, then waved her hand in the air. 'Very well, Alice. The kitchen is your responsibility. I'll leave you to sort it out.'

Alice beamed. 'Thank you, Connie. I'll get on with it.'

Alice had moved from the attic where she had slept as a servant to a bigger, more comfortable room on the first floor as befitted a housekeeper. Her new room was at the back of the house, on the opposite side of the building to Connie and Robert's room. It was quiet and overlooked the sizeable garden, which was now in full bloom with a riot of colour. In the still evening air, scents from the jasmine and honeysuckle mixed with the ever-present coal smoke and smell of the waste slag from the pits.

Alice stared through the still-open curtains, her hands cupping her chin. Life was going to change for both her and Connie. They would have to get used to a man being around the house. For the past year, there'd only been the three women and, much as she and Connie had plenty to chat about, she doubted Robert would wish her to join them in conversation.

It hadn't all been a bed of roses since Mr Copeland had passed away the previous year. Agatha received the house, but lacked the income to maintain it. She had been told that she might have to sell the house and move to something smaller, but had assured Alice there'd still be room for her. All the talk of selling seemed to have gone away, and Agatha had promised Holmorton Lodge to Connie on her marriage. Alice wondered what had made the financial problems go away, but it was none of her business. At least Holmorton Lodge would remain in the family.

Uncle James had his motor ready to take Connie and Robert to Stoke Station at ten o'clock to begin the journey to Llandudno. She was all packed up and ready when she turned to Alice.

'Now, are you sure you're going to be all right here, on your own?'

'I will be, Connie.'

'We could arrange for you to stay with Jean Adams. She'd be happy to take care of everything while we're away.'

Jean was lovely, but Alice shook her head. 'I'll not hear of it. I'm twenty-two. I think I can take care of myself, Connie.'

Agatha appeared on the step to bid farewell to the newlyweds. Connie hugged her, and the men shook hands.

'Come on. We'll miss our train.' Robert chivvied Connie along. 'Alice will be fine. She's got a sound head on her shoulders. After all, she's helped you to look after me on more than one occasion. I'm sure she's more than capable of looking after herself.'

Alice shot a friendly glance towards him. Yes, Connie had done well to choose Robert for her husband. 'I will. And I'll promise not to open the door to strangers an' all.'

'Come on, Connie – we'd best get a move on, otherwise we shall spend the night here because the train left without us!' said Robert.

They said their goodbyes and followed with hugs – even Robert. As he leaned over to plant a kiss on Alice's cheek, she could feel her face glowing. And when Robert winked at her, she couldn't think of a word to say.

–

The following day, Alice was up early. There were no fires to set, but both Agatha and Uncle James were due to depart for their journey to Urmston that morning.

Agatha smiled at Alice, making her want to curtsey, but felt relieved she hadn't when Agatha kissed her cheek.

'Please look after everything, Alice dear.'

'Come on, Agatha, love. I've got the motor running. We'll be stopping for petrol before we've started if you don't get a move on,' said Uncle James.

Agatha frowned at him but changed it to a brief smile when she saw the twinkle in Uncle James's eyes. Alice couldn't help but smile. He was good for Agatha, considering they would spend so much time in each other's company.

'Don't forget your walking stick, Mrs Copeland.'

'Don't fuss, Alice.' Agatha climbed into the motor and placed the walking stick in the corner beside her.

Uncle James nodded his farewell and sat beside her, pulling the door behind him. The motor rolled forward and turned left through the gates onto Hamil Road.

–

Alice returned to the house. She locked the front and back doors and relaxed. She returned to the kitchen and made a pot of tea with only herself and Patty for company for the first time in weeks.

She sat at the table, sipping her drink, thinking about the chaotic last few months. Since Mrs Williams had retired and Alice had taken over as housekeeper-cum-cook, she had done everything required of her, and now she was about to ask Patty if she wanted the job of housemaid permanently.

She crossed her fingers as she gazed out of the kitchen window into the vegetable garden. Patty walked in with her bucket and mop.

'That's everything done upstairs, Alice.'

'Thank you, Patty. Have a seat.'

Patty opened the back door and tipped the dirty water down the drain and returned, flopping into a chair opposite Alice. 'It's bin hard work, don't yer think?'

Alice poured her a cup of tea. 'Mm. Still, I'm glad it all went well. I couldn't have done it without you, Patty.'

'Thank you, Alice. I shall miss the house.' Patty gazed around the kitchen with its imposing range, its plentiful supply of cupboards and the enormous kitchen table taking centre stage. 'I've enjoyed my time here. D'yer think as Mrs Copeland or Mrs Caldwell will give me a reference if I ask them?'

Alice took a sip of her tea, glad she could give Patty the news.

'You won't need one. Mrs Caldwell has agreed that we keep you on doing much the same as you've been doing. What do you think of that?'

'Oh, Alice, I'd love to carry on here.' Patty jumped out of her seat and gave Alice such a hug she had to beg for mercy. 'I'm so pleased. I'll do a grand job, I promise.'

'I know you will. That's why I wanted to keep you. You'll even have time to work in the kitchen under my instruction, and I'll give you cookery lessons as well.'

'I don't know what ter say.'

'Continue to do a good job and you'll be fine.'

'Wait till I see me mum. She'll have me cooking for the family given half a chance, and she'll tell all the neighbours that we've posh dinners now I'm working for the Caldwells.'

Alice's tone turned serious. 'While it is okay to tell your family what you're doing and other bits and pieces, you must always respect the privacy of your employers. Discuss nothing you hear in this house with anyone. All information here is confidential. Do you understand, Patty?'

Patty nodded, but looked a little perplexed. 'Even to you or Miss Cope… Mrs Caldwell?'

'Yes. As servants, we see everything but say nothing.'

'I understand. You can trust me.'

'Remind me to tell you about my adventure in London with Connie and the suffragettes.'

Patty's eyes widened in shock.

'Anyroad, you'll be doing the same hours I did when I started here. You'll get one day a month off as well as one afternoon per week. One thing, though – you'll be required to live in. Will you be able to do that?'

'I don't think there'll be any problem. It's a bit of a tight squeeze at our house with me brothers and sisters.'

'At least you'll be able to pop home to see your family if you've any spare time during the day. I had no family when I came here, so there was nowhere for me to go.'

'That's a shame. So, what did you do?'

'Stayed here mostly. Did a lot of reading. Learned to bake some of Mrs Williams's lovely pies! I'll come home with you tonight to talk to your parents if you're still agreeable?'

'You bet I am.'

'You can bring a few clothes with you to tide you over.'

Patty beamed. 'This day keeps getting better and better!'

–

Alice walked with Patty to her home that evening. It wasn't far. Just around the corner. Nowhere was too far away from the next town in The Potteries, so called on account of the number of pottery manufacturers, or potbanks. Its full name was Stoke-on-Trent and was made up of six towns, Tunstall, Burslem, Hanley, Stoke, Fenton and Longton. These were interspersed with many villages. If money was tight it was easy to walk from one town to the next but a ride on the tram cut the journey time.

Again, it'd been a hot day and by six o'clock it had barely cooled. Many of the houses had all their windows open, some their front doors. Alice could hear tea being prepared, children playing in the street, and the chatter and laughter of men enjoying the nice weather. It was unusual to see so much activity on a Monday. It was the first day back at work. Most workers wanted nothing more than to rest their weary bones. The washing had been done, and the hot weather had dried it. Some women had done their ironing and would look forward to a little free time tomorrow.

They arrived at 42 Jackfield Street and entered through the open front door. Mr and Mrs Goodwin were having a cup of tea. Mr Goodwin looked as if he'd recently arrived home from work. There were no children to be seen.

Alice explained the situation to Patty's parents. Mrs Goodwin had a lazy eye, which made it difficult to know who she was talking to. One by one, the children returned, as word of their visitor from the big house spread. Before long, the house was full of children. Far more than the four Alice expected.

Despite the noise and interruptions from the children, Alice asked Mr and Mrs Goodwin if Patty could take up a permanent position of housemaid.

'QUIET, QUIET.'

The chatter subsided as the children stared at Mrs Goodwin.

'Now, all of you kids that dunner live here can get off home. I conner hear meself think. Us who live here'll be having us tea in a minute.'

Silence descended as the various children trooped out of the house until only the Goodwin family remained.

'Now, Miss Tucker, I was saying we're happy for Patty to take the job. She's a hard worker and very responsible for her age. It'll give her a sound start in life. Is there anything she needs to bring with her?'

'We're about the same height so there'll be plenty of work clothes that'll do. I'll have time before Mr and Mrs Caldwell return to sort out suitable clothes.'

'Are you staying there on your own now?' asked Mrs Goodwin.

'Until they return from their honeymoon.'

'I don't know if I like that. You never know who's hanging about. Everybody knows there's been a wedding. Do you want Rex to come back with you? He can sleep in the hall.'

'Oh no, Mrs Goodwin, I'll be all right. I couldn't have Mr Goodwin sleeping in a drafty hall.'

Mr Goodwin chuckled. 'No lass, me missus means the dog, not me – I hope.' He disappeared with *The Sentinel* under his arm.

Alice hadn't noticed the dog returning with the children. He had settled in 'his corner' without making a sound to have a nap. Alice laughed at her mistake, and the rest of the family joined in. He was a terrier, dark brown with a white bib, dark eyes and bigger than she had thought. He would need a large bowl of food to keep him fed.

'I could sleep there tonight and take Rex with me,' said Patty.

Rex didn't look capable of defending anyone. 'I'm not sure. Mrs Caldwell doesn't like dogs. I'm sure she'll know there's been one in the house.'

'He's a friendly dog, may not look much, but he's got keen hearing and a loud bark. He sounds very frightening,' said Patty in a persuasive tone.

'That's a bonnie idea, Patty,' said Mrs Goodwin.

It seemed a big step, and Alice didn't want to start off on the wrong foot. 'If you're sure?'

'Course I am.'

'Tell yer what, Alice, I'll send Patty's dad round. He can stay each night until Mrs Caldwell comes home. Between him and Rex, they'll look after the pair of yer.'

'Won't he mind? Shouldn't we ask him?'

Mrs Goodwin laughed. 'He does what I tell him, duckie. Dunner werrit about him. He won't see lassies like you and our Patty staying on their own in that big house.'

In walked Mr Goodwin. All eyes were on him.

'What?' He stared at them frowning, confused.

Mrs Goodwin patted his back. 'Tell yer later, love.'

'See, Alice. He does what he's told, my dad.'

Patty dashed upstairs wearing a huge grin, returning minutes later carrying a cloth bag. She slipped into a dark-brown coat and pulled on a hat. She collected Rex's lead from its hook on the door. On hearing the familiar sound, Rex jumped up, rubbing his body against everyone as if saying his goodbyes. On the short walk from Jackfield Street, Rex looked a different dog from the dog who had been about to fall asleep in the corner. His ears pricked, and he seemed changed after running around a building site, of which there were plenty now that building had started up again after the war.

They strolled back to Holmorton Lodge. It sounded quiet compared with the noise inside the Goodwins' house.

'How do you cope with all the noise at home, Patty?'

'They were excited to have a visitor, and a visitor from the big house. They didn't expect to see me, which added to the general mayhem. You get used to it.'

'You'll find it can be very quiet at Holmorton.'

'I'm glad, I shall do some reading. Being the oldest, I help with the younger ones, so I'm lucky if I get five minutes before being interrupted.'

They entered Holmorton Lodge through the kitchen door.

'We can shut Rex in the scullery.'

'He won't like that. He's allowed to go anywhere in our house. He'll behave himself. He just likes to follow you.'

'Very well, I'll try it.'

They set about organising the house. Patty would take one of the visitors' bedrooms opposite Alice's room for the time being. The bed was already made up.

'Tomorrow we'll sort out my old room in the attic. The bed's very comfortable, and you'll have your own privy and bathroom. As long as the range is running, there's plenty of hot water.'

'A bathroom for meself. I've never had a bath without worrying somebody'll walk in on me.'

Alice smiled. 'You'll get used to it.' She took Patty on her nightly task of checking all doors and windows were locked and bolted. It'd been Mr Copeland's task, but after he passed away, she had taken it over. It took about half an hour to complete, and Rex had behaved himself all the way. He was interested in every scent, but seemed to tire towards the end. There was a quiet stillness about the house as they walked from room to room, broken only by their voices as she explained to Patty what needed to be done. Now and then, a floorboard creaked. When Mr Copeland was alive, he'd retire most evenings to his library to smoke the cigars that Agatha refused to allow anywhere else, but Alice always knew he was in the house. It was reassuring.

There was a sudden sound, and Rex was on his feet, barking. Alice jumped, but Patty grinned. 'That'll be me dad.'

Alice's heart thumped inside her chest, glad of Patty's company.

'How do, duck?' His gruff voice was recognisable as he chatted to Patty in the hallway before moving into the kitchen. 'I wunner get in yer way.'

'I appreciate you coming, Mr Goodwin.' Alice held out her hand.

After staring, he wiped his hand on his trousers and took hers.

'I'll be gone be time yer gerrup in the morning.'

'Well, help yourself to breakfast and anything yer want for yer dinner.'

'Right yer are, miss.'

Patty went to bed and, to Alice's surprise, Rex stayed put in the scullery. He'd no doubt find Patty when he wanted. Alice sat on the chair in the little room just off the kitchen where the servants took their meals. That was in the days when there were five of them, Mr Bainbridge, the handyman-gardener, who died very early in the war at Mons, the two maids, Tilda and Sal, who left to earn more money in munitions work, and Mrs Williams. Alice smiled. It was going to be nice to have some company again.

Alice got to thinking about what would happen when the family came back together.

She popped her head round the door to Agatha's bedroom. Everywhere was as tidy as expected from someone as fastidious as she was. Agatha demanded a tidy room, just in case they had burglars. Alice smiled to herself as she closed the door and opened the next – Connie's room, now shared with Robert. This used to be Mr Copeland's bedroom before he passed away. The room, now redecorated, was light and airy. Connie had chosen modern colours and replaced the curtains and other soft fabrics. She had insisted that it was the only way she could sleep in there, with no reminders of her father.

Alice continued along the landing towards her own room, which lay at the far end. Connie insisted on Alice moving to a bigger room when she was promoted. She cherished the memories of her attic room, but the extra space brought her immense delight. She had made cushion covers, sewn a lace dressing table set and bought her own teapot, purchased from Kensington Pottery, together with a breakfast set from Chamberlain's.

Yes, everything had worked out very well for her and she couldn't have been happier.

By the time she returned to the top of the main staircase, Patty was asleep and Rex was lying at the top of the stairs. He came up to her and nuzzled his soft, cold nose against her hand. She pointed to the corner. To her surprise, he sloped towards it, circled it twice and then lay down with an enormous sigh. Alice got undressed in the bathroom next door. When she returned to her room, Rex was fast asleep on her bed. Alice pulled her nightdress to cover her modesty and then she remembered he was only a dog.

Visiting the Goodwins had reminded her that her life so far had been rather quiet. With no family, she was more used to adult company. She rather wished she'd had someone to share her life with, play with, talk to. Perhaps that's why she and Connie got on so well, and now she would lose that. She felt a touch of jealousy.

Chapter Two

July 1920

Alice called to see Ginnie and the new baby, Young Sam, named after his father. Ginnie White, a former workhouse girl herself, had become a close friend. She had married Sam White, her childhood sweetheart, on his return from the war last year.

Alice walked to North Street where Ginnie and her family lived. The sun had come out, and Alice was too warm in her coat. She knocked on the front door and heard boots thundering down the stairs. The door opened to a thrilled-looking Sam, grinning from ear to ear.

'How do, Alice?'

'I'm fine, Sam. I've brought a present for Young Sam.'

Sam stood aside. From upstairs there came the sound of a baby crying.

'He's got a hefty pair of lungs on him, sure enough,' muttered Sam with a sniff. 'You may as well go up and make his acquaintance. Ada and Jean are up there an' all. I'll put kettle on.'

Sam's infectious pride had Alice grinning in no time. She climbed the steep stairs to Ginnie's bedroom and peeped around the door. Ginnie lay in bed, holding the tiny baby, and a young woman sat at the foot of the bed. On the opposite side of Alice sat Jean Adams, who waved vigorously.

'Is there room for one more, Ginnie?'

Ginnie looked tired, but was sitting upright. She gave Alice a huge grin.

'Hiya Alice. How nice to see yer. It's a tight fit, but everyone's welcome. Come in and meet Ada Barlow. I've told you about her. She was in the workhouse with me.'

'Hello, Ada. Pleased to meet you.'

'Hiya Alice. You're the one what works for that posh girl what was a suffragette.'

'That's right. Ginnie came to Holmorton Lodge a few times. That's how we met, wasn't it, Ginnie?'

'I told Ada how good Connie was to me,' murmured Ginnie. 'She helped get my Sam out of the workhouse, an' all.'

Alice smiled again at the other two and then her eyes went to Young Sam. 'Anyway, enough of the past. I've come to see this little man.'

Young Sam had cried as people invaded the bedroom, but curiosity took over as he became the focus of attention. The visitors took great delight in cuddling him until Sam came in with cups of tea and took the baby into his arms, his eyes locked into the blue eyes staring up at him.

Alice looked at Ginnie. 'How's your Mabel? Is she out?' Mabel was Ginnie's married sister, who took her out of the workhouse when she was fourteen. Mabel was pregnant at the time with her daughter, Florrie. Her husband, Frank, was a little bit too fond of his sister-in-law as it got closer to his wife's time. But fatherhood calmed things down, and when he joined the army, the two sisters started to get on well.

'No, she's working in the Co-operative until six.'

Ada tiptoed around to the far side of the bed to make room for Alice and Sam. Alice reached out to hold Young Sam's finger, and his tiny hand grabbed hers, much to her delight.

'How are yer, Ginnie, duck?' Ada spoke in a broad Potteries accent, knowing it'd bring a smile to Ginnie's face.

'We're over the moon – aren't we, Sam?' Ginnie held out her free hand towards Sam, and he took it without hesitation.

Sam blinked. 'I always telled her she'd make the best mother in the world. Yer didn't believe me, did yer?'

'No, Sam.'

'You're looking well, but tired. I won't stay long,' said Alice. 'I've brought a few bits and bobs for the little one. Matinee coat, a couple of knitted hats and mittens to keep his little hands warm in case it goes cold early this year.'

Ginnie laughed. 'I dunner suppose it'll be that cold for a few months, but thanks. Young Sam here would say thanks an' all if he could talk.'

'Is Sam looking after yer all right?' said Ada, grinning up at Sam, who was now oblivious to his surroundings.

'Oh, yes. Him and our Mabel are doing all right between them. I'll be glad to get out of this room. Reminds me of the workhouse – being shut in one room.'

'Me and Ginnie shared a bed together.' Ada began chuckling. 'D'yer remember that time as I had chilblains, and you told me what to do to get rid?'

Ginnie laughed. 'Course I do.'

Their infectious laughter set Alice off too, even though she didn't know what they were laughing at. 'What did you say?' Her curiosity got the better of her.

'She told me to pee and rub it on,' said Ada.

Alice's eyes were open wide with disbelief. 'Ginnie – you didn't?'

Ada couldn't stop herself. 'Ginnie's ever so clever. I did what she said, and it went away.'

'Somebody at Haddon told me to do that, but I never did. I was glad it worked.'

Ada gasped. 'You mean you didn't know?'

Ginnie shook her head. 'If it hurt that much, you'd try anything, Ada.'

Ada shut up, but it wasn't too long before she joined back in again. She offered to make another cup of tea as Alice and Ginnie continued to chat. Ginnie allowed Alice to hold Young Sam. He wasn't very heavy. No heavier than a doll. She looked into the blue eyes staring up at her, and a faint stirring moved inside her. She held out her finger again and giggled when the little lad gripped it with his tiny hands.

'When are we going to hear summat about you courting, Alice?'

'Oh, not me. It'll be ages. I haven't got my eye on anyone.' Alice smiled as Young Sam made a murmur, seeking attention maybe. She bent her head over the baby, so they couldn't see the flush she had felt crossing her face. 'I need to talk over what Connie needs me to do when she gets back from Llandudno.'

'How is she? Have we heard from her?'

'They're having a lovely time. They're staying in a posh hotel that Mrs Copeland suggested cos she'd stayed there before. Actually, Jean, I was going to have a word with you about looking after the house. When you moved in with Stephen's mother, how did you take over from his mother in organising the household? Mrs Copeland's going to stay with her brother, so, knowing Connie, I think I shall end up doing all the planning and organisation. I don't know if I'm good enough.'

'Don't think like that, Alice,' said Jean, shaking her head. 'I'll help as much as I can, but I'm sure you won't need it. You're a capable woman.'

'If you're thinking about leaving Holmorton Lodge, have yer thought about coming to work at Royal Edwards Pottery, Alice? I could speak for you,' said Ada.

'I'll see what Connie says before I do anything.'

Ginnie took Young Sam back from Alice, and he settled down in her arms. She placed a kiss on his forehead. 'Well, girls, who would've thought that the four of us and Sam, who've spent our childhood in the workhouse, would be here cooing after this little man? We must meet again – sometime soon.'

–

The day had cooled a little, and Alice enjoyed her walk back to Holmorton Lodge. How happy Ginnie and Sam looked. She tried to think if she remembered Ada but couldn't recall her, so Alice must've left the workhouse before Ada arrived.

Even with the noise of the traffic and the railway, Alice was glad to be away from the crying of Young Sam. It was right what people said, the crying of a baby was annoying, and no woman, especially the mother, could ignore it. This got Alice thinking about what might happen when Connie and Robert started a family. She couldn't see a place for her in that house. Connie might look for a nanny at that stage. Alice shook her head. No, employing Patty was one thing; her wages would be low compared with the cost of a nanny. Employing both of them? Could they afford it?

Alice was so deep in thought that she never noticed the young man who had dropped into step beside her.

'Hiya, Miss Tucker. You're miles away by the looks of it.'

She jumped. It was Walter Latham, a man she had known to say hello to, but nothing more. She could feel her cheeks burning. He was attractive in a quiet kind of way. It was the first time they had spoken to each other.

'Hello, Mr Latham.'

'Did everything go well for Connie's wedding?'

'Oh yes. Very well.' What was she saying! 'The wedding was fine, but one guest went into labour just when they were about to sign the register.'

Walter guffawed. 'Just Connie's luck. I must tell our Ruth. She knows Connie from the PTC days. She'll laugh her socks off.'

Alice smiled shyly. He was quite nice when he was laughing. She wished they could be friends, but so far she'd only said hello. He was a few years older, about seven, she thought. He might find her rather too young for him. She couldn't help but smile back.

'I must go. I need to get things ready for tonight's meal,' she said when she could think of nothing more to say.

'Nice to see you anyroad, Miss Tucker.'

'And you too. Goodbye.' She took a few paces and smiled again. 'You can call me Alice if you like.'

She turned to walk away with a huge grin, and there might even have been a flounce in her step.

–

Alice soon got used to having Rex around the place. He was a very well-trained, well-behaved dog. He fell into the habit of sleeping on the landing, where he could see the guest room where Patty would sleep until Connie and Robert returned. Alice had found an old horse blanket from the days when they had a horse-drawn carriage. Rex seemed to like it, and that became his spot in the house.

In Patty's spare time, she had organised what used to be Alice's bedroom, ready for moving into before the newlyweds returned.

'Will you miss having Rex around the house?'

'Yes, I think I will, but he can't stop. In fact, I want him to go back to your house two nights before Mr and Mrs Caldwell return from Llandudno. We need to make sure that there's no dog smell in the house.'

'I expected that to be so.'

Before tea on Friday, Alice and Patty, accompanied by Rex, returned to Jackfield Street. Rex's return filled the family with joy, and soon he was back in his spot, awaiting a treat. Alice thanked Mr and Mrs Goodwin and promised to take care of their daughter.

–

Connie and Robert returned from their honeymoon on the Sunday afternoon at five o'clock. Alice was there to greet them, along with Patty. Alice had cooked Robert's favourite, roast beef and Yorkshire pudding, after which Connie invited Alice to the garden room so the happy couple could recount what they had done on their honeymoon. Not everything obviously, thought Alice, smothering a grin.

'You two look very well. You seem to have caught the sun,' she said.

'It was wonderful, wasn't it? Robert? The weather was pretty good all the time. We'd plenty of opportunity to take bracing walks along the promenade and even took the tram up to the top of the Great Orme. The view from there was spectacular, and the cafe where we had afternoon tea was splendid,' added Connie. 'I'd love to go back there sometime.'

'This tramway uses two long steel cables to pull the trams up to the top from the centre of the town,' said Robert. 'I must tell Stan Bristow the next time I see him. He'll be interested.'

Connie turned to Alice. 'He's the mechanic from the PTC. He loves anything with moving parts! He's walking out with Ruth Latham, isn't he?'

Alice's face tightened. 'Do you mean Walter's sister?' She hoped no one noticed.

'That's right.'

'We went from the pier on a day trip to the Isle of Man. It was a breezy day, and there was a bit of a swell on the sea. I doubt I'll be going on a boat again, but Connie was all right. Weren't you my love?' asked Robert.

'It was so much better when we went out onto the deck,' said Connie.

'We went on the train to Llanberis and caught the train to the top of Snowdon. The view from the Great Orme was spectacular, but from the top of Snowdon, it was unbelievable. A little narrow-gauge steam engine pushes a single coach up to the summit with several stops on the way. Many people took the train to the top and then walked down the mountain. I couldn't do that, not if I was going to be fit for other things.' He gave Connie a sideways grin.

'Robert! You'll embarrass Alice as well as me,' rebuked Connie.

'I meant for the walks along the promenade, which we both enjoyed so much, darling.'

'Yes, Robert, we all know what you mean.'

'I shall have to prepare tea, and would you like to eat in the dining room?' asked Alice.

'That would be nice. Once we are both back at work, we will not always have time to eat formally.'

'I thought it would be a good idea if we ate in the kitchen. It would make life easier for everyone,' suggested Robert.

'I agree, but this evening we will dress for dinner; it is the first night we are home. When you've finished serving dinner, Alice, could you come to see me in the library? I want to talk about running the house with you. Also, bring Patty along. I would like to welcome her to the household.'

'Yes, of course, Connie. Do you want me to bring my accounts book with me?'

'That won't be necessary. It's a general chat.'

–

Alice took off her kitchen pinafore and straightened her hair. She checked Patty was neat and tidy.

'I don't know how formal Connie is going to be, but it is normal practice for junior servants, like yourself, to speak only when spoken to. We shall remain standing and don't fidget.'

'I'm nervous, Alice. What if I should say something wrong?'

'It's not a test. All she wants is to speak to you. You'll be fine.'

Alice and Patty walked to the library. Alice knocked and waited.

'Come in.' Connie was sitting behind Mr Copeland's large desk. 'First, I'd like to welcome you to your new job at Holmorton Lodge, Patty. How're you getting on now that you're living in?'

'Very well, Miss Connie.'

'You do as Alice says to you and you'll not go far wrong.'

'Yes, Miss Connie. Thank you very much for giving me this chance. I won't let yer down.'

'Very good. And Patty – I think it'd be better to address me as Mrs Caldwell from now on, now that I'm married.'

Patty looked at Alice and then replied, 'Yes, Mrs Caldwell.'

'You can go now, Patty.'

Connie disappointed Alice, by asserting herself in such a manner in front of Patty. Did she mean what she said – or was she joking? It was obvious she couldn't be called Miss Connie – but was Mrs Caldwell necessary when they were at home?

'Alice, sit on one of the chairs by the window. I'll be with you in a moment.'

Alice made herself comfortable, and in a few seconds, Connie was sitting across from her.

'Alice, I thought it'd be a good idea to have a chat about how we run the house, especially now there's another servant to consider.' Connie continued, 'My mother planned that Mr Railsford would look after the finances of Holmorton Lodge in her absence, to take the burden off me and to make sure you had somebody experienced to talk to if you needed help.'

'Yes, Connie. Your mother mentioned something similar to me before she left.'

'Mother's decided to stay with Uncle James for the foreseeable future. As you know, she has given Holmorton Lodge to me as a wedding present, and she has insisted that it'll be my responsibility to run the house from now on.'

Alice thought her eyes must've looked like saucers. Fancy a woman like Connie being given a house like this – as a present!

'She's coming back on 20th July to pick up a lot of her personal effects to take back with her and is bringing a lady's maid, a Miss Doubleday. You must have rooms prepared for both of them.'

Alice nodded, surprised. She never expected this to happen. Holmorton Lodge would seem strange without Mrs Copeland.

'I want you to continue as housekeeper and look after all aspects of running the house. It looks to me that Patty will be a useful helper, given time.'

'Yes, Connie. But there's one thing I need to ask.'

'Go ahead.'

'Has the financial situation got better or worse?'

'That's nothing to concern yourself with, Alice. We will need to keep our belts tightened for the time being. I know what you're going to say – why have we employed Patty?'

Alice nodded.

'It's a necessary expense. You couldn't cope on your own. You need time for yourself. You've earned it, and I'll not take advantage of you. You'll continue your excellent work in reducing the cost of running the household. Robert and I are happy with the standard of meals you prepare, so there'll be no changes there.'

'That's good news. I was concerned that Robert would want something posher.'

'He's not like that, Alice. He's never had a servant. He'll be as concerned as Patty is!' She smiled. 'Besides, with him working different hours, meals won't need to be as formal as you're used to.'

'I was concerned that our time together had ended with your marriage.'

'No, Alice, that will never happen, but I can't deny things have changed. We've Robert to consider – having a man about the house again.'

Of course, Alice knew she couldn't expect everything to remain as it was, but a wave of relief shot through her. She was to be kept on, and the house wasn't to be sold. Nothing else mattered.

–

Tomorrow, Mrs Copeland and her maid would arrive to collect her possessions. Alice and Patty decided they would make up a bed for Miss Doubleday in the room next to Patty's. Mrs Copeland would have her own room, so Alice attempted to make sure everything was perfect.

Alice returned to the kitchen and prepared a joint of pork for their evening meal. There was a loud knocking on the scullery door, which made her jump. When she answered, a tall, imposing woman confronted her. Alice knew who this was, but before she could greet her, the woman said, 'Girl, you should be wearing a uniform, not your Sunday best. I'm Miss Isabella Doubleday, and I'm here to see Miss Tucker, the housekeeper. Look sharp and get her for me.'

The hackles on Alice's back rose. 'I don't need to. I'm Alice Tucker, pleased to meet you, Miss Doubleday.' The woman's accent was… different. Alice could've sworn it was Scottish, but she couldn't say for sure.

'You're a little young to be a housekeeper.'

'You're a little old to be a lady's maid, but we are who we are. You'd better come in.' Alice stood to one side, grinding her teeth as the woman entered. Already Alice knew she'd hate this woman.

'Well, I'm pleased to meet you, I'm sure. I would be grateful if you could tell Mrs Caldwell that I've arrived. I'm here a day early to supervise everything to Mrs Copeland's personal satisfaction.'

The woman held her head high, giving the impression she was looking down her nose at them. Alice took on a similar stance, arms folded.

Miss Doubleday had the grace to flush. 'Before I meet anyone, I would like to freshen up, so if you could show me to my room, I would be grateful, Miss Tucker.'

'Certainly, Miss Doubleday.'

Alice escorted Miss Doubleday up to her room. It was only going to be for a few nights and would be adequate. Miss Doubleday informed her that Mrs Copeland would arrive tomorrow, as planned, and a firm of removers would be arriving next Tuesday. She expected Mrs Copeland to leave here on Wednesday for Mr James Richardson's house, Lea Hill Manor in Urmston.

In speaking to Connie later, Alice was able to establish that Miss Doubleday was a Scottish lady's maid, originally from the Isle of Skye, and deeply religious, who had looked after Mrs Richardson, Uncle James's wife, until her death in 1912. Even Alice had to admit she didn't look as old as her sixty years would suggest, but doubted she would ever list the woman as a friend.

–

Everything went according to plan. Miss Doubleday came with firm instructions regarding what Agatha wanted to take with her to Urmston. She would retain a few clothes to see her through until she left, and the rest would be packed by Miss Doubleday and the removers.

Alice felt happy to leave Connie and Agatha to make the most of their time together. It would feel strange. She'd known Agatha longer than she had known Connie, who had been at boarding school when Alice arrived. She felt surprisingly choked up at the thought of saying goodbye, knowing that she might never see Agatha again. At least Uncle James would look after her.

For their final meal together, Alice made Agatha's favourite meal of roast beef, usually reserved for Sundays, followed by a summer pudding. As a thank you for her hard work, and friendship, Alice was invited to join them for the meal.

As it turned out, Miss Doubleday wasn't as bad as Alice had thought. Maybe the woman had been nervous when she arrived. She was completely different when Agatha arrived and it was obvious that the two got on well. It was only when she walked past Agatha's bedroom that she discovered Isabella Doubleday was also known as "Bella". Somehow, it made her sound more approachable.

Both Alice and Patty helped with the final packing on the Wednesday morning. Connie had hoped to have the day off work. Mr Railsford said the office was too busy, but she could go in an hour later to enable her to say her goodbyes face to face. After muttering under her breath, Connie had no choice but to obey.

Once all was packed, everyone gathered at the front door to wish Agatha and Bella a pleasant journey. Hugs were exchanged and a few tears made an appearance. A promise was made that Agatha would make the journey for Christmas. Five months seemed a long time, but privately, Alice wondered if brother and sister could stay together for so long without arguing.

Chapter Three

August 1920

Alice needed some additional items for that evening's meal, and the afternoon sunshine looked too inviting. She picked up her basket and took a ten-shilling note out of her cash tin. The note should be more than enough for what she needed to buy, and she needed some change too. Holmorton Lodge had accounts with most shops in the area, but after the Hesse family's appalling treatment, Connie insisted that if they'd to use the shop, then they'd pay cash.

Settled weather had persisted for most of the month, and there were several people chatting outside the shop upon her arrival, including Walter Latham.

'Good afternoon, Alice. It's a fine day, isn't it?'

'Yes, Mr Latham, it is.'

'If I'm to call you Alice, you must call me Walter. It's only fair, isn't it?'

Alice blushed. She had been wondering what she might call him the next time she saw him – at least she hoped she would see him again. That's why she'd been coming to this shop, wasn't it? Even Patty had commented that they always seemed to be missing something when they started preparing the evening meal, followed by a wink.

'You're doing a bit of shopping, are you?'

'Yes, I need some supplies for the dessert I'm making.'

'That sounds nice, whatever it is. Miss Latimer's thrown me out of the house. She says she doesn't want any clutter, by which

I assume she means me, in the kitchen. Somehow, I don't think I'll get a pudding this evening.'

'Who's Miss Latimer?'

'She cooks and cleans for Father and me. Been doing so for a few years. Our Ruth used to look after us, but she went to work in Stoke. Miss Latimer's an excellent cook, but doesn't hold with puddings.'

'That's a shame. Most people think it's the best part of the meal. I always try to make something every day. Have you been to work, or are you working tonight?'

'No lass, I'm on nights this week, but at least it means I can enjoy the fine weather.'

'So you do a week of nights. That must be difficult?'

'You get used to it. I've been down the pit all my working life, and shift work just comes naturally.'

'What do you do at the pit?'

'I'm a pit deputy.'

'No, I meant, what work do you do?'

'I'm the supervisor and safety inspector in my area of the pit. I'm also a shot-firer. I set the charges when we need to blast something out of the way underground.'

'Sounds dangerous.'

'Not really. You've got to respect explosives, and you need to be thorough. There aren't any shortcuts, despite what the management sometimes says.'

'You worked down the pit during the war, didn't you?'

'Yes, I did. I thought it was the safest place to be. My brother works down the same pit, but we're not on the same shift.'

'Did you know the family that used to run this shop?'

'Yes, I did. Bertie and Carla Hesse were my friends from school, along with our Ruth and her friend, Dottie Spilling. We spent a lot of time together.' He seemed to go into a bit of a dream, perhaps thinking back to his lost friends.

'It wasn't right what happened to the family. Whatever you think about the rights and wrongs of the war, they'd lived in

The Potteries all their lives and their parents had spent over twenty years in this country. Yet we still threw them out and destroyed their shop even though they were no threat to us. It doesn't seem fair somehow.'

'There's plenty of people around who'd disagree with you, Miss Alice. That's unlikely to change in the future. It'll take a long time for the wounds of that war to heal.'

'I expect so, Mr Latham.'

'Please call me Walter. Mr Latham makes me sound as old as my father.'

Alice turned her head away to spare her blushes. She'd better get on, but she was enjoying talking to Walter and wished she'd taken more interest in him before. 'Do you know what happened to the family?'

'Mr and Mrs Hesse opted for repatriation to Germany in 1915. Carla still lives in Stoke with Ruth and Dottie. They share a house. Bertie lodges with someone in Stoke as well. He was interned on the Isle of Man until the spring of 1919. He's a mould maker, but hasn't been able to get any work because of being German. It's a bit of a joke because he sounds more like a Stokie than I do. Bertie was two when the family came over here, but Carla was born in Stoke and, as far as the authorities were concerned, she was English. She couldn't go to Germany for the same reason. It was a real mess.'

'Bertie was married to Edith Wren, wasn't he? And had a little baby?'

'That's right. Luther was a bonny wee lad the last time I saw him. He'll be five or six now. Carla and I couldn't believe that Edith had left Bertie. We think it was her mother's doing. She never had a positive word to say about the Germans.'

'Yes, and after the authorities arrested Bertie, Edith went back to her mother's and the whole family moved to somewhere in Yorkshire – Bradford or Barnsley or somewhere else beginning with B. Nobody was sure where they went. He's going to look for them one day.'

'Didn't they keep in touch with each other?'

'It's a long story, but we never found out whether Edith left him of her own accord or whether her mother made her leave because it embarrassed her that her daughter was married to a German.'

A thought came to Alice. Mrs Williams had worked at Holmorton Lodge for donkey's years. She was a lovely person, but she enjoyed a bit of spicy gossip. She might know something about what had happened to the Wren family. She was celebrating her seventieth birthday soon, and Alice was planning to visit her.

She was about to mention it to Walter, but decided she should get the information first and then tell him – and it would give her another chance to meet him!

–

It had been over a month since Connie and Robert had returned from their honeymoon, and the household had settled into some sort of pattern. Patty was enjoying living in and had made her room quite welcoming. Alice's room extended over the kitchen, and she heard Patty getting up to start her day's work at half past six in the morning. It would be good to have someone else to lay fires in the winter.

Alice was up and dressed at her usual time of half past seven. As she moved around the house, the silence seemed to follow her. The weather was warm, and fires weren't lit until the evening unless required. When Alice walked in, Patty was outside with the door open, hanging out tea towels. The range was ready for cooking.

'Morning, Alice, it's a beautiful day out there. Mr Robert has left for work. I made him a cup of tea, and he took a slice of toast from yesterday's loaf. He said it makes better toast the following day.'

'Thank you, Patty. Miss Connie will be up shortly, so I'll start the breakfast.'

They continued to chat as they went about their work and stopped for a well-deserved cup of tea just after eleven.

'What should I do next, Alice?'

As a housekeeper, Alice's primary duty was to keep the house running and to make it appear everything just happened – as far as her employer was concerned. She now had a staff of one person to manage as well. Connie's upbringing didn't require her to consider such mundane matters.

'I think we can treat ourselves to a piece of sponge cake.'

'Oh yes, Alice, you make the most wonderful sponges. I wish I could. When I tried at home, it sank in the middle.'

'You'll succeed one day. We all have to learn, and you'll have disasters. I had plenty at first.' Alice took a sip of her tea. 'Now we're getting on top of the housework, we should have some free time and you can help me with the cooking. It's the best way to learn.'

'That would be nice.'

'On another subject, we need to agree on how we're going to address people. You've spent most of your time below stairs so far, but that won't be the case from now on and you'll meet different people. You must know how to address them.'

'I know. I got myself into a bit of trouble this morning when I called Mr Robert, "Robert". He said nothing, but I could see his surprise.'

'Yes, that's what I'm talking about. Always call Robert Mr Caldwell or sir, and always call Connie Mrs Caldwell or madam. When we're in the presence of Mr and Mrs Caldwell or any visitors and other family members, refer to me as Miss Tucker, and I'll refer to you as Goodwin. I know it sounds impersonal, but it's what they expect. A friend of mine was in service, and her mistress called her Edie – even though that wasn't her name – all because her previous maid had been called that and her mistress found it easier.'

'I understand. What about visitors?'

'Again, you call them either sir or madam and when you announce them to the master or mistress, you say their name in full. And one last rule of being an obedient servant is that you speak only when you are spoken to. Stick to this principle until you see how the land lies. There're other things, but I don't want to tell you everything at one go. It'll be too much. I struggled but I got the hang of it. You'll do the same.'

They ate the cake and finished the tea. Patty went off to dust the sitting room, leaving Alice on her own. Her mind strayed to other matters. Before Connie's wedding, she had pondered over what she wanted out of her life and was pleased when Connie asked her to stay rather than go with Agatha. Now she had more time to think about her future – could she see herself doing this job for the rest of her life?

The first big change was that Robert would be in residence and head of the household. She couldn't expect to have the same camaraderie with Connie as they'd had until now. And what about when children arrived? Would she be required to look after them, too? If so, Alice felt she would live her life through the Caldwells. She had been so busy that the thought hadn't entered her head until now. The sense of friendship they'd had before Connie's wedding was almost certainly over.

She was glad she was going to see Mrs Williams on her birthday. She would seek her advice.

–

There was a letter with a Birmingham postmark waiting for Connie when she arrived home from work. 'I wonder what Betty has to tell us now. Perhaps they've arranged a date for the wedding.'

'Oh, that would be nice.'

Alice had only met Duncan Kennedy a few times, but he seemed pleasant enough. Betty had strong opinions about a woman being able to work. This independent streak was something most men disliked, including Duncan.

'Alice, can you open the letter while I just wash my hands?'

Connie returned a few moments later.

'What does it say, then?'

'I think you had better read it yourself.'

'Oh, no. What's the problem this time…?' Connie skimmed through the letter. 'Same old thing then – both wanting their own way and neither willing to give in. Betty keeping her job versus staying at home to look after her family. That girl doesn't know when she's well off. Ever since she met Joe Cumberbatch, the union man, and they went to live in Birmingham, she's changed. I think the women she shares the flat with are a bad influence on her.'

Alice raised her eyebrows. 'Why?'

'Jessie and Rowena have got all these modern ideas, and although they seem to enjoy themselves in the company of men, I don't think they see themselves making a long-term commitment. They're too independent.'

'I thought you were like that at one time, Connie.' A thought flashed through Alice's mind. Was Walter like Duncan, looking for a wife to look after him and his home – or more like Robert, who gave Connie plenty of leeway in their marriage? Should she become a working woman or a housewife caring for a family?

'Oh, don't get me wrong, I believe in women's rights and I won't rest until all women receive the vote. But I'm also just as committed to having a family and growing old with the man I love. It doesn't have to be one or the other. That's where Betty goes wrong. She can't compromise, and neither will he.'

'Don't be too hard on Betty. Duncan lives at home with his father and sister. The last thing Betty wants is to become an unpaid servant to his family. Better if she takes her time coming to a decision.' Alice sighed. 'Relationships are fraught with problems. Thank goodness I haven't got one.'

Chapter Four

September 1920

Alice left Patty with some jobs to do and set off on her journey to Cheadle Hulme to visit Mrs Williams at just after eleven o'clock on Wednesday. She took with her a small leather-bound book of poetry by way of a present.

'I've told Mrs Caldwell where I'm going. You should expect me back about half past seven. The master and mistress will be in for their evening meal. It'll be something simple – a salad, and there's some cold pork I cooked last night. It should be fine to carve, but be careful with the knives and use the carving fork with the guard.'

'I will.'

'Nobody should be home until after five o'clock, but before preparing anything, be sure to ask Mrs Caldwell when and where she wants to eat.'

Alice walked along Park Road and took the next tram to Stoke. Arriving at the station, she bought her return ticket and waited on the platform for the Manchester train. She'd travelled on the stopping train, and by the time she arrived in Cheadle Hulme, she was feeling a little queasy.

Once out on the drafty platform, she walked down the flight of stairs to the street and, following Mrs Williams's directions, was soon standing outside a substantial-looking house in a terrace of four.

Her knock echoed on the half-glass front door. A young girl aged about twelve answered. She had blonde hair and blue eyes. She looked about the same age as Alice when she started working at Holmorton Lodge.

'Hello, you must be Alice.'

'Yes, that's correct. I'm here to see Mrs Williams.'

'Granny's expecting you.'

Alice followed the girl into the entrance hall. 'Would you like to take your coat off?' she asked.

It was then that she heard a familiar voice. 'Well, if it isn't our Alice. You're looking very well, my dear.'

'How are you, Mrs Williams?'

'Conner complain, the arthritis has got no worse now I'm not working. Come through into my sitting room.'

The room was light, with French doors opening onto a narrow garden beside the house. An alleyway with low walls ran behind each of the four houses. On the other side of the alleyway, each property had a garden sloping down to a tall wall shielding them from the railway tracks.

'You've a lovely room here.'

'Yes, I'm lucky. If I'm not able to get about some days, at least I can sit there and look out over the garden and watch the birds.'

Alice gave her a hug and handed over her present, which was very much appreciated.

The two of them talked about events and people, with Alice bringing Mrs Williams up to date about Agatha and Constance.

The girl brought in a tray of tea with Alice's favourite treacle tart, which Mrs Williams had made for her that morning. Alice poured the tea and served a piece of the tart to Mrs Williams and herself, bringing back memories of her early times at Holmorton Lodge.

'I don't expect Miss Constance will be too active in the household's running these days.'

Alice shook her head. 'No, she's happy to leave all of that to me. In fact, we all dine together in the little dining room off the kitchen we used as servants.'

'Was it their choice?'

'Yes, Mr Caldwell works different hours each day, but Constance arrives home around half past five most days. It seemed the best way to organise things.'

'Have you started your preparations for Christmas yet?'

'I wanted to discuss that. This Christmas will be my first since Agatha left to live with her brother.'

'Yes, but it shouldn't be any trouble for you. You've still got my book with all the notes, and you'll have your books, which I trust you've kept going since I retired.'

'Oh yes, they're invaluable.'

The two of them went through Alice's plans, which received approval from Mrs Williams.

'You should sit down with Constance and make sure she's happy with your plans, and then, if she wants anything different, you'll know sooner rather than later. You should also plan for uninvited guests and visitors, both for food and drink. Better safe than sorry. Without Mr and Mrs Copeland, I don't suppose there'll be as many guests, but you still need to be prepared. Any surplus food, I used to give to the people in those new terraced houses. As far as drink goes, it doesn't go off, and Christmas supplies, even when Mr Copeland was alive, lasted us until Easter. Another thing to make sure of is that you've paid all your bills up to date by November. When you owe tradesmen nowt they're far more amenable to helping you if you need it.'

Alice nodded, repeating the instructions as they went along.

'Remember, we're only servants. Whilst we can try to influence our employers, it's up to them what they do. If I was in your position, I'd continue in the same way as you worked with Mrs Copeland, and I'm sure that over time, Constance will surprise you.'

'What should I do if I can't cope?'

'Talk to Constance and explain the situation. You both know each other well enough, and she'll listen to you. One thing is for sure, Alice dear, she won't want to lose you! That young woman knows which way her bread's buttered.'

'Anyway, enough about work. Have you got a gentleman friend yet?'

'No, Mrs Williams. I've got my eye on someone, but it's early days.'

'Who is it?'

'It's Walter Latham. He lives in Dartmouth Street.'

'You mean Millie Latham's youngest lad?'

'Yes, that's right.'

'He's still single then. When I was there, most people thought that him and Carla Hesse would be married as soon as they could. They spent most of their youth together. After the argy-bargy at the shop and that anti-German stuff that went on around the time of the sinking of the *Lusitania*, she went to live in Stoke, and they didn't seem to bother with each other much after that.'

'I spoke with Walter a couple of weeks ago; he told me about Bertie Hesse and how internment caused him to lose contact with his wife and child. He's trying to find them.'

'That's not surprising. Mrs Wren was full of herself, and when the war started, it was an embarrassment to her to have a German son-in-law. Always had ideas above her station and ruled that house with a rod of iron. Mr Wren was too frightened to stand up to her. I felt sorry for poor Edith. She was a bit of a homebird. Never enjoyed living over the shop with her in-laws. Not that there was any problem. She'd plenty of space compared with that pokey little house. But Edith wasn't a bright woman. She was so used to being told what to do by her mother. I reckon she did just that.'

'Walter said they moved house soon after Bertie's arrest – to somewhere in Yorkshire, was it?'

'That story's still doing the rounds, is it?'

'What do you mean?'

'As far as I know, they went to live in Wolstanton. Mrs Wren told a neighbour, Mrs Curbishley, that story to put Bertie and Carla off the scent, and it seems to have worked. It's shameful

Bertie hasn't seen his son for so long. When did you say he came back?'

'Last year, he's been trying to get work and get himself back on his feet.'

'She should be ashamed of herself. There are enough children in this world who'll never see their father again. Listen – as far as I can remember, Mr Wren used to work in the offices at the Co-op in Newcastle-under-Lyme. He was a clerk. Mind you, that was three years ago, but it's worth starting there. I hope the lad finds his son.'

The afternoon passed in no time at all. It was soon time for Alice to leave. It was a pleasure to see Mrs Williams. Alice was feeling much better about the future, but decided she'd done enough thinking for one day and rested her head against the slats of the third-class seats. Soon, the train's rhythmic motion, punctuated by stops, lulled Alice to sleep. The guard's announcement of Stoke Station startled her.

When Alice returned to Holmorton Lodge, Patty had already carved the meat for the salad, and had prepared everything as instructed. Alice couldn't resist a quick look at the girl's hands, and yes, she still had the required number of fingers and thumbs on each one.

–

Later that evening, Alice took the first opportunity to visit Walter at home to tell him the news she'd discovered.

'I'm going out for a walk, Patty. I'll be about half an hour. I don't think Connie or Robert will want us again tonight, but keep your ears peeled, just in case.'

'Yes, Alice. Going anywhere nice?' enquired Patty.

'Never you mind.'

'So you are then,' she grinned.

Perhaps she was a little short with Patty, but Alice didn't want anyone knowing about Walter. If nothing came of it, she'd feel embarrassed, and although Patty had a lot of endearing traits, she had a sharp sense of humour. Alice donned her hat and coat and walked to Dartmouth Street.

Walter's father answered the door. She hadn't met him before, but had seen him about.

'Hello, what can I do for you, miss?'

'Is Walter in, please?'

The man turned around. 'There's a young lassie asking for yer.'

Walter appeared. He looked surprised, but introduced her to his father. They talked about the weather for a few moments while Walter put his cap and jacket on. When they got outside, Alice told him all she'd discovered about Edith and her family.

'That's interesting news. Our Ruth said that it seemed pretty conclusive they'd left the area.' He thought for a moment. 'One other thing you should know is Carla received a postcard from Bradford in Edith's handwriting a while back, telling her how much she was enjoying living there. They'd even changed their name from Hesse to Turnbull – to sound English.'

'Can they do that?'

'Don't see why not. The Royal Family have done it.'

Alice laughed. 'Good point.'

'I've never seen the card, but I know it intrigued the girls, although our friend Dottie Spilling thought it was a red herring.'

'What will you do now?'

'I'll tell Bertie at the first opportunity. In fact, we can nip down now, then you can tell him yerself.'

It was now almost eight o'clock, and Alice was conscious of her promise to Patty. 'I'll have to go back to Holmorton Lodge and tell Patty where I've gone.'

–

Ten minutes later, they were waiting at the tram stop on Moorland Road. They caught the tram through to London Road and were soon knocking at the door of number 14 Corporation Street.

Walter introduced Alice to Bertie, and she reiterated all she'd told Walter. Bertie took in everything and was looking happier as each moment went by.

'Bertie, show Alice the postcard, see what she thinks,' said Walter.

Alice blushed a bit, but when Bertie returned with the card, her interest piqued up.

'That's unusual.'

'In what way?' asked Bertie.

'Well, if I want to tell anybody anything important, I wouldn't use a postcard that anyone could read – and if she wants to remain hidden, why sign it with her new name?'

'That's what Dottie said, but the postmark's from Bradford.'

'Mrs Williams said that Mrs Wren's family came from there. You could post a letter containing the card to a relation in Bradford and get them to post the card back to Stoke – and you've got a genuine postmark.'

'You think they wanted people to know?' asked Bertie.

'I think she was trying to put you off the scent,' said Alice.

On the way back in the tram, Walter said, 'Miss Tucker, as a reward for finding out this information, I wonder if you'd do me the honour of coming to the pictures with me sometime?'

Alice's heart skipped a beat. 'Yes, of course I will. I'd like that.' She hoped she didn't sound too enthusiastic.

'Well, I'll be in touch with a date then.'

Returning to Holmorton Lodge, she felt pleased with herself. Not only had she been able to find out some information, but she'd now got an invitation to the pictures. Perhaps he was interested in her?

–

Two weeks later, as night-time approached, Alice overheard Connie and Robert having their first argument. Alice had collected the supper dishes from the garden room, and as she passed the library, she heard the raised voices.

Robert shouted something about how the house would be in Connie's name only, and that he might as well be a 'kept man'. Alice wasn't too sure what he was getting at, but he wasn't pleased.

Alice later found out from Connie that the main issue revolved around Robert's pride, and the fact that his wife owned the house and he lacked financial control. His only responsibility was to go out to work and contribute something towards the household income. Many men would've liked the idea of putting the onus on his wife to keep the family going, but Robert wasn't one of them. Robert still felt that there was a need for the man of the house to be just that – protecting and guiding his family through life.

Perhaps Betty's Duncan wasn't the only man who aspired to be in control of his own house.

–

A knock on the door had Patty rushing to open it. At nine o'clock, it was a bit late in the day to be receiving callers. Alice heard the murmur of voices before Patty returned.

'There's a handsome man outside who wants to see you. It's Walter Latham. It looks as if you'll be going on another one of your walks,' she winked with a loud whisper and waltzed out.

Alice checked her hair in the mirror and smoothed down her clothes after removing her apron. 'Keep an eye on things, Patty. And thank you,' Alice called, knowing the girl would remain in the hall to listen.

'Evening, Walter. Let's pop outside.' Then she raised her voice. 'Walls have ears in these parts,' she called over her shoulder, and closed the back door behind them. Together they walked towards the gate and talked.

Walter beamed. 'Excellent news, Alice. Your information proved to be accurate. Bertie checked the register of electors and found Mr Wren on it. He then went down to the Co-op in Newcastle, and he was told by a woman from the offices that there was no Mr Wren working there. Bertie didn't believe her and, with nothing better to do, he waited. He didn't have to wait long, as Mr Wren came out for his dinner.'

'Oh, that's so good to hear.'

'It gets even better. Mr Wren seemed very apologetic about what had happened and brought Bertie up to date. Edith and Luther are in rude health, and Mr Wren is certain that she will want to see him. He said it was Edith's mother who didn't want Bertie in the family.'

'The pair of them met that evening at a chess club, would you believe? It's the only place that Mrs Wren lets her husband go without asking questions.'

'To cut a long story short, Mr Wren has arranged for a family outing to see the autumn flower show in Crewe Park. It's taking place this Sunday, and all being well, Bertie will get to talk to Edith. He can't talk to his son because the little lad would be sure to tell his grandmother.'

Alice got emotional at that point. She didn't know any of the people involved, but she always cried when she got to a point in a book when something like this happened. She regained her composure and asked what was going to happen next.

'Our Ruth's going to organise for a group of us to go along with Bertie so that it doesn't look as conspicuous as a man on his own.' He swallowed and then took a deep breath. 'Would you like to come along with us?'

'Who'll be going?'

'Well, there's Bertie of course, his sister Carla, our Ruth and her fiancé Stan and me and you – if you agree?'

'I don't know many of them except Ruth – and you, of course. I might recognise them by sight. What will they think of me coming along?'

'Well, we wouldn't be going on this trip if you hadn't found the information. I'm sure you'll get on well with Ruth. And if the day proves to be a washout, then there's always the beer tent. Or we can return whenever you want.'

'I'd like that.'

Walter told her they were getting a train at eleven o'clock in the morning and would have some lunch at the show. Bertie was to meet Edith at three o'clock in front of the dobby-horses. This would coincide with the prize giving, so Edith could slip away unnoticed.

–

Walter called for Ruth the following Sunday in plenty of time to catch a train from Burslem to Kidsgrove, where they waited for the train to Crewe. Bertie and Carla, and Ruth and Stan would already be on the train, which had come from Stoke on the other railway line.

As the train pulled into the station, Walter saw Ruth waving out of a coach window. There was a general cacophony of voices as the group greeted and introduced each other. The only person who was quiet was Bertie.

Alice recognised Bertie and his sister, Carla, with her distinctive blonde hair and blue eyes. Although Alice had never met her, she had seen her working in the shop. But that was six years ago, and a lot of water had gone under the bridge since.

Alice whispered to Walter, 'Bertie looks anxious.'

'Yes, he took a bit of persuading to come along. The poor chap's worried she won't turn up and the whole thing will be for nothing.'

Alice squeezed Walter's arm. She didn't know why she did this, but it felt right.

The group wandered around the park looking at the flowers and then had a walk around the marquee to look at the exhibits. The inside was a riot of colour, none more so than the displays of chrysanthemums and dahlias, which were a particular favourite of many men who were lucky enough to have a garden or allotment. Mrs Copeland had never liked these flowers because they attracted earwigs, and the little creatures would drop out onto the table at the most inopportune moments.

The group made their way to the funfair, where the meeting was to take place. Throngs of people enjoyed the rides and risked their luck at various games.

As three o'clock approached, Bertie made his way over to the carousel and stood watching people enjoying the speed of the mechanical horses. The rest of the group broke into pairs, and Ruth took Alice to one side and talked to her about anything, as long as it made them look inconspicuous. Much to Alice's dismay, Walter went with Carla.

Ruth looked at her. 'So, are you and my brother walking out?'

The directness of Ruth's question surprised Alice, and she could only stutter a half reply. 'Yes, no, well maybe.'

'Oh, I'm sorry, I just thought you seemed so comfortable together. When I learned you were coming along today, all I got from Walter was that you were a friend of his.'

'No, we only met each other outside the shop a few weeks ago. He told me about Bertie's problem, and I thought our old cook at Holmorton Lodge might know something about the family.'

'Well, all I can say, Alice, is you've impressed him. He's a quiet man, but has spoken to me asking if I knew anything about you. I'd say you might receive an invitation to the pictures soon.'

'He said he was going to ask me when we were on the tram returning from telling Bertie about Edith, but I have heard nothing as yet and considering what I've seen today, I can now understand why.'

'Ignore what you've seen today, Alice. Any romantic involvement between Walter and Carla finished many years ago. Be patient, he'll get there in the end.' Ruth looked at her. 'Don't worry, Alice. If anything was going to happen between them, it would've happened by now.'

At that moment, Ruth caught sight of Edith, and they watched from a distance as husband and wife reunited. They talked for about fifteen minutes before Edith returned to the exhibition tent where the results were being announced.

'Just remember, Alice. Our Walter's a quiet man who likes to reflect on things. He doesn't rush. I suppose it comes from his work with explosives. You can't take liberties with explosives, so it's a case of check, check and check again. Which shows the regard he holds you in.'

'Thank you, Ruth.' From that moment, Alice's day got brighter and brighter.

For the rest of the day, Bertie could only talk about how he was going to get a job and get somewhere to live with Edith and Luther. He was keen to have a full and frank conversation with Mrs Wren, or to quote Bertie, 'tell that old witch where to go'.

On the return journey to Kidsgrove, the group were in high spirits. Carla seemed a nice person as she laughed and joked with the group. But she was never very far away from Walter, and this unsettled Alice.

As Alice and Walter were walking up to the Loop Line station, all she could think about was him and Carla. If she were going to have any sort of relationship with Walter, she needed to know his true feelings about Carla. They walked under the railway bridge and up the steps to the platform.

She blurted out, 'Walter, can I ask you something?'

'Yes.'

'What is your relationship with Carla?' Her face burned. He looked at her with a puzzled frown.

'Why do you ask?'

'I've spoken to Mrs Williams and Ruth, and they both said they expected you two would be married by now.'

Walter grinned. 'You've been making enquiries, haven't you?'

Alice immediately regretted her outburst.

His face became serious. 'We did promise to marry, but I was nine, if I remember. We're friends. Sometimes I thought we'd be good together, but we did nothing about it. She once told me, "It would feel like kissing my brother." That put me off a bit, if I'm honest.'

She bit her lip. His words didn't answer her question. Now that she'd started, she couldn't let it go. After all, they had been together all day.

'Carla and Bertie needed my help today – as a friend. I couldn't not help her. I'm not that sort of man.'

Alice pressed on. 'So, there's nothing between you?'

'No, nothing at all.'

With that, Alice had to be satisfied.

They had run out of things to talk about by the time they reached Holmorton Lodge, and Alice was desperate to keep him talking. She couldn't invite him inside at this hour.

'Alice?' He took her hand.

'Yes?'

'Would you do me the honour of coming to the Empire Picture House with me on Thursday?' He had never looked more serious.

She swallowed hard, as if something had lodged in her throat. She wanted to say yes please, of course I will, I'll go anywhere with you.

She didn't say any of those things. Instead, she said, 'Thank you for asking me,' and very nearly missed out the 'yes' bit!

Chapter Five

October 1920

'Patty, you'll be all right to serve tea on your own tonight?' asked Alice.

'Yes, I will. It's a simple tea. I've already made the pie, and all I've to do is boil some taters; I also need to prepare the runner beans and peas.'

'Don't forget to put some mint in with the peas. They taste so much better.'

'Yes, I will. You go and enjoy yourself. I can't believe you can be that old and never have been to the pictures with a man before. I can't wait to hear all about it.'

'You're too young to be thinking about such matters, young lady! There's plenty of time for that in the future.'

Alice heard Connie shout she was home and walked through to the hall to greet her.

'Hello, Alice.'

'Evening, Connie. You're home early tonight.'

'I had some papers to deliver to Hanley, and Mr Railsford said I could go straight home afterwards.'

'You've not forgotten I'm out this evening?'

'No, Alice. Where's Walter picking you up from?'

'Here, at about six o'clock. So you know about him?'

'Well, it's taken you long enough to find someone.'

'Servants don't get many opportunities to meet eligible young men. But even I was surprised to meet someone standing outside the local shop.'

'What are you going to see?'

Alice shrugged. 'We're going to the Empire Picture House.'

'You're going to the Empire, but you don't know what you're going to see. Mm, this could be serious.'

'Connie! It's far too soon to be talking like that. I might not see him again for all I know.'

Walter arrived at six o'clock. There was a tap on the door, and as usual, Patty rushed to answer it.

'Evening, Mr Latham.'

'Hello. It's Miss Goodwin, isn't it? You're looking very pretty this evening. Is that new face powder, or perhaps flour?'

Patty rushed to the mirror and rubbed the flour away.

'Stop teasing her, Walter, she's been very busy this afternoon.'

'Sorry, Patty, I won't tease you again.'

Alice saw Patty's face growing redder.

'Come, Walter, before you get yourself into trouble. We'll be back before nine o'clock. Don't forget the mint, Patty.'

'Have a nice evening, you two, and be good.'

Alice turned to see Patty's impish grin and a wink, and it was her turn to blush.

They hurried to the tram stop, arm in arm. Alice couldn't bring herself to look at him. This was different. Holding on to a man didn't come naturally to her, but she was sure she'd get used to it.

Alice was the first to speak. 'I'm so glad you came. I wondered if you might change your mind.'

'Oh, I wouldn't do that to you.'

'It's good to know. Patty asked me what we were going to see, but I couldn't tell her.'

'It's called *Charlie by the Sea*. Charlie Chaplin's in it. I thought you might fancy a comedy. *Eye for Eye is on and* there's a western too, but I'm not sure who's in it. I saw an advertisement in *The Sentinel*.'

'Oh yes. I haven't seen many films, just the odd one with Connie. I love comedies.'

'Then I chose well. Did you know the Empire was the first purpose-built cinema in Hanley?'

She shook her head. 'But I'm looking forward to the films.'

The tram arrived, and they were soon in Hanley heading towards Brunswick Street. The Empire stood out, looking quite impressive. Towering over three storeys, a large semicircular canopy sheltered the front doors, flanked by pillars.

It was nice to sit close to Walter. He felt comfortable to be with. She caught herself thinking that he could be the one for her. He was very much a gentleman and walked her home arm in arm, chatting more openly as he stood with her by the gate.

'I believe you enjoyed our night out, Alice.'

'It was lovely.'

'I hope we can do it again soon?'

She smiled. 'I do too.'

'I'll sort something out then.'

She couldn't take her eyes off him. She couldn't speak. She just nodded. He leaned close and kissed her cheek.

'I hope that wasn't too forward of me?'

'Not at all,' she squeaked, unable to swallow.

'Goodnight, Alice.'

He took his leave of her, and she strolled towards the back door, watching him as he walked away.

Alice entered the kitchen, to be greeted by a draining board full of pots, pans and plates and Patty sitting at the kitchen table fast asleep, head resting on her arms.

–

Alice received a letter from Walter inviting her to the pictures the following night. The evening would be dark, and he would call to meet her at six o'clock.

She sang as she watched over the pans on the range. Her happiness, however, was short-lived. It started with Robert arriving home late, looking ashen. Alice was setting the table in the dining room and saw him as he walked in and took off his coat. He stood still for long enough for her to go to him to ask if he was all right, worried he might have had a coughing fit or some such.

'Er…m, yes, thank you, Alice. I'm… sure I'm er…' With that, he shook his head and walked upstairs. Alice heard a door slam. She stared after him, waiting for the door to open again. It didn't. She scurried into the garden room, where Connie was sitting reading.

'Hello, Alice. Everything all right?'

Alice bit her lip. 'No, Connie. I don't believe it is. Robert doesn't look too good. He's come in and gone straight upstairs to the bedroom, with barely a word. He might be feeling poorly and doesn't want anyone to know.'

'Oh dear, don't like the sound of that. I'll pop up and see how he is.'

Connie disappeared, leaving Alice to walk downstairs on her own. She carried on laying the table.

Half an hour later, Connie reappeared, pale-faced and tearful. Alice clutched her chest. Something was very wrong. 'Come with me, Connie,' she said, leading her by her left arm into the kitchen. She called over her shoulder. 'Finish the dining room for me, will you, Patty? Now, please,' she added as Patty was about to speak. Patty nodded and shot off.

Connie sank into a chair and reached into her pocket, bringing out a handkerchief to dab her eyes. 'Robert's brought home the most terrible news. It's awful.'

Alice sat beside her and took her hand. 'He's not ill, is he?'

Connie shook her head, her eyes welling up again. 'Do you remember me telling you about the three young men from the cashier's office at the PTC who all joined up together to fight in the war?'

Alice nodded. 'I do.'

Connie licked her lips and nodded again. 'Only Tom Walton came back. He tried to fit in but couldn't, so he had to leave. Everyone felt sorry for him.'

'I remember you saying. It must've been awful.'

'Well, he nearly died earlier today. He tried to commit suicide.' The tears came, and it took Connie a little time to gain control. 'It happened last night, apparently. It must've been such a shock.'

Alice's eyes opened wide. 'Oh, my word!' Her hands covered her cheeks.

'That's right. After he left the PTC, he tried a few places, but couldn't settle. Apparently, he's been going downhill since then. Anyway, he went to stay with his mother so he had some company, and she could keep an eye on him. Unfortunately, his mother had a cleaning job in the evening. She arrived home and found him in the bathroom, collapsed. He'd tried to slash his wrists with a razor.'

Alice gasped.

'He's in the hospital. It'll be touch and go whether he survives. His poor mother's beside herself because she had to leave him to go to work, but she needed the money.'

'How awful, Connie. To have made it through that terrible war and then to feel so guilty about it you try to take your own life.'

'Robert saw a lot of the boys because he was based in Stoke. They could've had such fine lives.' Connie sighed. 'Could you keep the tea warm, and maybe Robert will feel like eating something later?'

'Of course I will.'

'I'll go back and sit with him and make sure he's all right.' Connie hugged Alice and returned to her husband.

Alice stared into the fire, watching the flames, feeling sick but unable to move. Damn that war. It had ended two years ago, and was still taking lives. Hadn't it done enough?

–

The following day, Alice wondered if she should cancel her date with Walter until a week or two later, sure that he would understand. Patty begged her not to, telling her she might regret it, not that she thought for one moment that Walter would resent her doing it.

The moment Connie heard what Alice was contemplating, she refused to allow it. At first, Alice felt guilty, but then her anticipation rose. During the day, Alice had been through all the emotions possible. What she felt now was exhilaration.

'If this is going to be a regular thing, Alice, you'd best get some new clothes,' said Patty.

'Why? Aren't these suitable?'

'They might've been for the Alice Tucker who was a housekeeper who went nowhere, but not for the Alice Tucker who is walking out with a man like Walter Latham.'

Unfortunately, there wasn't enough time for Alice to follow Patty's advice, so her Sunday best, a low-waisted dress with pleats and a lace collar in a soft lilac, would have to do. She would make something suitable for their next meeting – if there was to be one.

Her heart missed a beat when she walked towards the gate as she recognised Walter in the dark, misty evening. This time he didn't take her hand, but gave her a kiss that lingered longer than the previous one. They parted, and he offered his arm, and off they went.

She couldn't help telling Walter about Tom, and he tried to console her. She felt he understood even though he didn't know the man concerned.

He waited until she recovered herself and suggested they might go to the Theatre Royal, where there was a comedy called *Lord Richard in the Pantry* playing. Alice agreed. Walter said it was playing to crowded houses in London. Alice could see why. Sitting beside Walter, watching Charlie Chaplin she could feel Walter's body shaking throughout the film as she listened to his laughter.

There were one or two couples behind them who took advantage of the darkness to kiss each other. Although Alice couldn't bring herself to do such a thing in public, she felt a little jealous by the end of the evening.

The picture house emptied after the final curtain, and they made their way into the street. Conversation was flowing freely as they talked about the films.

They caught the tram to Burslem and walked up Moorland Road because she wanted to be with him for as long as possible. In a few dark spots, he pulled her close enough to kiss her. She waited with anticipation for his lips to catch hers. And when they met, her heart skipped a beat.

She hoped Patty had gone to bed by the time she arrived back at Holmorton Lodge. She would find it difficult to conceal the way she was feeling.

Chapter Six

December 1920

Alice and Patty were cleaning the silver in preparation for the festivities.

'Will I be required to work on Christmas Day?' asked Patty, rubbing a fork so hard her teeth chattered.

'No, I don't think so. There'll only be the three of us here, which I can manage on my own. So you can go home.'

At that moment, Connie entered the kitchen.

'Alice dear, could I have a word with you?'

'I'll go to the scullery and make a start on the boots.' Patty smiled and picked up the box containing all the shoe cleaning and polishing materials. She disappeared down the corridor, humming to herself, smiling at Connie as they passed.

'What can I do for you, Connie?' said Alice as she entered the kitchen.

'Before I tell you anything, I want you to promise me faithfully that you'll not tell a soul about what I'm going to say. I mean nobody.'

Connie's face was bright and flushed. Alice lowered the bread knife onto the table and stared at her. 'Of course, Connie, you know I'm very reliable at keeping secrets.'

'I know, Alice, but it's so important I get everything right.'

Connie took a deep breath, placed a hand on her stomach, and let the breath out slowly. Her glance went from her belly to Alice.

Alice gasped and put her hands to her hot cheeks.

'No!' she exclaimed. 'You're not… are you?'

Connie nodded, smiling. 'I'm expecting a baby, Alice.' The two friends hugged each other, both laughing and crying together.

'Oh, my word,' Alice squealed and then, remembering Patty was only down the corridor, covered her mouth. 'When's it due?'

'July, a few weeks after our first anniversary.'

'Well, that's excellent news. Congratulations. So who else knows?'

'Just Robert. I'll tell Mother when she arrives for Christmas and no one else until after that.'

'Is Robert pleased about it?'

'He's ecstatic.'

–

It was difficult to keep the news secret. When Jean came to visit the following day, Alice guessed Connie wouldn't be able to resist telling her. Alice took refreshments to the garden room, and as soon as she entered, one look at Jean's face confirmed it. She looked delighted. The three women chatted for several minutes about marriage and babies, and Alice took the opportunity to refresh the tea.

When she returned, the tone of the conversation had changed.

'—some people want everything,' muttered Jean with a stony face, now sitting with her arms folded as if creating a barrier.

Alice frowned. It wasn't like Jean at all. She placed the teapot on the table and sat beside her. 'What's up, Jean? Are you all right?'

Jean shrugged. 'I said that some people want everything. Like Betty, for instance.'

'Betty can't decide,' said Connie, musing. 'She's an intelligent girl. She doesn't want to be sat at home all day keeping house while her husband does something more interesting. We had a taste of that on the trams, and now that she has the job in Birmingham, I can see why she doesn't want to give it up.'

'Well, I can't imagine anything more interesting than looking after your own child,' said Jean.

Alice tried to be diplomatic. 'Her job in Birmingham sounds interesting, so why should she give it up to make Duncan feel better? They could make it work if they wanted to.'

'Well, I have to agree with Alice,' said Connie. 'Why should women give up all they've worked for?'

Jean shrugged her shoulders. 'Maybe they shouldn't have babies then.'

Alice raised her eyebrows at Jean's forthright tone, but she knew Jean would give up her job at a moment's notice if she should fall pregnant.

'Besides,' said Alice, 'Duncan's such a nice bloke, it would be a shame to let him go. She needs to be very sure of what she wants before she decides. She also has to consider her daughter's feelings.'

'I don't know why. Hannah has never been at the forefront of her mother's feelings,' said Jean.

'That's unkind of you. She's had to make some tough decisions in her life,' said Connie.

Jean shook her head. 'I'm sorry, but there are some of us who yearn for a baby and can't have one. It seems so selfish.'

Connie and Alice consoled their friend. After all, Jean and Stephen had been married less than two years. There was plenty of time.

'Wouldn't it be exciting if they got re-engaged at Christmas? And if it was snowing, and then she opens her present from Duncan and it's a ring…' By the time Alice had finished, the other two were helpless with laughter.

'Oh, Alice, duck, where would we be without you?'

–

A couple of days after Connie had spoken to Alice, Robert asked Alice to join him in the library to talk about arrangements. Was he taking an interest in the household? Most likely it would be about the baby.

After a few pleasantries, Robert told Alice about his plans.

'A new baby in the house will cause several changes to be made. The nursery will be redecorated. There will be a room for a nanny, two rooms for children, a living room and a small kitchen.'

'Yes, Robert.'

'That'll leave Patty's room and a smaller room to the side of it for servants.'

'I expected that. It's about time we put those rooms to good use.'

'Well, Alice, the other issue is your room on the first floor. It's part of the main house, and Connie and I want to use it as a guest bedroom again. So we suggest you move back to your old room and move Patty into the smaller room. Now that we've a bathroom and privy on that floor, it'll be far more pleasant than before.'

Alice's eyebrows shot up. Was she hearing it right? There was nothing wrong with the rooms on the second floor, but they were plain, and the windows were small, and she would lose her view over the gardens. Alice drew herself up.

'When will this happen, Mr Caldwell?'

'Just before the baby is born in July.'

'Has Mrs Caldwell agreed to this?'

He frowned. 'Of course.'

That night Alice lay awake. No matter what her own thoughts were, she was just a servant in their eyes. Robert had seemed such a nice man. She couldn't imagine him instigating this. Connie, her friend, wouldn't do such a thing – but Connie, her employer, might have changed her mind about the room. Would it help if she spoke to Connie? It didn't take long for Alice to come to the conclusion that speaking to Connie would be a bad idea. She would be asking Connie to choose between her husband and her housemaid. Best let sleeping dogs lie. Things like this have a habit of sorting themselves out.

–

On the Wednesday before Christmas, the household was readying itself for Agatha's visit.

'Mother should arrive in time for lunch. Can you make sure her room is ready? What arrangements have you made for Doubleday?'

'Mrs Copeland's room is prepared. I've put Miss Doubleday in the room next to Patty. They should be quite cosy.'

'I feel sorry for Uncle James. His two daughters, Amanda and Georgiana, and their families, are going to spend Christmas with their father for the first time in years. They do not get on with my mother. He has no sons, and his daughters stand to inherit sizeable fortunes. Mother thinks they are concerned he might do something different if he gets closer to her.'

Agatha, along with the infamous Miss Doubleday, was due to arrive before noon and stay until the 27th. Miss Doubleday had set ideas about the right and wrong way to approach all matters. Her ideas always fell into the 'right' category. Alice knew she'd have to put up with people, including many she didn't like, and Miss Doubleday was most definitely in that last group. She couldn't resist interfering. She enjoyed telling servants where they were going wrong. It would happen now, just when she needed to show Connie she was up to running the household.

Once Alice and Patty had carried Agatha's bags upstairs, Connie ordered afternoon tea to be served in the sitting room. Alice could tell how Connie was feeling by the sparkle in her eyes and the grin that stretched almost from ear to ear.

Alice decided it was about time that Patty began to serve afternoon tea. She had agreed with Connie that Patty should be given more responsibility. So, at four o'clock, Alice knocked on the door and opened it wide enough for Patty and the tray to enter.

'Ah, tea,' said Agatha. 'And how's Patty getting on? You seem to have grown, my child.'

Patty went several shades of red before replying. 'Very well, Mrs Copeland.'

Alice watched from the door. Patty concentrated on laying the tray on the table without spilling anything.

'Thank you, Patty.'

Once in the hall, Patty skipped into the kitchen, pleased with herself. 'They asked me to leave them in private. I think everything went well. No spillage and the spread looked just as you said it should.'

'There you are. I wouldn't have allowed you to do it if I thought you weren't capable.'

Later that afternoon, Alice received word from Connie that Agatha had been told, and Alice was free to tell Patty the good news. Patty almost screamed with excitement. It was indeed a happy day at Holmorton Lodge.

On the Thursday afternoon, Agatha was relaxing in the garden room as Alice walked by.

'Would you like some tea, Mrs Copeland?'

'Oh, that would be very nice, Alice. You are just the person I wanted to speak to. I believe that you're not quite yourself, my dear. Is anything the matter?'

Agatha's look of concern was comforting. Alice couldn't put Robert's ideas out of her mind, nor had she spoken to Connie, and it wouldn't be right to speak out of turn to Agatha. However, to speak to Connie about it would put her friend in the difficult position of having to support either her new husband or her maid. Best keep it to herself for now; after all, what happened at Holmorton Lodge was nothing to do with Agatha now.

Alice jumped. 'Er… no, Mrs Copeland. I'm fine. Really, I am. Christmas is always a busy time of the year.'

'Well, if you're sure…'

'Yes, I am.'

With nothing more to be said, Alice turned to go. She closed the door behind her, blowing out the breath she didn't know she was holding inside, and moved off towards the kitchen, glad Agatha hadn't pressed her too much.

–

This year, Christmas couldn't come fast enough for Alice. Why she should feel so excited about it, she had no idea. It wasn't as though she had a great deal to celebrate. There was just something about Christmas that set her body tingling with anticipation.

It was six o'clock in the morning on Christmas Eve and everywhere was dark. She lay in bed thinking of the day's events and what she was going to do. There was plenty to keep her busy, but she was happy to see the Christmas candles and garlands about the house, sprays of holly and the Christmas wreath hanging on the front door. Somebody – she suspected it might be Connie – had hung a piece of mistletoe above the doorway to the garden room. Maybe she might meet Walter there during the evening. He had promised to call.

Alice and Patty worked hard all day preparing savoury and sweet dishes and chattering away. Dinnertime came and went, and so did tea. Testing out the food as they went along meant they required little in the way of a meal.

Just after seven o'clock, there was a knock on the back door.

'It'll be for me,' Alice called as Patty rose from her seat. 'I'll get it.'

She hurried across the floor and almost skidded into the passage wall. She opened the door, and there stood Walter, wrapped up in a thick black coat, scarf, cap and boots. Only his eyes were visible. The cold air ensured bitter, icy conditions underfoot.

'Come in, Walter. Judging by what you're wearing, it must be pretty cold.'

'You're not wrong there, Alice.'

'Perhaps a glass of whisky might warm you up, Walter!' shouted Patty. 'Either that or Alice will, if you ask her nicely.'

They all laughed. Alice threw a pretend slap in Patty's direction.

Walter, coming from a house of men, was still a little uncertain about how much to say in the company of ladies, and it made Alice giggle seeing him looking discomforted. Nonetheless, he managed a grin and turned to her.

'Soon be Christmas Day, Alice,' he said.

'Yes, it will.'

At that moment, Connie walked in, and the room fell quiet. She smiled at Walter. 'Evening, Mr Latham. How nice it is to see you at last.'

'Good evening to you, Mrs Caldwell. Please call me Walter.'

'Likewise, you may call me Connie.'

Connie glanced at the two flushed faces and laughed to break up the silence. 'Come on, Patty, you can show me how your new dress is coming along.' Connie put her hand on Patty's shoulder and turned her towards the door, marching her off so that Alice and Walter had the kitchen to themselves.

'I'm glad Connie took the hint,' he said.

Alice felt a broad grin spread across her face. 'Me too.'

'Look, I know you're busy and I won't stay long… but…' He took a deep breath. 'But it being Christmas tomorrow and I won't see you… I wanted you to have this.' He pulled a small package from the pocket of his coat and handed it to her. 'Happy Christmas, Alice.'

Alice felt her cheeks grow hotter as she tried to swallow her embarrassment.

'But Walter, you shouldn't. I haven't got you anything.'

'I think I should, Alice. Go on, open it.'

She did as she was bid and unwrapped it. It was a stone. She had seen nothing like it before. Rectangular, it was about an inch long with rounded corners. It felt warm as she closed her hand over it. She opened her palm again and stared at it. Although colourless, there were a couple of streaks of grey running through it – like ice.

'I found it down the pit and have been polishing it to make it into a pendant for you. Will you keep it safe until then?'

'Walter, it's beautiful. But you shouldn't. It looks expensive.'

'Not as stones go. I thought it would look nice on a silver chain one day.'

Tears came to her eyes. 'I don't know what to say.'

'I'm glad you like it, Alice. I've been waiting for the right moment to give it to you.' He moved towards her, and she couldn't take her eyes off him.

'You've been so good to me. I don't know how to repay you.' Her voice was low, and she moved closer to him, her eyes unable to leave his, wanting him to kiss her. Not a peck on the cheek, but a passionate kiss that meant something had changed between them.

'I'm not looking for payment. But if you would allow me to kiss you…'

This time he moved towards her, and his arms drew her close. Then, at last, his mouth was on hers in a move that took her breath away, soft at first and then with a need she couldn't resist. Her heart pounded against his. As he drew away, she kept her eyes closed, too shy to let him see the effect he was having on her.

He lifted her chin gently. 'Oh, Alice. You don't know how long I've wanted to do that.'

She opened her eyes and gazed at him. 'Me too. I just didn't know it until now.'

They heard voices in the hall moving towards them and drew apart. Alice straightened her dress, and her hand went to her hair to tidy it, hoping she didn't look as dishevelled as she felt. But she was smiling – and so was Patty when she returned.

–

The family sat at a beautifully arranged table for Christmas dinner. Agatha, Connie, Robert, and Alice. Alice had given Patty the day off so she might spend Christmas Day afternoon and Boxing Day with her family. It seemed only fair. Patty had enjoyed working with her in preparing the Christmas dinner. It was a shame she wasn't there to sample it. Everything had been planned using Alice's journal, inspired by Mrs Williams: goose, beef and salmon with all the trimmings.

The kitchen door opened. Connie walked in and closed the door behind her. She folded her arms, frowning. 'Alice, I'm disappointed that you felt the need to go to my mother to tell her I was working you too hard. Why didn't you come to me?'

Alice opened her eyes wide. 'I've never said anything about work to her, Connie. She asked me how I was, and I said a bit tired because of all the preparations for Christmas – but that was all. She caught me unawares, but I haven't said anything.'

'Robert said he'd spoken to you about moving back to the attic.'

Alice nodded.

'That won't be necessary. I'll speak to him.' Connie relaxed a little. 'Does that feel better?'

Again, a nod from Alice. 'I'm sorry, Connie. I didn't mean to give the impression I was unhappy or nothing.'

'I'm sorry too, Alice, but remember that I'm the mistress of the house; you should come to me. We'll say no more about it.'

–

Robert's older brother, Stanley, had a week's leave from the Royal Warwickshire Regiment before being posted overseas and called in to see Robert to give him news about his family.

The youngest of the three, Andrew, was in the Essex Regiment and was now serving in the Middle East. They were a military family, which included both his brothers and their father, from whom Robert had been estranged for not joining them. Instead, he worked at the War Office in London. When the war started, Robert refused to enlist in the army, much to the chagrin of the family. Instead, he had joined the Friends' Ambulance Unit, preferring to keep people alive rather than kill them. His father had never given him the opportunity to talk about what he had done during the war. Thanks to Connie's intervention just before the wedding, both his brothers had turned up to see him get married. She got into trouble with Robert, who believed his father should have made the first move.

Alice was happy that Stanley had made it to see his brother, even if it was to say that their father was still refusing to acknowledge or talk about Robert.

Alice was taking out the crockery from the first course, ready to bring in the Christmas cake, when she heard low voices in the hallway.

'Now listen, Rob, we've been working on the parents to get them to receive you ever since the war ended. The old man's still insistent that he won't allow you in, but Mother has melted somewhat. I think she would've allowed you home sooner, but for him. She's given me a letter to say she wants to see you again. Especially when I tell her she'll have a grandchild before long.' He reached inside his breast pocket and handed over an envelope, his face earnest.

Robert took it and looked up to see Alice with her burden. His cheeks flushed. 'Thanks, Stanley.'

'It won't be long before Andrew is back in the country. He'll have to get used to the British climate again after the time he has spent in Mesopotamia. As for me – I don't know where I'm being posted to. But I'll be in touch. You'll not get rid of me now we're in contact again, and I hope the folks will follow.'

Connie invited her former tram girls friends together with their husbands – Jean and Stephen, Ginnie and Sam, and Betty with Hannah – to a Christmas get-together. Betty was staying in Birmingham this Christmas and couldn't come, which was a shame, as Connie planned to tell them of her pregnancy. Although Ginnie wasn't a tram girl, she had been a close friend of Connie's throughout that time. Alice and Patty joined the diners since Betty and Hannah were absent.

When Connie gave out her news, there was cheering and clapping. Out of the group, Connie was the last person they'd have expected to start a family so soon after getting wed, given her history with the suffragettes and campaigning on the rights of women. Even the men joined the conversation about the forthcoming baby. Alice and Patty chuckled as they left to bring in the next course.

When they returned, Jean was missing. Alice excused herself and ran upstairs. There was no sign of Jean. Alice tiptoed along the landing. She must be in the privy. Where else could she be? Alice felt uncomfortable listening at the door but wanted to make sure her friend was all right.

'Jean dear, are you in there?' There was a rustling of what sounded like fabric, and a cough. Nothing more. 'Jean?' Alice tried the door, but it was locked, as she had suspected. 'Jean.' At first there was no sound, then the chain was pulled. Moments later, Jean appeared, eyes watering. 'Oh, Jean, are you feeling unwell?'

Jean shook her head. 'No, and thank you, Alice. I'm just a silly woman feeling sorry for herself.'

'Whatever for? Is there a problem between you and Stephen?'

Jean dabbed her eyes with a handkerchief pulled from her pocket, almost as if she was expecting more tears. 'Look, my room is just along the hall, so come with me till yer feeling better.'

Jean allowed herself to be led to Alice's room. She glanced around. 'How lucky you are, Alice. It's a lovely room.'

'Connie felt it was time for me to move out of the attic room. Now, Jean, sit down and tell me. What's brought on all those tears?'

It all spilled out. 'It's with Ginnie having Young Sam six months ago and Connie's expecting and she's given no thought to having a family, as far as I know. Now you've got Walter, and you'll have a child before me, likely as not. And there's me, desperate to have a child of my own to cherish, and there's no sign of a pregnancy. I mean – it's so unfair, Alice.'

It all came back to Alice. When they'd been together chatting about life and who was going to do what when the war was over, Jean had never talked about jobs; it was children she wanted. And now here she was and most of her friends had children, or were expecting.

'To be honest, Alice, I've been thinking that being injured in the war might have decreased Stephen's... ability,' she said delicately, 'to become a father.'

As far as Alice knew, Stephen had received only injuries to his leg, so Jean's thought was unlikely, to say the least. She wondered how to respond. If she suggested it wasn't Stephen's fault because of the war, she was implying it had to be somebody's fault. Jean needed to concentrate on the home she had got.

'I need something to take my mind off... everything. I thought a job might help... but it hasn't.'

'There's still plenty of time, Jean.'

Part Two

Chapter Seven

January 1921

The former inmates of Haddon House Children's Hostel got together on 8 January at Ginnie's house. It was reminiscent of the workhouse, where Christmas always came in January.

They talked about the festivities, presents given and received, small things that meant a lot to the recipient. A book of nursery rhymes from Sam to Ginnie, which she could read to Young Sam. Ada had received a set of handkerchiefs from her neighbour, and Alice told them of the stone given to her by Walter.

'We are all so lucky, aren't we? At one time we had nowt, and now we have friends and are making families of our own.'

Young Sam must have heard them, as he came out with a series of chuckles as if he was listening.

Alice spied her chance. 'Ada, if I remember right, you were in the same position as me. Your mother left you in order to get work.'

'That's what the matron seemed to tell everybody. I've never heard from my mother since, and I'm not that interested in making contact.'

'Aren't you curious to know her reasons?'

'Not really. I suppose she did what she thought was best,' Ada shrugged. 'I never knew me father, so I don't suppose my mother had much to do with him. I did all right thanks to Ginnie and Sam, who showed me the ropes.'

'Same for me,' said Sam. 'As far as I can remember, me father was a sailor, which's a bloody rare thing in The Potteries, as we're a long way from the sea. I conner remember what age I was, but I know Father was looking after me one day, and next he left me with a neighbour while he went on a trip. Whatever that trip was, it must've been a bloody long one because I've seen nowt of him since. The neighbour put me in the workhouse cos she had umpteen kids of her own,' grinned Sam. 'That's where I met my Ginnie.'

'But Ginnie, you moved into the workhouse as a family. They didn't abandon you,' Alice said.

Ginnie shook her head. 'Well, I wouldn't say that was true. You see, my mother took to drink, and she'd disappear from Haddon, only to be returned by the bobbies when she was too drunk to get away from them. She always got herself sorted out, and then something would happen and she'd be back on the gin. Father was different. He'd something wrong with his eyes and couldn't do his job, which's why we ended up in the workhouse. They both died in there.'

'You've heard our stories, Alice. Now tell us yours.'

'We lived in a lovely house in Kidsgrove owned by the company Father worked for. It had a garden, and there were woods in front. One day, Father didn't come home. He'd been killed in a boating accident in the Harecastle Tunnel, a difficult canal tunnel. You have to lie down on top of the boat and use your feet to move along in the pitch black.'

The friends were silent. Ginnie and Ada looked horrified, and Sam hung on to every word. She caught her breath – and continued.

'I was six years old. There was less money coming in. Mother couldn't get enough work because of me. We had to move out of our lovely house to a horrible one on Napier Street, also in Kidsgrove. The windows let in water when it rained from a certain direction, the roof let in water when it rained from any direction, and we'd one privy between six families. The stink in the summer was horrible.'

Nobody said a word.

Alice continued. 'One day, Mother came to pick me up from school and told me we were going to a new place soon, where we'd be much better. She'd got somebody to take us on the back of a cart. I was eight. In Haddon Workhouse, we were separated, and I was put with the older children. It was the last time I saw her. Mrs Higgins told me Mother cried for days. Mrs Higgins was very good to me. I was so upset when she died. But I had one stroke of luck when I was twelve. I went to work for Mrs Copeland, and the rest you know.'

'Sounds awful,' said Ada, shuddering.

'Have any of you felt tempted to seek your parents?' asked Alice.

'Not me,' said Sam. 'If I met me dad, I'd lamp him one.'

'When I was thirteen, I thought about trying to find my mother, but they had no more information,' said Ada. 'I'm never sure whether they had the information but wouldn't tell us.'

'Well, I've been thinking about it,' said Alice. 'Mother had always been kind to me up to that point. It seemed out of character for her to abandon me. There must have been some reason. I wish I knew what happened to her.'

It was on Alice's mind as she walked home.

Alice settled in for the night. It must be possible to find out what happened to her mother. It was just a matter of knowing where to look. She lay in bed and let her mind wander back to her mother. Throughout her time at the workhouse, she had given little thought to her. There was a lot of work to do and little time for contemplation. At first, she'd been upset. Why had her mother abandoned her? One day she was there, and the next she was gone. Alice had been old enough to know how difficult it would be for any single woman to get work when there was a child at home and no family support. It was much later when she realised just how desperate her mother must have been to leave her in the workhouse. Alice was sure that once she had a job and was back on her feet, her mother would return to pick her up. That was over fourteen years ago, and Alice had heard nothing from her.

So why did she feel so unsettled now, after all this time? Could it be because of the changes taking place at Holmorton Lodge? The master had died, the mistress had gone to live with her brother, and her best friend, Connie, had married, and some of her friends were starting families of their own. Perhaps her apprehension came with the realisation that life at Holmorton Lodge would never be the same.

–

Alice got up the next morning shivering with the cold air. She hadn't had sufficient sleep, so she had difficulty keeping her eyes open. Patty, on the other hand, was as bright as a button. Alice tried her best to smile, but she wished Patty wasn't so happy.

'Mr Robert's already gone to work, and I've laid all the fires downstairs. I think we've got time to have some breakfast before getting ready for the mistress to go to work. How long do you think she'll work now that the baby's on its way?'

Alice shrugged. 'I don't know. Women working at the potbanks can work up to a few days before, but I don't think that'll be the case with the mistress working in an office. They won't want a pregnant woman wandering around. She might be asked to leave more or less straight away.'

'I wonder if she's told her boss yet?'

'I presume you mean Mr Railsford?'

'Yes.'

'She may have. He'll have to find somebody else.'

'She'll have more time to see how we're working and where things aren't being done to her standards.'

'Yes, Patty, and if we always do our best, it'll make no difference if she's at home.'

At that moment, Connie arrived in the kitchen looking pale and talked to Alice about household matters as she ate her breakfast. Patty grinned as she went about her morning duties. Morning sickness didn't seem to have spoiled Connie's appetite.

Once Connie had left, Patty, complete with her trolley and all the cleaning tranklements laid out, disappeared to start the dusting and cleaning downstairs.

Alice remained at the table, working her way through her notebook. She would need to buy some suet in order to make the jam roly-poly she was planning. It was one of Robert's favourites. Her mind kept wandering back to her mother and how she could go about finding her. In the end, she determined that the best place to start would be the workhouse to discover what information it held. They must know something.

Alice gave her excuses to Patty and had a rummage in the belongings she kept under her bed. She was pretty sure that she had received a birth certificate before she left the workhouse. After ten minutes, she found it.

She sat on the bed and scrutinised it, something she hadn't done for years. She noted her birthplace as Runcorn, and that her birth was registered there. All she knew about Runcorn was that it was on the River Mersey. Large boats brought china clay from Cornwall by sea, then loaded it onto barges and sent it down the Trent and Mersey to The Potteries. Most of the same barges returned with finished pottery ready for sale.

Would it be better to go straight to Runcorn? In the end, she opted to visit the workhouse on Turnhurst Road, between Burslem and Tunstall, at her earliest opportunity. The local choice seemed right for her first foray into gathering information.

Would it be a good idea to ask someone to visit the workhouse with her? If Mrs Copeland hadn't gone, she would have been tempted to ask her, since she had been a Workhouse Friend for several years. She may have been told something about her past.

Connie fell into the same category, but the last thing Alice wanted to do was to give Connie the impression that she was unsettled, and with the pregnancy looming, she thought it better to keep Connie in the dark for now.

It occurred to Alice to mention her intentions to Walter, but decided it was too early in their relationship for him to be involved in what was a very personal matter. She hadn't even told him that Mrs Copeland had taken her from the workhouse.

She had to decide for herself who to contact – and how. Mrs Hardcastle, the matron, could ignore a letter, leaving Alice waiting for a reply that never came. Answering the letter might raise more questions, causing another round of correspondence. This could take an age.

No – direct action was called for. She'd visit the workhouse and ask to see Mrs Hardcastle as soon as possible.

–

It was the end of January when Alice walked down to Burslem Station and caught the train to Tunstall. The station was at the bottom of Pittshill Bank, and the turning for the workhouse was on the left after about a mile. Continuing up the bank for about another quarter of a mile, the children's hostel stood on the right-hand side. They separated the children from the adults, believing the adults to be a bad influence. Alice continued on to the Big House, the local name for the workhouse.

The workhouse was close to an abandoned colliery, which closed during the reign of Queen Victoria. Alice remembered learning this at the board school on High Lane, which workhouse children attended.

The workhouse was a vast building containing an infirmary, farm, bakehouse, corn mill, workrooms and piggeries – plenty of work for the able-bodied or undeserving poor, as they were often called. In addition, there was a kitchen with a chapel above. Vagrants' wards and workshops were added later.

As she walked towards it, she recognised the red bricks and casement windows, but it appeared smaller than she remembered. On the opposite side of the road was the workhouse cemetery.

Alice thought back to her own arrival as a child. She couldn't recall having gone into that building until she was much older. Maybe her mind had shut it out, refusing to have any memories of something so tragic. Even when she and Ginnie had spoken of their pasts, Alice's memory refused to take part.

Alice's pace slowed as she came to the outskirts of the workhouse. She stared at it before making her way towards the porter's lodge. A lump had formed in her throat, making swallowing difficult. Without the Copelands' pity and offer of a home, she'd have ended up living there.

She knocked on the door, and an elderly man with a long, scruffy beard and wearing a flat cap and dressed in what looked like a workhouse uniform let her in.

'What can I do for yer, miss?' He grinned at her, showing only half a dozen yellowed teeth.

Alice looked away, shuddering. 'I've… er… I've come to see Mrs Hardcastle.'

'Got an appointment?'

Alice shook her head. 'I'm afraid I—'

'She wunner see thee if tha's not got an appointment.'

'I need to speak to her. It's urgent.'

His eyes narrowed, and his head leaned to one side as if trying to decide. 'Now what would a posh girl like you want with our matron, I wonder?'

Alice wished she were somewhere else rather than standing in front of this man. What could she say? He hadn't connected her with anyone who lived inside because she was posh.

She stood tall and lifted her chin. 'My name is Alice Tucker. I'm Mrs Copeland's housekeeper, and I'm here on her behalf. Would you be kind enough to ask Mrs Hardcastle if I could see her?'

She felt better now that she had asserted herself. At least she could say she tried.

The man sneered but did as she requested, disappearing through the opposite door and into the building. Alice closed her eyes and took a deep breath. He was gone some time, and she was giving up hope of finding out anything when the door banged open again. It wasn't the elderly man but a woman in a black dress that reached her ankles. Her white hair was scraped back from her face, showing off deep wrinkles around her nose and mouth. No smile passed over her lips as she stared at Alice. Then, as if making up her mind, she asked Alice to follow her. They crossed the yard and entered the main building, and went into an office marked 'Matron'.

Mrs Hardcastle sat at the desk and locked her fingers together. 'Now, young lady, I hear from the lodge-keeper you're here on Mrs Copeland's behalf. I remember you. You left us to work for Mrs Copeland. You seem to have done well for yourself. How can I help Mrs Copeland?'

Alice swallowed, unsure how to continue. 'I've come to ask for information for myself – not Mrs Copeland.'

'So, shall we start again?' Mrs Hardcastle leaned forward, locking her fingers together and frowning, her head tilted to one side, waiting for an answer.

Taking a deep breath, Alice began. 'My name is Alice Tucker, and I was in this place when I was a girl – well, not quite this place.'

Mrs Hardcastle's eyebrows lifted. 'And when was that?'

'1906. I was eight and with my mother. They sent me to the children's hostel. Mother stayed here.' She drew her hands together to stop them trembling.

Mrs Hardcastle took out a small notebook and wrote something down. 'And what was her name?'

'Margaret Tucker.'

'What about your father?'

'Dead. That's why we had to come in. We had no money.'

Mrs Hardcastle sucked in her tongue. 'So, what d'yer want to know?'

This was the difficult bit. Admitting to a total stranger that her mother had left her in the workhouse.

Alice licked her lips. 'My mother left here in 1906.' Alice blinked. 'She also left me.' Her fingers trembled, then lifted her head proudly. 'I don't know why she left me behind.'

Mrs Hardcastle leaned back in her seat – maybe to put some space between them. 'I see. We know even less than you.'

'I thought she'd have to sign out and leave her address or something, what with me being in the children's hostel.' Alice could feel tears welling as the painful memories were let loose. 'But Mother and I came here together, and then she left me and I never saw her again.' Alice dashed a tear away. 'She's the only family I have.'

Mrs Hardcastle stared at her long and hard as Alice tried to meet her gaze.

'One moment, please.'

The woman rose, and the rustle of her petticoat followed her out of the room. Had Alice said enough to persuade her? Where else could she go? Was she being thwarted from the outset?

Moments later, Mrs Hardcastle returned carrying a large book – a journal of some sort, maybe. She sat down again and flicked through the pages around the dates Alice had mentioned.

'Here we are – Margaret Tucker, born 17 January 1864, aged forty-two, formerly of 27 Napier Street, Kidsgrove in the parish of Wolstanton.'

'That's her! That's my mother.'

'Here you are on the next line – Alice Tucker, born 4 April 1898 in Runcorn, Cheshire, aged eight, daughter of Margaret Tucker, formerly of...'

Mrs Hardcastle skimmed through the notes beside the name. 'It's as I thought, Miss Tucker. She left the workhouse on 27 April 1906, but failed to return. She left no address or person for us to contact. And she left you, which of course was against the law, so she would have been in trouble if she came back.

She must have left in her workhouse uniform because she owes money for that.'

Alice was devastated. She'd hoped beyond anything that she'd pick up something that would help her next step. She was doubting the wisdom of approaching the workhouse, stirring up things that shouldn't be stirred.

'Now, let's have a look at your entry when you left.' A few moments later, Mrs Hardcastle's nimble fingers had arrived at Alice Tucker. 'Here we are, born on 4 April 1898, and at twelve, released into the care of Mr and Mrs Edwin Copeland, Holmorton Lodge, Burslem.'

'Is that all?' asked Alice.

'A note that you were abandoned, and it has your admission folio number. I'm sorry, but that's all I can do.'

Mrs Hardcastle rose, making it clear that the meeting was over. Alice thanked her for her time and left.

On the walk back home, Alice's mind was all over the place. She had been hoping that she'd got it wrong – about Mother leaving her in that place – but it was all true. Her mother had abandoned her. How could anyone do that to their only child?

Chapter Eight

February 1921

A few weeks later, Alice decided that it was time she told Walter about her early life and her decision to find her mother. She knew that when he was on days, he would usually go to the shop in the afternoon, so she made an excuse to be there around three o'clock. They decided to go for a walk around Burslem Park. Because it was a working day, there were few people in the park, and it felt quite private.

Walter listened to what she had to say. She loved how he allowed her to talk without interruption, only occasionally asking for clarification. When she got to her story's end, she stopped walking and turned to Walter.

'That's it, my whole life. Not very exciting.'

'It sounds as if you've had more excitement than most people.'

'What do you think I should do?'

'So the visit to the workhouse wasn't a lot of use?' said Walter, rolling a cigarette.

'No, I was disappointed, and now I realise that it's going to be a harder job than I thought.'

'What if, when you find your mother, she wants nothing to do with you?'

'I hadn't thought about that. I just assumed that any mother would want to meet with her daughter again, no matter what the circumstances.'

'That's what I find so attractive about you, Alice, always thinking the best of people.'

He touched Alice's hand during this conversation. It made her feel safe and wanted after the disappointment of the last few days.

'Unfortunately, there could be lots of reasons for not getting in touch,' he said. 'She may have got married again and not told her new family. Maybe she's too ashamed of what she did, and being reacquainted with you would be a constant reminder of that time.' Walter let go of her hand, and Alice felt she wanted to grab his back.

He cleared his throat. 'If you're agreeable, Alice, think it's about time that we told my family that we're walking out together, and you should tell Connie as well,' he said.

Alice stared into his earnest-looking eyes. Was he really asking her out? 'I don't know,' said Alice. 'It's difficult for servants to have friends, given the number of hours we do. I'd go as far as saying in the past that they've assumed that there was no gentleman friend on the horizon and never would be. They still look at me as a young girl. You can't be a servant and housekeeper and have a husband and children. What will they say?'

Walter shook his head. 'I didn't mean it that way, Alice. But I am falling for you. I know it's a bit soon, but, well – it's my turn to admit to not thinking things through. Forget it for the moment. Best keep it quiet until we're ready for any consequences.'

Now she had upset him. She couldn't leave him like this. She caught his hand as he let hers go. 'Walter, I want to understand my family before I make any firm plans for my future, and the sooner I do that, the better. Will you help me? Two brains are better than one.' She gave him her best smile.

Walter beamed. 'Of course I will. I'll always be here for you, no matter what.'

–

On the way back to Holmorton, Alice decided it was time she told Connie that she was planning to search for her mother. Surely she would be pleased to know Alice was taking her life into her own hands.

She looked in each of the rooms downstairs and concluded that Connie must've been taking a nap after work that day. Patty was looking after the meal, as they planned to eat at seven.

'Alice, can you go upstairs to see Connie in our room? She was asking for your company,' said Robert.

'Of course, Mr Caldwell.'

'Oh, and can we go back to you calling me Robert? Mr Caldwell sounds too formal to me. It makes me think I'm at work.'

'If you're sure – Robert. But I'll still call you Mr Caldwell when we've visitors.' Alice smiled and headed towards the door. 'Just so you know,' she grinned at the chagrin on his face and closed the door behind her.

She walked up the stairs and knocked on Connie's bedroom door.

'Come in.'

Alice entered. 'Robert said you wanted me?'

Connie was lying on the bed in the dress she'd worn for work that day, clearly exhausted. 'I don't know whether it's the pregnancy or whether it's the amount of work. The office was busy preparing papers for a number of cases.'

'Is there anything I can get you?'

'No, I just thought I'd like to have somebody with me, and we haven't had a chance for a chat. I sent Robert to make me a cup of tea. I thought it'd keep him occupied. He was fussing. I hope he's not going to be like this for the next six months.'

'Patty's in the kitchen. She'll help him if he needs anything.'

They chatted for a few minutes when they heard the sound of china on silver and in walked Patty with a tray of tea.

'Robert's got you to make the tea, thank goodness for that. He makes tea far too strong for me. You'll have to give him some lessons, Goodwin.'

'Yes, ma'am.' Patty nodded, and as she turned, she winked at Alice and left the room.

'She's coming on well. Pull up a chair, Alice.'

She did as she was bid. 'I think so. She enjoys the cooking the best but never complains about any task.'

Before Connie could say more, Alice launched into her plan. 'Connie, I've decided to search for my mother. I need to speak with her and try to understand just why she left me at the workhouse all those years ago.'

'I've never heard you talk about her before. What's changed your mind?'

'I've been speaking with Ginnie, Sam and Ada about their time in the workhouse, and it made me think. I realise Mother's decision must have been difficult for her to make, but I want to know why.'

Connie fell quiet, then caught her lip. 'It'd be incorrect of me not to say this, Alice, but are you prepared for it being a fruitless search?'

'I'll have to take that chance.'

'Suppose you don't like what you find?'

'At least I'll know. Connie, I keep turning it over in my mind. I can't go on like this.'

'Well, let me know if I can help. I could ask Mother if she knows anything that might assist you.'

'That would be excellent. They may tell Mrs Copeland more about me. Thank you.'

Alice took her leave soon after, pleased she'd included Connie after her recent doubts.

–

It was 20 February before Alice could get a Sunday afternoon off. Connie liked both servants to be working at the weekend, as it was the time she needed them most. She was still working with Mr Railsford at the solicitors, maybe because she wasn't showing much and her pregnancy seemed to be going well, now the sickness had ended.

Alice had arranged to meet Walter at Burslem Station. They were going to Kidsgrove to look at the area where Alice had been raised. She hoped there would be no ill-feeling between them after their discussion about setting their relationship on a more formal footing.

The Loop Line, as most people from The Potteries knew it, connected Kidsgrove, Goldenhill, Tunstall, Burslem, Hanley and Stoke before rejoining the main London-to-Glasgow railway line. When they arrived at Kidsgrove Junction, they walked up the main street, Liverpool Road. There were shops on their right and some nice-looking houses on the left. They turned left and headed up the steep bank that was Heathcote Street, with terraced houses on both sides. Every so often, there was a shop of some description. They turned right at the Lamb Inn and then left into Napier Street.

The demolition of all the houses Alice remembered and their replacement with new terraces shocked her, but she wasn't surprised. The house she had lived in was unfit and had leaked every time it rained.

Like many streets in industrial areas, people were always milling around. Women cleaning their doorsteps, chatting and gossiping, and men leaning against the sides of their houses, smoking until they had to go to work. Alice and Walter stopped to ask a few people if they remembered a woman called Margaret Tucker, but nobody they spoke to had lived in Napier Street back in 1906. Most were new to the area.

'I used to go to school further up the bank, but there's no point in going there on a Sunday. I think we should go to the house in St John's Wood.'

'Very well. Lead on,' said Walter, grinning.

The Loop Line railway bridge crossed the street near to the junction with Liverpool Road. It looked a prosperous little town. They crossed over Liverpool Road and walked down The

Avenue and on to St John's Wood. The houses here looked substantial and nothing like the terraces that they'd just seen. Although they were in the form of a terrace, each property was wider than normal, with a garden at the front and surrounded by a low wall.

'This was our old house,' Alice said with confidence. 'Number sixteen. And that window above the front door was my bedroom. We were happy here. I used to play in the woods across the road. There was a pathway leading to the scariest place in Kidsgrove – the cemetery.'

'Well, it's a cut above the houses on Dartmouth Street. I bet it cost a pretty penny to rent.'

'All I know is that it came with my father's job. Following his death, we had to move out, but they allowed us to stay until Midsummer's Day. Mother spent most of that time crying, and it wasn't until the week before we were due to leave that she attempted to find a place to rent. And what a place she found – Napier Street.'

Alice banged the large brass knocker, with Walter standing beside her. A gentleman of about forty opened the door a few moments later. His black hair was going grey at the temples, and his beard was almost white.

'Hello, young lady. How can I help yer?'

'Hello, sir. I'm sorry to trouble you on a Sunday afternoon, but I used to live in this house when I was a child, and I wondered if you knew anything about a family called Tucker that lived here until 1906?'

'I'm afraid I conner help you there, duck. I've only lived in this house for two years. Dunner know who lived here afore me, all as I know is that this house belongs to the North Staffordshire Railway, the NSR, we call it, so it may have had many tenants. What did you say the name was?'

'Wilfred and Margaret Tucker. I'm their only daughter, Alice.'

'I recognise the name Wilfred Tucker. I work in the engineering department at the NSR on the canal. Was he the one what died in an accident?' He scratched the top of his head.

'Yes, that's the man.' Alice paused for a second, wondering if he'd comment about the circumstances of her father's accident. However, if he knew any more, he wasn't about to tell them.

'There's a gentleman who lives in Long Row called Josiah Talbot. He seems to know everything there's to know about the canal in Kidsgrove. I think he lives at number 44. It might be worth your talking to him.'

Alice thanked the man for his help and left.

They continued their walk through a grassy area leading them back to Long Row and knocked on the door. A man, old in years with white hair and a long white beard, opened the door.

'Hello, and to what do I owe the pleasure?' He pursed his lips as he waited for their answer.

'Hello, Mr Talbot, we're looking for someone, and a gentleman from St John's Wood suggested you might be able to help us because you've lived here a long time.'

'Aye, I've lived in Kidsgrove a good few years now. There's few folk what I don't know. Best come in then.'

He stood to one side to allow first Alice and then Walter to enter. He shuffled in behind them. 'Have a seat, ducks, I conner be doing with standing up at my time of life.'

Alice and Walter sat on the dark brown settee while Mr Talbot lowered himself into the upright chair beside the fire, although it wasn't lit.

'Best tell me what you want to know then. Been living here all me life.'

Alice began. 'My parents lived in St John's Wood until 1904. They were called Wilfred and Margaret Tucker. They had a daughter. Mr Tucker worked at the NSR, but an accident killed him.'

Mr Talbot pursed his lips. 'Aye. I remember him. Top bloke. I had a lot of respect for him. Always treated men fairly, no matter whether they was bosses or labourers. How come you're asking about him after all these years?'

'I'm Alice Tucker, his daughter.'

His bushy eyebrows disappeared into his thick white hair. 'My word, I weren't expecting that.' He took up a pipe from the table beside him and put it in his mouth as if planning to stay seated for the rest of the afternoon.

Alice told him her story, how her mother had hit on hard times after her father had died.

'Aye, poor lass. That girl never hurt nobody.'

Alice smiled. It was the first time she had heard anyone praise her mother. That alone made her day worthwhile.

'Course, I remember Mrs Tucker having to leave the house cos it was an NSR house. There was summat to do with the accident – that's it, they said at the investigation that yer father had been drinking, but I've never seen him in any of the public houses roundabout. Most canal men drank at the Blue Bell, but not yer father. I remember this one day that yer dad had been chatting to Davy, one of the repairmen, while he waited for the engineering boat to arrive. Davy and some others would block the tunnel at both ends during the inspection. When the engineering boat arrived late, the two men seemed to be a bit on the merry side, but yer father ignored them. He started doing his job. The following morning we heard as he'd bin drowned. Davy tried to speak to the bosses, but they wouldn't listen. The company, which was a big employer in The Potteries, wanted it sorted. Everybody who wasn't dead had a vested interest in it being yer dad's fault. No insurance, no lost jobs, no costs, yer see. And – well, the dead conner talk, can they?'

During this speech, Alice's mouth had opened wider and wider, unable to believe what she had just heard.

'Is it possible to speak to Davy?'

'No lass, he fell on the first day of the Somme, like a few lads from around here. Like I said, duck. Yer father was a good man. It's only right that you should know the full story. The bosses used him as a scapegoat, nowt more.'

After a cup of tea, Alice and Walter took their leave of Josiah Talbot and walked back towards the centre of Kidsgrove to catch the train to Burslem. Neither of them said a word for five minutes. Then Alice gave a deep sigh. 'I suppose it was bound to happen, Walter. When you delve into people's lives, you never know what you might find.'

'Whatever you find, Alice, I'd bet a half-crown that your parents were decent folk and you should be proud of them. So, what do you want to do now?'

'To tell you the truth, Walter, I've no idea. My head's spinning. To think of all the heartache my mother must have gone through and with no one to share it, I really need to think this through. I mean, what else might I find out? You were right in questioning whether I was ready for it. That's more or less what Connie said. I'll need to think very carefully about what I do next.'

Chapter Nine

April 1921

Walter called by the kitchen at Holmorton Lodge, grinning from ear to ear. Alice couldn't help but smile. Looked like good news for a change.

'Bertie and Edith are getting back together, Alice.'

She clapped her hands. 'That's wonderful news. I'm so pleased for him. It's nice to see people settling down again after the war and the flu epidemic.'

'They've told anyone else yet. He and Carla are going to rent the house together. It makes sense, as Carla's already paying rent to Dottie. It'll mean Ruth and Dottie will have to find a bit more money, but they seem happy enough with the situation.'

'I expect Ruth's happy for her friend.'

'We're all pleased. Now, we just need to get you sorted out with your mother and then perhaps we can do some planning.'

Alice brought the conversation back to Bertie and Edith. 'I suppose they're concerned about what her mother's reaction might be. If they've got a home, they'll be able to move out.'

'Keep your fingers crossed for them.'

It must have worked, because by the end of the week, Bertie had got himself fixed up with a full-time job at the North Staffs Railway Company. Bertie and Edith could make their plans now.

–

Alice finished her shopping and visited Ginnie to see how Young Sam was getting on. When she arrived at North Street, she heard laughter and screams coming from Ginnie's house.

She knocked on the door, and Ginnie answered. 'Hello, Alice, come in.'

'Is everything all right? I could hear you at the top of the street.'

Ginnie laughed. 'No, Alice, nothing's wrong. Mabel's getting married to that nice Mr Bossons from the Co-op. She's been celebrating with the cooking sherry.'

'Hello, Alice.' Mabel giggled. 'Have you heard my wonderful news?'

Alice agreed with Ginnie about the drink. 'Yes, congratulations. Have you set a date yet?'

'No, but I told him there'd be no "divi" for him until we're married.'

Mabel waggled her finger in front of Alice's nose.

'But Alice, do you know what he said to me?' And without a pause, she answered her own question. 'He said I could have as much "divi" as I want once we're married.'

With a sigh, Mabel wandered back to the kitchen to refill her empty glass, leaving Alice and Ginnie doubled up with laughter.

'Come on, Alice, we'll walk Florrie home from school. Looks like our Mabel isn't fit at the moment,' said Ginnie. Florrie was Mabel's only child and had started school in September of last year.

As they walked through the streets after dropping off Florrie, Ginnie told her of the plans following the wedding.

'Mr Bossons only rents his present lodgings, so he'll move into our house with Mabel. Me and Sam'll need to find somewhere else.'

'Has Mabel got a date yet?'

'It'll be sometime this year.' Ginnie sighed. 'I'll miss them when we move out. Our Florrie's a cute little thing. I suppose I'm a second mum to her.' She paused. 'It'd be nice for our kids to live near Burslem Park. Those houses on Hamil Road look nice, but I think the rent's higher than we can afford. I wish I could go back to work. It'd make all the difference to us. But there's no one to look after Young Sam. Pity, those houses would be perfect for us. Sam would only be across the road from his job, and I've heard you say that the air's better up there. We've been trying to save up so we can rent somewhere of our own. We knew it'd happen one day.'

Alice let out a sigh. Nothing was ever straightforward in this world.

'Talking of getting wed. How're you getting on with this bloke of yours?'

Alice giggled. 'Not talking of getting wed yet – that's for sure!'

Chapter Ten

May 1921

There was a strong northeast wind blowing and everywhere felt cold as May Day dawned. About eleven o'clock there was a knock at the back door, and Walter and Ruth paid a visit.

'I thought I'd let you know Bertie hasn't let the grass grow under his feet. Him and Carla have found a house in Lime Street. If they pool their resources, then they can afford the rent and afford to eat. I think that's all Bertie wants.'

'Whereabouts is Lime Street?'

'It runs parallel to Campbell Road, where we live now,' said Ruth, 'and is within walking distance of the NSR. It has three bedrooms, so Luther could have a room of his own. Or at least he'll have one until more children come along.'

'It's very much the same as Dottie Spilling's. Close to the football ground where Stoke play. It looks a nice place,' said Walter.

'When does this happen?'

'Next Sunday.'

'Have they told Mrs Wren yet?'

'No, I don't think so.'

Sure enough, a week later, Alice heard from Ruth that Edith and Bertie had rented the house in Lime Street. It came as a surprise when Alice received a letter from Edith inviting her and Walter for tea on Sunday week. Alice thought back to the flower show at Crewe Park and how it helped them get back together. She could only speculate about how Mrs Wren felt. But no doubt she'd find out soon.

–

Ginnie called at Holmorton Lodge on Sunday, just before dinner. She was flushed, and had left Young Sam in the care of his father.

'Ginnie! How lovely to see you.' Alice gave her a hug. 'Are you here to see Connie?'

'Well, er, yes, I am. But I also wanted to see you Patty an' all.'

Alice glanced up at the clock.

'Dunner werrit, I'm not staying long.'

Ginnie smiled, causing an apologetic flush to burn on Alice's face. 'There's nothing wrong, is there?'

'I'm out of breath.'

'Sorry, I don't know where my manners are. Please sit down, Ginnie.'

A relieved-looking Ginnie sank onto a chair. 'I've got some news, and I wanted to tell you and Patty before I go up to see Connie.'

'That sounds exciting,' said Patty, her eyes lighting up.

A smile flooded Ginnie's face. 'I'm going to have another baby. I'm expecting!'

Patty squealed with delight while Alice clapped her hands. 'What marvellous news! Connie'll be that pleased. Is Sam looking forward to having another little one?'

'Oh, yes. He'd have a football team if he could.'

'He's like Walter's brother, Frank, and his cricket team!'

Patty burst out, 'When's it due?'

'December. I'd missed my monthly, but I wanted to be sure before I told anyone.'

'I'm so pleased for both of you. And I'm sure Young Sam will be glad to have a little brother or sister. Connie will be over the moon to hear the news.'

–

Alice wore her Sunday-best coat and a dress she had run up so she would have something to wear that Walter hadn't seen before – a soft, plain burgundy cotton, with a lace collar. It would be worth spending all those precious hours making it when Walter saw it.

She hurried into the kitchen, and there was admiration in Patty's eyes.

'Patty, have you got everything you need to finish tonight's tea?'

'I think so. It's only salad, and I've already made the dressing, one of Connie's favourites. I've made a fresh custard.'

Patty beamed at the cooling baked custard. Alice thought it looked every bit as nice as hers. During Patty's early days, she'd had several failures because she'd forgotten an ingredient. Two meals sprang to mind, both involving rice puddings. The first one was a pudding containing no sugar. The second was a rice pudding with sugar but with double the quantity of rice. Alice had to admit that she'd never carved rice pudding before. She bought Patty a notebook just like hers, so she wouldn't have to rely on her memory, and there'd been no failures since.

'We'll be back before seven o'clock. I should be here in time to help you tidy up the kitchen.'

'Thank you, Alice. I'm sure everything will go smoothly, or at least on the surface.'

'Yes, you're improving at organising things. I remember the first time you prepared a meal yourself. It looked as if you'd used every pot and pan in the kitchen, and when I returned, you looked exhausted. But I've every confidence in you.' Alice hoped Patty couldn't see her fingers crossed behind her back.

There was a knock on the kitchen door, and in walked Walter, also dressed in his Sunday-best suit, with a derby hat, which he had removed. It was the first time she'd seen him in such a formal hat and found it difficult not to laugh. She hoped she had concealed her amusement, not wanting to hurt his feelings.

Alice and Walter arrived at Lime Street at half past two. A very proud Bertie and Edith greeted them, along with a nervous-looking Luther. The poor lad had had to get used to the strange man who was his father. His mother had told him stories all about his father and how he'd return from abroad someday.

'Afternoon. Welcome to our home,' said Bertie.

'Thank you very much. We're glad you invited us.'

The group entered the house, its meagre furnishings highlighted by the faint tracings of former tenants' pictures on the walls. Alice was certain that a few weeks of settling in would transform everything into a proper home.

They entered the kitchen, and Edith put Luther down onto the red-tiled floor. They had a table, and four chairs, and a small stool for Luther.

'The last time I saw this little man, I think it was in the old shop.' Alice stopped short, realising that perhaps it wasn't the best thing to have said, but both Edith and Bertie seemed not to notice.

After a bit of general conversation and after Luther had settled down to look at a picture book of ships, Bertie filled them in on what had happened.

'I was renting a room from Pearl Langley on Corporation Street. Her and Daisy both work at the PTC. I went there for a few nights after I got back and stayed for two years.'

'Remind me not to offer you a bed!' said Walter, laughing.

'They were kind to me, especially at the beginning, and were always there to listen when I needed to talk things over. It was Daisy who discovered this house. I think she must know all the rent collectors in the area, because I believe she did the same for Dottie and her late husband, Donald, when they moved onto Campbell Road.'

Walter glanced around. 'Where's Carla?'

'She'll be here soon. She went back to Dottie's to see how they were getting on without her,' Edith said.

'So what happened next?' asked Alice, keen to get on with the story.

'Once we had the rent book for the house and I drew my first week's wages from the NSR, Edith and I met and agreed that there was no reason we shouldn't move in straight away. Edith had packed most of Luther's clothes beforehand and was ready for a quick exit if required.'

Edith took over. 'Mother suspected nothing. When he knocked at the door, Father went to let Bertie in. Mother was shocked. For a moment, she said nothing. Her mood got no better when she realised Father had known Bertie was back six months ago. I felt sorry for Father. Mother would make sure he suffered for defying her.'

'He looked like a condemned man on his way to the gallows,' added Bertie.

They all laughed.

'It's easy to laugh now, but it was deeply upsetting. She said Bertie wasn't welcome in her house, and neither would me nor Luther be if she ever saw us together again.'

Bertie took Edith's hand. 'I've got to know Mr Wren well during this time. I've even started to play chess again, and I see him at the club. I was proud of him when he told his wife to shut up. He said I was welcome around his table and reminded his wife it was his name on the rent book and she'd better be aware of that. He said this silliness had been going on long enough. Her concern about what the neighbours might think was too much. The war was over. She'd do well to remember that.'

Edith took up the story. 'You could hear a pin drop. Someone ordered my two younger sisters out, much to their dismay, as I think they were enjoying the spectacle. Mother could barely speak. She looked as if she was going to have a stroke. But a sudden calmness came over her, and she said that I was to do what I wanted to do. I was a grown woman, and she'd be pleased to have the space back in the house and not to have that screaming German brat under her feet.'

Bertie shook his head. 'I don't mind telling you, I was ready to hit her, woman or not.'

'Anyway, Father stepped in again and ordered her out of the room. If looks could kill, my father would no longer be with us,' grinned Edith.

'I found out from him at the chess club that the last two weeks have been heavenly. Mrs Wren isn't speaking to him, and that includes giving him orders and telling him what he's doing wrong. His two daughters seemed to have enjoyed the quietness too – their only function being to pass messages between husband and wife.'

'When I next saw Father, he said to me that all good things must end, and he was sure that now we'd moved out and Mother had worked out what she was going to tell the neighbours, things would return to normal.'

'What did you do next, Edith?' asked Alice, shocked.

'Well, I'd already packed all of Luther's things, and I rushed to put most of my clothes into a suitcase, and we left. Father has since brought me most of my belongings and even struggled on the tram with a box of toys for Luther. I haven't seen my sisters yet, but I expect they'll call when they feel it's safe to do so.'

Alice frowned. 'Why did the whole family move?'

'I never understood that. I guessed she'd rather move than face the prospect of Mr and Mrs Hesse visiting their grandchild. Mother's decision to move came before we knew of Bertie's internment for the duration, and we weren't aware that the Hesses had left the country. I was so glad when Father told me he'd met Bertie and that he was still in this country. You see, Mother had told me Bertie had been repatriated to Germany from the Isle of Man. I knew from the newspapers that some men like Bertie were appealing against repatriation, so I assumed either Bertie hadn't got a strong enough case or he hadn't bothered to appeal, and I have to admit I was upset.'

'I hope it's all behind us now. You'll still be able to meet your father and sisters, and let's hope your mother comes round, at least to where you and Luther can visit. I fear I'll be *persona non grata* with Mrs Wren for a long, long time,' murmured Bertie.

The group sat in silence for a few minutes until Luther said, 'I'm hungry, I want something to eat.' He looked at his father and said, '*Ich habe Hunger, Papa, ich möchte etwas essen.*'

Alice looked startled.

'That's Carla's influence. She hopes to teach him a little German so that when he meets his grandparents, he can greet them in either language.'

'*Also, mein kleiner Mann, sollen wir ein Sandwich und dann ein paar Apfelkompott essen?*' Edith said. 'I've been learning a bit as well.'

'What did you say to him?'

'I hope I said, "Well, my little man, shall we have a sandwich and then some stewed apples?"'

The group sat together for Sunday tea. Alice's happiness overflowed. A broken family brought back together again.

On the return journey to Holmorton Lodge, Alice and Walter chatted about the situation, and Walter said he would've loved to have been a fly on the wall.

Walter followed Alice to the back door. It was still light, but the building protected them from nosy neighbours. Walter took her into his arms and kissed her, with so much passion she felt quite lightheaded when he let her go.

'I hope we never have to go through anything like that; it'd be awful.'

They kissed again and then Alice stepped back. 'Walter, I've decided I'm going to look for my mother again. I'm going to visit Runcorn on a Sunday to catch most people at home. Will you come with me, please?'

'Yes, of course. I'd never miss an opportunity to spend a day with you.'

Alice wished him goodnight and entered the house to find a kitchen spick and span, ready for the following day.

The kettle was boiling, and there were two teacups on the table.

Patty smiled. 'Did you have a pleasant time?'

Alice nodded. 'We heard all about Bertie's encounter with his mother-in-law and the house. It's early days, but with a few more homely bits and pieces, it'll be very nice. Did tea go all right?'

'Yes, yes. Connie complimented me on the custard. In fact, she had two portions. I have to admit that I was proud of myself.'

'And I'm very proud of you too. This kitchen looks spotless, and you wouldn't have thought that you'd prepared a meal in here today.' Alice looked around. 'You've even put the pans in the correct order on the shelves.'

Patty gave Alice a big hug.

'What was that for?'

'For being the best teacher I've ever had. I feel I've achieved something. I don't care what people say about service being hard work; you get a sense of achievement.'

'Thanks. Nobody's ever said anything like that to me.' Alice's eyes watered a little. It might be because of the sentiment expressed by Patty, or it might have been the realisation that when she settled down with Walter, she and Patty would have to part ways.

On her way to bed, Alice pondered how things were moving on and leaving her behind. She had set her own path forward by not making any plans until she had completed the search for her mother. Now she regretted that. Would Walter be prepared to wait for her? Her heart lurched. She didn't want to lose him – but was it fair to keep him waiting?

Chapter Eleven

June 1921

At the beginning of June, Tellwright Street welcomed its newest family – the Whites. Alice and Walter, Patty and a very pregnant Connie helped with the move. Sam and Ginnie had little; she didn't hold with the tallyman, and she always said she'd never go into debt. Debt caused many families to end up in the workhouse.

Alice discovered later that Connie had lent Ginnie the deposit money for the house, and in that moment, Alice felt proud that Connie should help her friend.

Ginnie came walking into the kitchen with a big smile on her face.

'You're looking very pleased with yourself,' said Alice.

'Yes, I've just used my privy. I shall never take it for granted!'

They all laughed, and everyone raised their cups or tin mugs in a toast to the White family.

Mabel's marriage to Bernard took place a few days later. Nothing too elaborate. After all, she'd done the dressing up and celebrations before. She liked him, of course she did. But love him? Alice couldn't tell. How could anyone who had been married love the same the second time around? According to Ginnie, Mabel just wanted to get married so she wouldn't be on her own with Florrie.

And that was all.

–

The following Sunday, Alice and Walter set out for Runcorn as planned, searching for her Tucker relatives, or someone who knew something about her past. What might she unearth this time? She tried to be positive. Alice had arranged for Patty to work the day, and Connie approved. She had briefed Patty on everything that needed to be done, thankful that the girl could be trusted.

It was a complicated journey, involving several trains. The entire journey took around two hours. Once in Runcorn, they asked a policeman who was walking his beat for directions to Cawdor Street. It turned out to be a mere ten-minute walk from the station towards the River Mersey.

They turned onto Cawdor Street, and Walter remarked that the terraced houses were very similar to those in The Potteries. They found number 12 and knocked on the door, which was answered by a thick-set young man wearing no shirt, just a singlet with a pair of braces on top. He was rubbing his eyes as if he'd just woken up. Alice hoped they hadn't interrupted his sleep prior to going on nights, although he only looked about sixteen, so it was unlikely.

'Morning. Sorry to disturb you – but are you Mr Tucker?'

'I suppose you might call me that. I'm Henry Tucker. What can I do for you?'

'I'm hoping you might help me. I'm Alice Tucker, and I believe we are related.'

'Oh!'

He stood with his hands on the door, and it was obvious he didn't know what to do next.

'Do you think we might come in and explain? You might be able to help me.'

Without a word, he moved to one side to allow Alice and Walter in. He told them to sit on the settee.

'Is this bloke your husband or brother?' Henry asked, pointing to Walter.

'Sorry, I should've told you. This is Walter Latham, and he's a friend of mine. I've been trying to find out about my family, and I believe you might be my cousin.'

'Yer cousin? Yer kidding me.' His eyes grew wide and any sign of sleep vanished.

'My mother was Margaret Tucker and my father was Wilfred.'

'Our Pa's going to be surprised when I tell him you've been here. I dunner know much about Uncle Wilfred. I know he was killed on the canal in The Potteries; that's all. It were a long time ago.'

'I know nothing about Wilfred. Has he got any brothers or sisters I could talk to?'

'Well, my father, Thomas, he's the youngest, and Uncle George is the middle one. Wilfred was the oldest.'

'Would it be possible to speak to Uncle George or Uncle Thomas?' Alice nodded with a smile.

'I should think so. Uncle George lives on the next street, Suffolk Street, and knows everything about the family.'

Alice's eyes lit up. At last, someone who could tell her something about her family. How right she was to make this journey.

'I'll take yer round there now – if you've got time?'

Alice looked at Walter, who was also smiling. He nodded.

'That's very kind of you, Henry.'

Henry grabbed his coat and pulled a cap onto his head before turning towards the door.

'Follow me, Alice.'

The three of them set off at a pace. Henry said little, asking if they were likely to call again soon, as he was sure his ma and pa would be upset at missing them.

He banged on the door of 21 Suffolk Street and walked right in, beckoning Alice and Walter to follow.

Once the formalities were over, Alice explained who she was and that she was looking for her mother.

'She comes from The Potteries,' said Henry, as if that explained everything. 'Her says she's Aunty Margaret's daughter and is looking for her relatives. She wants some help.'

'Pleased to meet yer, Alice. Conner tell yer much about yer ma. All I know is she had a sister living in Widnes. Haven't seen Edna for years.'

'Really?' She never knew her mother had a sister. Excitement built up inside. At last she'd made a start. She had found her father's two brothers and her mother's sister – her aunty.

'Nancy!' George shouted. 'Nancy!' louder this time. A woman popped her head around the kitchen door. 'Nancy, love, come in here. We've a visitor.'

'Hello, miss, and who might you be?'

'She's our Wilfred's daughter. She was a babe in arms the last time we met her. Says she's looking for her mam. Do you have Edna's address anywhere?'

'I do, I'll go get it,' she said. A few minutes later her voice could be heard calling from somewhere, probably the kitchen: 'I'll just have a look in the dresser. No, it's not there. Best check upstairs… sorry to keep you, love.' Alice felt she was so close. Her heart was pumping in her chest. To teeter on the brink would be awful.

Nancy returned to the living room after ten or fifteen minutes. It seemed like an eternity to Alice. Good job she was patient, because Aunty Nancy hadn't found the envelope. Alice's heart sank.

'I'll look in the wardrobe – but it's almost time for dinner. You'll stop and take a bite to eat? You've had a long journey then?'

Alice didn't want to upset anyone, so she looked at Walter, and they both nodded their agreement. 'Yes, please. Seems a long time since I had my breakfast this morning,' added Walter.

'They say as travelling makes you hungry,' said Henry.

'Anything makes *you* hungry,' chuckled George. 'Sometimes I think you've got hollow legs.'

'It's only scouse. We got a nice piece of neck of lamb this week, so there's plenty for all.'

'What's scouse?'

'Oh yes, it'll be summat you've never heard of down in your part of the world. It's a type of stew with potatoes and carrots and anything else we've got that we can put in it. We simmer it on top of the range, so you can use the cheapest meat. It's ready when all the lamb stock has soaked in.'

Alice smiled. 'Sounds something like lobby. We make it the same way, except we add more water at the beginning and cook it until—'

'—There're two ways to make lobby,' said Walter. 'One way uses a thin broth, which itself can be soup. The other way has the broth thickened. There's considerable argument about which is best and, more importantly, about which is the correct way.'

'Walter, how do you like your lobby?' asked George.

'Oh, I like it with the thin broth. You can mop it up with your bread,' replied Walter.

'Well, I like it with the broth as thick as possible,' said Alice.

There was laughter all around. Alice shook her head, amazed that all her work on finding her family was about to end with a discussion on making lobby.

Nancy disappeared into the kitchen and returned with five plates of something that looked like a very dry lobby. She smiled at Walter and laid the steaming plates on the table.

'If you two are thinking about getting together, you need to decide how you want to have your lobby. Little things like that make all the difference,' said Uncle George, pointing his spoon at Walter.

They sat and ate, while chatting. Once the meal was over, Alice offered to clear the dishes, but Nancy refused her help. 'You're our guest. Tell Alice about Margaret and Wilfred, George, and I'll go to look for this address.'

'She was all right, your mam. The problem is that when you adopt someone, you're taking potluck, aren't you? Who knows what the kid'll turn into when he, or even she, grows up?'

A chill ran up and down Alice's spine. Why mention adoption? Had they got the wrong family after all?

'I'm sorry, I didn't catch that. Who's adopted?'

His mouth dropped. 'You were.'

Many feelings ran through Alice. No, no, no. They must be wrong. Margaret Tucker was her mother. How could she be adopted?

Alice stared at Walter, tongue-tied. He took over. 'Mr Tucker, I think – well, we both think we're talking at cross purposes. Alice lived with her mother after her father died, and they had to go into the local workhouse for a time, before Mrs Copeland took Alice in, gave her a job and brought her up.'

'I've got my birth certificate with me. It shows Margaret Tucker was my mother. There's no mention of adoption.'

Alice would never forget the emotion she saw on George's face as he shook his head. Was it pity – or something else?

'Aye, Wilfred and Margaret adopted yer when yer was about a week old. You see, Margaret couldn't have children and had wanted a kid of her own for years. One weekend, they turned up here, and Margaret had a babe in arms. They told the family you were adopted, but as far as the rest of the street was concerned, we were told to say that Margaret had been pregnant, but had hidden it well.'

At that moment, Nancy rushed into the room. 'I've got it. It'd got buried at the bottom of the wardrobe. Sorry to have kept you… er, Alice.'

She handed an envelope to Alice, who couldn't stop her hand from shaking as she took it. She read the name and address – Mrs Edna Anderson, 66 Peel Street, Widnes. She blinked several times. She saw the total shock written on Walter's face and wondered if hers looked the same. She couldn't feel her feet. She was going to faint.

Walter put his arm around her to steady her.

'I... er... don't know what to say. I've never heard of any adoption. I... er... I need to think about this. But I think we shall have to go now. It's getting late. I'll write to you when I... have thought about everything.'

'What have you been saying, George? I wish you'd think before you speak.' Nancy turned to Alice. 'Sorry, luv, for you to find out this way. I thought you'd know, but when you think about it, you've not seen your mother for a while. Why should you?'

'It was a surprise. I'd never considered it. I can't believe Mother never told me nothing about it. Are you sure we're talking about the same family?' Alice was on the verge of tears.

'Hearing this for the first time must be a shock. You go home and think about it. We've got no intention of going anywhere.'

Alice rose from the settee, and Walter followed, cap in hand. 'Thank you both for your time...' She could think of nothing else to say.

Walter added his thanks and guided Alice towards the front door. Nancy stood at the door to wave them goodbye until they came to the end of the street.

Alice was silent on the walk to the railway station. All the plans she had made to get this far had come crashing down.

'You don't think we could be mistaken, do you?' Her question was more of a plea. She knew he wouldn't answer unless he believed what he was saying.

He said nothing.

On the return journey, Alice had lots of questions. 'D'you think they were surprised to see us?'

'I think they were as surprised as anyone would be to find a relative they hadn't seen. The actual surprise might have been that you didn't know of the adoption.'

'If I'm adopted, do you think that's why Mother left me at the workhouse? Because she didn't want me?'

'You must have been a lovely kid, Alice. I defy anyone to walk away and leave you behind.'

Alice smiled a watery smile. Sitting in the railway carriage, she must've looked huddled and lonely because he moved into the seat next to her and put his arm around her. It felt just the right place to be. As they descended from the train, Walter still looked anxious.

'I don't think I want to leave you like this, Alice.'

'I shall be all right, Walter. No need to worry.'

'It's such a shock. One no one would've even thought of.'

'I know. I can remember M—mother talking to me about all sorts when we went out for walks, when I had a problem at school. She used to say I needed to work hard so I could get a good job – like my father had. I said I'd always work hard so that I could look after her when she got old.'

Walter grinned. 'Always thinking of others.'

'Thank you for going with me, Walter. I appreciate it, although I doubt I'll be going again.'

'What if they're your family? Don't you want to get to know them?'

'That's the whole point, Walter. They're not my family. I'm adopted.' Alice put her hand on Walter's arm. 'Thank you again.' She gave him a wan smile and then walked into the house. A single wave came just before she closed the door.

She walked into the kitchen to find an exhausted Patty finishing the dishes. 'I'll give you a hand with them, Patty.'

'No, I'm almost done. I've put yer dinner out and covered it over. It'll need warming before you eat it. I doubt you'd had time for eating on your way back.'

That was so thoughtful and kind of Patty. In her heightened emotional state, Alice almost burst into tears. 'Thank you.'

Patty chatted away about what she'd been doing all day, and Alice did her best to join in and ask suitable questions to show she'd been following. At that moment, she had said nothing about her day and what she hoped would come out of it. She needed to come to terms with a few things before she could talk without blarting.

She picked at the food but couldn't digest it. If Patty noticed, she said nothing. Maybe she was biding her time by waiting until tomorrow to find out the story. Instead, and so as not to upset Patty, Alice said she'd take her dinner up to her bedroom because she felt exhausted after such a long day. Patty looked even more curious when Alice asked her if she'd mind locking up for the night. It was a job Alice always did for herself. Patty looked quite chuffed at being given an additional responsibility – even though it was only for one night.

Alice lay on her bed, picking at the food until she had to give up. It was cold, and she couldn't bear to take another mouthful – nothing to do with Patty's cooking – she'd need to hide the remains so as not to upset that young lady who had come on well.

The word 'adopted' played over and over in her head, as if the world was laughing at her. She readied herself for bed and lay still, not touching the book she had been reading. She had heard others talking about being adopted, including Ginnie's friend, Ada. Until now, it'd been just a word. But no longer. It described her. Told the world who she was. Someone not wanted by her family.

She'd need to consider the ramifications of what she'd learned. Her first thought on learning of the adoption was who, if anyone, to tell. So far, she had Walter to rely on, but how long would that last? Was it fair to keep dragging him out to accompany her? She liked him a lot, and he professed to like her too, but would his view change now he knew what he knew?

–

Alice was not the only one who had a shock that month. Mid-afternoon found Alice and Patty taking tea and biscuits when a knock echoed on the back door. Alice had opened it to see Sam, almost collapsing on the doorstep.

'Sam! Whatever's the matter?' and then, 'Is Ginnie all right?'

'No!'

Alice put her arm around him. His eyes were bright with tears. She guided him into the hallway to a chair. 'What's happened?'

'My Ginnie's had a miscarriage. Twelve o'clock last night. It came on quick, and we got the midwife out straight away, but it was no use. She was in such pain, Alice. I couldn't help thinking it was all my fault.'

'But how can it be your fault, Sam?'

'It was me what put it there. Pardon me, Alice, but if I hadn't, then she'd be all right.' He put his head in his hands, looking done in. 'I thought as I was going to lose her.'

'How's she now?'

'In bed, washed out. Mabel's looking after her. Ginnie wanted me to let you and Connie know.'

'Poor Ginnie. She was looking forward to having another little one.'

The sound of a door opening revealed Connie rubbing her eyes and looking surprised at the gathering.

'What's going on?'

Alice explained, as Connie's hands cradled her face. 'I'll tell Robert and we'll come with you, Sam.'

'No.' He half raised himself out of the chair, but Connie pushed him back again.

'Stay there, Sam, and don't move.' It was the voice Connie used when she refused to take no for an answer. She moved towards the stairs and whispered to Alice, 'Don't let him move. He's not fit to be out on his own. We'll go with him. We'll be back as soon as we can.'

When they returned, it was obvious to Alice that Connie had been crying. She took Connie into her arms and held her.

'She looked so small in bed, Alice. Remember how happy she was to find out she was expecting again? And now...'

Fresh tears fell, and Alice felt her own eyes well up.

'And poor Sam didn't know what to do for her – and for himself too.'

Alice patted Connie's back gently. How unfair life could be, when those women who wanted children badly could lose them. Her thoughts turned to Jean, who was desperate for a child, but who, so far, had had no success.

–

Today was the last day of June. It'd been a month Alice would've liked to forget. She had taken every opportunity to visit Ginnie as she tried to come to terms with the events of the miscarriage. At least she had friends to help.

Alice had no one she could call on to help her with the devastating news she had received – except for Walter, and she was worried that she might frighten him off if she put too much onto him at this early stage in their relationship. She wanted to tell someone. Connie was out of the question. Patty, although she would be sympathetic, was too young.

Throughout the week, Alice pondered what to do. She would stand staring into space or wouldn't hear Patty when she spoke to her. Every now and then she caught the girl looking at her. Sometimes she thought Patty was going to ask her what the problem was. At these times, Alice sent her off on some errand or job to give herself time to regain her composure.

Alice decided. She would go to see her Aunt Edna. After all, it'd be silly not to use the information she had been given. She might even learn something that would help balance the rather bleak information she had received so far. Either that, or forget about her past forever.

She asked Patty if she minded working on her own again this Sunday, so that she might travel to Widnes. She hoped Walter could accompany her. Widnes was the next stop on the same train crossing the River Mersey by a modern stone bridge. Maybe it would take her to her real family.

Chapter Twelve

July 1921

'Do you know what you're going to say, Alice? I mean, it's going to come as much of a shock to her as it did to the Tuckers.'

'I don't know. I'll wait until I get there, I suppose.'

She sat in the carriage, biting her nails, wondering if she was doing the right thing. She still had time to turn back rather than set all those hares running. Walter's questioning had unnerved her, and it wasn't like him. What should she do?

After studying a map, they'd discovered that Mrs Anderson, or Aunty Edna as she might call her in the future, lived about two miles from the station in an area overlooking a large group of chemical factories. It took them over an hour to make the journey – and a lot of asking people for directions. Some regarded them with suspicion, but others were quite approachable. Most had a strong accent, which took a bit of deciphering, but Walter was good at that. In his job, he talked to men from all over the country.

Finally, Alice and Walter arrive at number 66 Peel Street.

'Ready, Alice?'

Alice straightened her skirt and adjusted her hat. Taking a deep breath, she nodded. 'Ready as I'll ever be.'

Walter knocked on the door and then stood back so that Alice might do the talking. He was just about to knock for the second time when a woman with a turban on her head and a cigarette between her lips opened it. Without removing the cigarette, she spoke.

'Yes?'

'I hope you don't mind, but might I enquire if you are Mrs Edna Anderson?'

'Who wants to know?'

Alice swallowed at the sharpness of her question, wondering whether to continue. This wasn't the welcome she was expecting.

'My name is Alice Tucker, and I believe you might be my Aunty Edna.'

'Somebody's pulling your leg.' The woman gawped at Alice. 'Your aunty? Who's told yer that, love?'

'George Tucker. I saw him last week.'

The woman frowned. 'You're our Margaret's girl?'

Alice nodded. She wanted to run and hide somewhere. How different to the welcome they had received from the Tuckers the previous month. 'This is my friend Walter, who's kindly helping me to look for my family.'

'Best come in then.'

Once inside, Mrs Anderson put out her cigarette and offered them both a drink of tea and a biscuit. It helped Alice to relax a little. Maybe it wouldn't be that bad after all.

'Happen yer might have come too late. Margaret died in 1918. Her heart gave up. Very quick.'

Alice gasped. 'Oh, no.' Walter quickly put his arm around her while Edna made her way back into the kitchen, murmuring about checking something.

She returned almost immediately, carrying a small wooden box and handed it to Alice. 'If you're her daughter, then she left this for you – if you ever came to visit.'

Alice took hold of the box, looking at it with awe. Did this truly belong to Margaret – her mother Margaret – or did it belong to some other poor woman named Margaret Tucker who was no relation whatsoever? She couldn't open it until she knew the answer. She laid it on her knee. 'Can you tell me a bit about her? As you can imagine, it's all come as quite a shock to me, Mrs Anderson.'

Edna lit up another cigarette and settled back in her chair. 'Margaret came back to Widnes in 1906 – the end of May, if I remember. Wilfred had died. She was skint and had to leave you behind. She said that you'd moved in with a family called Hardcastle, and that she would get you back when she could afford.'

Alice nodded and looked down at her hands. 'Mrs Anderson – the Hardcastles ran the local workhouse. I was put there, in the children's hostel.'

It was Edna's turn to gasp. 'Well, I never! You poor lass. That's not what she told me. She used to write to you regularly. According to her you were getting on well at school and it'd be a shame to take you out to bring you here. Then she told us you'd got a good job on a potbank, as you call them in The Potteries, learning to be a figure painter, and said it'd be much better than working in chemicals. As far as I was concerned, there was no reason to assume any different from what she'd told me.'

'But I never worked on a potbank. I never received any letters from her all the time I was in the hostel. It didn't seem wrong because she would've been in trouble if they ever found her.'

'Why's that?'

'She left me in the hostel for the parish to pay for – and that's against the law.'

'Margaret got herself a job in one of the chemical factories so she could pay her way. Mr Anderson, my husband, allowed her to stay as our family had grown up and left home by that time. When the war began and there was a surge in chemical jobs, she got a job at Spike Island. It's only a ten-minute walk away. From here you can see the chimneys and the like. The conditions were awful. She'd been complaining of feeling tired and washed out.' She flicked ash off the end of her cigarette into the fire. 'One day, she went off to work and didn't come back. She just dropped dead. She didn't suffer. She was dead before she hit the ground.'

'How awful.' Both Alice and Walter said the same thing.

'That box I gave you. Why don't you open it?'

Alice picked up the box gingerly and did as she was bid. It wasn't locked. Inside were some envelopes and a piece of paper.

'Thank you for looking after this for so long, Mrs Anderson. I appreciate it.'

At last Edna smiled. 'You do have a look of her.'

It was then Alice realised Edna had no idea she was adopted. Instead of blurting out what she was about to say, she bit her tongue. 'It's kind of you to say so.'

'Me and Margaret were never what you might call close. It would be nice to get to know yer. And if you're ever over this way again, you can call me Aunty Edna. Never thought I'd get called that again by anybody.'

It was time to leave. Alice and Walter said their goodbyes and headed back towards the station to wait for the next train to Crewe. Whenever she tried to find out anything about her mother, she discovered something unbelievable. She felt she was getting closer and then she was pushed back a step.

Alice and Walter spent a lot of the return journey in silence, taking in what they'd heard. She didn't know what to make of her mother after all of this, but closer inspection of the little wooden box's contents might shed some light on who she was.

'I'll bet you'll need a good few days to take it all in, Alice,' said Walter gently. 'I can't imagine what you must be going through. Finding your mother after all this time, only to discover she's died.'

Alice opened the box and examined its contents. There were a few cuttings from *The Sentinel* and some other papers. But there was nothing that related to Alice directly. 'I'll look at them in detail later. I feel a bit too wobbly just now.'

'I believe you're getting closer, Alice. Take heart.'

When they arrived back at Holmorton Lodge, she kissed Walter and let him go, only vaguely aware of his presence. She said goodnight to Patty and dragged herself upstairs.

With one last look at the box, Alice stowed it away at the bottom of her wardrobe, too emotional to discover yet more torment. Exhausted, she climbed into bed and fell into a deep sleep.

–

The following morning, she woke up later than usual, with a clear head. And then it hit her, like a bolt out of the blue. The box had a secret drawer!

She jumped out of bed and flung the wardrobe open. She reached inside and pulled out the box. She hadn't been dreaming. It was as she remembered. She sat on the bed, staring at the box, turning it slowly until the carving of the sailing boat faced her – and pressed on the sail. A drawer opened to reveal a sealed envelope addressed to Miss Alice Tucker. Inside, there was no room for anything else.

She stared at the envelope, unable to breathe. She lifted her hand to tear it open, but found she couldn't do it. Once she had opened it, she couldn't unopen it.

Minutes later, she decided. She would speak to Walter now. She dressed at speed and ran downstairs to meet a startled Patty in the kitchen.

'I'm popping up to see Walter, Patty. I won't be long.' She shot through the door without waiting for Patty's response.

She hammered on the door of 32 Dartmouth Street. Moments later, a dishevelled Walter appeared, rubbing his eyes.

'Alice! What're you doing here? Is something wrong?'

She pushed past him and into the kitchen just as Herbert Latham was leaving for work.

'I'm so sorry, but I need to speak to Walter.' She held up the envelope so that Walter could see it.

'Sorry, Dad. I'll deal with this. You get off.'

Muttering, Herbert did as he was bid.

'Alice, whatever's got into you?'

'I've remembered, Walter, it's got a secret drawer. This was in it.'

They sat at the table together, with the envelope between them.

'I'm so sorry, Walter, but I had to see you. It came back to me this morning – the secret drawer, I mean. It was a game Father used to play with me. He would put something in the drawer and close it and ask me to open it, but I couldn't. Then, one day, I observed him and – see the sail on the ship – he pressed on it with his thumb. You wouldn't notice unless you were watching – and a drawer opened. He passed it over to me, and I pretended to be none the wiser. Then I opened it, and he was so shocked, I laughed. Mother was there, and she laughed too, and said he would have to find somewhere else to keep his secrets.'

Walter's eyes bulged. 'And that was inside,' he said, pointing at the envelope.

Alice nodded. 'But now I've got to decide whether to open it.' She stared at him. 'I'm frightened, Walter.'

Alice watched him, seeing the sympathy crossing his face. 'Only you can make that decision, Alice. But you're so close now. It's what you wanted.'

'I know. What I keep thinking about is that Mother wanted me to have it. She planned to ensure I got the box. Don't you see – she knew I could open the drawer.'

'Have you decided yet?'

Alice nodded. 'You've been on this journey with me so far. I wanted you to be with me when I open the letter.'

Alice took a deep breath. Was the letter from the woman described by her sister, Edna, or the woman she had known and loved?

She slid her thumb under the sealed envelope and opened it. Inside was a letter, again addressed to Alice, and a slip of paper folded into quarters, nothing else. Alice looked at Walter, surprised.

She took the letter out of the envelope and unfolded it. Another, smaller slip of paper floated to the floor. Alice read out the letter, her eyes gradually filling.

> *1912*
>
> *My dear Alice*
>
> *I am so sorry to be away from you for so long. Please do not think the worst of me. You must realise, my darling daughter, that it is very hard for a woman who has lost her husband to make her way in this life. You may not think it now, but it is the best thing for both of us.*
>
> *You are getting three meals a day, a warm bed to sleep in, and an education. I cannot guarantee that if you live with me, my darling. I am staying with my sister, your Aunty Edna, and she has promised to keep this box safe until she can give it to you. I said you would know what to do with it. If you are reading this letter now, then I was right, my clever girl.*
>
> *You must make the best of what life offers, and one day, we might get together again and live the life we should have had.*
>
> *In the meantime, you will always be my little Alice.*
>
> *Your loving Mother.*

This was not a liar shirking her responsibilities – but a caring woman who was trying to do her best for her daughter. She burst into tears, only now able to understand just how deep the heartache had been. She passed the letter to Walter.

She would never know the woman in the letter, and it broke her heart. She had both found and lost a mother. Maybe it was her fault. If she had looked for her earlier, they might've had some time together before she passed away. She picked up the other sheet of paper, on which was written, in a spidery hand hardly recognisable as her mother's:

You were adopted in 1898. Your father arranged everything, and we picked you up from a nursing home in Holywell, North Wales.

Alice caught her breath. It was like a message from beyond the grave. A message for her. At last, she knew where she came from. But it wasn't enough. She needed more information, but of one thing she was sure: it was her mother's wish that she should find the woman who gave birth to her.

–

It'd been a few days since Alice had returned from Widnes. She now felt strong enough to tell Connie what she'd learned. The opportunity arose on the Friday morning. Alice wanted to confirm the butcher's order, and Connie was sitting in the garden room. She had given up her job with Mr Railsford to prepare for the baby's arrival. Alice checked with Connie, who approved the order. Alice intended to take it down to Burslem straight away, but then hesitated.

'Connie, can I have a word with you, please?'

'Yes, of course.'

'I'm sorry I haven't told you about my visits to Runcorn and Widnes, but I needed time to digest what I heard.'

'I thought you looked as if you'd something on your mind.'

Alice paused for a moment, and then the words burst out: 'I'm adopted and my mother, Margaret Tucker, died in August 1918.' Alice could feel her eyes smarting with tears. It was painful to say the words, but afterwards the relief was palpable.

Connie gasped. 'Are you certain?'

Alice nodded.

'Alice, my poor dear, how have you kept it all to yourself? Come here, you poor love.' Connie tried to hug Alice, but the baby got in the way and the pair giggled through their tears.

Alice told Connie everything she'd discovered.

'I didn't realise you'd been so busy. How nice of Walter to accompany you too. How do you feel now?'

'That's the problem. I don't really feel anything, except perhaps frustration with my mother for leaving me and anger that my birth mother also abandoned me. My uncle told me I was only a few days old when I arrived home with Wilfred and Margaret. My mother wrote me a letter which she never sent and left it with her sister, so I'm going to follow the Holywell lead as soon as I can, but now, it's a trip to see Mr Sutton, at the butchers, or we'll have no meat this week.' She blew her nose and got to her feet. 'I'll let you know if I find out more.'

–

It was only natural for Connie to want everything to be perfect for her first baby. The nanny would spend most of her time with the baby, so Connie interviewed and checked each woman's credentials before offering the job. Alice made a point of being around when each woman arrived and gave Connie the benefit of her experience too.

The successful applicant was Lily King, who appeared to be a strong-minded individual. Lily would arrive on 15 July, a Friday, and would start work on Monday, preparing the nursery for its new occupant. It'd be up to her to ensure everything was perfect.

Patty guffawed when she heard it. 'My word, Alice, this baby's going to be stifled – if you ask me.'

'Well, it's a good job nobody'll be asking for your opinion, Patty.'

'I'm just saying.'

'Well, don't. That's the best way to get yourself into trouble, my girl. Any new mother, like Connie, will want only the very best for their baby – especially the first one.'

'Most babies round here are lucky if they've got a bed to sleep in and not a drawer to make do.'

'I hope you're not suggesting Connie does the same, are you?'

Patty flushed. 'Course not.'

'Best keep your thoughts to yourself in that regard then.' Alice winked. Poor Patty! She hadn't yet worked out the difference between a joke and a sarky comment. Still, she was a fine girl and worked well. Alice had got used to having her about. Patty's absence would leave Alice lost.

The upstairs rooms, designed and built as a nursery, had served as storage until now. Decisions had to be made on what to throw away and where to put the rest, which took a while to sort out. After removing most of the items, they would have a nursery for the baby and a bedroom with a small sitting room for the nanny.

They'd tried to make it as pleasant as possible, under Connie's instructions. Fresh bright linen with a coverlet of spring flowers, and matching pillowcases, furniture that had seen better days in one of the guest bedrooms, now well-polished. A lamp graced a small bedside cupboard, lighting the way to the new privy down the hall if needed.

'Do you know anything about Lily?' Patty asked once they'd been told of the nanny's imminent arrival.

'I've been told she's in her forties and is a widow with no children of her own. Her husband died in the war.'

'Poor woman. I pity anyone what lost somebody during those days. How could they ever think about putting the war behind them when they'll never see their men again?'

'I believe she only takes jobs where she can live in.' Alice panted as she finished making the bed. 'That means she doesn't have to worry about renting somewhere.'

'I've heard as some nannies think they're a better class of servant than housemaids – so I hope she's not the bossy kind.'

As the two continued to chat, Alice put more thought into the woman who would soon join them. At the moment, Alice was in charge of the household, the housekeeper, so if Lily

King had any issues, she should always look to Alice before approaching anyone else.

'Lily King is going to spend most of her time with the child, taking her meals in the nursery, and will ask one of us to sit with the baby when she requires a personal break. When baby's asleep, she'll be upstairs in her room, prepared to deal with baby's needs.'

It was the hottest day of the year so far when Lily King arrived at Holmorton Lodge. She was smart and had a determined manner as Patty opened the door to admit her.

'Good afternoon, you must be Nanny King.'

'I prefer Nanny Lily, if you don't mind, Miss—'

'Miss Goodwin – Patty.' Patty stumbled the words out. She told Alice later that it was like opening the door and finding her old schoolteacher standing outside.

Patty brought Nanny Lily into the kitchen and introduced her to Alice, 'who is in charge,' she added, much to Alice's amusement.

'You can leave your belongings in here and I'll take you to see Mrs Caldwell.'

Nanny Lily nodded, removed her coat, folded it, and placed it on a chair, with her gloves tucked into a small, round grey hat that matched the colour of her hair – in fact, when she removed the hat it almost looked as if she was removing part of her hair. Alice bit her lip before she could let out any sign of amusement.

'Follow me, and I'll take you to the nursery.'

Alice strode towards the staircase. Nanny Lily looked the part. Her dress was pale green, and even though her journey involved a train for a couple of hours, there was no sign of creasing.

They arrived at the nursery door, and Connie, who had been sitting in there reading, rose and walked towards them, smiling, ready to shake hands.

'Welcome to Holmorton Lodge, Mrs King. I'm Constance Caldwell.' Over the last few months, Connie had grown larger and, as Alice looked at her with fresh eyes, she realised it wouldn't be long before the first Caldwell baby would be born.

'It's a pleasure to meet you, Mrs Caldwell. And please call me Nanny Lily. It gives a better understanding of who I am… if you don't mind?'

'Of course not.'

'I'll ask Patty to bring up a tray of refreshments. You must need something,' said Alice.

Alice nodded to Connie and walked to the kitchen, to be met by an excited Patty.

'Go on! What's she like?'

'I think you're right in your description, Patty.'

–

The next person to arrive at Holmorton Lodge was Nurse Kelly, engaged by Agatha as a private nurse to look after Connie for a month – or as long as necessary. Two weeks before and two weeks after the birth, in case of any problems arising. Responsibility for looking after mother and baby would fall to Nanny Lily after two weeks. Agatha was keen to have a qualified midwife on the premises for the birth.

Patty met Nurse Kelly, who arrived half an hour early, wearing a nurse's uniform, and so needed little introduction.

'I'm Nurse Kelly, the midwife, and I'm very pleased to meet you.'

The woman had quite a bouncy personality. Fair blonde curls cut just below her jawline, and on her face there was a broad smile. She took Patty's hand and gave it a resounding shake.

Patty reciprocated with a smile of her own. They were chattering away when they arrived in the kitchen.

'Afternoon.' Alice couldn't help returning the smile of her own.

'I didn't realise this house was so big.'

‘Yes, it is. The nursery’s on the top floor – all set up for the baby. You’ll meet Nanny Lily, as she likes to be called, there.’

Once again, Alice took their visitor upstairs to meet Connie. When Connie came down to the kitchen, it was obvious that Nurse Kelly had impressed her. Perhaps Nanny Lily might grow on them.

–

It took the two women no time at all to settle in. They were both seasoned workers used to moving their homes with their jobs. Nurse Kelly said it wasn’t very often that she was away from her home for so long. Nanny Lily’s employment depended on the age of the child or children in her care.

During their first week, the two women spent a lot of their time downstairs, and Alice could find out more about the pair of them and their work. She discovered Nanny Lily was a quiet individual and craved company, although she didn’t appear to know what to say to that company when she had it. Since she had lost her husband, she had taken live-in jobs where she could rely on other people being present. Perhaps it wasn’t so much companionship she sought – it was more about not being on her own. Alice felt sorry for the woman, something she never thought she would do when they first met.

–

Connie had been fidgety all day, complaining of feeling uncomfortable, so it wasn’t surprising when she went into labour at two o’clock on the morning of 28 July. Soon, everyone was awake, waiting for news, wanting to know that all was well. Alice was on hand to help Nurse Kelly, if required, while Patty’s orders were to keep everyone supplied with refreshments throughout the darkness of the night.

Alice kept popping out of the bedroom to cheer up an impatient Robert, who was on the landing looking like a lost boy sitting outside the headmaster's office waiting for his punishment. Alice felt sorry for him, but even she had no time to spend on the father when the child was due to appear in the world.

Just after seven in the morning, everything went silent. Alice, who had been talking to Robert, looked up in anticipation and slipped back into the bedroom.

'Quick, Alice! Give me a hand.'

Alice rushed to Nurse Kelly's side. Connie grasped her hand. As she did so, Nurse Kelly raised her voice. 'Push, Connie – as hard as you can – now!'

Alice felt Connie's push through her hands as she tried to hold them steady.

A little body slid towards the bed, and Nurse Kelly grabbed the waiting towel.

'Well, Mrs Caldwell – Connie – you have a gorgeous little boy.'

Tears sprang into Alice's eyes as she saw the joy on Connie's face shining through her tiredness.

'Congratulations, Connie, I'm so pleased for you. I'll get Robert.'

Alice popped her head around the door, and Robert jumped to his feet.

'You have a son, Robert,' she whispered.

'Tell Father he can come in now,' came Nurse Kelly's imperious voice.

There was no need to repeat the offer. Robert rushed to be at his wife's side. He put out a hand to pick up his son's tiny fingers, with tears in his eyes.

He looked up with a face full of astonishment. 'We have a son.'

Connie handed him the precious bundle. His arms closed around his son, and Alice heard him swear, in a low voice, to keep him safe. 'Why couldn't my father want the same for me? I'll keep you safe no matter how old you are, son.'

Then, with Connie's permission, Robert walked out into the hall and allowed everyone to meet John Robert, the latest member of the family.

As Alice watched the proud father showing off his infant son, she felt tears welling. It was the first time she had witnessed the birth of someone precious to parents who would travel to the ends of the earth for them.

Chapter Thirteen

August 1921

Alice had seen more of Jean since the dinner party after Christmas when Connie announced she was expecting, and they'd built up a friendship. Jean and Stephen visited Holmorton Lodge from time to time. Stephen and Robert's friendship had developed during the war years, and had grown as they worked together at the PTC. Both their wives served as clippies, fostering a close friendship among the four.

Stephen and Jean were to be their first guests since the birth of John Robert. As Connie had put it, 'We can get back to normal.' Alice thought that for most women in The Potteries, having children *was* the normal thing. Few people could afford a nanny.

Of course, John Robert dominated the conversation. Every time Alice took in a fresh course, he was the subject. Alice had noticed that Connie was becoming more and more like a married woman. Alice wondered where the demonstrator who had thrown a brick through the window of a government office in Trafalgar Square to support the suffragettes had gone.

The after-dinner conversation often turned to the PTC and, given that Alice knew them all, she could often join in. During one such visit, Stephen spoke to Robert.

'Did you hear about that young lad that's been seen in the depot, by the way? The night crew reported seeing him hanging around a lot. Caleb told him to…' He glanced at the ladies present, and Alice suspected he toned down his words. '…told him to get off home, where he belonged.'

Robert nodded. ‘Yes, I have. Have they seen him again?’

‘Last week, so Caleb said. He’s worried the lad might have something to do with the thefts we’ve had. Little things. But they soon mount up. We have to keep the depot running overnight to get the maintenance done. Anyway, Caleb grabbed him by the shoulder and warned him he’d get the constables on to him if he caught him again. Then he gave the lad a clip around the earhole and sent him packing. The lad doesn’t look much over nine or ten.’

‘You never mentioned it, Robert. Is it just Goldenhill depot?’ asked Connie.

‘Yes, dear. I didn’t mention it because I thought it was just lads playing around, but he doesn’t seem to take the hint, even when Caleb threatened to send the police round to his house to tell his parents.’

‘What did he say to that?’

‘He shrugged his shoulders and said he could try, but it’d make no difference.’

The voices were quiet, but Alice pondered over their words, unable to hear what they said next. This intrigued her. ‘Do you think the family may be hard-up?’

The two men turned towards her, causing a faint blush.

‘I mean, he may be looking out for a large family, or… who knows…’ Her voice trailed away.

Connie shook her head. ‘It doesn’t give anyone the right to steal from others, Alice.’

Alice persisted. ‘I know that, but his behaviour might be more complicated than stealing to line his own pockets.’

Jean then joined the conversation. ‘I agree with Alice. We feel we should blame someone, but we must also ask ourselves why he’s doing it.’

Stephen smiled at his wife. ‘You always see the good in people, my love, but I’ll need to investigate it; otherwise, every half-baked criminal in The Potteries will target us.’

Robert rose to his feet. 'With that, I think we men can retire to the library for a cigar and leave the ladies to ponder over whether to allow criminals to run amok.'

–

Two weeks later, Alice called in to see Jean and Stella, Stephen's mother, for an update.

'Stephen's tracked him down,' said Jean. 'I must admit to feeling happy about his capture, but also sad about the possibility of serious trouble if the PTC involved the police. I wish the boy had used his common sense and stayed away after his first capture.'

Alice nodded. 'Needs must, I suppose. Once it was brought to Stephen's attention, he couldn't ignore it, Jean.'

'I know. But I keep thinking about him. I mean… is he looking out for his family? If he is, then we can't blame him, Alice. Can you remember back to when you had no money and your mother left you in the workhouse? That may be the only alternative for him.'

'I'll never forget that place, Jean. What did he find out?'

Jean smiled. 'You sound as interested as I was, Alice. Anyroad, somebody saw the boy hanging around and, rather than give him a telling-off, Stephen followed him. He was late leaving, so it was going dark, and you'll never guess, Alice, the boy is living in an old, abandoned house near the railway tracks at Goldenhill on Colclough Lane – you know – it was a workman's hut before the North Staffordshire Railway finished the station.'

'It had a wooden roof, which had collapsed on one side, leaving it open to the elements. The lad boarded up the window and made a door out of the wood from the roof. He built a shelter under the intact part of the roof and covered it with a tarpaulin with NSR printed on it. There was a grate on which he could cook food. It was about a hundred yards from the railway. Provided he was careful, he could have a fire as long as it didn't make too much smoke. You can't see the building from Goldenhill Station.'

'But that place is derelict. The lad can't be living there. All alone?'

Jean nodded. 'Stephen hung back and waited until he'd gone inside. Then he opened the door. The lad tried to dash past him. Stephen may have a gammy leg, but he's quick with his arms. He used his stick to trip him up and then grabbed him by his coat, which he said had seen better days.'

'That was brave of Stephen. The lad could've attacked him, and nobody would've known where to look for him.'

'That's what I said to him when he told me. He calmed the boy down and said he wouldn't hurt him, but he wanted to talk to him, man to man.' Jean smiled as she said the words. 'Just like Stephen, to make a man out of the boy. Anyway, Stephen told him he was the depot manager and it was his responsibility to make sure everything was safe. If he had to report his actions to the police, then it may be prison or the workhouse for him.'

Alice was forming a picture of the boy in her mind. From what she knew of Stephen, he was a kind man, a man who spoke before his actions rather than after. 'Did the boy try to run away?'

Jean shook her head. 'No. Stephen has a calming voice and got the boy to listen to him. His name is Luke, by the way. He refused to tell Stephen his full name… which was understandable.'

'Luke – from the Bible,' said Alice, absorbed in the unfolding story. 'What did Stephen do?'

'He just sat on an old box and talked with him. Found out a few things. He's ten years old and a skinny-looking lad because of his irregular eating habits. He's tall for his age; Stephen says he comes up to his shoulders. It turns out Luke's on his own. He has no family and takes care of himself.'

'What a shame! I mean, it's thankful that he's only got himself to take care of, but… I don't know… what a lonely life – and him not yet eleven years old.'

Alice felt tears welling. She knew about loneliness. What it was like to have no one to lean on. 'So what're you going to do, Jean?'

'I don't think Stephen's decided yet. He's suggested that he take Luke to the workhouse. At least the workhouse will feed him and give him a bed. Luke refused. He said he'd run away if Stephen put him anywhere else. At least we know where he is, as long as he stays in that old house. We can get some food to him.'

'But… but what about the autumn and winter coming? How's he going to manage? He won't be able to find enough wood for fires. He'll need hot, nourishing food, not just bread or oatcakes and cheese, Jean.'

Jean stood up and walked up and down. 'Don't you think I know all that, Alice? But we've got to be careful. The last thing we want is to rush things and frighten him off.'

Alice could feel Jean's dilemma as she paced the room.

'I believe I know what I'd like, Alice. I'd like us to get to know him. Build his confidence up a little. Take him food and water and, by building his trust, we might find somewhere for him to stay. I might even ask Stephen to take me with him so I can talk to him.'

'You won't know what to advise until you've met the lad. I hope you can get something sorted for the poor boy.'

Later, as Alice walked to the tram stop, she couldn't stop thinking about the situation her friends were facing. She even wondered whether they might think about taking the lad into their home. Jean was desperate to have a child, and although a boy of ten might not be what they had in mind, it could solve a problem for all of them.

Chapter Fourteen

September 1921

Alice went to Holywell as soon as Walter could get the day off work to accompany her.

'All I've got to do now is tell Connie,' Alice said to Patty.

'She'll let you have the time off, won't she?'

'It's not that I'm worried about. I feel guilty about leaving her with such a young baby.'

'I don't know why. She's got Nanny Lily and Nurse Kelly, and we never get called up to help in the nursery. They don't know we exist down here.'

'Yes, you're right.'

'I can cope with the meals for everyone. Just leave me with the menu,' said Patty.

'It's going to be homemade pâté, followed by turbot, beef Wellington and then a summer fruit pudding. Easy enough?'

'Yes, Alice. Soup, boiled ham salad and rice pudding – I can manage that.' They both laughed.

Alice left the kitchen and found Connie in the garden room. Connie liked this room the most, just like her mother did.

'What can I do for you, Alice?'

'Will it be acceptable for me to have the whole day off on the tenth? Walter and I are going to follow up on the information we got about Holywell.'

'Of course, Alice. Hope you find whatever you're looking for.'

'Well, it's twenty-three years and a war since it happened. I don't fancy my chances, but I'll have to go.'

'As long as you tell me everything when you get back.'

'Of course.' Alice smiled. She got the idea that if John Robert hadn't been born – or was older – Connie would've wanted to come too!

Walter grinned when she told him. Almost immediately, Alice said, 'Do you think my mother – adopted mother – wanted me to know about the woman who bore me? I mean, why else would she leave me the message? It would have been easier for her to have let sleeping dogs lie.'

'She's given you the choice.'

'She's left it up to me to decide whether I follow it through.'

'I'm worried about you, Alice. This isn't turning out to be what we thought. Are you sure that's what you want to do?'

'Don't you see, Walter, my actual mother may still be alive!' Alice's face looked determined. 'I'm going to do it, whether or not you agree. It was meant to be.'

'Well, in that case, we're off to Holywell then.'

Alice kissed him to thank him. He rubbed his forehead and gave a wry grin.

'It'd be worth it just to get another kiss like that.'

'I'm sure I can accommodate your request, Walter.'

–

The journey to Holywell went smoothly despite the number of connections they had to make. It was a relief when the train pulled into the station.

Holywell was a small town, and the walk from the station to the cottage hospital took a mere ten minutes. Alice's plan was to ask for details of nursing homes within the area.

They found the cottage hospital and knocked on the door. The nurse asked for Alice's name and apologised for her own lack of knowledge, as she hadn't worked there long. She disappeared down the corridor to find a staff nurse or someone who might help.

The young nurse soon returned in the company of an older woman wearing a dark blue uniform and a white cap. As luck would have it, this new nurse had worked at a place called Bryn Celyn before the war.

'I can tell you a little about the place, Miss Tucker, but can you tell me why you're looking for it?'

Alice explained the note from her adoptive mother. 'I believe she wanted me to find out more; otherwise, why mention the nursing home?'

The nurse nodded. 'I understand. I can tell you that the nursing home closed at the beginning of 1915 and was taken over by the army as a rehabilitation centre for injured soldiers returning from the war.'

'Is it very far away?'

The nurse shook her head, although her face had a sad look to it. 'It's empty now and in poor condition. The army pulled out in March. I believe the builders are in there now to renovate it back to its former layout before handing it back to the original owners. It's about a mile away. No harm in your going down there, I suppose. You're not likely to get inside, mind you.'

The nurse pointed them in the right direction. It'd be a walk down the lane opposite, where they'd have views of the River Dee estuary from time to time. 'You'll find the walk pleasant even if you don't get any help with your research. Still, I wish you well, Miss Tucker.'

The nurse shook hands with both of them, and they turned towards the lane for the start of the next part of their journey.

'D'you think they'll let us in to have a look around? I'd like to see if there's anything that might be helpful to us.'

'If it's in a poor state, they might think it is too dangerous. You might have to be prepared for disappointment, my dear.'

They arrived at Bryn Celyn twenty minutes later, expecting to find a ramshackle building. On the outside, there looked to be no problem. Men inside whistled, chatted and shouted. The front door was open. Walter thumped on the door three times in the hope someone might hear. A second attempt brought a tall man in an army uniform. The person in charge directed them to a small office just inside the main entrance.

A man was leaning over a desk, looking at what appeared to be a large plan. 'What can I do for you?'

Alice stepped towards him. 'Hello. My name is Miss Alice Tucker, and this is Mr Walter Latham. I'm here to look at this building. I understand it was a nursing home before the army took it over during the war.'

'Good afternoon, ma'am. I'm Corporal Durham. I'm in charge of getting this building ready for occupation again, and yes, you're correct regarding its former life.'

'I believe I was born here, and I was hoping I could have a look around. The building looks quite impressive from the outside.'

'Yes, it does. But I'm afraid I can't let you in. The ceiling requires reinforcement; we haven't yet assessed the stairs.'

Not to be put off, Alice tried again in a sort of pleading voice. 'We live in The Potteries, Corporal, so we've come a long way on many trains. You might be my only chance of finding my mother.' Alice forced tears into her eyes and saw Walter looking askance at her. She gave Corporal Durham her full attention. 'We wondered if any documents or paperwork might have remained here.'

Alice watched him. He looked torn between granting her request and telling her to make herself scarce.

He hesitated. 'It's more than my job's worth, Miss Tucker. I could be in serious trouble if anything happened.'

Walter jumped in at that point, sensing, as Alice had, the hesitation in his voice. 'You'd be doing this young lady a good turn. You can see how upset she is.' He pulled a quarter bottle of whisky out of his pocket and handed it to him.

This had the desired effect. Corporal Durham took them down to the storeroom and let them in.

'For God's sake, be bloody careful and don't speak to anyone.' He walked off, returning to his post for a nice cup of 'Scottish' tea.

Alice and Walter proceeded to the back of the building, taking care as instructed. They found four offices; two had boxes and tea chests that looked prepared for removal, but no one had returned for them. At least the metal linings would've protected documents from damp and vermin. The tea chests had lids nailed down at each corner. Their careful packing suggested they contained important information. Corporal Durham had been kind enough to leave them with a crowbar, and soon all the chests were open. Not wanting to waste any time, Alice looked for ledgers, which she assumed would've been used to keep track of patients, just like in the workhouse. There were several of these chests and, between herself and Walter, they began a systematic search looking for documents referring to births around 4 April 1898.

'And Walter, make sure you look about two weeks before, in case there was a delay in registering the birth.'

Walter grinned and saluted her. 'Yes, ma'am.'

It didn't take long before Alice found a bound ledger. She opened it at the first page. It contained a list of names, date of admission and date of leaving, and what looked like a reference number.

'This must be it, Walter. They had one like this at the workhouse.'

'Yes, but look at the first date.'

Alice had been so eager that she hadn't noticed the first date was 20 January 1906. Her shoulders dropped.

'Not to worry, love. There's bound to be others.'

They set about looking for similar books. It didn't take long. Alice found the ledger starting on 1 April 1896 and ending on 31 December 1899.

'I've found it!' She lifted the ledger onto the small table, and they looked for leaving dates after 4 April 1898. Alice turned the pages slowly. Each double-page spread contained the person's name, address, next of kin, date of admission and date of leaving and a page number. There were ten names on each sheet.

They found three women who gave birth to girls, but as soon as Alice saw the entry, she knew she was the one – Ethel Barnes. Her heart pounded. This record stood out because the name was the only piece of information. No date of birth, address, next of kin – nothing – a dead end, just right for someone wanting to hide information.

They hurried to turn to the folio number quoted, and there she was. Still no more information, but there was a list of invoices and payments received. The invoices were for medical care and her stay at Bryn Celyn. All in immaculate handwriting. It looked as if she had spent the whole of her pregnancy here. There was a flurry of invoices for medical care dated 28 March 1898. The last entry was on 11 April 1898, and the last payment received on 20 April 1898.

'We need to find copies of the invoices. They must be somewhere.'

'How do you know there'll be copies?'

'It's just sound business practice. We'll concentrate on Ethel, but I've got the addresses of the other two if I'm wrong.'

They turned their attention to files containing administrative paperwork, but finding the right file was going to be difficult given the sheer number of files.

'It's going to take ages to find anything; let's hope we're lucky.'

'The lack of alphabetical storage tells me whoever packed these thought they weren't important,' said Alice.

'Or maybe the poor sods who did the packing knew they'd never have to find anything.'

'That makes sense. As Miss Doubleday would say, "Men canna pack correctly; they havna got the brain for it."'

After an hour of searching, they found some of what they were looking for – a cardboard wallet containing invoices, statements and other documents. Unfortunately, there was no personal information, no home address. The contents of the wallet contained only one address – Ethel Barnes, c/o Turnbull, Gregson and Turnbull, Solicitors, Manchester.

Alice and Walter looked at the array of papers.

'We've not got a direct link, but this one looks too good to be left alone. Remember, I've got details of the other two women, which we can investigate if we've no luck with Ethel,' said Alice.

'It could just be the woman who paid the bills at the solicitors,' said Walter.

'Yes, but there must be a reason for the secrecy. All this wasn't cheap. I think we should start with the solicitors.'

'I agree. Let's have another hour to see if we can find anything else.'

'We haven't got time to look through everything. I'm sure Corporal Durham will want to throw us out. We need to get moving.'

'If we go too quickly, we'll miss something.'

'Then we'll take the papers with us.'

'You can't just take important documents away. We'll be in serious trouble. I'm surprised at you.'

'Look, Walter. They left all this paperwork here with no regard for privacy or confidentiality. Perhaps someone removed all the medical records, disregarding the other paperwork.'

'That's taking a lot for granted.'

'Well, I'm going to take them with me. We've come so close to finding my mother and I'm not about to leave anything behind that might help us. You stand by and I'll stuff them in my bag.'

Walter kept watch while Alice thrust what she could into her bag, thankful that she had seen fit to bring a sizeable one with her. They placed the rest of the documents back into the tea chests more or less as they'd found them. Then they placed the tea chests side by side so it all looked the same as they'd found them. Walter nailed the lids down using the flat side of the crowbar, and together they returned to Corporal Durham, with Alice doing her best to pretend her bag was as light as when she walked in.

'Thank you so much for letting us go inside,' said Alice.

'Did you find anything, Miss Tucker?'

'No, I didn't. It looks as though I might have been mistaken. I'm so disappointed.'

The corporal looked down at the bag and frowned. Alice looked, and to her dismay, found some paper sticking out of the top. She felt herself flushing.

'Papers never stay where you put them, do they? We're off to see the solicitor, so I hope it's not raining; otherwise, they'll be unreadable.' She pushed the papers down hard into the bag.

'You should've told me, Walter.' She tutted at him as they walked towards the door. Corporal Durham had already returned to his own plans and paperwork. They need not have worried after all.

There were no other passengers in their carriage and so there was plenty of room for the two of them to spread out and look at the papers. Nothing seemed to jump out at them as potential clues about her mother. It might just have been a complete waste of time but for the name of the solicitor who paid the bills and the name Ethel Barnes. Could this be another blind alley, sending her on to yet more distant places? She didn't even know if Ethel Barnes was the patient. Like Walter had said, it could be the name of a clerk who paid the invoices. But she knew one thing – she must discover who Ethel Barnes is.

Walter was looking through some of the papers and he exclaimed, 'I've found another name – David Turnbull. He signed the document which allowed you to be adopted. He signed using his power of attorney. Below the signature there, it says "signed under power of attorney, a copy of which is attached", and an embossed seal in the name of the solicitors.'

Alice looked at the paperwork, but there was no copy attached. 'Dash it, we'll have to look through every sheet again, because it might contain my mother's address. Ethel Barnes – we're getting closer.'

The train pulled into the next station, where there were quite a few people waiting. Alice sighed and began collecting everything together in case anyone walked into their carriage. Walter slid his arm around her shoulders. It felt so comfortable. She needed a document stating that Ethel Barnes had given birth to a daughter named Alice. *Then* she might believe she had got the right person.

A wave of tiredness flowed through her. It was hard work looking for information that was so important to discovering herself. How lucky she was to have Walter by her side. She smiled and leaned on him, her eyes becoming heavy, making it hard to focus on what they should do next. She gave up and, with her head still resting on his shoulder, she fell asleep.

It seemed no time at all when he woke her. She stretched. No one had joined them. She arrived back home at ten o'clock. She let herself in and was met by Connie.

'How'd you get on?'

Alice told her she'd found a likely candidate who could've been her mother. 'Have you ever heard of a woman called Ethel Barnes?'

'Is that the woman?'

'I think so.'

'No, I don't recall knowing anybody called Barnes, but I can ask Mother next time I speak to her. She might remember something from her time in Manchester.'

'I'm going to write to the firm of solicitors we found and ask them if they can put me in contact with her.'

Connie wrinkled her nose. 'I don't think they will. Mr Railsford always told us to reply asking for the solicitors of the person enquiring, and then he would write directly to the other solicitors. You should make an appointment to see him. He'll write the letter on your behalf. Turnbull's are bound to reply to him.'

–

Over the next few days, Alice couldn't get the thoughts of the trip to Holywell and what she had found out of her mind. Whenever she had some spare time, she would look at the documents to see if she had missed anything. Something inside was telling her she was getting closer.

It was Saturday, and Alice and Walter were sitting on a seat in Burslem Park. It was such a glorious day that it seemed a shame not to be enjoying the late afternoon sunshine. She would have to rush off to start the evening meal. She couldn't leave everything to Patty.

'Do solicitors open on Saturdays? I mean, suppose they're not open. We don't want to go all the way to Manchester to find them closed.'

'They'll let you know when they write back, Alice. That would be the correct thing to do. You're getting impatient. You can't hurry them along by just turning up on their doorstep. Besides, travelling's expensive. You need to make sure you'll be received before you go.'

'You're right, Walter, of course, but you needn't worry. I've been able to save money out of my wages. I had little to spend it on – until now.' She could feel herself blushing. 'Sometimes, when I feel we're making a little progress, I want to rush ahead. I'll just have to learn to be patient. Unfortunately, I've discovered it's not one of my strengths.'

–

'Stephen met Luke a few times after the initial contact,' said Jean to Alice when she popped over later in the week to have a chat. 'At first Luke kept his distance, but with the promise of food being available, he's become a regular at the depot. He always sits close to the door, to enable a quick getaway – or so Stephen says. Stephen has told his workmen to keep an eye on him but not to approach the lad, fearing he might run away again. At least Stephen knows where he is when he's in that rickety old building.'

'Have you seen the lad yet, Jean?'

Jean looked glum. 'I'd like to. Now he's more settled.'

'Autumn's ending. Winter'll be with us before you know it. What'll happen to him then? He can't live in that rundown place when there's snow on the ground.'

'I know. I'm working on that, Alice. I'm planning on getting Stephen to take me to see him next week, otherwise I might never get to see him. I want to see where the boy's living. Stephen says it's derelict.'

'Oh, poor boy. Has Stephen been able to find out anything about Luke's family? I mean, does he have any?'

'He doesn't have any now. He told Stephen he's better off on his own. He said he wouldn't recognise any of them if he saw them.'

'How awful.'

'Anyway, no one may go to the building without checking with Stephen. The mechanics find him errands to do, and he gets paid in food. Stephen has had a word with the shop owners in Goldenhill, who all seem to know of him, but nothing about him. He seems to do errands for everyone.'

Alice smiled at Jean. 'He's fortunate Stephen's looking out for him. Maybe he can talk some sense into him. I'll maybe knit him a couple of jumpers – and maybe socks too.'

'It sounds just like we were during the war, knitting to keep our boys at the front warm. At least Luke hasn't got Germans shooting at him.'

–

Alice felt quite uncomfortable waiting to see Mr Railsford. She'd been to the offices once before when Connie worked there. She glanced around at the dark wood-panelled walls, the tall windows letting in lots of light, but frosted glass at the bottom prevented people in the street looking in.

Mr Railsford appeared at the door. 'Come in, Miss Tucker.' He pointed her to a nice green leather-covered chair then took his own seat. 'How can I help?'

Alice filled him in regarding her plans to find her birth mother, careful not to tell him about the stolen documents. She said a nurse had been helpful and remembered there had been one woman where everything was shrouded in secrecy. Ethel Barnes was unique as the accounts were sent directly to Turnbull, Gregson and Turnbull, a firm of solicitors in Manchester. 'I wondered if you would write a letter to them on my behalf. I've been told solicitors like to talk to other solicitors and may not talk to me directly. How much would the letter cost me?'

Mr Railsford coughed. 'I charge one guinea for sending the letter and handling the return. But for you, I will write the letter pro bono, which is legal speak for no charge. The Copelands have been excellent clients for many years. I'll arrange for the letter to be written and despatched at the first opportunity. I'll let you know when I get a reply.'

'Oh, thank you very much, Mr Railsford.'

Alice stepped outside into the sunshine with a smile on her face and tried to look forward to another period of waiting.

Surprisingly, she received a reply together with a handwritten note two days later, informing Alice that he had sent a letter to Turnbull, Gregson and Turnbull and was awaiting a reply.

Chapter Fifteen

October 1921

Two weeks later, the telephone rang, and Alice answered to find Mr Railsford on the other end.

'Good morning, Miss Tucker. I've received a reply from Turnbull, Gregson and Turnbull. They're aware of the client in question, but no longer act for that person. They've forwarded the letter to the person's current solicitor. They haven't provided their names, which is normal.'

'So we're no further forward.'

'It's frustrating, I know, but as I said, the wheels of the law grind slowly, I'm afraid.'

'Thank you, Mr Railsford. I appreciate that.'

She and Walter discussed the matter, but neither could say much about what to do next. At least they knew that Ethel Barnes wasn't the woman at the office who paid the bills. Perhaps this other solicitor would not bother to reply, or Miss Barnes was no longer their client, and her whereabouts were unknown. Then the matter would be taken out of Alice's hands.

–

It was now well into October. The weather was changeable and growing colder. Alice had resigned herself to not finding more information. She considered ringing Mr Railsford to see if he had any news, but decided not to bother him. She trusted he would let her know as soon as he knew anything.

So, it came as a tremendous shock when she received a letter from him, short and to the point. He had received a letter from another Manchester-based legal firm called Solomon, Solomon and Penfold, and would she like to arrange a meeting to discuss the contents? She stared at the letter, turning it over in her hands. The time had arrived. Could she face the upset that might come with it?

She took a deep breath, and tore open the envelope containing the copy letter. Excitement mixed with dread. Her hands shook. The letter was from a Mr Penfold, who invited her to a meeting at his office in Manchester. They had something of interest to discuss and requested that she should bring along her birth certificate and any other relevant papers she had about her birth, her identity and early years. They would be obliged if she could attend a meeting at ten o'clock on 9 November at their chambers in Charlotte Street. Could she confirm her attendance as soon as possible? Mr Railsford's letter said that he awaited instructions once she was ready to discuss this matter. She picked up the telephone and was soon speaking to Miss Cheeseman, who had taken over from Connie when she left to have John Robert. She put Alice through to Mr Railsford.

'Good morning. You've received my letter, I expect?'

'Yes, Mr Railsford. Are these the solicitors that the other firm passed my letter on to?'

'It appears so. What do you want to do?'

'I want to go to the meeting, but I only have my birth and christening certificates.'

'Very good, I'll reply, but if you agree, I'll ask them to send me copies of any documents they give you. Also, and this is very important, don't sign any documents or indicate verbal acceptance of any agreements.'

'Yes, I'll make sure I do that.'

'Are you going to take someone with you?'

'I wasn't planning to. Do you think I should?'

'Yes, it's always good to have someone on your side at any meeting like this. No doubt Solomon, Solomon and Penfold will have access to their entire staff should they require it at the meeting. I'll arrange for my junior solicitor, Mr Moreton, to attend the meeting. Miss Cheeseman will make the travel arrangements, and she'll let you know. I hope you find what you're looking for.'

'Thank you, Mr Railsford. I hope I do too.'

She hung up the receiver and sat for a few moments. Then she sent Patty to Walter's with a note asking him to come to see her that evening, as she had received the response she was waiting for. Patty soon returned.

'Walter's on days. Miss Latimer said she'd give him the note as soon as he gets in.'

'Thank you, Patty.'

–

Alice was on tenterhooks for the rest of the day as she waited for Walter to arrive. She was beginning to regret ever starting this quest.

It was around three o'clock when he arrived. She hugged him. How lucky she was to have a man like him to rely on.

'This letter came from Mr Railsford in this morning's post.' She gave the two documents to Walter, who read them.

'On the first reading, I'd say it looks promising. He must have something to tell you; otherwise, there'd be no point in setting up an appointment. Unfortunately, I won't be able to go with you. I'm working that day.'

'There's no need for you to ask for time off work. Mr Railsford is sending a junior solicitor with me. He stressed the importance of taking legal counsel to the meeting.'

Walter lifted his eyebrows. 'That sounds heavy-handed. I bet that'll cost a pretty penny.'

'No, Walter, he's doing this for free.'

'Lawyers do nowt for free.'

She nodded and smiled at him. 'We've done a few of these visits now, and I know what I need to do. I shall put together several questions so as I don't forget.'

'Very well. I'll give you a hand.'

She gazed into his eyes and was about to kiss him when his lips touched hers. It was only a whistle from Patty that drew them apart.

–

Alice popped over to see Jean and Stella to find out how things were going with the boy, Luke. They were sitting in the kitchen having soup for dinner, made up of the leftovers of the previous day's meal, and had heard a van pull up outside. The front door flew open.

'Jean, Mother. Come quickly.'

It was Stephen, panic-stricken.

The three women jumped up and scurried into the hallway to see Stephen carrying a young boy in his arms. He wasn't making a sound.

'Is this… this… Luke?' asked Jean.

Stephen nodded. 'Quick, Mother – phone for the doctor. Jean, help me get him to bed. He's so cold. We need to warm him up.'

The women jumped into action, seeing nothing but the deathly pale face in Stephen's arms.

'Get me a bed warmer and I'll fill it and bring it up to you,' said Alice. Within seconds, she was running up the stairs, following the murmur of voices. Jean was ashen. Luke was shivering and sweating, throwing off the blankets almost as quickly as Jean could cover him.

'Whatever's happened to him, Stephen?'

'A mechanic popped into my office saying he was worried about Luke. He hadn't seen him for a couple of days.'

Stephen laid Luke out on the bed while Jean stripped Luke of his dirty clothes and dropped them on the floor.

'He'll have to wear one of Stephen's nightshirts, Alice, until I can get something more suitable.'

Stephen muttered, 'I don't think he'll care much about what he wears as long as he wakes up.'

Stella arrived in the bedroom to see Jean bite her lip at Stephen's utterings. She placed a hand on Jean's shoulder. Alice heard her whisper, 'He doesn't mean it, my dear. It's his worries getting to him. They always do.'

'I'll go back downstairs and wait for the doctor, Jean,' said Alice, aware that her friends were going through a difficult patch.

At that moment, Luke's eyes fluttered, and he murmured something that nobody caught.

Alice bounded down the stairs and paced about the sitting room, waiting until, at last, there was a knock on the door.

She shot to answer it. The man waiting was short and tubby, with round spectacles and carrying a case.

'Dr Trainor… Miss? I received a telephone call?'

'Oh yes, please come in. I'm Miss Tucker. It's the little boy upstairs. I think he must have a fever.'

The mechanic, who had been waiting by the van, said he'd go back to the depot and inform them that Mr Adams was dealing with an emergency. Alice nodded and shot back inside. She showed Dr Trainor upstairs to the spare room where Luke lay, surrounded by the three people who cared about him.

'Oh, Doctor,' said Stella, relaxing, 'it's good to see you. We have this b—'

Dr Trainor ignored her and strode to the bed. 'How long has he been like this?' It was obvious he didn't take too much notice of the niceties of conversation when he had a patient to take care of. After a series of sharp questions no one could answer, the doctor sighed. 'I can't do anything just now. Can you keep him here for a couple of days, and I'll look in on him again tomorrow?'

Stephen looked up, clenching and unclenching his fists. 'Do you think he'll be all right, Doctor?'

'We'll have to wait and see. If he doesn't improve, we might have to take him to London Road Hospital. He looks malnourished and, once he's on the mend, he'll need to build his strength up.' His eyes narrowed. 'Are you his parents… or guardians?'

'No,' said Stephen. 'One of my employees discovered him.'

Alice raised her eyebrows. Surely the doctor didn't think the Adams were responsible for Luke's condition.

Jean picked up Luke's hand and stroked it with her fingers. 'He needs looking after, Stephen. We can't let him go to the hospital. He'll be all on his own.'

It was Stella who showed the doctor out of the house. Stephen stayed with Luke, sitting beside his bed, while Jean and Alice made their way back to the kitchen. Jean heated the kettle again, but when she looked at Alice, her eyes were misty.

'I feel it's my fault, Alice. I should've made Stephen bring him home, but I didn't know what'd be best. I didn't think Stella would agree to bringing home some boy off the street – but I know now I should've asked, for the boy's sake.'

'It's not your fault, Jean.'

'It is – don't you see? I've been so wrapped up in my dreams of having a family of my own that I haven't given this poor boy a thought. I've let him live a life on his own, without for one moment considering what we can do to help him.'

'But it's not like that, Jean. Didn't you say that Stephen had tried to get him to pay a visit but Luke wouldn't? You can't kidnap him, Jean.'

Jean smiled wanly. 'I know. But why do I feel that the poor boy needs a mother?'

Alice shook her head. 'It's hard to watch any child fighting an illness. Take care of him while you can. Now he's in your house, he might feel tempted to stay awhile… you never know.'

'A last resort, for someone like me, you mean. All my friends have children. Ginnie, Connie, Betty – all except me. What if we can't have children, Alice? Every time I go into the town, I see mothers with perambulators and pushchairs, and every time I wish it was me. I'm getting older, Alice. I don't want to wait until I'm too old to enjoy them.'

Alice stared at Jean, hearing everything she had tossed around in her mind. She had mentioned several times that she and Stephen were hoping for a child or children to complete their family, but hadn't realised just how much the waiting was tearing her friend apart.

Later that evening, Jean, Stephen and Stella, together with Alice and Walter, sat round the dining table while Stephen told them what he knew.

He had not seen the lad for a few days, nor did he remember hearing his steady whistle. A mechanic appeared in his office and said he was worried and asked Stephen if he could nip down to the building to check out what, if anything, was happening down there. Stephen went with him. They shouted for Luke, but there was no answer.

Once they got inside, they discovered Luke lying in a corner, covered with the blankets Jean had sent to keep him warm. He didn't speak. His forehead felt hot and clammy, and his breathing was irregular. The boy's lack of weight had left Stephen stunned. They laid him in the van, and Stephen sat with him. They knew they needed to get him warmed up and food in his belly.

'I had to bring him home. I couldn't think what else to do,' Stephen finished.

Walter shook his head. 'Poor bugger.'

Alice bit her lip, seeing Walter moved by Stephen's words. Her eyes turned towards the stairs and the poor boy who lay up there.

–

Alice and Patty were sitting having a cup of tea after washing up all the pots and pans after Sunday dinner. Connie and Robert had taken John Robert for a walk around the park in his pram. There was a knock at the kitchen door.

'I recognise that knock,' said Patty. 'It's time for me to find something to do.'

'You don't have to go straight away. Walter will think you don't like him.'

'No, Alice, I think he'll be relieved.'

Alice answered the door and invited Walter into the kitchen. Patty said hello to him and made her excuses to leave. Alice thought back to a few years ago when she was doing the same for Connie and Robert.

Walter stood by the table. His eyes wandered about the room before he lowered himself into the chair by the range. Alice poured him a cup of tea.

There was silence. Alice almost wished Patty would come back. 'Something on your mind, Walter?'

'No. Well, maybe. Yes, I have.'

'That seems to cover every possibility. Which is it?'

There was a pause that seemed like an eternity, and then Walter spoke.

'You remember when we first walked out together? You said you didn't want to think about marriage until you found your family?'

'Ye – es, I think that's what I said.' Alice spoke slowly, wondering what was coming.

'Have you done much thinking since? I don't want to push you but, as far as I can see, I think you've found your family. You know what happened to your mother, and you've found uncles, aunts and cousins.'

'But they're not my family. I'm not related to them by blood.'

'I think they are. I saw your face change when we met them in Runcorn. You looked happy that you had a family.'

'I agree. For a couple of hours, I had a family, and then it was taken away from me.' Alice could feel tears starting to run down her cheeks. 'I'm adopted – if you remember. I'm back where I started. Don't you see?'

Walter jumped up and put his arms around her. 'Don't cry, Alice. I'm sorry if I've upset you – that wasn't my intention at all, dearest.'

Alice dabbed her eyes with a handkerchief, and they sat there for a few minutes, holding hands across the corner of the kitchen table.

'I understand what you're saying, Walter, but I felt nothing for them. I'm alone again. Just the workhouse girl. I expected to feel… different.'

'No, you're not just a workhouse girl. You've got me, and the Caldwells – and many friends.'

Alice regained her composure and smiled at Walter, squeezing his hand. They kissed. The love she had for him coursed through her body.

'Carry on then. I interrupted you.' She held her breath.

Walter paused and swallowed a few times. 'I don't think you're ever going to find out why Margaret did what she did, and it could take many more months to trace this Ethel Barnes. We still don't know if she has anything to do with you. And all the time we're not getting any younger.'

'What're you getting at, Walter?'

'I think it's time that we got married.'

Alice's mouth fell open. 'You want to marry me even though I don't know who I am?'

He held her close. 'Of course I do. You mean the world to me.'

'Oh, Walter.' Her eyes filled again.

He looked confused. 'Do those tears mean you're saying yes?'

'Yes, of course I'll marry you.' They kissed more passionately than ever before.

It was as if she had known the question was coming all along. Now it was out in the open, and she was more thrilled than she'd imagined.

'You've been so patient, Walter, and have always been there for me. I'm sorry I asked you to wait so long. You're the only man I've any intention of marrying. I know a good man when I see one.' She lifted her face towards him. As their lips met, Alice heard a giggle coming from the doorway. But she didn't care anymore!

'I'll make some fresh tea, and would you like a piece of cake?' said Patty. After preparing the refreshments, they sat down at the table. Patty left them to themselves again.

Walter picked up Alice's hand and kissed it. 'When are we going to tell everybody?'

'Apart from Patty, you mean? Well, when I was a child, I read a book where the heroine got engaged at Christmas, and I so wanted it to be me. If you don't think I'm being stupid, can we keep it quiet until Christmas?'

'Yes, I'll be quite happy to do that. We need to do some planning first, and we don't want people trying to butt in and tell us what we should be doing. We're old enough to make up our own minds.'

'You realise I'll have to leave and will not be able to work in service unless I am extremely lucky.'

'There's more to work than service. Your job must be one of the worst you can have. I don't know how you've managed it for all these years. It's hard work down the pit, but at least I know once I finish my shift, it's finished. I can go home and do what I want to do, but you're on call all the time.'

'I realise that, but it's all I know.'

'But, you'll have time for yourself to decide what you want to do. Somebody who can cook as well as you must be able to work for themselves at something – if you want to. Set up your own catering business, for instance.'

'I assumed I'd be single and spend all of my life at Holmorton Lodge or something similar, just like Mrs Williams. Well, I have to admit I didn't expect all this today when I got up.'

Walter smiled. 'Have you got any idea when you'd like to get married?'

'A spring wedding would be nice. The weather is improving and everywhere looks nice with the spring flowers. It'll give us time to find somewhere to live. I like your father very much, but I think it'd be worth waiting to get somewhere on our own. I don't know whether I could share a kitchen.'

'I don't know whether Miss Latimer would allow you to.' They laughed. 'She has father right under her thumb now.'

'So that's it – at Christmas we'll tell everyone we're engaged and plan to get married at Easter,' said Alice, beaming.

'Do you want a church or a chapel wedding?'

'I'd like to have a church wedding, but it seems absurd to have a religious wedding when neither of us attends church.'

'We can get married at the registry office.'

'Jean and Stephen got married at Hanley Registry Office and then had a do at the Albion Hotel. They went to a dance at the Victoria Hall. That was where Connie and Robert took their first steps together, and now look at them. I think a registry office would be fine. We can save some money and put it to better use. I'm just happy I'm getting married to the man I love.'

'I'll put my name down for a company house to rent. I should stand a very good chance, being a deputy.'

They kissed again. Alice embarrassed herself when she thought she could've taken him to bed right there and then if she'd given way to her feelings. Who'd have thought it? Would she be able to wait until the spring?

Once Walter had gone, she sat at the table hugging herself, mulling over the events of the evening. It couldn't have been any better.

There was a tap on the kitchen door, and Patty's head appeared.

'Why didn't you come straight in?'

'I didn't want to burst in on you, just in case. So I thought it best to knock and see what happened.'

'I don't know, Patty, you've a very fertile imagination for someone so young.'

'I'm almost sixteen,' she said with a proud grin.

'I'd say you've only just turned fifteen.'

Patty thought for a moment. 'I'm fifteen years and seven months, so that makes me nearer to sixteen, so I'm right.'

'Let that be a lesson to you, Patty. Two people can spend time together on their own with nothing like that happening.'

'I'm sorry, Alice. I didn't mean to suggest…'

'Don't worry, Patty, you've said nothing wrong.'

'So, have you got any interesting news for me?'

'No, Miss Goodwin, no news.'

'Funny, when I saw you kiss, it looked very much as if you'd something to tell me. I've got it all planned out. The pair of you are to get wed, and you move to a delightful house, one suitable for a pit deputy. And I cook and clean for you. That would be just perfect.'

Alice could only grin and touch her nose. 'Now where would I get the money to employ you, Patty Goodwin?'

Chapter Sixteen

November 1921

Happily, Jean could keep Alice informed about Luke thanks to the telephone. She had asked Alice to visit her on Saturday, as she had some news for her. Patty had taken the message, and didn't ask what it was about. Mind you, if she had asked, then there'd be no point in a visit. She would just have to be patient.

Alice walked from Pittshill Station past the park, where several little kids were collecting a 'penny for the guy' – old clothes stuffed with newspaper and straw in the shape of a body and a head made with an evil-looking face painted in black. Alice thought some looked very good and gave a penny.

At one gate, a lad about seven or eight called out, 'Penny for the guy, missus!' Alice looked at the guy. Very little work had gone into it. 'No, I've given my change to the better one down at the station,' she called back.

'Well, in that case, missus, can I have yer hat and coat? They look about ready for the bonfire.' Alice stopped in her tracks, and the lad bolted off into the park through a hole in the fence. Cheeky blighter, she thought, and then realised that might have been Luke if he hadn't been ill.

Alice and Jean sat in the front room, and Alice told her, half laughing.

Jean tried her best to hold back her giggles. 'Perhaps it is time for a new hat and coat.'

'There's nothing wrong with this coat, Jean Adams. It has plenty of use left in it.' Alice changed the subject. 'How's Luke?'

'He's coming along now he's being looked after and I hope he continues to improve. I broached the subject of him staying with us for the winter with Stephen.'

Alice took a sharp breath. She might have whistled if she could. 'That's an enormous commitment, Jean. Are you sure you're ready for it?' asked Alice, frowning.

'Stephen agreed straight away. Maybe he felt guilty that he wasn't stronger with Luke when they first met, and that if he had been, then Luke wouldn't have become so ill. Anyway, we both talked to Luke. It wasn't as if I didn't trust Stephen; it was more a case of showing Luke it was what we both wanted. I couldn't bear for him to be living outside all winter, and I didn't want to be the one to put him in the workhouse. I know what Ginnie went through – and you too, Alice.'

'So what did you do?'

'We sat him at the kitchen table, and I let Stephen speak first. He asked how Luke had felt staying with us, and Luke, his face a little red with embarrassment, said he had enjoyed having a place to stay that was warm and where he could have his tea cooked every night. He was certainly honest. We all laughed. I took hold of his sweaty hand and looked him in the eye to show I meant every word. I told him we'd been concerned about him living outside for several months now and, with the winter coming, and this illness, we thought it was a bad idea for him to go back to the old house. We're afraid he might end up with pneumonia or worse. So, I asked him if he would consider staying with us for a while.'

'What did he say to that?'

'Well, his face turned bright red, and he asked me if I meant it. I remember smiling and stroking his hand and saying, of course we meant it. He would stay as a friend of the family, and if it didn't work out, he could leave at any time. I almost cried when I saw the shy smile. Do you know what he said, Alice?'

Alice couldn't help but smile at the look on Jean's face. 'Tell me.'

'He said he was proper chuffed and that nobody's never given him anything before. Then he asked if we were sure we wanted a stranger living in our house?'

Alice's eyes welled up. 'Oh, Jean. I'll say it again. Is it wise?'

'I see it as a sign of trust between us, and I hope he sees that too. Then he told us his name – Luke Prentice.'

'That's a definite step forward. He must trust you.'

'We then told him if he stayed with us, he would have to promise to go to school in January. We explained that schooling was compulsory and would help him get a decent job in a few years' time. He said he could read and write and do sums, so he needed no more schooling.'

'So he's had some education then, which means he had or has a family.'

'If he has, he is saying nothing about them. No doubt we'll find out someday, but not yet.'

–

The early frost of the winter settled on the bushes in the garden at Holmorton Lodge as Alice stood at the front door talking to Ruth Latham. She had promised to bring over a pattern for a going-out dress for Alice to make up for Christmas. The scene took Alice back to her early childhood.

'I remember how the canal used to freeze and local kids would dare each other to walk on the ice. Did you?'

'Not really. I wasn't allowed anywhere near it,' laughed Ruth.

Alice sighed. 'I remember Father telling me I should never do that. It was dangerous, and if I fell in, I might not get out again.' Even now, a deep-seated distrust of the water, especially the canals, lingered within her. She hated walking past the locks and always stayed well away from the edge. 'My father… well, my adoptive father, would tell me to be careful near the water.'

'He's still your father, Alice, and I know your circumstances have changed, but you owe everything you are to your mother and father. Whoever you are going to be in the future will be up to you.'

'Shall we go inside? It's cold out here.'

'Yes, let's,' said Ruth. 'But at least my friend Dottie will be happy to get frost on her sprouts.'

'I beg your pardon!'

Ruth burst out laughing. 'I'll tell yer over a cup of tea, but first I've got some better news. That's why I popped over on my way to Burslem. Bertie Hesse has got a job as a mouldmaker for Mintons.'

'That's excellent news. He'll be able to make use of his skills, and they'll have more money coming in.'

'It turns out that his foreman from Royal Edwards is now working there, and he knew Bertie to be a skilled and hard worker. Let's hope that none of the feelings during the war are still strong. Bertie deserves a chance.'

-

The big day arrived. She met Mr Moreton from Railsford's in the entrance hall of Stoke Station. The afternoon train wasn't full, but it felt crowded to Alice. He was easy to pick out, wearing a black coat with grey pinstriped trousers, a homburg hat and carrying a small case.

'Good morning, Miss Tucker.'

'Morning, Mr Moreton. I believe you have the tickets.'

'That's correct. Miss Cheeseman is as efficient as usual.'

They made their way to the first-class coach and entered. Very much the gentleman, he remained standing until Alice was seated.

They chatted about the weather and other subjects until Alice asked what would be happening today.

'I expect it will be a fact-finding meeting. I know nothing about the client, but the solicitors aren't the cheapest. They're a well-established and respected firm of Jewish lawyers.'

'I was concerned when Mr Railsford suggested I needed someone with me.'

'He's following normal procedure. You'll meet lawyers well acquainted with the case. You'll have travelled to a strange town. The information you receive will be a surprise for you – likely shock you. You need someone with you to advise, listen, and take notes. It is the safest way to proceed. It is unlikely you'll remember everything said. I'm here to make a record of the event.'

'You make it sound as if they might try to cheat me.'

'I expect nothing like that with this firm. But not all lawyers are, shall we say, as ethical, so as a practice we always prefer the cautious approach. Don't worry, Miss Tucker, I'm sure everything will be all right.'

They made their way down the platform and through the ticket barrier. Once outside, Mr Moreton hailed a taxi, and they were soon in Charlotte Street.

The receptionist, a lady in her fifties, greeted them. They handed their coats and Mr Moreton's homburg to her, and she hung them in a cupboard behind her desk.

'Take a seat. Mr Penfold will not keep you waiting.'

It wasn't long before a young man called Reuben appeared to escort them to Mr Penfold's office. Mr Penfold looked to be in his early fifties. He smiled and rose, and shook hands with them both.

'Greetings, Miss Tucker, and you must be Mr Moreton. Mr Railsford mentioned you would be attending the meeting. My name is Philip Penfold, and I understand you are looking for a lady named Ethel Barnes?'

'That's correct, Mr Penfold, but I'm intrigued to know how you know I'm looking for her?'

'Although Manchester is a large city, the legal community is small, and we all know each other. I received a phone call from the solicitors you wrote to telling me that enquiries were being made, and was given your name and address.'

'I see,' said Alice. 'It's just like the people on our streets. Something happens, and everybody knows within a few hours.'

'Yes, we aren't very different, Miss Tucker,' said Mr Penfold with a smile. 'So to business. I can confirm my firm is acting on behalf of Miss Barnes regarding this matter.'

'Are you able to tell me anything about her? Is she my mother?' Alice's shoulders dropped. If Ethel Barnes was the lady in question, then the very fact that she was 'Miss' Barnes seemed to show they had the wrong person. 'Or…'

'Not yet. As Miss Barnes's legal adviser, I'm bound to take all reasonable steps to protect my client. To divulge any information, I must first verify your identity. So to further that work, I'd like to take your photograph and to photograph any documents you've brought along.'

'I've never had my photograph taken before. Of course, if it's necessary, you can.'

'Well, I'll make sure we put an extra copy into your file.'

'Thank you.'

'If it's acceptable, I'd like to ask you several questions. It's not a test. I just want to ask you about your childhood, where you lived, schooling and the like.'

They talked for about an hour. Mr Moreton stepped in on several occasions, seeking clarification. Mr Penfold was easy to talk to, and he didn't make his questions seem as if she was on trial. She had little to tell him, but he still made copious notes.

'There we go. That wasn't too bad, was it?'

'No, I've only just noticed how long we've been talking.'

'Right, I think I need to tell you we'll be using an investigator to verify some of this information. It's normal procedure, and the person we use is very thorough and, more importantly, very tactful. So if any of your friends tell you somebody has been asking about you, then you'll be aware.'

'Oh, I didn't think you'd have to do something like that.'

'I'm afraid it's standard procedure. The investigator leaves a card with his telephone number and address when a person or place refuses to give him information before contacting you. He returns to speak to them when he's sure they're happy to talk about you.'

'It all sounds very intriguing... like reading a mystery book.' Alice chided herself for making an unprofessional remark, but he didn't seem to have noticed.

'So, do you have any more questions, Miss Tucker?'

'I have got many of them, but until I know what's what, they'll have to wait.'

'I have a request, if I may?' asked Mr Moreton. 'Could you make sure you send any correspondence for Miss Tucker to my office, and I would be grateful if you could ask your investigator to make himself known to us prior to starting work in The Potteries?'

'Yes, I'll leave instructions to that effect.' He turned back to Alice. 'About our next meeting, I suggest Friday the ninth of December, at ten o'clock. At these offices?'

'Yes, that's acceptable to me. Is it suitable for you, Mr Moreton?'

'Yes, of course.'

'All that remains is to wish you a safe journey home, and I'll say goodbye until we meet again.' He rose and held out his hand. It was a warm handshake, and she felt very much a lady.

Reuben Solomon entered the office, carrying their outside clothes, and they made their way out of the office. Reuben led the way with Alice. Mr Moreton followed.

Outside, the pavements bustled with activity.

'The photographer's is just around the corner, Miss Tucker. It's getting cold outside, but we won't be there for very long.'

They turned the corner, and after about twenty yards, there was an entrance to a photographer's studio. Mr Moreton caught up with them, and the party entered.

'This is somebody we use regularly. His name is Mr Goldblum, but we all call him Goldie.'

It didn't take long. Goldie took pictures of Alice from the front and the side, with and without a hat and with and without her coat. He photographed the documents, finishing within twenty minutes.

'Thank you, miss, you've been an excellent subject, and especially for you I'll do a discount on any copies of the photographs you want.'

Alice didn't know what to say.

'Now, come on, Goldie, you know Mr Penfold doesn't like you doing that,' said Reuben.

'A man's got to earn a living. I have a wife and five children to look after.'

'Hold on, you only had four children last month.'

'Is it my fault that I'm so attractive to my wife?'

'Well, as much as we enjoy listening to you, these good people need to catch a train. Goodbye.'

'Goodbye, Goldie,' said Alice. The man bowed to her and wished her a safe journey.

When they got out onto the street, it didn't take Reuben long to apologise for Goldie, but Alice said that she thought he was a nice man. Mr Moreton flagged down a taxi, and they were soon on their way to the station.

The journey back to Stoke seemed to pass in no time at all. All the way back, she could think only of the events of the afternoon and what they might mean. She couldn't wait to tell Walter everything and see what he thought.

Mr Moreton took some documents out of the case and read them.

'How do you think that went, Mr Moreton?'

'I think they're being very professional and very careful. It would imply there are some complications we don't yet know about. I expect everything will be clear after our next meeting. I'll have my notes typed up for the file.'

'But why the private investigator?'

'As Mr Penfold said, it is normal in this type of case to undertake these checks. It's become more important since the war, as there are many families who've lost younger members in the conflict. The natural order of things meant fathers left their estates to their sons, and so on. But the war has altered so much. There are families where all the sons perished and the inheritance line is no longer clear. Many obscure members of families need to be traced and informed of their elevated status. It all takes time.'

The train pulled into Stoke Station, and they took a taxi, which dropped Alice off at Holmorton Lodge, and Mr Moreton proceeded on his way.

She walked into the house and prepared to say nothing at this stage. She had learned nothing new, so there'd be no point.

–

After a meal and several cups of tea, Alice felt refreshed. They'd finished the day's work earlier than usual, thanks to Patty.

'I need to pop up to see my mother, Alice. I shouldn't be long.'

'You take as long as you need. I'm too tired at the moment to go to see Walter, and he'll not be expecting me till gone nine o'clock.' Alice took a moment to rest in the armchair in the room next to the kitchen.

The next thing she knew was Patty tapping her on the shoulder.

'Come on, sleepyhead. It's almost nine o'clock and Walter'll be expecting you.'

'Thank you, Patty, I must have dropped off.'

Alice shot out of her seat, tidied herself up and donned her hat and coat and rushed off to see Walter. He was getting ready for the morning. The underground workers in the pit took food in with them, always in a tin box to protect it from the environment – and the rats.

After the normal greetings, Alice told Walter what had happened during the day. He listened intently.

'Sounds promising. I don't expect they would've gone to all that trouble for nothing. I think we may have your birth mother.'

'I don't know if we can say that, but I feel I've found something. Mr Penfold referred to her as "miss" – she still might not have had any children.'

'Alice, my dear, that could well be the reason for all the secrecy. Someone is paying a lot of money to check your identity.'

–

'It's lovely to see you again, Jean. Do come in,' said Alice. 'Take off your coat. Connie's in the sitting room with Robert.'

'Thank you, Alice.' Jean slipped out of her coat and removed her hat and gloves.

'How's Luke? Is he better now?'

'He's much better. The doctor says he should be well enough to attend school in January.'

Alice smiled. 'That must be good news.'

Jean frowned. 'I'm not sure, to be honest. We've mentioned it twice and, by the look on his face, he doesn't seem too thrilled. He changes the subject.'

'Kids rarely want to go to school from what I've seen, Jean. Once he's settled in, he'll be fine, I should imagine. It'll be good for him to be in the company of other children. I know you look after him well, but it must be a little boring for him to only have three adults for company.'

Alice walked Jean through to the sitting room, where she was to have afternoon tea with Connie and Robert.

Connie jumped up and gave Jean a hug while Robert dropped a kiss on her forehead. Alice disappeared to pick up the trays laid with afternoon tea. When she returned, Jean was talking about Luke.

Robert looked pleased the lad was settling in, but Connie shook her head. 'I still think you've taken such a responsibility,

Jean. You know so little about him. What if he turns out to be a troublemaker—?'

'Oh, he's not a troublemaker, Connie. Life has dealt a bad hand to a nice boy. We've always wanted kids ourselves, so why shouldn't we give this boy a start in life?'

'You say that, but… we shall have to see… but don't say I didn't warn you.'

Alice watched Jean's face turn cold. Alice was sure Connie didn't mean what she said, but Jean looked none too pleased. Only when the conversation revolved around Connie and her baby did Connie look interested. Even Robert looked a little taken aback by Connie's disinterest.

Alice gave Connie the benefit of the doubt. John Robert was only fifteen weeks old. Alice thought Connie wasn't enjoying the feeding, but she had Nanny Lily to help her with everything else. As Patty had said, all she had to do was fill John Robert up, and Nanny dealt with the rest. However, it was a shame for Jean. Next April marked her third wedding anniversary, yet she remained childless.

-

Alice called in at Walter's house before tea on the Sunday closest to the anniversary of the Armistice. Many places observed two minutes of silence at eleven o'clock on the eleventh day of the eleventh month, and even Alice and Patty had stopped work and thought about everything that had gone on. Thoughts of Bertie came to mind, and Alice paid the Lathams a visit to see how he had got on at work.

She knocked on the door. Ruth answered.

Alice gave her a smile. 'I thought I'd pop round to find out how Bertie's getting on now that he's back at work.'

Ruth spoke first. 'He said he was a little rusty with some techniques, but after a few days, he was getting back into the swing of things.'

Mr Latham added, 'Good to see yer, Alice, love. He's working in a small shop with about a dozen men, and they all seem to be pretty good sorts. But on Friday when the factory observed the two minutes' silence, some blokes from the casting area had heard that Bertie was German. I'm told they were all up for striking, but the foreman nipped the trouble in the bud. He told the men that Bertie was as British as any of them. He had lived in Germany for only two years and had been interned for four. He pointed out to the men that the two minutes' silence was there to remember those who couldn't return.' He shook his head. 'You'd think that people had had enough of war.'

Ruth nodded and continued. 'Although from what Bertie said, only a few were involved. He came home quite despondent that evening. He expected a repeat of the aftermath of the *Lusitania* sinking in 1915. But Carla managed, with Edith's help, to make him see that the vast majority of people have had enough of conflict and to keep his head down and see how things go.'

–

The following Sunday, Alice went to see Walter. She apologised for calling so near to dinnertime. She asked him if he'd heard anything about Bertie.

'According to our Ruth, a group of blokes came up to him yesterday, all of whom had served in the army, and they told him not to worry. He couldn't help where he was born any more than they could.'

'That was nice of them. I hope everything goes well for Bertie.'

'I think it will, Alice. There's more to worry about at the moment. We're all worried about keeping our jobs. Germany is selling coal and lots of other goods, like pottery, so they can pay their war reparations. Sales of pots haven't increased as expected and there's a lot of unrest in the coal industry about cutting wages. Everybody around here depends on pottery or coal. I'm sure the government knows what it's doing.'

At that point Miss Latimer came in and everybody said hello to her. Walter whispered that she'd taken to having her tea with them on a Sunday, and winked. Alice was confused for a moment and then the penny dropped.

Chapter Seventeen

4 – 9 December 1921

It was the first Sunday in December. Robert and Connie were in the garden room, chatting. Patty was completing everything for the morning and would go to bed soon. She had to. She was always up at five in the morning to get an early start to the day.

'I'm going to see Walter, Patty.' Alice flashed her a broad grin.

'Take your keys with you. I'll lock everything up and drop the latch on the front door.'

'Thank you, Patty.'

'Goodnight – and be good.'

There were matters she needed to discuss with Walter about her upcoming meeting on Friday. She had so many questions she needed answers to. She stepped outside into the darkness, the dim light from the gas lamps making her journey hard going. The ice-covered paths were slippery, so she had to tread carefully. At least it wasn't snowing.

She knocked on the door and waited. Walter answered.

'Alice, darling, come in. If I'd known you were coming, I would have called for you. We're in the front room.'

She stepped inside and hung up her coat. She couldn't avoid a brief gasp as Carla Hesse greeted her. So that was the 'we' Walter was referring to.

'Hello, Carla, I didn't expect to see you here.'

'Hello, Alice, want a cup of tea?' asked Mr Latham.

'Yes, please.'

Carla smiled. 'Walter and I were just talking about Christmas.'

'That sounds cosy!' Alice glared at Walter. 'I came around to see if Walter was all right.' Walter sat on the settee, and Carla flopped beside him.

'Yes, Alice, of course I'm all right, why shouldn't I be?'

'You tell me.'

Carla squirmed and shuffled in her seat. Alice couldn't help feeling pleased. Mr Latham brought in a cup of tea. Sensing something was amiss, he returned to the kitchen.

Carla rose. 'Best get my skates on if I'm going to catch that tram.' Walter helped Carla into her coat and the two went outside. As the door closed, Alice thought she heard Carla say, 'You can tell her—'

Alice bit her lip, now feeling ashamed of her behaviour, but with a sense of panic about what Walter was going to tell her.

Walter returned almost immediately.

Alice couldn't hold her words back. 'What was all that about? I didn't expect to see her here, not at this time of night and with it being a work night.'

'Is my little Alice jealous?' He tried to grin, but Alice remained aloof.

'No, just surprised. I wanted to talk to you. You haven't been very happy recently. Have you got something or someone on your mind?'

Walter sighed and sat back on the settee. 'Yes. He's a shot-firer. He trained before me, accepted the call-up in 1917. The army assigned him to a mining regiment of the Royal Engineers.'

'What did they do?'

'Before a major offensive, they'd tunnel under the enemy trenches and fill the chamber with explosives. Then, at the start of the attack, they'd detonate the mine, hoping to create a sizeable gap in the enemy lines for our attackers to exploit. Both sides did this, and defenders would sink shafts and use listening equipment to detect activity. There were even cases of each side digging into each other's tunnels and having to fight their way out in the pitch black.'

'Sounds horrible. Just thinking about the enclosed space is enough for me. How did they stay sane?'

'Most escaped, but those caught in these underground battles suffered, and many still suffer today.'

'Anyway, this shot-firer set his charges and checked them. A switch box, which generates an electric charge, operates the detonators. The explosives will blow up once the switch is thrown. I wasn't on shift that day, but they told me he didn't do a second check, and when one bloke reminded him, he told the man not to bother. He set the charges off, and they blew, cracking the rock as planned. He allowed a team of men in to clear the rock out of the way and start the extension to the gallery. Unfortunately, one charge didn't go off, and when he was packing away, he hadn't set the safety, so when the wires touched, the remaining charge exploded. These types of switches have enough charge in them to fire several detonators, so...'

'Was anybody hurt?'

'The explosion injured three men, causing burns and a broken arm. It could've been worse.'

'None of it was your fault, was it?'

'No, but I was on the next shift, so I had to do an accident report, which doesn't make pleasant reading for him. At worst he'll lose his job, or at best they might demote him to a surface worker. No one will work underground with him again.'

'I'm sorry, I could tell there was something wrong. So that was what Carla was talking about on the way out?'

'No, but you need to know about Carla as well.'

Alice wondered what it could be.

'I don't know how to tell you this.' Walter paused.

'It can't be that bad, can it? Is it something you've done? You aren't seeing Carla again after everything you said to me?' Alice could feel the thumping in her chest. If he were, where would that leave them?

'It's nothing like that, but it is about Carla.'

'What about her?'

'We've known each other since we were at primary school, and in the last year she was at school, she must've been thirteen, we experimented…' He went bright red. 'She stopped me after a few minutes and the next day told me she was sorry, but wanted to make sure—'

'Make sure of what?'

'She said she didn't want to be with me, or any boy, for that matter. She preferred girls.'

'Well, what did that mean?' Alice thought she must've preferred to be with girls – you can't get into trouble like you can with boys.

'She meant she… she preferred girls.'

'Oh…' She didn't know what he meant, and then the penny dropped. 'You mean…'

'Yes. I'm the only person who knows, and now you're the second. She wanted me to tell you so you might understand our position. You see there's nothing to worry about, don't you?'

Alice paused and thought for a moment. 'I wish I hadn't been so nasty to her. I won't know what to say.'

'Say nowt – just keep her secret. She could get into trouble if it became common knowledge.'

–

Alice felt eager and a little nervous when she entered the offices of Solomon, Solomon and Penfold in early December. She was getting close. Even though very little had happened since meeting Mr Penfold, she could feel in her bones it could only be a matter of time before she had the whole truth. It'd been a long month, but now the day had arrived.

Once again, she made the journey to Manchester, accompanied by Mr Moreton. Her heart had been thumping ever since she had risen that morning. She didn't want to get too excited – she had thought she was getting close before. But this journey felt different, and if she came away with no answers, she would feel utterly dispirited.

Once again, Mr Rueben Solomon escorted them to Mr Penfold's office, and this time she went straight in.

He rose from his seat and smiled. 'Morning, Miss Tucker, Mr Moreton.'

It must mean good news. She swallowed, her body shaking. Was she prepared for this? She wished Walter was with her, or even Connie. Somebody strong to hold on to. Mr Moreton was a very capable man, but she couldn't squeeze his hand if she felt the need.

Mr Penfold returned to his seat and leaned back, quite relaxed. She tried to follow his example.

'I believe we've some good news for you, Miss Tucker. Since your last visit, I've checked various records and spoken to several people to ensure we have the right person. It'd be unprofessional to raise a client's hopes without reviewing all the paperwork. I have now completed that to my satisfaction.'

Alice wanted to urge him onward. Something of her frustration must have been communicated to him. He stopped talking and clasped his hands together. 'Miss Tucker, I'm now satisfied that you are indeed the daughter of Ethel Barnes.'

The breath Alice was holding in exploded with such force she had to cough to regain control. She almost swallowed her tongue. Tears welled up in her eyes. So much water had gone under the bridge since she had discovered that the woman she had called 'Mother' all her life wasn't the woman who had borne her. She rummaged in her pocket for the clean handkerchief she had placed there – just in case – although she never thought she would need it. Yes, she could admit it now. She had anticipated that something might go wrong, forcing her to start again.

Mr Penfold rose from his seat and gathered his papers into a neat pile to avoid looking at her wet face, she suspected.

'I need to sort out a few things with your solicitor. We'll be in the next office. Would you mind waiting for a few minutes?'

Alice shook her head, grateful for the time to gather herself together. The look on his face told her he was relieved to disappear. It almost made her smile.

At that moment, Rueben returned. 'Are you feeling all right, Miss Tucker?'

Alice couldn't speak, just nodded.

'I believe you're in need of a cup of tea, and a more comfortable place to sit,' he whispered.

'If you're sure? Mr Penfold asked me to stay here.'

Reuben shook his head. 'It's not a problem. I'll tell him you needed somewhere to relax. It must've been quite a day for you.'

Alice followed him to the end of the corridor. On the way, he indicated the facilities before showing her into a sitting room. She sat at a small table on which a pot of hot tea was waiting for her.

She gazed around the walls, covered in portraits of elderly, well-dressed, stern-looking gentlemen. No ladies.

'They're partners and founders of the business, Miss Tucker. That gentleman there is my father, Mr Elijah Solomon, and most of them are my relations,' he added with a touch of embarrassment. 'I'm following in his footsteps.'

About ten minutes later, the door opened and admitted a fine-looking woman in her fifties. Alice watched her take the seat opposite. She removed her hat and gloves and made herself comfortable. She was well-dressed with a three-quarter-length coat and a straight black skirt and reminded Alice of a younger version of Agatha, who always sat with a straight back. Alice caught herself wondering who she was there to see. If Mr Penfold was involved, he faced a busy morning.

The door opened again to admit Reuben bearing another tray, complete with teapot – the same as Alice's – and he laid it on the table. He smiled at Alice as he left the room. Alice wished the woman hadn't sat opposite her – she didn't know where to look without giving the woman the idea she was watching her and that she had nothing to say.

'The weather isn't too bad for the time of year,' the woman said, pouring tea into her cup.

'No. I'm glad it stayed fine.' Alice swallowed. She wasn't into small talk. What could she say now that would interest such a well-dressed woman as this? Her upbringing as a servant was ingrained into her – not to speak until spoken to. Well, the woman had spoken to her, and she had replied. Should she say anything more? What would Connie say? 'Er… I've come up from The Potteries – on the train. I'm hoping it stays like this for the journey home. I've got my best shoes on.'

Alice cringed. Who'd want to know she had her best shoes on, for goodness' sake?

The woman smiled. 'I've the same trouble. You live in The Potteries, do you?'

Alice nodded, smiling. 'Yes, I've lived there quite a long time now. Do you live in Manchester?' She hoped that didn't sound too nosy.

'No, I live near Knutsford.'

Alice nodded again. She hadn't heard of Knutsford, but she didn't like to admit it. Having talked about the weather and their respective homes, Alice couldn't think of anything more to say. She felt pleased; she had engaged the lady in conversation and could now relax.

'Alice, I'm so glad to meet you at last.'

Alice gasped. This woman knew her! How was that possible?

'I, er – I'm not sure…'

'My name is Ethel Barnes.'

Alice froze. She couldn't speak. Here, after all this time, was the woman who had given her life. The woman she had never heard of until this year. The woman who didn't want her, who'd given her away as a baby. The woman sitting opposite her right now was Ethel Barnes. She couldn't swallow. The lump in her throat was too large.

All this time, Alice had wondered what she would say when she found her mother. She had expected her mother would be working-class like herself, but this lady looked far too grand. Could she really be her mother?

Then Alice remembered what the nurse at the cottage hospital in Holywell had said about the clientele of the nursing home – and everything fell into place. She had thought it'd all go wrong – and it had. She was Ethel's bastard. That was why she wasn't wanted. She caught her bottom lip with her teeth, shaking her head. No, no, no. How could she be?

'I'm sure I didn't know how to approach the matter when Philip Penfold told me he'd found you, Alice. It's come as quite a shock after all this time and… I'm sure it's been a shock to you too, my dear.'

Alice nodded. She opened her mouth to speak, but the words wouldn't come. Her throat was dry. She tried to swallow two or three times before she managed it, and even then she didn't know if she could trust herself to say the right words. What *were* the right words in this situation?

'I'll give you a moment to compose yourself. If you're feeling anything like me, you'll be comatose with shock.' The woman said nothing more but concentrated hard on refilling her cup with tea.

Alice watched her, her ears pounding. She couldn't imagine what Walter would say when she told him this news!

'Did Mr Penfold tell you anything about me?'

Alice shook her head. 'Only your name.'

'Well, let's clear up the name first. My actual name is Elizabeth Hamilton.'

Alice's mouth fell open. This was getting weird. The Ethel Barnes she was expecting wasn't Ethel Barnes at all – she was called Elizabeth Hamilton. Her head spun; her eyes must've been like saucers. She was trying so hard to take it all in, but it wasn't easy. 'I… er… I—'

'Ethel Barnes was the name my family gave me at the nursing home.'

'Why?'

'That will become clear in a moment.'

'Whatever your name was… someone should've told me.' Alice felt a wave of indignation well up inside. She blinked. No! There would be no tears. She lifted her head with dignity.

'You poor thing. Mr Penfold should've prepared you better. I'll have a word with him.'

'Please don't, Mrs… Miss? Hamilton. They've done well in bringing us together. I don't suppose it's something they do every day.'

'It was, in part, my fault. I wanted to see you once Philip told me he'd found you. He gave me some information about what he'd discovered, and I knew, with little doubt, you were my daughter.' Her face had grown pink.

Alice, too, felt her face reddening at the woman's use of the word 'daughter'. She couldn't believe that the woman opposite was her mother. How long would it take to sink in? What would Connie and Agatha say? And Walter?

Elizabeth began again. 'Would you like me to tell you a little about myself?'

Alice wanted to say no – not yet. She wanted to know why Elizabeth didn't want her, but perhaps it would be better to talk about less… painful matters first?

'Yes, please,' she said in the end.

'My parents were Reginald and Mary Hamilton, who are no longer with us. My father owned Hamilton's Empire Ales, in Knutsford. I have two brothers, both of whom are older than me, and they run the brewery. They're both married with families of their own. I was never close to them. Father was busy with the business and Mother led a hectic social life, which left little time for her children. In fact, I was closer to Nanny.'

She took a sip of her tea and licked her lip as if unsure how to continue and then resumed.

'As soon as I was old enough, they sent me to boarding school. Attending an all-girls' school prevented me from having experience with boys. When I came home from school at the end of each term, my parents would take me out to meet various influential people, hoping to find me a suitable husband.'

'That sounds like my employer's daughter.'

Elizabeth smiled. 'It doesn't take much imagination to know what came next. I met a man. He was in the army, in the Lancers, as a matter of fact. We courted and soon we were engaged to be married. His mother wrote to me one day, informing me of his death in South Africa while on active service. I was heartbroken.' Her voice broke up.

Alice didn't know what to say. She waited for Elizabeth to regain her composure.

'I was thirty-four when I met your father. We started a stimulating and passionate love affair, until I discovered I was expecting. He wasn't sure what to say when I told him. He was married, you see. He'd a wife and child of his own. What I'd done was wrong, but I was in love, and adultery seemed a small price to pay. My parents sent me off to a nursing home to await the birth of my baby. When you were born, my dear, they took you from me and gave you to a couple who couldn't have children, with the agreement that neither party would contact the other under any circumstances. I didn't know where they lived or anything about them until Mr Turnbull contacted Mr Penfold.'

'I wrote to Turnbull's asking if they knew of you after speaking to some relations of my moth… Mrs Tucker.'

'Alice, please understand, I'm not trying to take your mother's place. That has been Mrs Tucker's privilege all these years. I only hope that there may be some space in your life to accept me.'

'So, you've known nothing about me all this time?'

Elizabeth shook her head. 'My father saw to everything. He suggested I should enter the nursing home under an assumed name. He was worried someone would find out about my terrible deed. I was unaware until my mother told me that

Father had warned your real father not to see me again or to contact me. He didn't know where I was, even if he had wanted to. As far as I know, he never tried to contact me, let alone show any interest in his daughter.'

'I see,' said Alice. 'So why did I receive a letter from Mr Penfold?'

'I spent six months at Bryn Celyn. At first I was too upset to function properly, but as time went by, I thought more and more about your future. I'd have no control over who you went to. You'd also have no identity, as Father had already made me sign a power of attorney, giving Mr Turnbull full power to arrange the adoption. Father was adamant that there was as little information about me as possible – hence the assumed name.'

'How did you feel about putting me up for adoption?'

'I never did that, Alice. I'd have kept you. It was my father's bidding, and he wasn't to be argued with. He was used to getting his own way – in everything. He was worried about my misdemeanours and how they would affect the business. My father sent me to the nursing home until the pregnancy was over and the baby was adopted. I saw you only once after you were born. A nurse told me you'd gone to your new home. Never, ever think I didn't want you. You meant a lot to me. I loved your father. There has been no one else.' Elizabeth's eyes were wet with tears. 'I'm so sorry it happened as it did. I thought about you often in the early days. I ached for you. I made milk but had no one to give it to. Those were lonely days.'

Alice felt so sorry for this woman.

'Who was my father?'

At that moment, there was a knock on the door and Mr Penfold appeared, followed by Mr Moreton. Alice found she had been talking to Elizabeth for nearly two hours, which surprised her. Mr Penfold asked if they wanted more to drink or anything else.

If her own face was anywhere near as bad as Elizabeth's, then he would see that they'd both had a traumatic time. Alice felt strained. It seemed to her that this was an opportunity for Elizabeth to avoid her question about who her father was. She was determined not to let that happen.

'Mr Penfold, could you give us a moment, please?'

Both he and Elizabeth looked surprised at her request.

'Very well, Miss Tucker.'

He closed the door behind him. Alice turned to Elizabeth, who had put on her hat and was about to put on her gloves.

'Miss Hamilton, the question I need you to answer is, who was my father?' Only now did she realise just how much it mattered to her.

'I'm afraid I can't tell you, Alice.'

'Why not?' She didn't mean to be sharp but, having come this far, it might be her only chance to discover the answer.

'I promised my father and mother and your real father not to give anyone that information, including you, to avoid embarrassment to both families, and I intend to abide by it.'

'Is he still alive?'

'He might be, but we didn't want to involve other members of his family.'

'But I need to know. I've only got half the story otherwise – can't you see that?'

'I'm sorry, Alice. I wish I could help. But even if I wanted to tell you, I'm bound not to.'

Mr Penfold reappeared and stood waiting.

'We shall have to leave it there for now,' said Elizabeth. 'I need to get home. Would you like us to meet again once you've considered our discussion today, Alice?'

Alice was determined to discover the full story of who she was and wouldn't leave matters as they were. So she agreed to another meeting.

They said their goodbyes, with a formal shaking of hands. Elizabeth departed, leaving behind a very bewildered Alice.

Mr Penfold accompanied Alice back to his office, where Mr Moreton was waiting.

'It's a lot to take in, isn't it?' Mr Moreton said, helping her on with her coat.

'What if I don't want to see Elizabeth again?' She gave a wry laugh. 'I never even asked what I should call her. Ironic, isn't it, Mr Penfold?'

'Alice. I understand what you might be going through.'

'And the assumed name.'

'I believe Mr Hamilton was adamant about keeping this matter under his control.'

'Do *you* know who my father is?'

'I do.'

There was a pause.

Before she could say more, Mr Moreton took her to one side and whispered, 'He's bound by client confidentiality. He'll say nothing.'

'Very well, but he says he knows.'

'I've gone through the paperwork relating to your meeting. He'll take instruction from you on the way you want to proceed.'

'Wouldn't going through these documents be a waste of time and money for everyone if we don't meet again?'

'You must go through them, Miss Tucker, irrespective of what your decision is regarding a future relationship with Elizabeth Hamilton.'

'Or should you say, Ethel Barnes?'

'Quite.' Mr Moreton nodded to Alice.

She let the subject drop – for the time being. Alice promised to read through all the paperwork.

'Safe journey to you both, and I hope to see you soon.'

Alice was getting used to Mr Moreton, and their return journey was more relaxed. Alice bombarded him with questions, which he answered as best he could.

The taxi pulled up outside Holmorton Lodge just as the church clock struck the quarter hour. It was already dark. Today, she'd discovered she was a bastard.

Connie and Patty would be on pins waiting to find out all that had happened and, frankly, she didn't feel able to talk about it. Not yet, when she was still trying to come to terms with it and trying to work out how she was going to tell Walter.

She rubbed her forehead, feeling tired. Was her life to be an ever-changing story, with no one taking responsibility for the girl trapped within it? She had already let Connie and Patty into her story by telling them all about the Tuckers, and her visits to Runcorn and Widnes, only to find out her mother had died, and the Tuckers weren't her real family. What on earth would they think of this latest development?

Alice took a few deep breaths before making her way towards the house. As she drew near, she checked, but could see no one at any of the windows. Perhaps she was being paranoid.

She opened the front door. This was it. She just hoped she was ready for the deluge of questions she would face.

'Hiya, Alice. Here, let me take your coat and bag.'

'Take my coat, Patty. I'll keep my bag. I'll take it upstairs and get changed.'

'Of course.' Patty hung the coat up and placed the hat and gloves in the sideboard next to the coat stand. 'I'll put the kettle on, and you can tell me all about it.'

As they headed towards the kitchen, Connie walked out of the garden room.

'I thought I heard your voice, Alice.'

'Yes, I've just got back. Patty has offered to make a pot of tea.'

'That's fine – I'll join you both. I'll pop upstairs to see Nanny and check if John Robert needs feeding first. Don't start without me!' Connie's last words were an order rather than a request.

Patty linked arms with Alice, and the two walked into the kitchen together.

Patty put the kettle on to boil and set out the Royal Edwards teapot and cups. 'I think we need the posh set to celebrate you finding out more about your family.'

'And I'll have some of your lovely shortbread biscuits, Alice,' piped up Connie as she walked into the kitchen. John wasn't hungry, or he was asleep. Alice didn't think Connie would rest until she knew all that had happened.

Once they were all sitting at the table, Alice closed her eyes, wondering where to begin.

'Did you find her? Did you find your mother?' burst out Connie.

Alice kept the news brief, giving a mere outline of the day. She wanted to save the full story for Walter. That was his privilege, after all.

Alice went up to her room to get changed into her work clothes, still bemused by everything that had happened. She would need to check with Patty on what jobs needed to be done before she could go to see Walter. She came back downstairs. She was making her way to the hall when she heard Connie on the telephone. When she heard her name mentioned, she stopped to listen. Of course, she could hear only Connie's side of the conversation, but it sounded as if Agatha was asking a lot of questions.

'She said she saw a Mr Penfold. There was a lot of talk about getting paperwork confirmed and so on.'

'...No, she went on her own.'

'...How could I go with her when she went by herself? I expect she didn't know what they were going to tell her and she preferred to find out before involving any of us.'

'...Yes, Mother. She said she had to wait in a room for Mr Penfold to come back, and a woman in her fifties came in and took a seat, and they started chatting.'

'...I know Alice doesn't chat to strangers.'

'...Yes, Mother. That's what I thought too.'

'...Well, I discovered the woman was a lady named Ethel Barnes from Knutsford.'

'…I know. Anyway, the woman's real name was Elizabeth Hamilton, and I think, from what she said, she may be related to the brewery owners. Do you remember them?'

'…Mother? Mother – are you there?'

'…Are you all right? I thought we'd been cut off.'

Hearing only one side of the conversation while interpreting events proved perplexing. Connie was quiet for a time – listening to her mother talking. Alice clicked her shoes on the hall tiles as she walked into the hall, heading towards the kitchen.

Connie jumped, or so Alice thought, and changed the subject. Alice had never seen Connie's face turn so red.

–

The last thing Alice had to do on this momentous day in her life was to tell Walter about all that had happened. They'd agreed to meet at nine o'clock at his house, and Alice thought, as she walked in the crisp, frosty air of that December evening, how her life had changed in just one day.

Alice arrived on Dartmouth Street to be greeted by Walter.

'We've got the place to ourselves. Father's down at the cricket club, putting seats out for the kids' Christmas party. He feels he should be there as he's playing Santa Claus.'

Alice laughed as she pictured Herbert Latham in costume.

They sat at the kitchen table. For a moment or two, Alice didn't know where to begin.

'Cutting to the chase, Alice – is Miss Barnes your mother?'

'It's not straightforward.'

'Nothing ever is.'

Alice licked her lips. 'I went in and Mr Penfold, the solicitor, told me they'd done all their enquiries and said he believed they knew who my birth mother was.'

Walter raised his eyebrows. 'At last, and was it Ethel Barnes?'

'Yes and no. She's one of Mr Penfold's clients. The other firm knew that, and they passed details on to him so he could check into it for himself.' Alice stopped to take a breath.

'That's got to be worth celebrating.'

'We'd found the right woman, but the name Ethel Barnes turned out to be false. Because she was expecting out of wedlock, her family decided everything had to be kept quiet. That's what they did in those days to ensure nobody found out who the mother was if a child was involved. Her real name is Elizabeth Hamilton.'

'Mm, interesting. Ethel Barnes is Elizabeth Hamilton, is she? They went to all that trouble to protect their reputation.' Walter frowned. 'I wonder why.'

'Apparently, her family owns Hamilton's Empire Ales.' Alice stopped to let her words sink in.

He whistled. 'You're having me on.'

Alice stared back. 'So you think for one moment I could mock something as important as this, Walter Latham?'

His face coloured. 'I'm sorry. But bloody hell, Alice, they're loaded.'

'If a girl like her gets into… trouble, she can be sent to relations, if they have any, away from the area, for the rest of the pregnancy and return when the problem has gone away.'

'And you're the result?'

Alice nodded slowly. 'It seems so.'

They both sat staring at the wall.

'What happens now?'

'Mr Moreton received several documents that require a solicitor's review. I'll then know what they're asking me to do. How I understand it, there are two parts which need to be resolved together. She needs to persuade her brothers to accept me as her daughter, for which she'll give up her share of the brewery, and the second part is the financial arrangements, which she's made on my behalf. I'll make an appointment to see him on Monday.'

'Are you telling me you'll inherit some of this wealth too? Let's hope things are clearer before Christmas when we tell people we're engaged.'

'I expected nothing like this, Walter. I thought it might be as simple as a visit to the workhouse. What a story! I learned that my mother abandoned me and that they wrongly accused my father of causing the accident that killed him. In Runcorn, I discovered my adoption. In Widnes, I learned of my adoptive mother's death. Then I thought I'd found her in Holywell, and that turned out to be a false name, and now at last…' Alice blew out her disbelief as Walter stared at her, unable to say a word. '…and now I discover I'm illegitimate.'

'Did that possibility never occur to you?'

She shook her head, 'No, it didn't.'

'Would you have done it if you had thought of the possibility?'

Alice stared at him. 'I don't know.'

'Well, Alice, you've done very well, considering you had so little to go on.'

'No, Walter, *we've* done very well. It's been a partnership all the way through.'

As Alice returned to Holmorton Lodge, she wondered what Agatha would think if she knew the full story about the girl she took in from the workhouse.

Chapter Eighteen

10 December 1921

Alice and Patty were working in the kitchen when they heard the doorbell ring. Patty wiped her hands on the tea towel, frowning.

'I wonder who that could be?'

She hurried into the hall to find the door open with Agatha and Uncle James removing their outdoor clothes.

'Good afternoon, Mrs Copeland.' Patty smiled. 'We weren't expecting you.'

'No, I appreciate that, Goodwin, but needs must.'

Agatha's eyes caught Alice's. 'Good afternoon, Alice. Is Connie here?'

'I believe she's upstairs with John Robert, Mrs Copeland. I'll pop up and tell her you're here, and I'll get rooms ready for you.'

'Thank you, Alice.'

'Would you like some tea?' Alice's glance took in both of them.

'Most definitely, Alice,' said Uncle James. 'And a slice of cake too – if it's not too early. That journey from Urmston seems to get longer, if you ask me.'

'Bring the tea through to the garden room, would you?'

'Of course.'

Patty took their outdoor clothes to hang up, and Agatha walked off, removing her gloves without another word. Patty disappeared into the kitchen to prepare a tray of tea and cake for their guests.

Alice shot upstairs to speak to Connie. It was most unusual for Agatha to turn up unannounced. If Connie had known about her mother's visit, she would have told Alice to get the rooms prepared. This sudden appearance was out of character.

An hour later, Connie walked into the kitchen looking pale but collected. The last time she had seen Connie looking like that was when her father had passed away. Alice had been pondering over the happenings in the garden room and what had brought Agatha and Uncle James hurtling back to The Potteries unannounced.

'Mother wants to see you, Alice. In the garden room. And Patty, would you take them some fresh tea?' She turned and left the kitchen without waiting for a response from either of them.

Patty pulled an anxious face. 'Whatever's happened now?' She rushed to boil the water in the kettle, still warm from the last pot.

Alice entered the garden room, swallowing hard, unsure what lay ahead, followed a second or two later by Patty with the tea.

'Thank you, Goodwin. We aren't to be interrupted by anyone, whatever reason they might have. Do you understand?'

'Yes, Mrs Copeland. Certainly, Mrs Copeland.'

After a quick glance at Alice, who remained standing, Patty left. Agatha turned to Alice. 'Sit down,' she said, waving a hand towards the chair opposite.

An attack of butterflies made Alice feel weaker than ever. Was this all about her? Was Mrs Copeland going to sack her for spending so much time searching for her family? Come to think of it, Agatha looked more troubled than Alice had ever seen her.

'I believe you have been looking into your ancestry, Alice. Would you like to tell me what you have discovered?'

Agatha's interest after so long surprised Alice. She owed Agatha a lot, so she filled her in on her discoveries so far.

'After last Christmas, I thought more about my mother; she was all the family I had,' Alice began. She told Agatha everything.

Agatha nodded from time to time, not taking her eyes off Alice. Alice's voice became stronger.

'So, you met the woman who says she's your mother in the solicitor's office.'

'Yes, Mrs Copeland. You can imagine how difficult that was.'

'Of course.'

'She said she went by the name of Ethel Barnes, but then she told me her real name was Elizabeth Hamilton. Does that name mean anything to you, Mrs Copeland?'

Agatha stared back at Alice, unmoving, as if frozen.

'Are you all right, Mrs Copeland? Shall I call Connie?'

Agatha shook her head.

'Then let me call Patty for another cup of tea.'

'No, Alice. There are matters we need to discuss – confidential matters – before you let anyone in.'

Silence fell. The sideboard clock boomed the hour.

'I can confirm that Elizabeth Hamilton is your mother, Alice,' said Agatha.

Alice's mouth fell open. Her face felt hot and clammy. 'But how could you know – unless you knew all along?'

'No. I knew nothing about Elizabeth's part in your story. I know her from my past. We spent some time together at school and parties because we were of a similar age.'

'Then I don't understand, Mrs Copeland. Didn't the two of you get on – or did you have a falling-out?'

Agatha took a deep and shuddering breath. 'Alice – I hoped this moment would never happen, but it has – and you need to know.'

'Know what?'

'Edwin Copeland was your father.'

'Mr Copeland – he was my father? But, how? I mean – was he married before he met you?'

'No, Alice.'

Agatha granted her the opportunity to contemplate it alone. Alice's brain wouldn't let her. 'He can't be. If he was married to you...'

Alice's face was on fire. That would mean... had Mr Copeland known about her when she first came to the house? If he knew, he hid it very well. He even made her sit in a third-class railway carriage because of some trouble that Connie had got her into. Overnight, Alice, the woman with no family, had become a daughter, sister, aunt, and sister-in-law. She looked as shocked as Agatha.

'Could you tell me anything, Mrs Copeland?' Even now Alice was finding it hard to believe.

'I'll tell you what I can, but please bear with me. It's difficult for me too – given the circumstances.' Agatha looked towards the window rather than at Alice. Perhaps it made the words come more easily.

'Mr Copeland had met Miss Hamilton at a business event in Manchester. Elizabeth was there with her father and two brothers. They danced a few dances together. Nobody discovered until later that the two had become close until Elizabeth confessed she was with child. Elizabeth's behaviour appalled her family, and it caused an uproar. They insisted she had nothing to do with Edwin Copeland in the future and nothing to do with the baby. Society sent away women and girls like Elizabeth to conceal their wrongdoings, bringing them back only after any evidence of their "misfortune" disappeared.'

Agatha stopped talking.

Alice knelt in front of her. 'It must have been awful.'

'It was. Naturally, the news devastated the Hamiltons. They had meetings to decide what to do to save the family from the scandal. I almost left your... Edwin. I didn't think I could stand it. In the end, it was in my interest to let sleeping dogs lie, provided Edwin had nothing to do with the Hamilton family in the future. I didn't want to be reminded of what he'd done. As far as I know, he kept his word, and so, I think, did Elizabeth. I understand Edwin met with Elizabeth's parents and agreed that everybody would remain silent until both sets of parents and I had passed away. That way, the silence would protect everyone from hurt.'

Alice jumped up and began pacing the room. 'Everyone! What about me? The baby!' Her eyes watered as her hand patted her chest. 'Abandoned by my mother and my adopted mother. I spent my childhood in the workhouse. How could that have been right for me? Didn't I deserve to have a family? Oh yes, you were kind to me and gave me a job; you didn't know who I was. And why would you? I was a servant. That didn't stop me from missing out on what I wanted – a family.' She tapped her chest again, harder this time. 'I've never had that, Mrs Copeland.'

Agatha looked startled. But Alice was beyond caring.

'I needed a maid to help Mrs Williams, and you were recommended to me... Is there anything else you'd like to know, Alice? I can't guarantee the answers, but I'll try my best.'

'Yes. I have a question.' Alice's heart pounded. It was the most difficult question she would ever ask of anyone. 'Did you know who I was when you took me from the workhouse?'

Mrs Copeland was silent, stony-faced, not the woman Alice had grown fond of over the years. Alice refused to turn away. She had to know. She swallowed. 'Did you know?'

Mrs Copeland shook her head. 'No. I found out when Connie telephoned.'

And then, the last question from Alice. 'Would you have taken me in if you had known who I was?'

There was silence.

Alice had her answer. Her head sank towards her chest. Still no voice came. Just the thumping of her heart doing its best to escape. She muttered, 'What about Connie? What have you told her?'

'Everything.'

Alice said nothing and headed for the door. She looked back at Agatha sitting alone, staring out of the window. What thoughts were going through her mind at that moment? How difficult it'd been for the families. Agatha was blameless – except for prohibiting Edwin and Elizabeth from ever meeting again.

She opened the door to see Connie pacing up and down the hallway. Nothing was said.

–

Alice was in her bedroom. She didn't know how she got there. Her mind was blank, remembering part of the conversation she'd had with Agatha, but not what she herself had contributed to it. She sank onto her bed and lay staring at the ceiling. Of all the stories she had picked up on this journey to find her mother, what she'd heard today had stunned her. From this point on, nothing would ever be the same again. How could it be? The events destroyed her life – and the Copelands too.

Her icy body melted. She had enjoyed her work at Holmorton Lodge. Over that time, friendship had overtaken her relationship with Connie and they had become close. Now, everything had changed. Connie was married with a child and the mistress of the household, and Alice was Agatha's step-daughter and Connie's stepsister. How could anything go back to what it was, given all that had happened? Would they hate her for who she had turned out to be?

Alice didn't know how long she had lain there. The room had darkened, but still she didn't move.

A light tap came on the door, followed by Patty's voice.

'Alice – are you in there?'

Alice didn't move.

'Are you all right, Alice?'

Then there was the sound of footsteps moving away.

She couldn't face anyone, knowing what she now knew.

Still, Alice lay there, unable to make any plans to get up. Another knock on the door. This time louder, with more force. And then Connie's voice.

'Alice, can I come in?'

Alice's eyes turned towards the door, unable to face her sister. It was that thought, more than anything else, that felt so unbelievable.

'I'm coming in, Alice. We need to talk.'

Trust Connie! She always got what she wanted. Alice brushed away her tears. She must remember she wasn't a servant any longer. She had a choice. She sat up on her bed as Connie, entering sheepishly, slowly walked towards her.

Sitting on the bed beside her, she took Alice's hand.

'How are you?'

'Numb. I can't seem to feel anything. When I started out on this journey to find my mother, I thought I was ready for anything that came out of it. I couldn't have been more wrong.'

Connie shook her head. 'I don't believe anyone could be prepared for what you discovered, Alice.'

'I've always been happy here. You and your mother have treated me very well. I know that. But how can things continue as they are, knowing what we know now? I couldn't continue to be your housekeeper and your sister, could I?'

'We need time, Alice. Time to sort everything out.'

'I can't think what I might say to Mrs Copeland when I see her tonight. How much I must have hurt her without even knowing.'

'You mustn't talk like that. It's not your fault, and it's not Mother's.'

'But what did you think when she told you who I was?'

Connie pursed her lips. 'I thought that, after all this time, I'd gained the sister I always wanted.' Connie gave a watery smile. 'I suppose that was selfish of me, but that was all I could think of. That and being unable to believe that my father and this woman could do such a thing to us.'

'Elizabeth seems to be a fine woman forced into difficult circumstances. Her family demanded she give me up. I believe she would've kept me if she'd had a choice.'

'She did,' snapped Connie.

'That may be the case, but not everybody can stand up to their family, especially their father.'

–

There was a lull in the day's events. Agatha and Uncle James were resting. Connie was feeding John Robert, and Robert would be at work until nine o'clock. Alice needed to tell Walter her latest news. He would be… well… sympathetic? She wasn't sure. Although he had been on her side throughout, he had been very clear in telling her she might not like the outcome of her searches.

She ran downstairs and was slipping into her coat when Patty appeared and rushed to give Alice a hug.

'What's that for?'

'What's happening with Connie? Is there something wrong with Mrs Copeland? Everyone seems serious, and anytime I approach, everyone goes silent. You're going to sack me, aren't you?' Patty was biting her lip until blood appeared.

'No, Patty, it's nothing like that. I can't tell you anything, but I'll tell you soon, I promise.'

'Where on earth are you going?'

'I'm just popping out to clear my head. I won't be long, Alice.'

'Would you like me to come with you?'

'No, I'll be all right. I'm not going far.'

Patty frowned. 'You sure? I feel I should tell someone. Shall I go to get Walter—'

'No! Don't do that.'

With that, Alice hugged Patty back and let herself out through the back door and headed off to see Walter.

Walter beamed, delighted by her presence, but gradually, the smile changed to anxiety.

'I didn't expect to see you today. Santa Claus told me there was a posh car at the big house. I guessed you had some important visitors, or perhaps Santa had got a bit too much Christmas cheer in him.'

Alice walked into the kitchen, where she discovered Santa sound asleep in his usual chair.

'Can we go somewhere, Walter?'

He glanced at her with a worried frown. 'Go through to the backyard,' he said.

Once out there, Alice paced up and down and she told him that the car belonged to Uncle James and Mrs Copeland. 'I don't think I told you last night, but I heard Connie ringing her mother, telling her I'd found my mother and about Elizabeth. Today, Agatha's on the doorstep.'

'The news must have been important to drag them here in the middle of winter.'

'Walter, Edwin Copeland was my father.'

'Bugger me!' His mouth fell open.

Alice shook her head. 'I've been wrestling with the news ever since I found out, and I don't know what I'm going to do.'

'So you're going to be posh.'

'Why should I be? It's going to make no actual difference. I know Connie will be my half-sister, and I'll have to leave Holmorton Lodge. I can't work for Connie now, can I?'

'Come here.'

Alice walked into Walter's arms, but he didn't answer her question. A sudden chill ran through her body as she stood embraced by him.

'Oh, Walter! What have I done?'

–

As the meeting with Mr Railsford approached, Alice grew more nervous, wondering what the legal agreements contained. She and Connie had agreed not to tell Mr Railsford about their father unless they had to.

The meeting went well, and Alice came out happy. She called on Walter on her way home to tell him all that had happened.

Walter looked at Alice as she stood on the doorstep in the rain. Her best hat got soaked, and her hairpins had fallen out.

'Come in, you look like a drowned rat.'

'Thank you. If a drowned rat feels like I do, then he has my sympathies,' Alice muttered sharply.

'Not a good day with Mr Railsford?'

'Exact opposite, it was all excellent. But this news brings problems with it. I shall have to go through each item in order and try not to wander off the subject, so pin your lugs back.'

'Yes, ma'am. But might I suggest we make ourselves comfortable first? And could I give my wife-to-be a kiss?'

'But your father might see us.'

He winked. 'We're getting wed, aren't we?'

What could she say to that?

They settled themselves at the table, and Alice began. 'The agreement requires Elizabeth to sell her shares in the brewery to her brothers, Spencer and Aubury. They each receive 50 per cent. In return, they'll pay Elizabeth a sum equivalent to the dividends she would have received.'

'What does that achieve?'

'In a minute. Let me go on. The next agreement acknowledges that I'm the daughter of Elizabeth Hamilton and grants me the same rights as a daughter born in wedlock. I can't use the name Hamilton in any context for myself or my children. I may not own or rent property within a twenty-five-mile radius of the Market Cross in Knutsford for my lifetime, and I may not own shares in or a controlling interest in shares owned by a third party in the brewery. I will receive a salary of £100 a month, payable for the rest of my life.'

'Did you say £100 per month?'

'Yes, you heard right.'

Walter whistled. 'Even the pit manager doesn't get that much!'

'Mr Railsford said that this gives the brothers full control of the brewery. I can't own shares, and will never inherit shares from Elizabeth.'

'So you've got nowt at the moment and you are giving nothing up, so you are losing nothing.'

'Correct, I thought that, but Mr Railsford explained to me I was mistaken. Without this agreement, if Elizabeth leaves me all her shares, then there's nothing the brothers can do. A third of the company would be mine, and who knows, that could be a lot in future years. But nevertheless, his advice is to sign the agreement and take the salary. As they say, "a bird in the hand is worth two in the bush."'

'Is there more?'

'Yes.'

'I'll make a cup of tea.' Walter made it.

That's a good start. At least he knows the recipe for tea. She continued as they drank. 'From the day I was born, Elizabeth has made contributions to a trust fund held in my birth name. She registered my birth in Holywell as Edwina Hamilton. This fund is worth a tidy sum. I will receive income from 28 March 1923, my twenty-fifth birthday, when the fund will be transferred into the name of Alice Tucker.'

'So you're called Edwina. Bit of a clue in the name! There must be a catch to this.'

'No, there are no conditions that compel me to meet, talk to or acknowledge Elizabeth. That's up to me.'

'You'll be a rich woman.'

'That is what it looks like.'

'You'll not want me. You can choose who you want, and there'll be plenty of suitors for a rich single girl. I'll be holding you back if you wed me.' There was anxiety written on his face.

Alice laid her hand on his brow. 'Yes, but *this* rich single girl has decided who she wants. It's you.'

He leaned forward and kissed her. She pulled away and, with a hand on each of his cheeks, stared into his eyes. 'Dearest Walter, I want you to know that I have no intention of letting you go. No matter what!'

'Where do we go from here?'

'Mr Railsford says that apart from a few wording changes, he can get everything ready by 23 December, which is the last day for the agreements to be signed.'

'Do you plan to sign?'

'Yes, this money is compensation from her family for forcing me away from my mother, and the fund is Elizabeth's estimation of what she would've had to spend to bring up a child.'

'So they're using the money to relieve their conscience?'

'It doesn't matter to me what their motives are. I've spent the last fifteen years cleaning and cooking and being at everyone's beck and call, but with this money, that stops. Unless you want to do something different, we're telling everyone we're engaged and we can plan our wedding and be together at last. I will change my name from Alice Tucker to Alice Latham.'

–

Just before Christmas, Robert fell ill again. He had been gassed at the beginning of the war and was prone to lung infections more than most.

Preparations dominated the week before the festivities. Agatha was arriving for Christmas on the twenty-third, so rooms had to be prepared for her and her constant shadow, Miss Doubleday, who had become Agatha's trusted companion. Alice and Patty had got used to her manner and realised that whatever the subject was, she always had an opinion, and her opinion was always correct.

In the meantime, Alice and Patty were busy with the preparations, and Nanny Lily was busy with a sniffly John Robert, leaving Connie to look after the bedridden Robert for three days. She said his body felt like lead, his movements sluggish and laboured. She was worried and had called the doctor out on two occasions. Alice thought with all the changes of the last month and it being December with so little light, both Connie and Robert were at a low ebb. Connie tried to minimise contact with John Robert, just in case. She spent most of the time upstairs with Robert in their room. Alice could hear Connie reading to him.

Patty did a lot of the running about with meals and drinks for both the patient and the carer. She enjoyed the new role and seemed capable of managing many tasks on her own, which was a considerable help. She always called him Mr Robert now and Alice could detect they both felt more relaxed. Nanny Lily, being that much older and experienced in the ways of posh households, was quite at home with Robert and always referred to him as Mr Caldwell. Nanny Lily would stand at the open door to Robert's bedroom so that he might wish his son good morning. Connie refused to allow her to take John Robert in for fear of infection, even though Robert wasn't infectious. Connie's answer was always – it's a precaution.

Then, like before, his body got on top of the infection. By Agatha's arrival he was up and about, but he didn't go into work, to keep out of The Potteries' smoky atmosphere. It'd not gone unnoticed by both Connie and Alice that Robert's cough was always worse during prolonged periods of settled weather when the lack of wind meant that the air didn't seem to change.

Everyone was glad when the household returned to normal. Alice was getting used to her new relationship with Connie, but in public, it was business as usual. They'd learned to treat each other as friends again rather than as mistress and servant. The next thing would be to treat each other as the sisters they now were.

Chapter Nineteen

Christmas 1921

What had started out twelve months ago as a mission to find the mother who had abandoned her in the workhouse had ended in a way no one could have predicted. Alice sat in Mr Railsford's office on the Friday before Christmas and signed all the agreements between a family she hardly knew and herself.

'So what happens now?'

'Miss Cheeseman will take the sealed documents to the brewery's solicitors in Manchester and receive in exchange an identical set of documents which have been signed by the two brothers. They will also release the cheque for your first month's salary, which she'll pay into your account on her return.'

He handed Alice her passbook for the Potteries Municipal Bank, in Kingsway, Stoke-on-Trent. She didn't like to count her chickens before they hatched, so hadn't allowed herself to get excited about the money until she had evidence of it in her hand. Mr Railsford had set up a bank account for her where she could pay in the cheque from the brewery. She looked at the passbook, and on the front page, there was her name and address. It looked impressive. Not something that would belong to her at all. She turned the page and looked at the balance, £84 12s 7d, and it looked unreal. She gazed at Mr Railsford and back at the book in her hand.

Mr Railsford took a moment to let it sink in. 'Well, Alice, the balance consists of £100 granted from your trust, authorised by Miss Hamilton and myself to "set you on your way". I've also taken the liberty of deducting my account from the trust money; a detailed bill is included in your copies of the papers.'

Miss Cheeseman came into the office ready for the journey.

'Hello, Miss Tucker. I'll need your passbook so I can pay in the cheque when I return. Thank you,' said Miss Cheeseman.

Alice looked at Mr Railsford.

'It's all right, Miss Cheeseman will take good care of it.'

That was it. In a few days, she would be an independent woman.

–

Agatha was due to arrive that afternoon and Alice wondered what the atmosphere would be like over the festive period. She was determined not to let anything get in the way of her engagement to Walter. After all, everybody liked a romance at Christmas.

Alice had convinced herself there'd been an irreversible change in their relationship when Agatha had returned to Urmston. In the past, Agatha had treated Alice well. Perhaps the happiness of Christmas and the prospect of a wedding would heal the rift between them. After all, it wasn't Alice's fault.

Miss Cheeseman arrived at Holmorton Lodge at half past three. Patty answered the door and went to find Alice.

'Good afternoon, Miss Cheeseman. I trust you had a safe and successful journey.'

'Oh yes, miss. Everything was in order.'

Alice took her through to the kitchen, where Patty had two cups of tea ready.

'In this large envelope are your copies of the agreements, which will be checked by Mr Railsford. I thought you would like the contents of this small envelope a little more.' She handed it to Alice, who took out her passbook.

They talked for a few minutes and finished their tea, and then Miss Cheeseman left.

Alice returned to the kitchen and opened the passbook. There was the balance Mr Railsford had written down for her – £214 4s 0d. A fortune. She whirled round a few times before steadying herself. She ran out of the kitchen to her bedroom and placed the passbook under her pillow. All the excitement had made her sweat and she had to swill her face in cold water to help calm down.

When she returned to the kitchen, Patty had cleared the crockery and was sitting at the table.

'She was a nice woman, and by the look on your face it was good news.'

Alice lifted Patty out of the seat and gave her a big hug. At the same time she pressed into her hand two half-crowns. 'Merry Christmas, Patty, treat yourself to something nice.'

–

Christmas Eve was as busy as ever. Alice and Patty worked tirelessly. By the time Patty left to go to her family for the night, both of them were exhausted. They had agreed Patty would return on Christmas morning, having seen her family open their presents. Patty had saved all year so she could buy her family a little gift each. She was so looking forward to seeing her brothers' and sisters' faces when they saw the additional present in the stockings so carefully hung in front of the fire.

Alice remained on call for the rest of the family. Occasionally seeing Bella or Lily. Bella asked if Alice would like to partake of a "wee dram of whisky", but she wanted to keep a clear head. John Robert had been grizzly, but Lily seemed to have everything in hand.

By the time Alice finally made her rounds, it was nearly midnight. As she walked around, she thought of past Christmases and knew nothing would ever be the same. For her, everything had changed. It would be her last Christmas at Holmorton Lodge, and the thought frightened her. All the bad feeling Agatha had bottled up. So much better if nothing was said and Alice simply moved out and never saw her again.

Instead, she had the anticipation of her future with Walter. It was time to make her own way in this world. Nothing else mattered. Connie had built her life with Robert, and they were Connie's priorities now – just as Walter should be Alice's. She had been putting off their marriage because she was frightened to acknowledge what the future might hold. Deep down, Alice knew there would be problems ahead; nothing ever flows smoothly, but with Walter by her side she could cope with anything.

Alice realised it would be impossible to work for Connie from now on, and what's more, she didn't want to. That time has passed. Their wedding would have to be planned, and the registry office booked as well as somewhere for the family to get together afterwards. Their house would have to be furnished and, of course, being a married woman, with all that entailed, would keep her busy.

She would talk to Connie in the New Year to agree her leaving date and give Connie plenty of time to find her replacement.

–

At last, it was Christmas Day. Alice went over her plans a final time. She and Walter would tell Patty of their engagement as soon as Patty returned, although she doubted it would come as a surprise. Then they would speak to Connie, Robert and Agatha and get that over with. In the evening they would tell Walter's family. By the end of the festivities, everybody who should know would know that Alice and Walter would be getting married in the new year. The identity of Alice's father would not be mentioned.

As promised, Patty arrived bang on time. She was followed into the kitchen by Walter.

'Look who I found lurking around outside,' Patty grinned.

'I wasn't lurking around; I was waiting for you so that we could come in to wish Alice a Merry Christmas together.'

'Well, whatever the reason was, a Merry Christmas to both of you.' Alice gave Patty a hug and asked if her presents went down well with her family. After taking off her coat, Patty chatted away until Alice put up her hand to stop her.

'I…' Alice swallowed, '…I mean we—' she turned to Walter, – 'have something to tell you, Patty. It's good news.' She took Walter's hand. 'We're getting engaged today and we want you to be the first to know.'

Patty clapped her hands. 'Of course, I knew all along, and I have to say it's about time an' all.'

'You knew?'

'Course I did. You've had a smile on yer face every time you come back from seeing him. I expected it, but I've been very good and not gossiped about it to anybody.'

Well, mind you keep it that way for a few more hours. I need to tell Connie and Robert, and afterwards, Bella and Lily need to know too.

'Yes, ma'am.' Patty smirked and sank into a curtsey.

They hugged each other, swirling round until Alice begged Patty to stop. 'Enough of that. We'd best get some food prepared, don't you think?'

The two got to work, although the smiles never left their faces. Walter disappeared to join his family's Christmas dinner and promised to return so that they could announce their news to the Caldwells.

–

Alice supervised the serving of the meal to Robert, Connie and Agatha, which was easier when compared to the numbers she had served in the past. Patty, helped or hindered by Bella Doubleday, put together the servants' meal for later on. Alice felt run off her feet as on a couple of occasions Patty wasn't to be found. Since the passing of Mr Copeland and Mrs Williams's retirement, Alice had eaten with the family at Christmas, but this year she hadn't been invited. An oversight – or was it deliberate? If the truth be told, she would prefer to eat with her friends below stairs.

By two o'clock, the Caldwells were tucking into the Christmas pudding and mince pies. Alice had taken a pot of coffee and placed it on the sideboard in the garden room. Alice and Patty quickly cleared the dining room and placed the used crockery in the sink.

'We'd better lay the table and start getting the meal out of the warmer. Good to see you've washed up as much as you can.'

'Bella helped me. She dried and put away. She's nipped upstairs to check on Lily.'

'I was wondering where she was. She's never normally late for food.'

'Everything is taken care of. We are going to eat in the nursery. We've organised everything and you can tell Bella and Lily your news.'

'That's where you kept disappearing to.'

Alice clapped her hands in excitement. It was all beginning to feel real.

Bella and Lily were beaming when Alice and Patty walked in.

'Alice, dear,' said Bella, warmly. 'We want to thank you for your kindness to us, don't we, Lily?' said Bella warmly.

'Yes, we asked Patty if we could prepare something a little special for you.' Lily moved towards the stillage in the corner and brought out a trifle, which was likely to be enough to feed twice the number.

Alice looked askance at Patty. 'Did you tell them?'

'How could I? You've only just told me!' Patty grinned.

'Tell us what?' asked Bella, frowning.

Alice flushed as all eyes turned to her. 'Walter and I are getting engaged today.'

There was much joviality as congratulations, hugs and laughter followed. Even Bella lost some of her normal reserve.

They had a wonderful time, but it was over too soon.

'We needed this, didn't we, girls?' said Alice as she wiped her eyes with her sleeve. 'It'll be our last Christmas together.'

While Lily took care of John Robert, the other three carried down all their used crockery and cleared up after the meal ended. Surprisingly, Bella volunteered to dry the dishes. Alice wondered if it was wise, but she hadn't got the heart to stop her. After all, the pots and pans had survived.

–

Walter arrived, on time, but soaking wet, at four o'clock, dressed in his Sunday best. Patty had gone up to her room to get changed. She was going to spend the rest of the evening with her family. Bella, after the excitement of drying dishes, decided she needed a nap in her room. The two were alone. Alice could almost feel the brightness in her eyes as she gazed at Walter.

'This is it, my love,' he murmured as he kissed her. 'You haven't changed your mind?'

Holding his eyes with hers, she shook her head. 'I want nothing more.'

His face became serious. 'I know we agreed not to buy a ring until the new year, but I've got this for you.' He took a little green ring box out of his jacket inside pocket. Alice opened it, to reveal an exquisite gold ring with a single diamond.

'It was Mother's engagement ring. She wanted me to have it "to give to my girl". She said it was because she couldn't be with me, and this was the next best thing she could do.' His eyes were bright.

'Oh, Walter, it's lovely.' They kissed again, more urgently this time. And then, as Alice gazed at her left hand, she could barely contain the tears threatening to fill her eyes. It looked just perfect. She, Alice, could never have aspired to such a beautiful thing.

Alice was still in his arms when Patty entered the kitchen.

'Oh, Patty. Look at my ring.' She eased herself out of Walter's arms.

Patty's jaw dropped. 'Yer never said as you was getting a ring an' all.'

Alice laughed. 'I didn't know myself until now.'

'Have you told Connie?'

'Not yet. She's next on our list.'

'Good luck with that. I've just been into the garden room to make sure they'd enough coal, and all three of them look as if they'd lost a sovereign and found a penny. Mrs Copeland had a face like thunder, and the conversation stopped as soon as I knocked.'

'No doubt I'll find out. But thanks for the warning.'

'What time do you want me back tonight?'

'I shall be back at ten o'clock. You can have another night at home.'

'Thank you very much for that, Alice, but one night a year sandwiched between my two sisters is enough. I missed my bed last night. I won't miss it again tonight.' Patty kissed Alice on the cheek and approached Walter, who seemed to be surprised. Perhaps he was thinking about telling Connie. Patty paused, and then reached around Walter and picked up her scarf from the coat stand and left the kitchen with a cheery goodbye.

'Phew. I thought she was going to kiss me again.' He stood silently as if not wanting to move.

'Walter, are you worried about telling Connie and Robert?'

Walter shrugged. 'It's all so real now.'

'But you *are* sure, aren't you?'

'More than anything. Let's tell them now and get it over with.' He took a deep breath and held out his hand.

Alice took it and squeezed it gently. Together, they left the kitchen. She knocked on the door of the garden room, let go of Walter's hand, and entered. Connie and Robert were sitting on the settee while Agatha and Uncle James each had a comfortable chair.

Alice didn't know if she could go through with it, in the presence of Agatha. She took a breath and raised her head. 'Hello, everybody. I— we, have something to tell you.'

Walter stepped forward and nodded each of them.

Connie smiled. 'Hello, Walter, compliments of the season. Have you come to take Alice away from me?' asked Connie.

For a moment Alice wondered whether Connie knew, but suddenly discovered it no longer mattered. Her confidence returned. She lay a hand on Walter's arm and smiled at him. 'In a manner of speaking, Connie. Walter and I have got engaged.'

'We plan to marry in the new year,' said Walter.

'That's wonderful news,' squealed Connie. 'It's about time. When did you propose, Walter?'

'At the end of October, and Alice said yes straight away, but we made it formal today. It's what Alice wanted.'

'You sly creature, Alice Tucker! How did you keep it to yourself all this time?' said Connie.

'With difficulty,' Alice grinned. 'But there was so much going on.'

Robert stood up and kissed Alice on each cheek, and shook Walter by the hand. 'I'm pleased for you both.'

Alice showed them the ring.

Robert sat down and said, 'I think we should have a celebratory drink.'

Alice looked at Connie, who was looking at her mother. Up to that point, Agatha had been silent, and Alice found this strange, but she wasn't prepared for what followed.

Agatha turned towards them and said, 'Did he propose before he knew you were rich, or afterwards?'

Everything went quiet. You could hear a pin drop. Alice looked at Walter, and she had to admit he looked shaken. No, not shaken. His eyes burned with anger.

'Mother! How can you say that? It's not fair and unlike you!'

'I'm only saying what I think and what other people will say.'

'You've upset Alice and Walter. I think you should apologise.'

'I won't apologise for telling the truth.' Agatha turned from Connie to Alice, her nose up and her eyes cold. 'Alice, you will no longer be welcome in this house when I am visiting. I will not be resident here with my dead husband's bastard. I will go to my room now for a nap. I don't want to be disturbed.' Agatha rose out of the seat and walked past Alice and Walter with no acknowledgement.

A wave of nausea rose within Alice. Connie looked horrified as she turned to Robert for comfort as she watched her mother leave the room. The garden room remained as muted as an empty church.

Walter's face was white. 'I think I need some air. I need a walk.'

'I'll come with you,' Alice whispered.

'No, I want to be on my own.' Walter left the room and Robert followed.

Connie threw her arms around Alice. 'I'm so sorry. I must apologise for my mother.'

'I can understand. It's been a terrible shock, and seeing us both together was too much. I never thought she would take against me like that. I thought she liked me even though I was only a servant. I should've been more careful in talking to her.'

'No, Alice, you've done nothing wrong. I'm sure when she thinks about it, she'll realise that she should've directed her anger towards my father or Elizabeth Hamilton, but not at you. You're the innocent party in all of this.'

Alice sat down, trembling at the unexpected turn of events, and Connie poured them both a small tumbler of whisky. 'Well, at least we can celebrate your engagement. I don't think we need our men to be present.'

About a quarter of an hour later, Robert returned.

'Where is he, Robert?' said Alice, rising.

'He went straight home. He asked me to tell you he'll call for you at seven o'clock this evening and he'll talk to you then, but he will not step inside this house.'

Alice thanked Robert and went up to her room. She had a good cry. Not over what Agatha had said, but as a release from all the tension of the last few weeks. She hoped Walter was all right. No doubt she would see tonight. She kept herself busy for the rest of the day, looking at the household journal – anything to take her mind off things.

–

Alice glanced at the clock for the umpteenth time. It was a minute after the last time she'd looked. It was five past seven and still no sign of Walter. It was very unlike him; he was usually so prompt. Her heart was in her mouth.

She walked up to Dartmouth Street. At least the rain had stopped now, and the clouds looked as if they were clearing. She arrived at about quarter past seven and knocked on the front door as usual. Walter answered it, complete with a cardboard hat and his brother Frank's youngest, Anthony, hanging onto his leg demanding that his siblings come to get the fire-breathing dragon.

'Hello, Alice, is it that time already? I've lost track. We were just playing a game. Let me free myself from Anthony and I'll put my cap and coat on, and we'll have a walk.'

Walter was soon back, and they strolled up Dartmouth Street. 'I'm so sorry for losing track of the time.'

'Are you all right about what happened this afternoon, Walter? I'm so sorry. I never thought Mrs Copeland would be so cruel. She as good as called you a gold-digger, and I'll never forgive her for that.'

'I wasn't thrilled when I left. More than anything, the comment surprised me. But what she said was right. People will say that I'm only marrying you because you've now got some money.'

'They might, but we know the truth. Connie and I talked about what had happened, and she thought it was unfair to you.

Her mother was taking out her frustrations over events from twenty-odd years ago.'

'That's what Robert said, but he also said that he could understand how something like that would knock me for six. He said that when he married Connie, although she'd had money troubles after Mr Copeland passed, her mother's side of the family, in other words, Uncle James, stepped in. I think we now understand why.'

'I hadn't thought of that.'

'Robert admitted to me he had thought long and hard before asking Connie to marry him, and even after they were married, it took him a while before he came to terms with the fact that his wife would always be worth more than he was.'

'I know they had problems at the beginning, and Connie is so used to money, she often makes tactless remarks without thinking about the consequences. But Walter, that won't happen to us. We're both from the same class, no matter how much money I get in the future. I'll still find it hard to take a tram down to Burslem, because it's cheaper to walk, and it's all downhill.'

'You know, Alice, what's bothering me is if we decide to buy a house instead of renting, I'll be the only man at the pit to own the house he lives in.'

'It'll be a while before we're able to buy a house, but I don't think we should apologise for our money or lock ourselves away just because of what people think. We should enjoy the money, not waste it.'

'That's what Robert said. He said not to let money stand in the way of our happiness. We'll get used to it, but we shouldn't be apologetic about it. You don't have to be rich to be happy.'

'So, where does this leave us?'

'Walking around the streets of Burslem on Christmas night when people are enjoying themselves. I can't understand why Mrs Copeland said what she said, but I'll not let it bother me. I agree we shouldn't apologise for your good fortune. You've earned it. So, I think as soon as we can, we get ourselves down to the registry office and organise this wedding. In the meantime, we've got a house full of people wondering where we are.'

By this time, they were turning back onto Dartmouth Street, and soon they entered the warmth of Walter's family.

Everyone was sitting in the front room laughing and joking.

'The wanderers return. We'd thought you'd got lost,' said Mr Latham.

'Come on, Alice, have a seat here,' said Ruth.

'Before you sit down, Alice, we might as well tell everybody our news.' Walter put his arm around her shoulder. 'We're engaged. We're planning to marry in the new year.'

Cheers went up from the men, and Ruth rushed across to embrace her sister-in-law-to-be. Joan put Anthony on the floor and then she, too, embraced the new member of the family.

Alice thought to herself how marvellous it all was. For years she'd had no family and thought she was all alone in this world. Now she had a family and was on the verge of creating her own. What a change since last Christmas.

Joan and Frank left around eight o'clock as the kids were getting tired and were missing their beds.

Walter and Alice updated Ruth and Stan on Alice's search for her mother. They knew Alice had found her, but very little else. So Walter and Alice decided they'd tell the full story, omitting anything about who her father was.

'Where are you planning to live?' asked Ruth. Alice noticed Miss Latimer seemed unsettled by this question. 'Are you planning to move in with Father?'

'No, we're going to look for a place of our own. It'll be around here and, as you know, Alice will have to leave her job at Holmorton Lodge.'

'Why is that?' asked Ruth.

'I can't do my job there and live somewhere else. It'd be impossible.'

'So you're going to become a housekeeper for our Walter, instead of being a housekeeper for the Caldwells?'

'Yes, you could say that. But I haven't decided what job I'm going to do. The most important thing at the moment is to get the wedding organised. We are going to have a registry office wedding and a "do" afterwards for all the family. You can meet my mother, Elizabeth.'

'Has Elizabeth got any children other than you?'

'No, but we're still learning about each other.'

The conversation moved on, and Alice and Walter ceased to be the subject of the hour. At ten o'clock, Alice rose and put her coat on. 'I've got to go to work now.'

'On Christmas Day?' asked Mr Latham.

'Oh yes. That's the problem with service. You have to be available when your employer wants. When Walter comes home, he gets to sit down and read the paper. I've always got some task to finish, and although Connie and Mrs Copeland are fine bosses, there is never any doubt. I'm asked to do something, and I do it. I can't sit in a comfy chair and put my feet up.'

Everybody said goodnight, and Alice and Walter walked back to Holmorton Lodge, taking their time. Since the news about Elizabeth, she'd given a lot of thought to what she would do. She had choices now, something she'd never had before.

The sky had cleared, revealing a bright moon. But as always, there was the glow from the steelworks and some kilns that were still being fired.

'I think that went very well,' said Walter.

'Your Ruth is good at asking questions.'

'Oh yes, I think she's intrigued to know about Elizabeth.'

'I noticed you said we were going to get a place of our own, but didn't mention that we might buy a place.'

'No, I chose my words. No one in our family has ever owned any property. That piece of news can wait until we've decided what we're going to do.'

They arrived at the front door about the same time as Patty. Alice said her goodbyes to Walter, and Alice and Patty opened the door. It was quiet. Alice noticed that there was a note on the post table. It read: 'We're all tired and have gone to bed. See you in the morning. Breakfast at half past eight. Connie.'

Part Three

Chapter Twenty

New Year – 1922

New Year's Day, 1922, was one of those damp, dull days often found in mid-winter. Falling on a Sunday, as it did this year, meant New Year's Eve celebrations resulted in a hangover at home and not a lost day's pay, or worse, a hangover at work. Alice bundled up in her heaviest coat, a woollen scarf, and her best hat as she made her way to Walter's house.

Walter answered the door, a warm welcome on his face, still in his mining clothes.

'Oh… you're going out? Is there a problem?'

'No. I was called in to remove an outcrop of granite in one of the galleries. I went in at two o'clock and have just got home.'

'I didn't hear any noise or feel any vibrations.'

'It was only a minor explosion. I think we set the shots off just after five o'clock. Then I had to do all the paperwork. At least there's one thing about being called in today – I get the whole day off tomorrow.'

Alice chatted to Mr Latham while she waited for Walter to have a wash. After a few minutes, Walter returned and gave Alice a kiss on the cheek. She smiled. 'I came round this evening to see if there was anything you think I should ask Elizabeth tomorrow?'

'She's been on my mind. But no, nothing so far. When am I going to meet her? It'll be good to put a face to the name, whether it's Elizabeth Hamilton or Ethel Barnes. I'll likely have some questions once I meet her.'

'Why not come with me tomorrow? I'm sure she won't mind, and it'd be nice if you were there. We can tell her we're getting married.'

'I'd like that. What time will you need me in the morning?'

'It's a late start. We should leave here at about half past eight to catch the Stoke to Manchester train.'

–

With the legal matters concluded, Alice decided to treat them to a more comfortable journey. Today was a good deal colder than yesterday, with a biting wind. She purchased two first-class return tickets at the ticket office, and they waited for their train to arrive.

'How much do I owe you for the ticket?'

'It's my treat.' She beamed, happy to give a treat instead of being on the receiving end. The blaring noise of the approaching express train heralded the beginning of their journey. Smoke belched out of its chimney, filling the station and causing the waiting passengers to cough and splutter. Alice approached the carriage with a gold number one emblazoned on the doors. Before she could reach the handle, a porter's hand appeared and opened the carriage door.

'Let me do that for you, miss.'

'Thank you.'

Walter looked on, frowning.

They found a seat in a compartment with two women reading, who nodded a greeting and returned to their books. Alice got out her precious notebook and settled down to write out a list of questions for her meeting with Elizabeth.

Walter whispered to Alice, 'We're in first class. They'll chuck us out.'

'No, they won't. We both have the correct tickets. I'm treating us to a comfortable journey, Walter. We've sat on enough third-class seats over the last year.'

'It must have cost a fortune,' he muttered, sitting back in his seat.

It wasn't long before the ticket inspector came around. 'Tickets, please. Tickets, please.'

Alice handed them to him. He glanced at each of them and back at the tickets before clipping the tickets in the appropriate place.

'I wonder if he thinks we don't look like first-class passengers?' whispered Walter.

'Thank you, miss. Is everything all right for you?'

'Yes, thank you,' Alice said with a little smile on her face.

The inspector nodded, lifted his cap, and continued on his way, closing the door behind him. Alice was pleased to be proved right. From now on she would have every right to sit in the first-class carriage. No one spoke for the rest of the journey. The next stop was Macclesfield, then Stockport and finally Manchester. They alighted from the train and strode to the taxi rank. Walter couldn't help grinning as Alice marched along, a determined look on her face.

They arrived at Solomon, Solomon and Penfold's offices. Alice made her way towards the stairs and the reception on the first floor, with Walter just behind her, gazing at the opulent surroundings he wasn't expecting. They were asked to take a seat. Reuben would come along to collect them.

Walter hadn't said a word since getting out of the taxi.

'Are you all right, Walter? You're very quiet.'

'I... I'm a little nervous, if you must know. This place looks so grand. Not what I expected at all.'

'Not to worry. Everyone here is very nice. I think I'll ask Reuben's opinion on whether we should go in together or wait until I've explained the situation to Elizabeth.'

'Dunner leave me out here on my own—'

'Hello, Miss Tucker.'

'Hello, Reuben.'

'Oh, a change of lawyer this time, I see.'

'No, Reuben, I'd like to introduce you to my fiancé, Mr Walter Latham.'

'Apologies, sir. I'm Reuben Solomon.'

'Pleased to meet you.' Walter shook Reuben's hand without hesitation, which seemed to put Walter at ease.

'Reuben, do you think it would be acceptable if we went in together?' asked Alice.

'I think that's a splendid idea.'

Reuben led the way to the sitting room, where she had first met Elizabeth. He opened the door and announced them.

As Alice approached, Elizabeth broke into a warm smile.

'Hello, dear. It's good to see you.'

'And you too. I'd like to introduce my good friend, Walter Latham. He's been helping me to find my family.'

There was a momentary pause and a look of surprise on Elizabeth's face, which she turned into a smile.

'Pleased to meet you, Miss Hamilton,' Walter said, smiling. 'I've heard a lot about you.' Walter held out his hand, which Elizabeth took with a slight shake while glancing at Alice, looking confused.

Alice felt her face redden. She should've made his position clearer; otherwise, it might look as if she was ashamed of him.

'Pleased to meet you too, Walter. You must call me Elizabeth. Miss Hamilton sounds far too formal and makes me feel like my old housemistress when I was at boarding school.'

Alice butted in. 'Elizabeth, when I described Walter as a friend, I'm afraid I misled you. He's more than that. We've been walking out for just over a year. He's a pit deputy at the large coal mine across from the estate. We grew up in the same area. We got engaged at Christmas. I'm still getting used to it.'

Walter relaxed visibly. Thank goodness she had given him the courtesy of a proper introduction.

Elizabeth beamed. 'Congratulations. I'm so pleased for you both.'

Elizabeth's tray of tea arrived and, after pouring a cup for everyone, they talked about the weather, the journey, and so on. The conversation came to Alice's childhood.

They sipped their tea. Alice remembered being in a happy place until everything changed. She recounted the story of her father's death and the assertion that he was drunk. 'But he wasn't, Elizabeth.'

'How long ago was this?'

'Eighteen years.'

'And the gentleman who told you this, what age was he?'

'About seventy, I think.'

'Don't let one man colour your view of the events. You don't know if he had an axe to grind concerning the company or the other men involved, or just wanted to make trouble.'

'I wondered the same thing, but I decided there was no point in talking to the company about it. Whatever the facts were, it was too late.'

'So what happened next?'

'Everything I found disheartened me.' Alice took another sip of her tea and stared at the table. 'So I stopped thinking about it. It wasn't until the spring of 1921 that I started to search again. I had a birth certificate in the name of Alice Tucker and an address in Runcorn. With Walter's help' – she smiled at him – 'I journeyed to Runcorn and discovered my father's family still lived in the same area, and one of his brothers lived in the same house as I was born in – or at least the same house I thought I was born in.'

By the time Alice had finished talking about that part of the world, Elizabeth knew about the adoption by the Tuckers and that her mother had died in August 1918.

'Oh, that must've been traumatic for you.'

'Yes, her sister gave me a box with some personal stuff inside, including a letter Mother had written to me but never sent. It partly explained why she abandoned me at the workhouse, but didn't say why she never came back.'

Elizabeth sighed. 'Some things are too important to put in writing. They need to be talked about and explained. My dear Alice. After a year, I'd have moved heaven and earth to see you, but as time went on, I learned to live with the pain. It was better to pretend it had never happened. Then you find something occurs and everything comes flooding back.'

'But why didn't you look for me?'

'In the agreement, I made promises to my parents and to your biological father's family that I wouldn't interfere. I didn't know your new name, nor where you lived.'

'When I first worked for Mrs Copeland, I dreamt my mother would come along and take me back to the way we were, but just like you said, after a while, you start to think it was all a dream.'

Elizabeth frowned. 'So how did you connect with the nursing home in Holywell?'

'From my mother's scribbled note I found in the box. She must have died a few weeks after she put it there. All the note said was my name, and that I was born in Holywell. So, with Walter's help, a lot of luck and a quarter bottle of whisky, we found references to Ethel Barnes. And I think you know the rest.'

'I'm intrigued. What was the whisky for? I hope you didn't mean to hit someone with it.'

'I thought it might come in useful if we had to persuade someone to help us,' grinned Walter.

They all laughed.

Elizabeth continued. 'You did very well to piece all of that together from one visit.'

'My solicitor wrote a letter to David Turnbull. He said Ethel Barnes was no longer a client of his and that he had forwarded the letter to another firm of solicitors, who may or may not represent her now.'

'Oh yes, David's very careful. They've represented my family and business since its inception. I find they can be more protective than my brothers.'

'Well, it would've worked. I'd run out of ideas,' said Alice, eager to continue. 'It'd be hard to find a specific man in a big city like Manchester, but finding a woman who could have been married and changed her name was even harder.'

'When Philip informed me that someone had enquired at Turnbull's about Ethel Barnes, hearing that name after all these years shocked me. I told Philip to follow it up. I had to know if you were my daughter.'

'He appears to have done a good job for you.'

'And I couldn't be more pleased.'

'Before we go into that, Elizabeth, I've got a confession to make, and I feel quite bad about not mentioning it as soon as we arrived.'

'What's that, my dear?'

'I've discovered who my father was.'

It was the first time Alice had seen Elizabeth lost for words. Perhaps she shouldn't have come out with it that way. Everything had been so tied up. Perhaps she had never prepared herself for such an event occurring.

'I... see,' said Elizabeth, her face flushed. 'I never in all my wildest dreams thought this situation would arise.'

'How did you find out I worked for your...?'

'Lover?'

Alice bit her lip. 'Yes, that was the word I was looking for, but it sounded so rude after all you've done for me.'

'Not in the least. To answer your question, I knew only about a week before our meeting in December. Philip Penfold'—she turned to Walter—'my solicitor, you might recall, had his private investigator looking into the matter. As we were working through his report, I saw the name of your employer. I was shocked beyond words.'

Elizabeth was distressed. Her hand came up and rested on her chest, fingering a row of pearls Alice had only just noticed. 'Philip and I discussed how to proceed, because of the agreement with my brothers.'

'Mrs Copeland told me about your affair, the pregnancy, and her agreement – if that's the right word – to give Mr Copeland a second chance, provided he never saw you or spoke of you to anyone.'

'Of course, now that Agatha's let the cat out of the bag, I'm released from the promise I made never to speak of it.'

The room fell silent. Alice stared at Elizabeth. Dare she go on? She had to. It may be her only opportunity to discover the full story. She had heard Agatha's side. She should give Elizabeth the same courtesy. She pressed on.

'I hope you don't mind me asking, but Mrs Copeland gave me the impression that it was an affair like you read about in those dreadful magazines. Was that the case?'

Elizabeth shook her head. 'Not at all. I'd have married Edwin at the drop of a hat if he had been free. I was thirty-four at the time and thought that love had passed me by, but when I met Edwin, it was love at first sight.'

'How long did it last?' Alice asked quietly.

'Edwin and I were together as often as we could be for over a year. It sounds a long time, but it wasn't. Meeting unnoticed was difficult for us. I knew he would never leave his wife, but that didn't matter – those hours we spent together were reward enough for me.' Elizabeth sighed. 'Then you came along and all hell broke loose. I depended on my parents and did what I was told. Within days, they packed me off to a nursing home. It was what families did in those days – protecting the family name, they called it.' She laughed, but there was no happiness in it.

Both Alice and Walter hung on to every word. Alice was having difficulty swallowing as Elizabeth continued talking.

'What shocked me was that Edwin seemed to accept being warned off by my father and never seeing me again. His concerns, of course, were for Agatha and his daughter. I wondered if he ever thought about me during the years that followed. Did he ever feel as much for me as I did for him? I don't think he did.'

'So what happened?'

'Oh, the usual things. I gave birth and you were such a pretty little thing. Then you were taken away from me and I never saw you again. Oh yes, they told me I'd had a little girl, and that I should feel lucky because they'd already found a home for you. And that was it.'

'You never saw me?'

Elizabeth shook her head, her eyes watering. 'I thought about you often, how you were growing up, and what sort of life you were having. My father took care of the paperwork, and he was the one who gave me a new name and arranged to channel any correspondence through his solicitor.'

'Did Mr Copeland ever try to see you?'

'Not that I'm aware of. Then again, nobody would tell me. It was in my best interest not to be told.'

'And Agatha?'

'I'm sure that she also took a pragmatic point of view.'

'How so?'

'Better to be married to a man with money and a roving eye than married to a poor man or not married at all. I don't believe it was Agatha's fault, if I'm being kind. It was the doubt drilled into her by that family of hers. People who have money always want more. Very like my own brothers,' she sniffed.

By this stage, it was time for a visit to the privy, and when they returned, someone had replaced the tea. They returned to their seats, and Elizabeth continued the conversation. 'What happened when you told Mrs Copeland what you'd discovered?'

'Agatha had been staying with her brother, Uncle James, for a while, so she wasn't around when I told Connie, but I heard Connie on the telephone to her later that day. Agatha must have asked lots of questions, but I only heard Connie's side of the conversation. Then Agatha turned up at Holmorton Lodge, with Uncle James, who I think knew about everything that had happened.'

'Ah... James is still around, is he? He and I don't get on. One day I will tell you about Uncle James, but not today.'

'Agatha told me first, which I suppose was the right thing to do – then she talked to Connie.'

'I thought Agatha would. Once you'd told her about your discovery, I'm sure that my name triggered lots of unwelcome memories. How did she take it?'

'I'm grateful for her kindness to me over the years. Although I was a servant, we'd grown quite close. But since discovering who I am, her attitude towards me changed in an instant.' Alice continued. 'She's living with her brother for the time being, and said there'll be no need for her to see me again. She said she will visit Connie and her family, but left me in no doubt that I must not be present.'

'Agatha had a nasty streak – when she had a mind to use it. She'll regret that one day. What did Connie say when she found out she'd got a sister?'

'She was shocked, but I hope she was pleased too. She said that if she was going to have a sister forced on her, she couldn't think of anybody better than me.'

Alice took a deep breath. 'I'm afraid I have some bad news for you, Elizabeth. Were you aware that Mr Copeland had passed away?'

Elizabeth nodded, and her bottom lip trembled. 'Word gets around in our circles. Perhaps now is the right time to start a new chapter in all our lives. I'm glad the story has come out and we can come together like this. I hope it'll be one of many meetings in the future. It's been an intense morning, but I think we can say that we've both learned something about each other. Now tell me about your wedding plans. I'm sure Philip won't mind our staying here a little longer.'

'We haven't made any yet,' said Walter. 'But Alice is very good at making lists, so she'll keep us on the straight and narrow.' He took Alice's hand again. 'Somewhere to rent once we're married will be high on the list. I've already put our name down for a colliery house, and we should stand a good chance of getting one, due to me being a pit deputy.'

'So you plan to rent to somewhere first?'

'When I put my name down, I knew nothing about Alice's money and salary thingy, so I just assumed we'd be like every other couple. We'd rent for the rest of our married life.'

'It doesn't have to be like that. It'll only take you a few months to save enough out of your income to buy a house outright. In the meantime, you could draw money out of your trust fund, Alice.'

Alice and Walter stared at each other.

'I can take money out of the trust fund?'

'It's your money. The terms of the trust require any advance payment to the recipient to be approved by the trustees. But that won't be a problem, as Mr Penfold and I are the two trustees.'

'So we could buy a house and furnish it now and not have to bother about renting?'

'As long as we bought somewhere close to my work and we had a garden for the children,' grinned Walter. 'It'd be an excellent start in life.'

'So you'd be happy to do that?' Alice smiled at him, her anxieties all but disappeared.

Walter rubbed his forehead. 'At one time I'd have said no, but as you've explained to me, the salary and the trust fund are compensation for your earlier life. And I don't see why you shouldn't have a house of your own.'

'It wouldn't be mine; it'd be ours. Both of our names would be on the deeds.'

'Well, in that case, I'm more than happy to go ahead with it. We've just got to find a house to buy.'

'Very well, before I leave the offices today, I shall instruct Mr Penfold to draw up a document for us all to sign,' said Elizabeth. 'I'm so pleased we've sorted it all out. I imagine you'll want to get the wedding organised next. Have you and Connie decided anything about your job yet?'

Alice shook her head. 'Not as such. The one thing I know is that I can't continue working at Holmorton Lodge under Connie. As a servant, I'd have to leave when we get married.' She paused. 'Connie's been a good friend to me over the years, and I don't want to let her down. I'm planning to leave at the end of January. That should give her sufficient time to find a replacement.'

'I think you're right, Alice. When you grow up with servants, you find it difficult to adapt to changing circumstances. We don't realise we're doing it. So I can imagine Connie will still, deep down, treat you as a servant.'

'That's why I've got to leave at the end of the month. Walter's in full agreement.' Alice licked her suddenly dry lips. 'I've something to ask you, Elizabeth. When the wedding takes place, would you do us the honour of attending? It'll only be a small affair, at the registry office in Hanley, and a celebration for friends and, I hope, family.'

'You don't want a church wedding?'

'No, neither Walter nor I are religious. So we thought that a family celebration would be the best.'

'If you're sure. I should hate to cause trouble at the very start of your life together.'

'I'll introduce you to everyone as my mother. I'll say that we'd been searching for each other for a long time and came together, with Walter's help, only a few months ago. Unfortunately, my father had already passed away, but meeting my mother was one of the best things that has happened to me.'

'I'd be delighted, my dear.' It was then Alice noticed the tears in Elizabeth's eyes, and her own eyes filled.

When the two women had regained their composure, Elizabeth asked if the couple would like something to eat before the return journey. The mention of food made Alice realise how hungry she was, and they accepted the invitation readily.

They left the solicitor's arm in arm to walk the few hundred yards to a small restaurant that Elizabeth used whenever she was in Manchester on business.

It had been a good day. Everything had gone well. Elizabeth and Walter appeared to get on. It'd meant so much to bring the two of them together. Alice just hadn't realised until now.

On their way back to The Potteries, she relaxed – and fell into a light snooze on Walter's shoulder as the train took them home.

–

Connie and Alice sat at the kitchen table the following day, as Connie was eager for news. A gale buffeted the house, shaking some windows. Alice was glad she wasn't travelling today. Yesterday had been tiring and would've been much worse in the weather they were currently experiencing.

How relieved she was that she and Walter had committed to each other before her changed circumstances came to light. They loved each other, and the money played no part in it. She was glad Robert had talked to him after Agatha's disparaging remarks at Christmas. He must have been in the same position as Walter, and he'd been able to overcome the difficulties.

'Alice! I'm talking to you,' muttered Connie. 'You're not listening.'

Alice shook herself awake. 'Sorry, Connie. It was a long day yesterday.'

'I asked if you've a date for your wedding?'

'No, but we'd like it to be soon. Walter and I are going to see the registrar next week to plan it out.'

'I only ask because I need to plan for your replacement. I never thought I'd be saying that. Somehow, I thought you'd always be here.'

'It's the same for me.'

'It goes to show there's no point in trying to predict the future. So, would you be quite happy to work until just before your marriage? If not, I'll need some notice.'

'I've made some plans, and I thought it only fair to give you one month's notice from today. I'll leave on 3 February.

Although we've not decided on the date, our friendship is too important to put at risk by my continuing to work here. Like it or not, I'll always be Alice, the servant who has spent her working life at Holmorton Lodge. It'll lead to tension, and we could end up arguing with each other and that wouldn't do.'

'I think I understand what you're saying, Alice. Although I don't necessarily agree with you. I wouldn't treat you as a servant, and I'd hate for us to argue.'

Alice said nothing. 'My plan is to find somewhere to stay in the short term until we're married. And then we can meet as sisters as often as we want to.'

'How am I going to manage without you? First Father died, then Mother went off to live with Uncle James, and now you're leaving and there'll be just me and Robert left.'

'And John Robert – and maybe another one or two little Caldwells in the future.'

'I suppose so. Surprisingly, I'm growing accustomed to the idea. But I won't have anyone to talk to like we used to. Remember going to join Sylvia Pankhurst's call to arms to the suffragettes? I ended up in prison and you in the safe house?'

Alice nodded. 'Mm, I do. I was only fifteen, but I'd every faith in you sorting it out, Connie.'

'It seems ages ago now – but if I have a little girl, I'm going to call her Sylvia Alice.'

Chapter Twenty-One

January 1922

Robert arrived home early from work, coughing and spluttering. Alice heard him before she saw him. His face was flushed. It could be influenza or the recurring problems with his lungs again.

'Are you all right, Robert? Do you want me to get the doctor?' she asked.

'No, Alice. I've just seen a doctor, and I feel a lot better. I'm going up to our room. Can you find Connie and ask her to come to me?'

'Yes, do you want any help?'

'No, just Connie.'

Later that afternoon Connie told Alice that he'd been taken to London Road Hospital as an emergency after he collapsed at work earlier in the morning. A doctor familiar with gas injuries from war service had seen him. He had given Robert the name of a specialist in Birmingham and a letter of introduction.

'I have the telephone number here. I'm going to contact him now and make an appointment. I hope it's nothing serious, Alice. I don't know what I would do.'

'Does Robert want anything?'

'No, he's going to have a nap until teatime.'

–

Alice and Walter made their way to the registrar's office beside the town hall to sort out their wedding day. They were lucky.

Nothing was taking place, so Alice hoped they'd get speedy answers to some of her questions. Walter knocked on the door and stood aside to let Alice enter first. A gentleman was sitting behind a large oak desk containing several files and papers. He was wearing a dark suit, and on his face he wore a pair of round spectacles, which gave him an air of importance.

Alice swallowed, but did as she had seen Connie do many times. She lifted her head high and strode towards him. She was wearing her best hat and coat because it gave her confidence, something she was a little short of at that moment, having done nothing like this before.

The man looked over the top of his glasses. 'What can I do for you?' he said in a deep voice, not unlike Uncle James's.

'I... we... want to get wed quickly and want to know how long it takes.' Alice's words came out before she had time to think.

His eyes travelled down to her belly. Her face burned as she realised he had made a wrong assumption.

Alice didn't know if Walter had seen the look she'd received, but he stepped in front of her and took over. 'My intended and I wish to marry as soon as possible because we love each other and conner see the point of waiting. Could you tell us how long it takes to get married and what's involved?'

'I see.' He looked a trifle suspicious, but opened the drawer of his desk and drew out a sheet of paper. 'You'll find everything you require in here, Mr...'

'...Latham, and Miss Alice Tucker of Holmorton Lodge.'

A smile crept onto his face. Alice saw at once how easy it was to get someone to believe you if you first believe in yourself. And Walter did. Perhaps the registrar was more used to talking to men.

'I see.' He sat back in his chair. 'Have you got a date in mind?'

'As soon as possible, like the lady said.'

'I'm assuming you're talking about a Saturday wedding?'

Alice nodded.

'That won't be possible. We're booked through the summer.'

'Well, why offer it if you've no vacancies?' Walter closed his eyes. He tried again. 'When could you do it?'

The gentleman pursed his lips. 'Most likely, it'd be September.'

'September! That's an eternity.'

'What if we get wed on a weekday?' said Alice.

'Weekdays are much easier.'

'What do we have to do to get a weekday?'

'In short, Mr Latham, you'll need to give this office twenty-eight days' notice of your intention to marry, and you've got to get married within twelve months of giving that notice.'

Alice nodded. 'I see.'

'You can apply for a special licence which would allow you to marry sooner, but that would cost you thirty pounds.'

Alice gasped.

'Might I assume you're both residents of England or Wales?'

'You may.'

'You must have two witnesses who'll attend with you and sign the document.'

'Is there anything else?'

'No, Miss Tucker. That paper explains everything.'

'Thank you. That's very helpful.'

She turned to Walter, and they skimmed through the information the registrar had given them. 'What d'yer think?'

'I checked the rota yesterday, and I think we should try for mid-February – say, 17 February. Would that be all right with you?'

Alice nodded. 'That's a Friday.'

'Could you check that date, please?'

The registrar flipped a couple of pages forward. 'I could do that date if it could be late afternoon – say four o'clock?'

'Are you happy with that, Alice?' Walter's eyes burned into hers.

Alice felt her heart miss a beat. She was getting married! Committing to a date made it all real. She couldn't breathe.

Her voice came out like a squeak. One word. 'Ye…s.'

'That's it then. Four o'clock on 17 February. Fill in the paperwork and return it to this office, giving us that twenty-eight-day notice.'

He rose to his feet and bowed his head. 'Good day, Miss Tucker. Mr Latham.'

Once they were outside again, Alice took a deep breath.

'We've done it, Walter. We're getting married!' Alice felt like doing a dance in the street, but she didn't know how Walter would take it. At one point she had thought Walter might come to blows in there. Thirty pounds for a special licence – how on earth could people afford such a luxury? Then she remembered. Of course she could afford it. She was a woman of means now. But thirty pounds was more than a year's wages! And that was just for the marriage. Then there was the celebration meal and welcoming their friends to join them for the evening. No, Walter would never agree to spending all that money.

'I felt like punching him on the nose,' muttered Walter.

'Walter! He's doing his job. No point in getting into a tizz.'

'It's not that, Alice. That'll be our special day, and I want what's best for you.'

'Don't think like that. I agree. It's our special day. Ours, Walter. Let's go to the Albion Hotel and see if we can hold our reception there.' She grabbed his hand and hurried towards the main road.

The Albion Hotel was just opposite the registrar's, at the top of Lichfield Street. Overall, it was a splendid-looking building in red brick with fancy windows suggesting three floors. She had never walked into a place so grand. Now she was inside making enquiries for her wedding celebration with her intended.

She lifted her head high and opened the door, with Walter on her heels. In front of them was a desk at which sat a man who appeared to be making up invoices.

Together, they walked towards him, and it was Walter who asked the questions this time. Someone showed them to a seat to await the catering manager, who could give details about the food and check the date's availability. Alice waited anxiously until he returned and confirmed their reservation. They gave him a few details with a promise to send an initial ten-pound booking fee to reserve the date.

Alice felt like singing all the way back to Holmorton Lodge. The wedding was happening, and she couldn't be happier.

Once all the wedding arrangements were booked, Walter took his leave and hurried off to work the afternoon shift, leaving a happy Alice to make her way back to Holmorton Lodge. She scurried round to the back door as usual and rushed into the kitchen, where Patty was completing Connie's dinner.

'I'm glad yer back, Alice. Connie's been wandering around and watching what I'm doing. Can you take her dinner into the dining room? I've got an idea she's looking for somebody to talk to.'

Alice smiled. 'Of course.'

Alice picked up the tray, complete with sandwiches and a pot of tea, and set off. She felt like singing, but hummed instead.

When she opened the dining-room door, Connie glanced up. 'Oh, thank goodness you're back, Alice. Did you get everything done?'

Alice beamed. 'Oh, yes, and I've got good news. We've set the date! 17 February, which means I can give you a month's notice like we agreed.'

'Oh, right. I mean – sit down, Alice.'

Alice pulled out a chair and sat beside her. She had hoped Connie would be happy. She had done as they'd both agreed.

'The time will go past so quickly, it might leave you wishing you had longer. What about staying here until you get married? It saves you looking for somewhere for such a short time.'

Alice had been keen to move out before the wedding so she could prepare herself for the days ahead, but also because she didn't want to feel put upon by Connie. With hindsight, and the short period until the wedding, it would be to everyone's benefit to remain where she was.

'That sounds perfect, Connie.'

With faces alight with smiles, they chatted through the plans Alice had made so far.

–

On the Saturday, Alice and Walter took a walk up Dartmouth Street to High Lane, and a building site on Marsh Avenue where a Mr O'Donnell was building four semi-detached houses. He had already built six houses on High Lane. These four houses were almost finished. Mr Railsford had told Alice they would be an excellent investment and assured her that the builder had a good reputation. Alice agreed to meet the builder at three o'clock, as Walter was on the early shift.

'Good afternoon, you must be Miss Tucker. I'm Pádraig O'Donnell.'

'Good afternoon, Mr O'Donnell. This is my fiancé, Walter Latham.'

'I gather you're in the market for a new house. A worthwhile investment, I'd say. But you'll have to be quick. I'll finish these four houses in February, and then I'll start on four more opposite. I've sold the first, third and fourth ones of these, but the second one's available now.'

'Can we see inside?'

'Yes,' said Mr O'Donnell. 'Follow me.'

Alice waited a moment, picturing how they'd look when finished. Fields lay at the road's end. The distant village of Bradeley boasted a cluster of new houses and their allotments.

Walter and Alice stepped inside.

'It's well built, and the joinery's very good. All the internal walls are brick. The floors will be redwood, which I'll polish if you wish,' said Mr O'Donnell, scratching his head.

Alice walked through the house. Downstairs, there was a front room, dining room, kitchen, scullery, and outbuildings. Upstairs were four double bedrooms, a bathroom and a separate toilet. There was a toilet downstairs and another one outside, and best of all, it had electric lights and no smelly gas lights.

'This is the kitchen, Miss Tucker.'

Alice's mouth dropped open. 'How big is it?'

'It's twenty-four feet by eighteen feet. You could feed an army in there. I hope you like cooking.'

'I like to cook.' Alice turned to Walter, her smile infectious. 'It sounds perfect, Walter. How much is all this going to cost?'

Mr O'Donnell had the gift of the gab, telling them every reason it should cost more. In the end he said that, finished with tiled floors downstairs and polished floors upstairs, the cost would be £399. Alice put a hand on Walter's arm to stop him from speaking.

'That's a lot more than we had in mind. What do you think, Walter?'

'It'll make a dent in me savings.' Walter was getting into the swing of Alice's strategy.

'It's a very well-built house. You'll not find a better-built house in the whole of The Potteries. Across the road, the houses we're building will be £425 finished like this one.'

Alice turned to Mr O'Donnell and said, 'You'll have the money, in full, from us on the day it's completed. Bearing that in mind, I think a fair offer would be £375.'

'You're taking the bread out of my children's mouths. I'll need more than that.'

'Mr O'Donnell, we're a young couple just starting out. It's all we've got. But the money is in the bank account right now.'

Mr O'Donnell thought for a moment and then spat on his hand and offered it to her to shake. Alice closed her eyes and reciprocated – it was a small price to pay. She was pleased with her first exercise in bargaining. Alice insisted Mr Donnell shook hands with Walter too.

On their return walk, they talked about the house.

'My word, Alice, you played a blinder in there.' He was surprised, even impressed, by her newly developed negotiating skills.

She linked his arm. 'I asked myself what Connie would do,' she giggled.

Most of the way home he talked about the garden and, for the first time, she could see how much the prospect of a garden of his own excited Walter.

'There'll be plenty of room for our children.'

Alice felt her cheeks redden – and changed the subject. 'Yes, and a proper kitchen!'

–

Alice sent out invitation cards, and collected the replies as they came in. Most people had said yes, much to her delight.

By the return post, she received a friendly letter from Betty, who was still working in Birmingham. She was hoping to attend the reception, and would bring her daughter, Hannah, along too, if that was all right. There was no mention of Duncan, the man she had been engaged to, before changing her mind, yet again. Alice was sure they loved each other in their own way and was puzzled that they hadn't resolved their differences. They made a lovely couple. She couldn't wait to talk to Betty to see if they might get back together. Now that she was feeling more settled, she wanted all her friends to feel the same.

Alice's first job on Monday morning was to go down to Burslem to see Mr Railsford and to confirm that she and Walter were going to buy number 4 Marsh Avenue at a price, agreed with Mr O'Donnell, of £375. She instructed him to include the extra tiling and polishing, and that the purchase must be completed by 7 February, as they wanted to move in before their wedding on 17 February.

She walked around Burslem, feeling very proud of her accomplishments so far. She had seen the look of surprise on

Mr Railsford's face as she passed him the list she had written out.

'Thank you for your help, Mr Railsford, and good day to you.'

She gave him her hand and held her head high. As she left him she had to cover her mouth for fear she might burst into laughter.

–

In less than a month, Robert's breathing problems returned. Each time he took ill, it seemed to be worse, and lasted longer.

Connie and Alice were sitting in the kitchen with a cup of tea and some toast. It was Alice's usual time for breakfast, but Connie had risen early to see Robert off on his visit to the specialist.

'He should be on the train by now,' said Connie as she glanced up at the large kitchen clock. 'I hope he's going to be all right. I wanted to go with him, but he said there was no point and John Robert might need me.'

'He'll be fine, Connie. I should think a man who works as an inspector on the trams in Stoke can find his way to Birmingham by train.'

They laughed.

'I'm still worried about him, though. These coughs are getting worse – and more frequent.'

Alice said nothing, but she too had noticed Robert's coughing had been getting worse. 'It's that horrible weather we've had in the last few weeks. The smoke from the potbanks never seems to clear. It just hangs around. I've had to dry all the clothes inside the scullery. He'll be better when the spring comes.'

'I'm so worried about him, Alice. And it's all due to what happened during the war. It was a relief for him, no doubt, to get out of that carnage – but it seems it'll be with him for the rest of his life.'

'He's never going to get better?'

Connie shook her head. 'His doctor said that if we stay here, in The Potteries, it could shorten his life. The smoke and poor air are having a detrimental effect on him.'

'Oh, my word. Poor Robert. So what did he recommend?'

'He says we should think of somewhere near the sea.'

Alice pursed her lips. 'You can't get much further from the sea than here.'

'I know, but if we don't, his future doesn't look rosy. If we do nothing, he could be dead in three years and even if he gets an inside job, perhaps six years. If we move to somewhere more suitable, away from industrial towns and the like, then it could be near normal again, if he looks after himself. We'll know better after today – after he's seen the specialist.'

Alice shook her head. 'I can't believe it. Not of Robert. What does your moth—Agatha think of this?'

'She's shocked by it all, naturally. She said, "damn the war," in the heat of the moment. She even surprised herself, Alice. Can you imagine her saying that? I've never heard her swear.'

Robert arrived home just after two o'clock. Alice heard the front door close and hurried out of the kitchen just as Connie, having heard Robert's voice, joined him in the hall.

'Let me take your coat, Robert, and you can sit down while I make you a drink. Do you want anything to eat?' Alice asked.

'No, Alice, thank you. I had a sandwich at the station buffet. I also had a cup of tea, which was feeble.' He gave a wry grin. 'The woman behind the counter said I need to be reminded that tea is expensive and what did I expect for tuppence?'

'I should go up to have a rest if I were you.' Connie gave him a kiss on his forehead. 'I'll come up with the tea once Alice has made it.'

'Yes, Connie, I'll make it straight away.'

Robert walked up the stairs slower than usual, as Alice and Connie gave each other a concerned look.

Alice prepared a tray for Connie to take up, and didn't see her again until teatime.

After they'd eaten, Connie, Robert and Alice settled themselves in the sitting room where it was warmer with the thick curtains closed, shutting out the rain that appeared to be turning to sleet.

'The specialist's view was identical to the doctor's thoughts. I need to rest. There's no cure for my lungs. Moving to a cleaner environment, like the seaside or countryside, could reduce my susceptibility to infection.'

Connie stared at Robert. 'We'll have to sell the house.' Connie waved her arms around. 'Leave all of this… everything.'

'Yes, I can't see any alternative.'

'But where will you go?' said Alice.

Connie took charge. 'It's obvious that we can't let things continue as they are, but it's going to be hard to find somewhere like this, anywhere.'

'I'm thinking of somewhere much smaller, but with a large garden. And a dog.'

Alice smiled to herself and wondered if Rex was interested in moving.

'You'll miss the PTC, won't you?' said Connie.

'Well, yes, I suppose I will, but I wouldn't let that stop me if I thought it was the right move for us to make.'

'And do you? Think it's right?'

Robert's shoulders sagged a little. 'Yes, I see it as the only solution, but I don't want to force you to leave your home.'

'Our home, Robert.'

'No, it's yours, Connie. I could never think of this place as ours.'

Connie exploded. 'Well, that's it then! I don't care about this house, Robert. I care about you, and if that means we need to move, then move we shall.'

All this time, Alice had been watching their reactions to each other's comments. They were trying to do what was best for the other, just like her friends, just like she was with Walter.

'What do you think, Alice?'

Alice jumped as Robert said her name. 'Oh, I… er, suppose there's no point in having a lovely home that's causing you to be ill, is there? But have you thought about where you might go?'

Robert shrugged his shoulders. 'Norfolk would be my first choice, on the coast.'

'But Robert, I've never been further than Birmingham – apart from that trip to London for the suffragette march, and we all know what happened then.'

'You'd love it, Connie. When I worked in London, before the war, I'd travel up to the coast just to take in that sea air. The whole county is farming, with little in the way of industry. There are mainline railway stations at Norwich and King's Lynn, so visiting here wouldn't be a problem. On the coast in the north of the county, there're strings of small villages with flint cottages. I'm sure we could find somewhere we like.'

'Well, it seems like you've already made your choice, Robert,' said Alice, smiling. 'The coast sounds lovely. I can see you walking a dog,' she said, and noticed Robert winked as if thanking her for her support.

Alice was happy to bow out at that point. In her opinion, Robert was the likely winner, and they should set their sights on Norfolk. But how much she would miss them.

–

Later that evening Connie sat down with Alice. She looked pale-faced and her shoulders drooped. 'We're going to follow the specialist's advice and move to the coast. I've spoken with Mr Railsford, and his advice is to sell both the house and the contents by auction. We can't possibly take everything with us.'

'Of course, I understand, Connie. I thought it might be the likely outcome.'

'He'll co-ordinate the sale, but he needs us to work on a full inventory, splitting the contents between those to be sold at auction and those items we're keeping.'

'That will be a task.'

'I'd be grateful if you'll help, as you know so much about the house.'

'Have you decided when the auction will take place?'

'The auctioneers have suggested it takes place in the week before Easter, giving time for the catalogue to be drawn up and the house viewed by prospective purchasers. Besides, we need time to find somewhere in Norfolk. We're going to rent in case we don't enjoy living away from The Potteries.'

'Have you told your mother?'

'Not yet. We need you to keep this to yourself until I've had a chance to speak to her.'

'Are you worried about telling her?'

'I'm concerned for her, given everything that has gone on the past few months. She always said that the house was mine to do with as I wished. But I'm not sure she thought I'd ever sell.'

'What's the plan then?'

'We're going to visit Norfolk and will be back before your wedding. I wouldn't miss that for all the tea in China. Nanny Lily will stay here with John Robert. I'm no longer breast-feeding, so my presence isn't required.'

'What does Nanny Lily know?'

'We've told her we're going on holiday to help Robert recuperate. When we move, we'll take her with us, if she's agreeable.'

'What about Patty?'

'Oh, she's too young to consider taking her. We'll need an experienced cook and someone to manage the house. She's not ready for any of those tasks.'

Connie looked away for a moment and then turned towards Alice with tears in her eyes. 'I don't know how I'm going to manage without you. You always keep me on the straight and narrow.' Connie picked up Alice's hand, showing off the beautiful ring that Walter had placed there. 'My friend, and now my dear sister. We should get closer together, not further apart.'

'Oh, Connie. I worry about you. Since Robert's illness, I've thought about you even more. It's made me wonder if I should leave getting wed until later – when you've settled yourselves in Norfolk.'

Connie stared at Alice, open-mouthed. 'Did you just say what I think you said, Alice Tucker? That you'd postpone your wedding because of me?'

'I… I suppose I did.' Alice couldn't believe she had blurted out what was on her mind. Whatever would Walter say? She put her hands to her cheeks. They felt as if they were on fire. She regretted her words – but they were out. How could she take them back?

Connie was staring at her, unable to utter a word.

'You're my sister,' said Alice, simply.

Connie burst into tears, pulling Alice towards her. 'Oh, Alice, dearest Alice. I'm going to miss you so much.'

They hugged each other, both of them in tears.

'To think you'd do that for me.'

Alice was glad Connie couldn't see her face. She was putting Connie before her beloved Walter. How could he forgive her for that?

'I'm glad that we've become sisters, Alice. I could never hope for one as good as you. And it is for that reason that I'd have to say thank you, but no, I can't allow you to do that for me. You have your own life to lead now, and I won't let you begin by letting Walter down. He worships you, and I know how much you love him.'

More hugs followed.

'We'll keep in touch, you and I, and let no one come between us.'

–

On the Tuesday, Robert received a call from Mr Taylor, the manager of the PTC based at the main offices in Stoke. He'd frowned when Alice told him who was calling and passed the earpiece to him. Connie, too, had heard the telephone ringing and had come into the hall to see who it was. Telephone calls were rare. Few people could afford them.

They could hear Robert's side of the conversation, but that was all. Robert's face grew solemn. 'I'll see you at five o'clock on Friday. Goodbye, Mr Taylor,' he said replacing the earpiece.

He turned to Connie. 'He's coming to see me at five o'clock on Friday. He wants to discuss how I am, he says. I very much doubt he's going to bring me a present.'

He walked off towards the library, with Connie trailing behind.

Patty stared after them. 'What do you think about that, Alice?'

'I suppose we shall find out soon enough.'

By dinnertime, Connie looked to have perked up. 'I've had an idea, Alice. I've thought about what I can do for Robert.'

'What is it?' Alice's head tipped sideways.

'I need to talk to his family again. Tell them he's poorly. Tell his brothers to get his mother and father here. They were supportive when I asked them to come to our wedding. Between them they might convince Mr Caldwell – I think.'

Alice shook her head. 'And it didn't do any good. They refused to come to your wedding, and you got a telling-off from Robert.'

'But this time it's different, Alice. If they don't come to see him soon, they might be too late.'

'You'd go as far as that?'

Connie lifted her stubborn chin. 'I'll do what it takes to get them together again.'

'Even if Robert's told you not to.'

Again, Connie nodded – with less conviction, but nonetheless, it carried the sound of a woman who had decided. 'I shall go to their shop in Newcastle; it's only the other side of Hanley. I'll think of something to tell Robert. I need to get something for your wedding. If the Caldwells choose not to let me in, so be it. At least I will have tried. Besides, if I let it be known in the shop that he's ill – they can hardly throw me out, can they?' Connie said. 'I'll decide whether to tell Robert once I know their answer.'

'Then I'm coming with you.'

Connie's eyes opened wide. 'You'd come with me?'

'Why not? I'm your sister, aren't I? I can provide moral support even if I say nothing.'

Connie blinked away more tears as they gathered. 'Thank you, Alice. I have to feel I'm doing something for Robert. His family show no interest in him. And all because he never followed his father and brothers into the army. His brothers have accepted it – so why can't his father and mother?'

'There are some people who just won't listen, Connie.'

'They should at least know Robert is ill. What if something happens to him and they haven't resolved their differences?'

'You got into such trouble with Robert for ignoring him last time.'

'I need to do it, Alice. And I shall take John Robert with me. Maybe he'll succeed where I failed. How could his grandparents see him and not want to have more to do with their grandson?'

They agreed not to take the perambulator with them, enabling Connie to order a taxi, which arrived at half past one. The Caldwells' shop, a haberdashery, was in Newcastle-under-Lyme, which most people living in that area would insist wasn't part of The Potteries.

'No second thoughts then, Connie?'

'None whatsoever. They need to know, Alice. Supposing Robert gets worse. I'd never forgive myself for not telling them – no matter what Robert said. I'm sure that, deep down, he wants to build bridges.'

Alice nodded. 'Well, I hope you're right!'

'Anyway, how're you and Walter getting along? Have you got everything ready for the wedding? Anything I can help with?'

Alice's cheeks flushed. They had talked little since the engagement. Connie had been so busy with John Robert and Robert's health that they had barely spoken.

'We're doing fine, Connie. I'm more than pleased. I've been a little worried that my discoveries about my family might put him off.'

'Why?'

'I'm not the woman he fell in love with, am I? Sometimes I think it would've been better if I'd found nothing.'

'But then we wouldn't know we were sisters, would we?' Connie linked her arm through Alice's as the taxi headed down the hill towards Newcastle.

Connie was right. Sometimes a chance must be taken to make things happen. Alice smiled, crossing her fingers.

-

The Caldwells' shop was empty when Connie opened the door, with Alice holding John Robert. She felt a certain amount of relief that this first part of the meeting would take place without onlookers. Much as Connie had sounded well-prepared, Alice wasn't sure she could take on Mr Caldwell, a former soldier of the old school, used to getting what he wanted, going by what Connie said after meeting him almost two years ago. Two years was a long time, and she didn't blame Connie for doing what she could to bring them together again.

The curtain that hid the entry to the back of the shop swished to one side and an older woman entered. The smile on her face disappeared.

'Can I hel— oh, it's you.'

'Good afternoon, Mrs Caldwell. I hope you're keeping well.'

Mrs Caldwell nodded.

'This is my… friend, Alice. Alice, meet Mrs Adelaide Caldwell, Robert's mother.'

Their eyes turned towards Alice. Connie's introduction came out of the blue and, for the first time in her life, Alice felt an equal. 'Pleased to meet you, Mrs Caldwell,' she said, extending her hand so as not to disturb John Robert.

The woman looked at her and then at the baby, no doubt wondering whether she was its mother.

'I'll get somebody to come down and look after the shop if you give me a minute.' Without another word, Adelaide disappeared into the back and returned with a woman who looked to be in her early twenties.

'Come with me,' Mrs Caldwell beckoned to Connie.

They walked through a room full of shelves laden with boxes of stock, Alice presumed, and continued towards a staircase leading to the family living quarters.

Mr Caldwell was stoking the fire as Connie and Alice entered.

'We've got visitors, William.'

'Oh, it's you. Has Robert sent you?'

'He doesn't know I'm here. I've brought your grandchild to see you, Mr Caldwell.' Connie moved to one side so that Alice could bring forward the baby.

'Oh, my word!'

Mrs Caldwell was almost in tears, and Alice knew the battle was won.

Connie lifted John Robert into her arms and walked towards Adelaide Caldwell. 'He's your first grandchild. His name is John Robert. Would you like to hold him?'

Adelaide put a hand to her chest and then took him from Connie with great care, cradling him in her arms. 'How is Robert?'

'That's why we're here. He's been unwell and is getting worse. The last bout he had was just last week.'

Adelaide motioned to both of them to sit down. 'I see.'

'No, Adelaide, and forgive me, but I don't think you do.'

Startled, Adelaide took her eyes from John Robert to Connie, and then to her husband before returning to Connie.

'He's been getting worse these last couple of years, but last week he had to go to see a specialist in lung diseases.'

Both Caldwells opened their eyes wide, but again, it was Adelaide who replied. 'Is he… is he getting better?'

'No, he isn't. He's been told he has to move away – to the coast – or somewhere where the air is better for his lungs.'

Adelaide took a sharp intake of breath. 'Oh, my poor Robert.'

'He's had problems ever since he returned from the war—'

'Dunner tell me he took part in the war, my girl. He never joined up. He was never a soldier. Why should we welcome him back into our home when he let us down so badly? Our Stanley and Andrew are still serving out there, doing what they can for their country. And what's Robert doing? Inspecting trams, for Christ's sake.'

The outburst came from Mr Caldwell. Connie's eyes blazed. 'How dare you talk like that about my husband? He didn't go to war to kill people. He went to save lives, Mr Caldwell. He deserved a medal for what he did. Going out onto the battlefield with no protection to help bring back the wounded. Working in casualty stations and all sorts. Don't ever hint he didn't care for his country.'

William looked startled at the venom in Connie's voice. Alice, shocked, felt the need to say something. 'Mr Caldwell, Robert is very ill, and he needs help. He'll die if he doesn't leave. Connie wanted you to see your grandchild before they move away.'

Connie took John Robert from Adelaide and cradled him in her arms.

Alice's words had given Connie the chance to calm down, as Alice hoped they would. There'd be no benefit in losing her temper. But Robert's self-righteous father had rubbed Connie up the wrong way again – just like the last time she had tried to intervene on Robert's behalf.

'We shall take our leave of you now,' she muttered. 'Our door will always be open to you, if you wish, and I'll write to let you know our new address when we move.'

With that, they said their goodbyes and left.

Alice felt sorry for Adelaide, who wanted Robert back in her life. If anyone could talk William round, it'd be her.

–

It fell to Alice to open the door to the very smart-looking man. He walked into the house at Alice's bidding, and she took him to the library where Robert was waiting to receive him.

Before she could announce him, the man strode forward. 'Ha, Robert, good to see you.'

Alice closed the door behind her and returned to the kitchen to be met by an inquisitive Patty. 'What's he like?'

'Mr Taylor, he's well-dressed, hair turning grey at his sideburns, wearing round spectacles, tall and possibly ignorant. Do you know he ignored me completely?' Alice continued without stopping. 'Is there anything else you want to know, Patty?'

'I suppose not. I was interested, that's all.'

She walked off in a huff.

Alice was sorry for being short with her, but she couldn't get over her own anxieties.

As Alice and Patty were preparing the tea, Connie came in. Alice pushed her thoughts to the back of her mind and watched Connie's face to see if she could make out whether she had good news or bad, although she wasn't sure what good news would sound like. She stood beside the table. The two workers stopped what they were doing. Connie's face held no emotion as she spoke.

'As you're both aware, Mr Taylor from the PTC called to speak to Robert about his health this afternoon. He's decided that Robert has done enough for his country and it was time he looked after himself. Reading between the lines, the PTC doesn't want an inspector who can't do his job because it involves him being outside in the dirty air of The Potteries.'

'Oh dear!' Patty murmured before she could stop herself.

Connie ignored her. 'Mr Taylor is sorry to lose him, but believes Robert must look after himself and, if it requires Robert to give up his job, then that's what he must do.' She sent a quick glance towards Alice – to warn her to say nothing more. 'Thank you, both of you.' She turned on her heel and left.

Patty came round the table. 'That looks bad for us, doesn't it? If Mr Caldwell loses his job, they're never going to keep us both on. Don't suppose it'll matter to you, cos you'll be leaving any road, but it looks like I'll be looking at the jobs page in *The Sentinel* from now on.'

'Wait and see, Patty.'

'D'yer think I'll need to look for another job?'

'I don't know, Patty. Just get on with your job – while you still have it!'

Alice didn't mean to be harsh, but she needed time to think. Patty backed out of the kitchen and disappeared.

Damn! All these secrets were hard work. But she had given her word to Connie and would have to let it run its course.

–

Uncle James arrived at Holmorton Lodge about half past ten and took Connie and Robert to Mr Railsford's offices to discuss the sale. Alice couldn't get the thoughts of the sale out of her mind as she worked. Patty was silent and preferred to work upstairs on her own. Alice let her, not wanting any responsibility for keeping Patty in the dark about her future.

When the Caldwells returned, they told Alice Mr Railsford had contacted a local surveyor and they would draw an accurate site plan of the inside and the outside of the house and the boundaries of the land. The house would be auctioned together with its contents, so anything that was not to be sold should be removed prior to the sale.

Mr Railsford said this type of sale attracted all sorts, but the auctioneers would arrange and manage viewings.

'We don't even have to be there,' said Connie. 'The auction will be held on 12 April, a Wednesday.'

'It all sounds so clinical. It's your home we're talking about.'

'It's only possessions. But I know they mean a lot to people, which is why both Mother and I are taking items of sentimental value. Mark up any items you want to take, by the way. I think you should have all the pots, pans and cooking crockery because they'll come in handy for Marsh Avenue.'

'I will, and I was hoping you would say that. I'm so used to using them.'

'Well, they're no use to me.'

They laughed, as Connie's culinary skills had always been a source of amusement between them.

–

Mr Finney from Butters Auctioneers arrived at nine o'clock in the morning and got straight down to business. They started the inventory in the kitchen. They did the same in each room, even down to the contents of the outbuildings.

'Well, ladies, thank you very much. Everything was organised and easy to catalogue. The draft should be with you in a few days. I've also made a list of items which I consider worth inspection by specialist dealers.'

'What's the reason for that?' asked Connie.

'In all auctions of properties like this, there are items which can be of considerable value. Where I think this is the case, we get a trained eye in to look at them to enable us to fix a realistic guide price.'

'Was there anything in particular you had in mind?'

'Some paintings are originals by lesser-known artists, and it's always difficult to judge the market. The house's decorative china is also in demand, as several pieces are rare.'

'I shall wait with interest to see what the catalogue says.'

'I'll bid you ladies goodbye.'

He popped his bowler hat on his bald head and marched out of the front door without another word.

On the Thursday of that week, Alice discovered how things were in the Adams household. With everything going on, she'd had no opportunity to ask Jean about Luke. So when Alice heard Robert mention Luke by name, she stopped collecting the dirty plates and leftovers.

'Jean told me they were taking Luke in, to give him somewhere to stay, when I saw her last. Have you heard how it is working out?' she asked.

'Well, once the boy was well enough to be up and about, Jean told him he would need to go to school. She said he looked shocked. I don't think the idea had crossed his mind, or he'd conveniently forgotten.' Robert grinned. 'He's an interesting lad. Got something about him. Anyway, it seems he wasn't too keen, but they talked him into it. A couple of weeks later, the teacher called and asked Stephen why Luke had registered as a pupil but had only attended twice. He hadn't been in school, so the teacher hadn't been able to question him. Were they aware that it was a requirement for children to attend school?'

Alice's eyes bulged. 'Oh, my word.' Alice lowered herself into a seat at the table.

Connie shook her head. 'Poor Jean. I hope she hasn't bitten off more than she can chew.'

Alice frowned. 'Has Jean said why Luke didn't turn up, Robert?'

'The boy's exact words were, "That wasn't part of the deal." Cheeky little tyke.'

Alice covered her mouth with a hand to hide a grin. She thought Luke had got a nerve to suggest that school was not discussed. You have to admire his cheek. She remembered that workhouse children resented the forced school attendance, where they frequently faced ridicule and bullying. Parents might keep kids home from school to run errands or work to supplement family income. Workhouse kids had no choice.

'Anyway, Stephen says he's laid down the law and told Luke he must go to school. Luke might not have thought it was part of the "original deal", but it was now. Jean asked Luke if he wanted to see Stephen in trouble for keeping him out of school. Luke argued it was his own decision, but Stephen said it wasn't for him to decide to break the law. Anyway, he's agreed to go back to school.'

–

There was further news. Connie received a letter from Mrs Caldwell to inform her she and Mr Caldwell intended to pay them a visit on Sunday, 29 January. Connie was relieved, but now she had to break the news to Robert – and no doubt face his wrath again.

Connie was quite crafty. She told Robert when Alice was with them, knowing full well he wouldn't be too confrontational in public.

'Robert, dear. Your parents are coming to see us on Sunday. I invited them so they could see John Robert.'

'You did what?'

'I invited your parents to visit.'

'After all I said when you tried to get them to come to our wedding? Have you got no sense, Connie?'

Alice bit her lip. She hadn't wanted to be around when Connie told him, but Connie had insisted: 'You know I did the right thing by asking them, Alice. Now, I need you to be on my side.'

Connie explained her reasons about them making up before it was too late – although she hadn't elaborated on the 'too late' bit. She had left that to him to digest. But she tried a different angle.

'I did it because we're thinking of moving away – hundreds of miles, Robert. They might never see their grandchild. They need to know that.'

Robert turned, frowning at Alice. 'Were you in on this?'

'I told Alice to come with me to help with John Robert. She didn't know what I was going to do.' She let that sink in for a few seconds. 'I gave them the opportunity to see our son. Your mother was quite overcome when she saw him.'

'She was?'

'How could she resist? You underestimate a baby's powers, my love.'

Robert sighed, but Alice could see signs he was relaxing.

Connie spied her moment. 'One more try, Robert – that's all I ask.'

–

Mr and Mrs Caldwell arrived at two o'clock on Sunday afternoon and were welcomed by a smiling Patty, who was now aware of the issues around Robert and his family. Alice had made her promise not to mention a word of it to anyone else.

The atmosphere became tense as both parents walked into Holmorton Lodge. In her letter to Connie, Mrs Caldwell had said she had told her husband to behave himself and to forget about the war. Their other boys had insisted to her that Robert had been just as brave as them. The war was over and pray to God nothing like that ever happens again.

Mr Caldwell had called Robert a coward during the war for refusing to join the army. What he hadn't acknowledged was that his son had played a far more dangerous game by joining the Friends' Ambulance Unit who would go out into no-man's-land to pick up casualties, without weapons, to protect them.

After Connie had persuaded the brothers to go to the wedding, Robert had received letters of commendation from both of them, for whom the army was a way of life.

Connie invited Robert and his father to have a chat in the library while she took his mother upstairs to see John Robert again. The two men were still in there when Connie returned, much to her relief. She had checked with Patty that there'd been no raised voices.

Alice watched Connie's face as she sank onto the settee. She looked so much better seeing Robert interacting with his family after all this time. He'd been so alone – but no more. It'd take time to heal completely because there'd been a lot of hurt on both sides.

Robert's parents stated their intention to visit again regularly until Robert and Connie moved. Once Holmorton Lodge was sold, Robert told them he would invite his family to visit their new home.

They stayed for a couple of hours, and when they decided it was time to go, it seemed with sadness that the afternoon had ended. As she left, Mrs Caldwell gave Connie a hug, and Alice saw her whisper something in her ear.

'Anything you'd care to repeat?' Alice asked as the two of them walked arm in arm into the sitting room to tidy up.

Connie smiled. 'She said thank you for bringing the buggers together again.'

Alice's eyes widened in shock and the two burst out laughing.

'I think I'll get to like my mother-in-law after all!'

Chapter Twenty-Two

February 1922

Alice brought her household journal up to date with everything she had ordered for the next month from each of the shops she frequented for the family. It was the same journal she had accepted from Janet Williams when she retired.

She remembered buying another journal a little while ago, when she started looking into her past, and wanted to write it all down, but so far, she'd done nothing with it. Perhaps now would be the time to begin. She rummaged through her chest of drawers before discovering it at the bottom of the wardrobe.

She ran her fingers over the soft cover, flicking over the crisp white paper. She would have to write neatly, with no mistakes. It would be something she could give to her children, if she was lucky enough to have any. She would show it to no one but Walter. He had become her soulmate. She could keep nothing from him, nor would she want to.

She took out a pen and a bottle of ink and stared at the blank page. Where should she start? She held the pen against her teeth as she thought, then nodded to herself.

This is the Journal of Alice Tucker, soon to be Alice Latham.

February 1922

Dear Journal

My name is Alice. I started my life as Alice Tucker – or at least I thought I did, but that wasn't the full story, which I soon discovered. The fact was I'd two names, and when I get married this month, I shall add a third. Born a Hamilton, adopted as a Tucker, and, I hope, married as a Latham. And now my life is taking another turn. Living at Holmorton Lodge has been an ordeal of late. Sometimes I feel I belong there, and then at other times, it's as if I am an outsider and the camaraderie I once felt has disappeared. I shall write about my experiences before I forget; after all, this will be the last month we will live in this house.

Connie and Robert are currently in Norfolk looking for a house, possibly a rental to start with, to ensure they are both happy with their new home. They have promised to be back in The Potteries for my wedding. I cannot imagine getting married and not having them to wish me – us – well. Not to have her with me would be unbearable. I also hope, for their sakes, that they can find somewhere to settle, although even now I cannot imagine my life without them once they are more than a tram ride away. We'll be separated by hundreds of miles.

I shall begin my life with Walter in Marsh Avenue. He's been so good to me, and I love him for it. He is the most caring man I know. I feel safe with him. But living with him – just the two of us – makes me feel nervous. It's the thought of committing for the rest of our lives. There has been little commitment in my life so far.

When I decided to search for my family, I was warned not to expect too much and that things might not turn out as I expected. I'm only now beginning to realise how true that was, and how unprepared I was for the discoveries I would make.

Alice looked up from her journal and sighed. The words she had written were neat, but could be neater. She would write as much as she could while she remembered her discoveries and how they had made her feel. She never wanted to forget her feelings.

She wrote for an hour, pouring out all she had gone through, leaving nothing out, then placed the journal in her desk drawer and took out the shopping list she had written.

–

Friday was Walter's last day of noons, and because he started nights on Sunday at ten o'clock, he got the whole of Saturday off, so it was an ideal opportunity to look at their new house and to plan how they would furnish it.

Alice put on her regular outside coat and thought back to last bonfire night, and the discussion that followed about her coat. Perhaps she would also look for a new coat today. Just as she was about to leave, the telephone rang. It was Mr Railsford.

'Good morning, Miss Tucker.'

'Morning, Mr Railsford. I hope you've got some good news for me.'

'Yes, the building inspector and the architect have agreed that the property at 4 Marsh Avenue is now complete and ready for occupation. The corporation's water and sewerage department have checked the drains. Mr Moreton went up himself yesterday and checked that all the electric lights worked and the gas supply was available. Mr O'Donnell has started the coal boiler, which appears to be working. I believe Mr Latham spent some time with Mr O'Donnell going over how various appliances work.'

'Oh, that sounds good. It'll be nice not to have to lay fires every day just to get warm.'

'All that remains now is for Walter and you to come into the office to sign the conveyance. Mr O'Donnell has already signed it and his solicitors are waiting for our payment, and then we'll exchange. I expect the exchange to take place this afternoon, and you should be able to collect the keys by four o'clock. The house will then be yours. I've received the purchase price along with my legal fees from your trust fund.'

'The entire process has gone smoothly. Walter told me that the builder has completed everything we asked him to do.'

'Yes, Miss Tucker, not all legal matters flow this smoothly, but I believe Mr O'Donnell wanted the money to start his new houses across the road and you want the house to move into after your wedding. It's surprising what a keen seller and a willing buyer can achieve. I look forward to seeing you soon.'

'Thank you, Mr Railsford. Goodbye.' Alice put the receiver back onto the cradle and took a moment to calm herself down. She put on her hat and picked up the shopping bag, and went to collect Walter.

An hour later, Alice and Walter left the solicitors having signed the conveyance and exchanged the documents and banker's draft for the keys. The house was now theirs. Everything seemed very real to Alice. In only two more weeks, they'd be married.

It took them twenty minutes to walk to their new house, which looked splendid in the sunshine on that frosty morning. Walter put the key into the lock and opened the door to their new house.

'Ladies first,' he said, giving her a bow.

'I feel quite weak inside.' She took a breath and entered.

They spent most of the morning looking around and measuring room sizes and windows for curtains, all of which were written in Alice's new journal. The early morning sunshine had given way to grey clouds, suggesting rain might follow. They locked the house and hurried to the tram stop at Smallthorne.

Once they arrived in Hanley, they treated themselves to a warm Parker's meat and potato pie. Alice recalled that Betty Dean's friend, Martha, was the daughter of the owner of these shops. The pies were delicious, made even more satisfying by seeing their new home.

Alice had decided to furnish two bedrooms and one room downstairs, and the dining room. There were so many things she would need. Her first priority was to decide on the large items. She sorted those, but the rest would have to wait.

They ended the day with a meal at the North Stafford Hotel and a taxi ride home.

Alice called at Burton & Dunn on Monday morning with a shopping list. The manager agreed to deliver the large items by 14 February as they were in stock at the warehouse. Alice selected a long list of other items for delivery, together with the furniture. She even negotiated a discount on the entire order.

Next she went to Cartlidge's, the drapers, and left orders for six sets of curtains. That too would do, for starters.

–

Patty had finished a pile of ironing and was tidying her hair and dress before going upstairs to put the clothes in their appointed places.

'The man who invents an ironing machine will make a fortune. I'd buy one,' she laughed. 'I'd better get the irons. I put them outside to cool.' Patty returned with three irons and checked they were cool enough to be put into the cupboard.

'I think we should talk to your mother about what will happen when I leave here and the house is sold. Have you said anything?'

'Course I have… and she's ever so pleased you're getting wed. Walter's a lovely man.'

'Very well, put your hat and coat on and we'll have a word with her.'

They chatted away as they took the short walk to Patty's house.

Rex, who always seemed to be eager to see Alice, was the first to greet them.

'Come in Alice, duck, and sit yerself down.'

The house was quiet. Mrs Goodwin grinned. 'It's all right, I haven't sold the kids. The boys are upstairs doing their homework – sums – and I think the girls are reading. No noise is often a sign they're up to mischief, but we were just enjoying the silence before the storm breaks.'

'Patty has told you I'm getting wed to Walter on the seventeenth, and I shall leave Holmorton Lodge. What do you want Patty to do? I can have a word with Mrs Caldwell about keeping her on?'

'Is Mrs Caldwell going to get a replacement for you?'

'Yes, but I don't know when. I thought she might have done so by now. I told her in January.'

'I dunner want Patty to stay working at Holmorton Lodge if you're not there. You've taken time to show her how to do things, and she enjoys the cooking so much. I'm worried if she stays there, she'll just get put on. She's too young for that.'

'I know what you mean. I'm concerned that they might try to manage without replacing me, so I'm glad you feel the same. Patty? How would you feel about coming to work for me?'

'To come to work at your new house? Yes, please!'

'I'll need a lot of help to get the house finished. I've decorated none of the walls, so there'll be a lot of work. When we've time, we can continue with the cooking lessons.'

'Will I have to live in?'

'I'm happy either way.'

'I'd like to live in, if that's possible.'

'How would you feel, Mrs Goodwin?'

'Couldn't be better as far as I'm concerned.'

Alice agreed to pay a little more than Patty was getting at Holmorton Lodge and allow her to have Saturdays and Sundays off.

Patty was so eager, a visit to the privy was called for, and Mrs Goodwin asked Alice if she wouldn't rather be on her own with Walter, as they'd be newlyweds. It took a few seconds for Alice to make the connection, and then she became embarrassed but regained her composure.

'That's what Saturdays and Sundays are for, and Patty's a sound sleeper.'

They laughed. Alice added, 'She will have her own facilities for privacy.'

'Can I move in as well? I'm getting too old for the tin bath,' said Mrs Goodwin, chuckling.

–

During the second part of February, the weather was mixed. Alice dressed in her Sunday best, a new black three-quarter-length woollen coat and matching hat, and headed off to Jean's house in Tunstall. She took with her the jumpers and socks she had knitted for Luke and hoped they would fit.

She boarded the tram at three o'clock and stared out of the dirt-streaked window, watching people going about their business. She stepped off in the centre of Tunstall, near to the public library, walked past the memorial gardens, and turned into Park Road.

Jean opened the door in response to her knock, and they hugged each other.

'It's good to see you, Alice. I've so much to tell you. Let's get comfy, and I'll fill you in.'

As she took off her coat, Alice couldn't tell from Jean's demeanour whether it was good news or bad. She hoped it was the former and that, if it was the latter, it didn't include Luke. The couple had been so good in welcoming him into their home that it'd be a great shame if their well-meaning actions had failed.

'Have a seat in the sitting room, Alice, and say hello to Stella. I'll be with you in a second or two.'

Alice obeyed, and Stella, sitting in the upright chair beside the fire, greeted her.

'I'm sorry, Alice. I'm afraid I can't get up.'

'Oh, are you unwell, Mrs Adams?'

Stephen's mother was about to reply when Jean reappeared bearing a large silver tray and carrying cups, saucers, teapot, milk jug, sugar bowl and an assortment of biscuits. Alice jumped to her feet and helped Jean to lay out her load on a table that was there for that purpose.

'Talking of not being well, Robert's having trouble with his chest again, Jean. He's coughing almost continuously, and it takes his breath away. Connie's had the doctor in twice, poor Robert, and he's seen a specialist.'

They all had their cups of tea and biscuits. Alice was about to ask Jean about Luke when Stella piped up.

'Has Jean told you that young Luke saved my life?'

Everyone went quiet.

Alice felt her mouth open and close like a fish. Not quite knowing what to say, she turned to Jean, her eyes full of questions.

'It wasn't quite like that, Stella.'

'It might not have been to you, Jean dear, but it felt like that to me.'

Alice felt herself to be in the middle of an argument between two women who each felt they were in charge.

'Would you like to tell Alice?' Jean's face was full of disappointment, but she had realised that the way to keep on favourable terms with her mother-in-law was to let her take charge.

'Well, it was a Wednesday, and Stephen and Jean were at their places of work, of course. Luke had gone to school, or so we thought.' Surprisingly, Stella giggled before carrying on. 'I was upstairs in my room sewing a nightdress that had a tear at the bottom where it must have caught on something. I decided some lace around the hem would hide my repair. I walked into the spare room to get the lace from the sideboard in there – or did I go straight downstairs? I'm not sure now.' Stella paused, her index finger on her chin.

Alice nodded, but Jean was on edge, as if she couldn't wait for Stella to get to the point. Stella winked at Alice. She was doing it on purpose! How did these two women live together? Alice tried her best to keep a straight face. There was no way she was going to side with either of them.

'You might as well carry on, Stella,' muttered Jean, sitting back in her chair, her arms folded.

'Well, Alice. I walked downstairs, and I came over faint. My head didn't feel my own. Believe it or not, I slipped and fell down the rest of the stairs.'

'You fell downstairs?' Alice's mouth fell open.

'She fell down two steps, Alice,' butted in Jean.

'And it was excruciating too, I don't mind saying.' Stella pursed her lips.

Jean relented. 'I'm sure it was very painful. Are you comfortable now?'

Stella nodded. 'I suspected I'd broken my ankle, and I was all alone in the house. Then I heard somebody whistling. I knew it was Luke. He often whistles when he's happy. I shouted to him, and when he saw me at the bottom of the stairs, he ran to me and asked me where it hurt. I told him about my ankle, and he lifted me up and put my arm around his shoulder and helped me to a chair. I lifted my dress a fraction, and I could see my leg was turning blue. He looked pale and said he would make me a cup of tea, and then he would get the doctor.'

'It was fortunate he was there and able to help,' said Alice. 'It must've been such a relief that you didn't have to lie there until Jean or Stephen got home.'

At that moment, the door to the sitting room opened. Luke stood in the doorway.

'Oh, I didn't know you had a guest, Mrs A. Just called to check you were all right.'

'Yes, I'm fine, Luke. Come and meet Alice. She works for Connie, Mr Caldwell's wife.'

He walked in. 'Pleased to meet you, Miss Alice.'

'She'll soon be Mrs Latham. She's getting married on Friday.'

'It's good to meet you at last, Luke. Jean has told me you're staying with her at the moment. Good job you were here to help Mrs Adams.'

'I only did what anyone would do, Miss Alice.'

Alice watched him as he was talking, taking in his straight dark hair, which needed a cut. He was taller than Alice had imagined, given that he was only ten. His hazel eyes were gentle.

'Call me Alice, Luke. I'm not used to being called anything else.'

Luke grinned, then turned to Stella. 'Best get on, Mrs A. I told Mr Adams I'd do some tidying in the garden.' With a nod, he strode towards the door and was gone.

'What a nice boy,' said Alice. 'He'll steal some girl's heart when he gets older!'

-

On the Monday before the wedding, Burton & Dunn delivered all the large furniture items, placing them in the rooms as Alice instructed.

She stared at the new furniture and furnishings now placed in the house belonging to her and Walter, unable to believe that it was all theirs, and hugged herself.

The house still looked bare, but it'd soon look like a home. Alice thought to herself that there were lots of things at Holmorton Lodge she would like, but she would put in bids for them at the auction in April.

-

As promised, Connie and Robert returned home in time for the wedding. They had good news. They'd found their perfect house, a furnished flint cottage with a large garden, on the edge of the village of Blakeney, and Alice was delighted for them.

Connie reported Robert's happiness after the discovery of five inns in the village. He laughed when he talked about them, but he said that it was more about the choice rather than the number of inns he could frequent. A considerable number of inshore fishing boats operated out of the port, which was one of the busiest in the Middle Ages, but the sea had receded, and the harbour was only accessible during high tide.

Alice was pleased for her sister, which she had now taken to calling her – in her mind, at least. More good news followed when Connie told her that Nanny Lily would be moving with them. It made sense.

All too soon, the day of Alice's departure from Holmorton Lodge arrived. Alice looked around her room, everything packed in suitcases and boxes. Not that she had very much – it would have fitted into one of Agatha's steamer trunks.

It brought back so many memories. Mrs Williams, for example. When she arrived, Alice couldn't boil an egg, and now she would try almost anything. She'd remembered the exciting journey to London with Connie for the demonstration in Trafalgar Square, Connie getting caught by the police while Alice spent a month in a safe house, near to Holloway prison. Mr Copeland had sacked Alice on the spot, saying it was all her fault. She was made to sit on her own in third class while he and Connie went first class, and all she could think about was being sent back to the workhouse. Connie and Agatha pleaded her case until Mr Copeland relented. Elizabeth may have been in love with him, but Alice's own views of Mr Copeland were very different.

She remembered Mr Bainbridge, the gardener and handyman. A reservist called up when the war started, who died at Mons. She remembered Connie being jilted at the altar and meeting her friends Jean and Betty when Connie became a clippie on the trams. And then there was fellow workhouse inmate Ginnie, whom Connie taught to read and write.

And then Connie, falling in love with Robert, had given Alice her first opportunity for matchmaking. When he was ill, Alice left them together by trotting off to buy something he needed – he must've had ten pounds of sugar in his food cupboard by the time he returned to work. She giggled as she closed the door.

It was gone eleven o'clock when Alice made her final rounds, checking windows and doors. She remembered Rex, Patty's dog, had followed her around, nuzzling her hand at each stop. She might think of having a dog one day. It would keep her company when Walter was working late.

–

The day of Alice's wedding was sunny, but with a bracing wind. Everything that had seemed to be beyond her reach was coming together. She had received a letter from Elizabeth confirming her attendance – and Alice had told Connie before her nerves got the better of her. When she first discussed the matter, Connie had agreed with her; she must invite her mother to the wedding celebrations.

Alice's excitement and apprehension had been building in equal proportions as the day passed. Connie must have realised and had kept her chatting, and Patty followed suit. They'd had a hectic morning. Alice couldn't help being surprised at the number of people who passed through Holmorton Lodge, leaving their best wishes together with a small present for her new home. Now, it was mid-afternoon, and they were ready to show off their new outfits. Alice wore a plain white cotton dress with a lace overlay and neckline that flattered her slim appearance, complemented by a wide sash at her waist and just short enough to show off her neat ankles. Connie's dress was similar but in a pale ivory.

Alice and Connie were together in the garden room ready to leave when Patty walked in carrying three posies and gave them one each, keeping one for herself.

'I thought it might make things special.'

'They look beautiful, Patty. What an excellent idea!' Alice hugged the girl, who blushed at the compliment.

'When you're on edge, Alice, it's best to find summat to do with your hands. It helps to calm you down. I felt a posy each might just do the trick. Sam picked them from his allotment's greenhouse, and Ginnie made the posies.'

Robert appeared at the door. 'Are you three beautiful ladies ready to leave?'

The three hurried towards him, and he gave each a hug.

When he came to Alice, she clasped him tightly. Why on earth she had been afraid of this man, she didn't know. 'Thank you, Robert.'

'It's the least I can do, Alice.' He looked into her eyes. 'With the number of times you've looked after me in the past, it's my pleasure to look after you on your special day.'

A car, polished until it glowed, waited by the front door, and they all stepped into it. They were meeting Frank, who was to be a witness, at the registrar's office. Robert sat in the front beside the driver, leaving Alice to chat with Connie, the second witness, and Patty, who insisted she was there to provide moral support and who'd wait for Alice to re-emerge from the registrar's office as Mrs Alice Latham.

They were shown to the room reserved for them while they waited for their appointment. Walter was already there. He watched her enter without saying a word. His eyes told her everything.

'Good afternoon, Miss Tucker. I'm pleased to see you,' said the registrar.

The happy couple moved forward with their witnesses. Connie felt for Alice's hand and squeezed it twice. 'For good luck,' she whispered, grinning, while Patty blew a kiss across the room.

Walter was looking so handsome, and he would soon be hers. Her eyes never left his. How wonderful this day was going to be!

'I must be the luckiest man in the world,' he whispered in her ear.

She crushed his hand, too choked to say anything.

'If you're ready, we can begin,' said the registrar, his face now serious.

They nodded.

He read the solemn words of the marriage ceremony, and Alice and Walter pledged themselves to each other, for better or worse.

It seemed to be over before it'd even begun. And then Walter kissed her, and it no longer mattered. They belonged to each other – forever.

Alice linked her husband's arm as they made their way over to the Albion Hotel, where the head waiter was standing at the door to welcome them. Another waiter led them to a private function room where their guests were waiting.

Herbert and Ruth Latham were the first to greet them. 'Mother would have been proud of you, Walter,' said Ruth.

His father gripped his son's hand. 'Well done, son.'

Alice caught sight of Elizabeth, who had just entered the ballroom, looking very smart in a pale blue dress with a matching jacket fitting tightly at the waist, emphasising her slimness. Even though Alice was expecting her, it still came as a bit of a shock to see her walk in alone. How brave she must be.

Alice hurried across the floor to greet her. 'I'm so glad you made it, and I do like your outfit.'

'Thank you, you've made an old woman thrilled. Congratulations, my dear! I'm so pleased for you and Walter.'

Alice kissed her mother and whispered, 'Thank you for everything.'

Connie and Robert, and Frank and Joan, made up the family party.

Alice was glad she had chosen a hot and warming meal of soup, roast chicken, and trifle for afters. The surprise of the meal was an exquisitely decorated wedding cake carried in by Patty.

'I've bin practising the icing while you've bin gallivanting about with Walter. One day you came back early, and I didn't half curse him,' she chuckled.

'You mean Walter was in on it?'

'Patty asks in such a way you conner say no,' muttered Walter, rubbing his nose.

Frank, as best man, made his speech, and Walter thanked everyone for coming. Alice broke with tradition and stood up to offer her thanks. 'Many of you will know I've spent some time searching for my family. I'm pleased to introduce you to Elizabeth Hamilton, my mother, who I think you all know of, but now you can put a face to the name.'

Everyone clapped, causing Elizabeth slight embarrassment, but Alice had linked her arm, determined to support her. The fact that Agatha and Uncle James weren't present didn't matter. They had their excuses planned; 'Illness prevented them from travelling.'

Frank announced, 'We've got this room until seven o'clock, when we can move through to the ballroom and join the rest of the guests. The ballroom opens at six o'clock, but there'll be no music until seven.'

Alice thought Frank managed that very well, as she had never heard him speak in public before. Walter said that even after winning the player of the year award at cricket, he had accepted his trophy with a 'thank you'. That would've been a long speech by his standards. Alice smiled at Frank, her new brother-in-law.

The staff moved in to clear the table and placed coffee, tea, and slices of the wedding cake on a side table. Now Alice had to carry out an important introduction. It was time to introduce Connie and Elizabeth to each other. She gulped. Introducing her newly found mother to her newly found sister had her panicking. Suppose it all went wrong? As they approached, Alice noticed Connie's flushed face.

'Connie, this is my mother, Elizabeth. I've told her so much about you.'

'Yes, you have. Hello, Connie, I'm very pleased to meet you.' Elizabeth lowered her voice. 'And I'm glad to find that Alice has a splendid sister. I couldn't wish for anything better for my daughter.'

A trickle of goosebumps ran up and down Alice's back. It'd been so long since anyone had called her 'daughter'. It brought tears to her eyes on this most emotional of days.

'I'm pleased to meet you… Elizabeth. Is it all right to call you that?' Connie held out her hand.

'Elizabeth, this is Constance Caldwell. She used to be Constance Copeland.'

'Call me Connie, Elizabeth, everybody does.'

'I see. Hello… Connie. I'm pleased to meet you too.'

'Alice has spent a lot of time looking for you.'

'Yes, I'm aware of that, and I hope to make it up to her.' Elizabeth's face flushed a little at Connie's tone. 'I agree, Connie. Life can be quite difficult. But nothing is insurmountable. Wouldn't you agree?'

'Yes, Elizabeth, I believe I do!'

To Alice's surprise, she witnessed a twinkle in Connie's eyes.

–

Alice and Walter waited outside the main entrance to the ballroom and, on a signal, the doors opened and Alice burst into laughter as the men from Walter's shift formed a guard of honour, with pickaxes crossed above their heads. The guests clapped and cheered.

Alice asked Walter to say a few words of welcome, and then she spoke. 'I too would like to welcome you to celebrate our wedding with us today. Many of you know I've spent some time over the last year trying to find my mother, and today, I'm happy to say that I've not only found her, but can introduce her to you, my friends.' Alice held out a hand to Elizabeth, who had turned pink. 'I'd like to introduce you to my mother, Elizabeth Hamilton.'

Elizabeth nodded to everyone. 'And I'd like to thank my daughter, Alice, for inviting me along to what must be the best day of her life.'

First to greet them were Ginnie and Sam, followed by Ruth and Stan. Of course, Jean, Stella, Stephen and Luke were there as they fell into line to pass on their best wishes to the happy couple. It was a pity Mrs Williams hadn't been able to join them, but she had been quite ill and had, given her age, spent the week prior in bed. Still, perhaps she could pop over when things had settled down.

The happy couple mingled with their guests, who had joined in the celebrations. Someone brought a fiddle, and everyone danced Strip the Willow, the Gay Gordons and the Dashing White Sergeant, and had a wonderful time.

At nine o'clock, Walter whispered in her ear that the car had arrived to take them home – to Marsh Avenue. Alice nodded and made her way around to tell her guests she was leaving.

There were plenty of hugs all around. It took another half an hour before they were sitting in the car. Connie and Patty went with them to say their last goodbyes, and the two of them stood together, arms around each other, before waving their goodbyes.

Alice leaned back in the car, glad to be on their own at last. She had enjoyed the wedding and being the centre of attention for the day. Now, she was just happy to be going to her new home with the man she loved.

Stan stopped the car outside 4 Marsh Avenue and jumped out to open the door for Alice. A biting wind sliced through the dark. If anything, it was worse than earlier.

'Thank you so much for bringing us home, Stan,' she said. 'Now it's over, I can't believe how tired I am. Would you like to come in?'

'No, I won't. You two will need some time on your own, and I'll not be the bloke that stops you.' Stan grinned and patted Walter on the back. 'You can do the same for me when I get wed, Walter. Ruthie kept me waiting a good while. I'm hoping that when she sees the pair of you happy ever after, she'll decide it's time!'

'She's a good lass, Stan. Worth waiting for.'

Stan's face became serious. 'I dunner need convincing.'

They waved Stan off and opened the front door. Without warning, Walter scooped her into his arms and carried her inside. Her joy in the day was complete. She tried to quell the squeal of excitement. She couldn't. Gently, he lowered her to her feet.

She had never envisaged that she would marry and have a house of her own. She walked through each of the rooms downstairs, the parlour, the kitchen and scullery, and the dining room. She hugged herself.

Walter slid his arms around her waist. 'What do you think now, Mrs Latham?'

A trickle of anticipation ran through her. 'I think it's the most beautiful house I could wish for, Mr Latham.'

'I'm so glad.' He bent his head, and she felt his lips brush the top of hers. What felt like a bolt of lightning shot through her. She caught her breath.

'Happy?'

'Blissfully.' She twisted in his arms to look at him. Her husband. What more could she want?

His lips met hers. Only now did she realise how much she had wanted him. They'd kissed before, but not like this. She couldn't breathe, wanting his kiss to go on forever.

He took her hand, and she followed where he led without protest. He pushed open the bedroom door, pulling her after him, sinking onto the bed with her following. She was on top of him now, kissing him back, and nothing had prepared her for the explosion of passion that followed.

Chapter Twenty-Three

March 1922

Walter came into the kitchen. He'd taken a bath as soon as he got home from work, and had a shave. Alice kissed him. 'You smell very nice.'

'Oh, thank you, my dear. It's Mr Boots's best.'

'Have you washed the bath out?'

'Just like you showed me. As a reward, can I have some apple crumble?'

'Yes, I'll make some custard to go with it.'

'Yes, please,' said Walter.

Alice set about preparing the custard, and they chatted.

'Have you seen today's *Sentinel*, Alice?'

'I had a quick look. Why?'

'Did you see the article about the sale of Holmorton Lodge? Mr Butters has done an excellent job. Even have pictures as well.'

'No. I didn't get that far.'

The milk and cream came close to boiling, and Alice added it to the mixture of egg yolks, cornflour, caster sugar and vanilla. She stirred it together and allowed it to sit for a minute, and then poured it over the crumble. She noticed Walter's eyes looked surprised. 'What are you looking at with such wonder?'

'At you.'

'Are you in awe of my beauty and how lucky you are to have married me?'

'No, I'm not surprised by your beauty. I'm surprised because I've never seen you make custard before, and you made it look so easy.'

'So you only married me for my custard?'

They laughed. She took the crumble over to Walter and sat next to him.

'So you know, I married you because I love you so much and want to spend the rest of my life with you. But the custard helps.' They kissed, and she would've taken him there and then, but she hadn't the heart to deprive him of his pudding. She startled herself with where her thoughts were heading. And suddenly, she didn't care. He was hers and nothing could change that.

Sure that her face was bright red with her thoughts, she moved towards the sink so he couldn't see.

He picked up the newspaper and handed it to her. There it was, in black and white. Even though she'd known about it since the end of January, her stomach churned when she saw it.

'Do you think anyone will buy it?' asked Walter.

'I think so. It's a lovely house for a family. You could convert it into a school, a hotel, or even a nursing home. Bryn Celyn wasn't any bigger, and there's plenty of land at the side.'

'Perhaps someone will buy it and knock it down to build houses.'

'Don't say that. It's too upsetting to contemplate.'

–

Later that evening, Alice went for a walk to see Patty to agree on when she would move into Marsh Avenue. The decorators were coming in next week, and Alice wanted Patty to choose colours for her room.

Mrs Goodwin welcomed her and they went through to the kitchen. Patty and her sisters were sitting at the table, their eyes full of tears.

'What's happened, Patty?'

Patty couldn't speak.

'Poor old Rex died overnight. He'd been quiet for a few days, and when Mr Goodwin got up to go to work, he was dead. Lying on his favourite sheet,' said Mrs Goodwin.

Whether it was the emotion of Holmorton Lodge being put up for sale, or the sad look in Patty's eyes, she didn't know, but soon Alice had joined the three girls shedding a tear for Rex.

–

Luke's progress had impressed Jean and Stephen. He had settled in very well and, as far as Alice could make out, had done everything requested of him. Stephen had given him responsibility for laying the fire at night and lighting it during the early hours. As the winter passed, everyone got used to wandering into a nice warm kitchen at the start of the day. Jean had insisted on making porridge for his breakfast, and he had filled out, Jean told Alice, proudly. She was positive he'd added to his height too.

Since Alice's marriage, Jean had visited Alice on Saturday afternoons. Today, she popped her head around the back door and was beaming. Alice hadn't known what to expect, but it looked as if all was fine in the Adams household.

'Luke's doing all right, Alice. When he first arrived, he kept himself to himself pretty much. I think he'll turn into a fine-looking young man. You mark my words.'

'So you've a mind to keep him, have you?' Alice had lifted an eyebrow at Jean's words.

Jean flushed, then shrugged. 'I suppose he may as well stay here now. He's doing well. I mean, where else would he go?'

Alice had made a pot of tea and directed Jean to sit at the table before joining her. 'It's a tremendous step, Jean. Supposing something goes wrong? You couldn't just throw him out, and you know nothing of his background.'

'I know, and I wouldn't throw him out, as you say. I'm sure Stephen will keep him in line. Luke respects him. He wouldn't want to jeopardise his place here by doing anything untoward. With him being at school during the week and out most weekends, he seems to use us as a bed for the night. He brings an odd rabbit home – he says it's his contribution for his stay. What else he gets up to, I don't know. But at least he's got a roof over his head.'

'Well, I'm glad he's settled in. And you're looking so well, Jean. I think he's done you some good.'

Jean smiled and leaned towards Alice. 'You should see Stella. Ever since he found her after twisting her ankle, he can do no wrong in her eyes. He reads to her most nights before he goes off by himself. She won't hear a bad word spoken against him.'

As Alice walked home in the frosty evening air, she was pleased that everything seemed to be going well for Jean at last.

–

Connie and Alice were having a cup of tea. It would be the last time they sat in the kitchen. Tomorrow, the Caldwell family would leave for their new life in Norfolk, and by the middle of the month, the sale of Holmorton Lodge would be completed. The pair had been talking about the past and reminiscing when Connie put her cup down and very matter-of-factly said, 'I've some news for you, Alice. I wasn't sure I should say anything yet, but I wanted to see your face when I tell you.'

'Oh, yes?'

'I think I might be expecting again,' she whispered.

'Expect—'

'Shush.' Connie put a hand on Alice's arm, silencing her. 'I don't want anyone else to know. Not yet. I'm still trying to come to terms with it.'

'Oh, Connie, I'm so pleased – and I'm sure you'll be pleased too.'

'I love John Robert, Alice. But the thought of having another makes me feel… old.'

'When's the baby due?'

'By my reckoning, if I'm expecting, then November, sometime in the middle.'

'So it's opportune that Nanny Lily is moving with you.'

'Yes, I'm so thankful. But why couldn't it happen before we move rather than after? I'd still have my friends to help me.'

'I'm sure they have midwives in Norfolk, Connie.'

–

The day of the move arrived; the Caldwell family was travelling by train to their new home.

The sun was shining, as if Holmorton Lodge wanted to look its best for them.

'You'll come to see me, won't you?' said Connie, as she gave Alice a last hug. 'And write every week! I'll miss you so much.'

'Me too, Connie, dearest. I've found a mother and a sister. I won't let either of you disappear. I give you my word.'

Alice turned to hug Robert. He kissed her cheek, then shook hands with Walter.

'Take care of her, Walter. We'll miss her. And if you ever decide to move to Norfolk…'

Walter roared with laughter. 'Very few pits in Norfolk, Robert.'

Alice couldn't see Walter moving out of The Potteries. It was in his blood.

A car arrived to take them to Stoke Station. They'd sent several items ahead and put their remaining possessions into storage until needed. The car rolled to the gates and waited for a gap in the traffic. Alice could see two faces: Connie with tears in her eyes and Robert, thoughtful.

Alice and Walter went back into Holmorton Lodge. Connie had asked her to lock the doors and windows after they left. There was no sound. Even the Westminster chimes had been silenced, packed away in a box for Alice to take home. She strolled through each room and could almost picture it as it was when the house was full of visitors. Even if she hadn't discovered that Connie was her sister, she'd begun to think of her that way. She hoped they could see each other from time to time, and there was always the post, wasn't there?

Tomorrow, the men would come to take away everything that was going to Marsh Avenue and to Agatha at Urmston, and then it would be over. She hoped it'd be a nice, friendly family that bought it.

The first room she walked into was the one she had spent most of her life in – the kitchen. How bare it looked now. She walked around, checking windows and doors, opening the odd cupboard doors, now empty.

The garden room was next, with its large windows and door into the garden. She took out the largest key and locked the door, then closed the shutters until the room grew dark. She did the same upstairs and worked through each of the bedrooms, the bathroom, and the nursery. As she stared around, she wondered what Connie was thinking at that moment. Did she have any regrets about leaving this house with so many memories?

She reached the attic and popped her head around the door that had been her bedroom when she arrived from the workhouse. A small room – but one of her own. Tears came to her eyes. Not of sadness, but a saying goodbye to a life that had been hers for so long.

She headed back down to the hall. Walter was talking to the man from Butters. She felt his eyes watching her as she handed over the keys. That was it, the last time she would enter the building.

'Right, Mrs Latham, we'll take over now.'

–

Walter returned from a visit to his father's. When he walked in, he looked flushed. He took off his jacket and cap and hung them on the peg. Then sat down to take off his boots. He placed them in the cupboard under the stairs.

'Guess what my father's just told me?'

'The cricket club has asked him to be president.'

'No, something a lot more important than that.'

'I thought Father thought nothing was more important than cricket.'

'So did I until today. You'll never guess. He's proposed to Miss Latimer, and they're getting married on 10 May at Hanley Registry Office.'

'Well, I'll be b— blowed,' said Alice. 'I thought she was spending a lot of time at Dartmouth Street, but I never expected that. Has he told Frank and Ruth?'

'I didn't ask.'

'Oh well, he's old enough to know what he's doing.'

'I never thought he would marry again after Mother died, but it looks as if there's life in the old dog yet.'

Chapter Twenty-Four

April 1922

It was the beginning of April, about four o'clock in the afternoon, when a loud knock came on the back door. Alice was sitting at the kitchen table working through her journal, not expecting any callers. She rose and opened the door to see Luke standing there.

'Oh, it's you, Luke,' she said, smiling. She'd got used to Luke calling by, as he enjoyed helping Walter with the garden. Alice was sure he had a crush on Patty too. Today, he looked flustered and upset. Her smile disappeared.

'Is Patty here, please?'

Alice opened the door wider and beckoned him inside. 'She's in the garden, collecting some washing, you can go and help her if you want to?'

'I dunner think she'd appreciate that.' He stared at his dirty hands resting on the table as if lost for words now that he'd arrived. They were not the hands of a child returning from a day at school.

Alice poured out a glass of milk and handed it to him, and sank into the chair next to him. She would need to tread carefully. 'You look troubled. Has something happened?'

'I think I've gone and put me foot in it. I dunner know why I thought as I could get away with it.'

Alice frowned. 'Get away with what? You haven't got yourself into trouble? Thieving or some such? Mrs Adams was telling me the other week that you were doing well.'

'I think the schoolboard man will be coming to see mister and missus next week.'

'Why?'

'I think he's going to tell them I've bin bobbing school.'

'You've been… Oh, no, Luke. Why would you do something like that, for goodness' sake?'

'Some of the other lads were bullying me cos I was different. Cos I've got no family. I ignored them at first, but it just got worse. I swear I didn't start the fighting.'

'You've been fighting?'

Luke sniffed. 'Couldn't let them get away with what they was saying about me, Alice.'

At that moment, Patty walked in with a basket of washing that needed ironing.

'Hello, Luke, what're you doing here? I thought you'd still be at school.'

Luke said nothing, so Alice outlined what she had been told so far.

'You've bin bobbing school? Whatever possessed yer, Luke? You could get the Adams into trouble. You wouldn't want that, would yer?'

'Luke says the schoolboard man might call round,' said Alice.

'He only comes round to see a parent when you've played truant a lot. So you've only told us cos you've bin found out, Luke.' Patty folded her arms under her breasts.

Luke's face grew redder by the minute.

Patty put the basket of washing down and sat at the table opposite Luke. 'How long were yer bobbing school, Luke?'

If his face was red before Patty came in, it was now scarlet, as if he'd been told off in front of the entire school.

'How long, Luke?' asked Patty.

'A few days.'

His words were so soft that neither of them heard him.

'How long?' Alice pressed on.

'Eight weeks.'

'Oh, my word!' exclaimed Patty. Her hand covered her mouth.

'Whatever possessed you, Luke? I mean, how could you do that when Mr and Mrs Adams have taken you into their home?' Alice couldn't stop the anger from pouring out. They were her friends, and this was how he repaid them.

'I didn't mean to do it, Alice. I promise.'

'Then why did you, Luke?'

His eyes went to Patty and then returned to Alice.

Luke shrugged again. 'Dunno. I hate school.'

'That's no excuse.'

'They laugh at me.'

'Who does?'

'The other kids. Sometimes the teachers.'

'Why do they laugh, Luke?' asked Alice quietly.

'Cos I ain't got no family. They say I'm no better than a workhouse kid.'

Alice looked at Patty, not knowing what to say, and turned back to him. 'But eight entire weeks, Luke. What did you do with yourself?'

Luke shrugged. 'I just avoided everybody. Instead of hanging around the PTC depot, I went to the other side of Tunstall. I ran errands for people, and they gave me coppers. Doesn't sound much, but it kept me going for a while.'

'I thought everything was fine. Mrs Adams was only saying how well things were going the other week. And all this time, you were playing truant.'

'I went to school on that first day, and nobody said much to me. The teacher said I was joining the class and that they should make me feel welcome. He shouldn't have said that. It felt as if he was treating me different from the others, and that's not right. People shouldn't treat children differently. Kids pick up on that soon enough, and it ends in fights with the other boys to show I can do whatever they can do. I spent a lot of time on me own in the playground. Two girls spoke to me, but the lads said I acted more like a girl and pushed me into the girls' privy. They said that was the best place for me.'

'That was cruel, Luke. No wonder you were upset,' said Alice. She glanced at Patty in time to see her eyes bright with the onset of tears.

'You know I like to read, Alice, cos I still read to Aunty Stella. Bits from the paper, books and stories and such things. When we had to read aloud in class, they had a go at me again and said I was a cissy cos I read books. One day, they caught me on the way home across the park. There was no one about. They took my trousers off and dressed me in a skirt. They said I acted like a girl, so I might as well look like one.'

'Have you talked to Mrs Adams about any of this, Luke?'

'I was ashamed. I thought she wouldn't want me.'

'For goodness' sake, lad. Didn't it occur to you we'd all be on your side?' Alice felt like shaking him.

'Nobody's never been on my side afore, and I was only good at reading and writing. Anyroad, I stopped going to the classes. I walked to school and stood outside the gates until everyone had gone inside. Then I'd bugger off… pardon me, Alice. I'd take meself off into Tunstall, down by the canal. Sometimes I'd do some fishing. If it was raining, I'd sit under a bridge and wait until it stopped. If it was sunny and warm, I'd swim in the canal. It's good for yer.'

Patty covered her mouth to avoid letting out a gasp of shock at imagining Luke in the water. 'You swam in the canal? There're all sorts of things in there, and most of them are dead.'

'Sometimes the canal boatmen would give me odd jobs to do while they were waiting to go through the lock, and they'd give me summat to eat for my trouble. Other times, I'd do odd jobs for the shopkeepers in the town, and they'd give me money or bread or some such. I can manage on me own. Done it often enough in the past. I had to if I wanted to stay alive.'

'And you did that for getting on eight weeks? Why didn't the schoolboard man tell Jean and Stephen sooner?'

'Perhaps the teacher didn't report it because I was too much trouble.'

'But it wasn't your fault, by the sounds of it,' said Patty.

'Mrs A knew I hated school. She tried to tell me it was for my own good. But then I heard about the schoolboard man who went round to see families where kids had been truanting. I worried I'd get Mr and Mrs Adams into trouble. I thought about going back to school, but by then I couldn't. I was afraid to go back. When I got back today, I saw a man dressed up all posh like, and I panicked cos I thought it was him, so I scarpered. I come here cos I couldn't think of nowhere else.'

'And is that everything?'

Luke pursed his lips. 'Conner think of nowt else.'

'Listen, Luke,' said Patty. 'Don't you think it'd be a good idea to go back and talk to Mr and Mrs Adams? Tell the truth. I'm sure they'll see your side in all of this. They'll help you. Best you tell them rather than the schoolboard man.'

'It's too late, Patty. I think he's there now.'

'But you need to tell them what you've told us – now. They'll see you right.'

After an hour of talking, Luke agreed to return to Park Road and tell Jean and Stephen everything. Alice accompanied him, not that she didn't trust him – well, partly because of that – but more because she could help him explain everything to Jean and Stephen. She apologised to Patty, but she was in complete agreement. She left Patty with a few instructions regarding the evening meal and promised to be back as soon as she could.

As the two set off for Tunstall, Alice kept a close watch on him. She didn't hold his hand – he wouldn't thank her for that – but she chatted to him and tried to keep him talking to take his mind off what lay ahead. He was sorry for his behaviour. Jean would just hug him, relieved to have him back again, but Alice didn't know how Stephen would take it. She hoped, for Luke's sake, he would show the boy some compassion.

'You aren't the only one to be left on your own, Luke, or sent to the workhouse, and it's not a sign of you being a criminal or anything like that.'

Luke kept his eyes on the road, saying nothing. Alice was unsure he was even listening. She took a deep breath. 'I was in the workhouse as a kid, and so were Mrs White, Mr White and their friend, Miss Barlow, and look how well we've done for ourselves.' That got him interested, as Alice had hoped it would.

'Did you get mistreated at all?'

'Workhouse kids always get treated unfairly. And if no one gave us a job, we got called the "undeserving poor". They thought of us as wanting things for nothing. It wasn't our fault we couldn't get jobs.'

'I didn't know.'

'It's not something you want to talk about. But mark my words, the best thing you can do is to stay with the Adams, and they'll do right by you. I have Mrs Copeland to thank for getting me out of there, and there's never a day goes by when I'm not thankful.'

They arrived at the tram stop and had to wait a while. Luke never said a word. Alice hoped he was taking it all in. No doubt she'd find out soon.

Stephen looked exasperated as he opened the door wide. 'Luke, thank the Lord you're here. Wherever have you been? Why is Alice with you?'

'Are you all right, Luke?' said Jean, who moved towards him to check he wasn't hurt. 'You had us so worried.'

Stella tutted. 'Let the boy get in before you bombard him with questions, Stephen.'

Alice smiled at her, thankful that at least Stella would be on Luke's side. 'May we come in?'

All three moved to one side.

'I'm here because Luke came to Marsh Avenue late this afternoon, and he was upset. Patty and I talked to him, and we got out of him what was going on.' Alice turned to Luke. 'Now that you're here, you'll need to tell these good people what you've told us, Luke. Would you like me to stay to help you?'

Luke stood in the hallway, looking around him almost as if he was refreshing his memory.

'I'll be all right, Alice. I've caused all this trouble, and I need to sort it.'

Alice nodded. 'Good lad,' she murmured, and stroked his shoulder as she headed towards the door.

Stephen and Stella walked Luke into the sitting room while Jean remained in the hall with Alice.

'Thank you so much for bringing him home. We've been so worried.'

'That's why I came with him, Jean. I believed he's sorry. It sounds like he's had a bad time. Tell Stephen to go easy on him.'

Jean nodded. 'I will, and thank you again, Alice.'

–

Alice returned home, hoping that nothing had gone wrong in her absence. Once inside the house, she hung up her coat and hurried into the kitchen. Patty was laying out the fruit puddings, and the potatoes and vegetables seemed to be ready.

'The fish is ready to be fried as soon as Walter gets home.'

'I'm sorry I had to leave everything to you, Patty. I panicked in case he went off by himself. I'd never forgive myself.'

Glancing over the meal, Alice was satisfied it was ready. 'Well, Walter will be coming home from his father's, and we can cook the fish whilst he is getting his boots off. We'll start the vegetables shortly, but you can get some water boiling and—'

'Remember to put some mint in the peas,' grinned Patty.

–

On 8 April, Alice received a letter from Connie. She had been waiting to hear how the move had gone and how they were settling in. She hoped, for Connie's sake, that everything had gone well.

She took the small stationery knife out of the set of drawers in the hall and slit the envelope, and returned to the sitting room to read what she hoped would be a newsy letter.

Keeper's Cottage,
Blakeney
Norfolk

My dear Alice,

It seems ages since I last saw you, even though it is only two weeks. I keep telling myself the days will pass more quickly as we settle in. Everything we brought with us is now put away in cupboards and drawers, and the cottage feels quite cosy now. Robert has taken the rest of the month to recover from the move – it's taken a lot out of him – and will look for some form of office work. He believes he will need something other than his illness to concentrate his thoughts on – as if he hadn't got enough to think about with John Robert, who will soon be crawling. He is keeping us awake, cutting his teeth. Thank goodness for Nanny Lily.

On the mention of Nanny Lily... I have some further news for you. I was right! I am expecting again. I have missed two monthlies now, and the last time that happened resulted in John Robert. Please don't worry. When the time grows near, I shall employ a midwife as I did before, and with Nanny Lily here too, I shall be well taken care of. It would be nice to have a daughter, but another son would be a pleasure too.

I hope you are enjoying married life and your new home. Do keep in touch, and hopefully we will see each other again before too long.

With warmest wishes from your sister and friend,
Connie x

–

The telephone in the hallway rang. Walter answered it. 'Good afternoon, the Tucker residence.' Alice still got excited every time she heard that.

'Alice! Alice, can you come to the telephone? Oh, there you are. Jean Adams wants to speak to you.'

'Thank you very much, Walter.' Alice took the telephone and raised it to her ear, hoping Jean had resolved everything after Luke's recent problems. She crossed her fingers. 'Hello, Jean. How are you?'

'Fine, thank you, Alice. I just wanted to tell you that things are more settled now. I think Luke appreciates the problems he's caused, and I'm hopeful it won't happen again. Incidentally, I can also tell you that the schoolboard man did call.'

'Oh, no. Poor Luke. I'm sure he didn't think he'd get you all into trouble.'

'Don't worry. Stephen has spoken to him and explained the situation. We've undertaken to ensure he'll attend school in the future. The man said that truanting happens everywhere, but it's the first time he's come across someone doing it for so long. He'll need to be a brave lad when he goes back. To be honest, Alice, I believe he admires Luke for his boldness! Of course, I haven't told Luke any of this – I didn't want him to feel demotivated or admired. Anyway, he's gone to school now, and I hope that's the last we shall hear of "bobbing" school!'

When Alice put the telephone back in its cradle, she found she was smiling. Luke had a way about him. Jean and Stephen would have their work cut out to keep him on the straight and narrow. But he could be a godsend too.

Alice decided to let Connie tell Jean about her pregnancy. She would no doubt be writing to everyone very soon. How sorry she felt for Jean, another baby on the way and yet again, it isn't hers.

–

Uncle James came from Urmston to watch the auction taking place and called to see Alice to tell her what had gone on. He seemed pleased with the way it went. The house had fetched a lot more than expected and most of the furnishings had been sold. Alice gave him tea and cake before he made his way back. It wasn't long before he changed the subject to Elizabeth Hamilton.

'How are you getting on with Elizabeth?'

'Very well. I like her, and she seems happy that we've found each other.'

'Elizabeth Hamilton was always an amiable woman, if a little naïve. She was engaged to a young man who died in South Africa. He was in the army, and was killed in a Boer skirmish near the Kimberley diamond mines. The loss devastated her, and she became reclusive, rarely seen at social events. By the time she met your father, my brother-in-law, she looked more like an old maid than the striking heiress she was.'

He stopped talking for a moment, as if reliving his past. 'Agatha didn't have a very easy confinement, and she suffered with her nerves after the birth of Constance. I know Agatha and Edwin slept in separate rooms and hardly spoke to each other.'

'Things between me and Edwin went downhill after he purchased a competitor. The founder of the company had died with no children. His wife had no intention of running the company, and Edwin got in there with his charm and persuaded the woman to sell at what I considered to be a giveaway price. If he'd paid the market price, it still would have been a worthwhile purchase for him, as the two companies fitted together so well.

'We had words about the transaction, and Edwin told me that everything was legal and open, and she was happy with the deal and he was happy, so why worry? I told him his actions were unethical, but he said, and I quote, "Ethics are optional in business."'

'The affair was the final straw. Agatha was told by Mr Hamilton, Elizabeth's father, and between them they hatched a plan, which required Edwin to behave himself and Elizabeth to give you up and never see you again. Edwin never knew the part that Agatha had played. They agreed to keep your existence hidden from the world. I don't like to say this about my sister, but she can be very stubborn when she wants to be.'

Alice couldn't get out of her mind all that Uncle James had told her about Agatha, and how mean she had been both to Elizabeth and Mr Copeland himself. She had thought of Agatha as the person hardest done by ever since she had discovered the truth about all that had happened. But it was Agatha's version of the truth – that of a woman let down by her husband. Only now was she beginning to understand that there was another side to her, a side that shocked Alice – and presented to her by her adoring brother, who loved her despite her obvious flaws.

Poor Elizabeth.

'I'll take my leave of you now, Alice. I dare say we shall not see each other again. You'll take care of yourself, won't you, lass?'

Alice could think of nothing to say. Instead, she crushed him into a hug, and that would have to do.

–

Luke turned up at Marsh Avenue a few days later. He had knocked on the door, arms behind his back, waiting to be given leave to enter. Once inside, he withdrew his arms and presented each of them with a small posy of flowers from an unknown source.

Alice smiled at him. 'Why, Luke – that's very kind of you. Everything worked out for you, did it?'

He nodded and grinned as he passed the second bunch to Patty.

'I'm right glad for yer, Luke,' she said.

Luke flushed, looking unsure of what to do next.

'Have a seat, Luke. Want to tell us about what happened?'

He scraped a chair back from the table and sank onto it. Patty gave him a glass of water, and the two of them waited for him to speak.

'I told them everything as I told you two. I left nowt out. I told them how the other kids treated me and how upset I'd been. I'd always planned to go back to school, but the longer I stayed away, the worse it got, until I couldn't bring myself to go back. What could I say? Teachers wouldn't believe me. Nobody would. When I finished telling them everything, I didn't dare look at them. In the end, I looked at Mr Adams. He had his head on one side as if he was unsure what to think. I told him I was telling God's truth. He said that if I was going to stay with them in their house, they'd need to know I could be trusted. Then he told me he'd talk things over with Mrs Adams and Mrs A. As they live in the house too, he said it was only right to talk to them and that we'd talk again after tea.

'He said they'd all agreed to let me stay on the condition that I return to school. He said they couldn't have me wandering around willy-nilly whenever the fancy took me. He said he'd find me a job when I was old enough to leave school, doing odd jobs at first to see how I got on.'

Luke beamed as he finished speaking. 'I promise, Alice, I won't let them down. He told me I could call them Aunty and Uncle. I've never had an uncle or aunty before.'

'Well, you have now!' beamed Patty.

Chapter Twenty-Five

May 1922

The following week, Alice paid a visit to Ginnie. She took the letter from Connie with her. She thought it was likely that Connie had already passed her news on, but went, just in case the news hadn't filtered through.

She arrived at Tellwright Street and knocked on the door. Ginnie answered.

'Oh, Alice, do come in. Sam's at work all day today, and I shall be glad of your company. I've some news for you.'

Alice stepped inside. So, Connie had been in touch. She would've been surprised if Ginnie didn't know. 'It's good news, isn't it? Connie must be over the moon.'

Ginnie looked puzzled. 'I suppose she is. It's a shame she's so far away. We could've met to talk about baby things. Compare how they're—'

'Compare? Are we talking about the same thing – Connie's baby?'

Ginnie's face looked blank. 'Connie's baby? What baby?'

Alice rummaged in her bag. 'I've had a letter from her. She's expecting again. Due in November.'

Ginnie burst into laughter, and Alice looked puzzled.

'Trust Connie. I was going to tell you my news. I'm expecting in November too.'

'You are? Oh, Ginnie, I'm so pleased for you.'

They hugged each other. 'Fancy that! And here's me thinking you had second sight and telling me I was pregnant – unless you were about to tell me you were?'

'Oh, no. I'm only just getting used to being married – but I'm so glad for both of you.'

–

Walter changed his shift to mornings on the day his father remarried. Alice and Walter arrived at Dartmouth Street at three o'clock.

'You look very handsome. I've never seen you in a suit before,' Walter said to his father.

'I never expected to wear it again until they buried me in it. Life's unpredictable, son.'

Walter grinned. His father scratched his head as if confused about how he had come to the situation he found himself in.

'You got everything you need?' asked Walter.

'Yes, Jane made sure of that last night.'

'Father! Not in front of my wife. Anyway, come on,' Walter pushed his father towards the door. 'We don't want to be late.'

Alice turned away, biting her lip so as not to burst into fits of giggles. She had never heard him so lewd in front of ladies. Maybe that's what Jane liked about him.

Herbert Latham had grown on her, and she was pleased to see the happiness radiating from him all afternoon. He deserved to be happy. He had waited long enough.

They returned from Hanley as soon as they could. She and Patty had completed all the preparations before dinnertime. Patty had been looking after the joint of best rib of beef, basting it regularly, just as Alice had shown her.

'How'd everything go?'

'Fine. Jane looked quite stunning, and Mr Latham cut a fine figure of a man.'

Alice opened up the door of the range's oven and inspected the joint. It looked perfect. Using a skewer, she checked the joint and was pleased to see it cooked to perfection.

'Well done, Patty. That looks perfect. I'll transfer it to the warmer and let it rest.'

They set about preparing the rest of the meal.

Alice asked Patty to sit next to Dr Latimer, Jane's brother; then the table would be balanced.

At the end of the meal, Mr Latham and then Frank made speeches.

It'd been a long time since she'd prepared a meal for fourteen people. Alice was so glad she had decided to take the dining table from Holmorton Lodge. It was a clever design comprising three additional sections, added as required.

When everyone had gone, Alice and Walter sat in the sitting room.

'We've done Father proud tonight. It was a lovely meal. I've never tasted beef like that before.'

'Rib joints are the tastiest. The right amount of fat has to be blended into the meat to enhance the taste and keep the moisture. It's expensive. I ordered that piece two weeks ago. Not all butchers do the cut, but they know me there and they made a special effort.'

'I can see marriage to you is going to be tasty,' said Walter, dropping a kiss on her lips that grew increasingly urgent.

–

Alice was thankful she had agreed with Connie to take all of the crockery and utensils she needed prior to the auction. She and Patty washed all the crockery before finding a home for it. Walter hung the pictures under direction from Alice. Patty and Alice placed the occasional tables and other small pieces of furniture. China ornaments, some made in The Potteries, added a final touch to turning their house into a home.

Elizabeth paid her first visit to Marsh Avenue on Whit Sunday afternoon. Alice ran around the house, making sure everything was in order, and then began peering through the curtains, awaiting her arrival.

'I doubt she'll arrive any quicker if you're looking for her,' shouted Walter from the sitting room. 'You'll wear yerself out.'

'I want everything just so. What's wrong with that?'

'Nothing, my love, but she won't think any less of us for not being organised when we've had so much to do.'

He walked over to her and put his arms around her waist. 'Take a few deep breaths. Elizabeth will be here when she comes.'

They were about to move away from the window when a large car pulled up outside. Alice watched as a man in a plain, dark suit jumped out and hurried to open the door for Elizabeth.

'She's here!'

'Slow down, Alice. Take some more deep breaths.'

Alice did as Walter requested, and they made their way to the front door.

'Good afternoon, Elizabeth. Welcome to our home.'

'Hello, my dear Alice.'

Elizabeth stepped in and hugged Alice and did the same to Walter, much to his surprise. He took her hat and coat.

Elizabeth gazed around as she sat in a chair while Alice produced a two-tier cake stand full of delicacies to have with their pot of tea, announcing that tea would be served at six o'clock.

Alice couldn't help grinning as she watched Walter instructing Elizabeth on the different time names for meals in The Potteries.

'It is breakfast, dinner and tea, not breakfast, lunch and dinner. You'll get used to it,' said Walter.

'I can see why you chose this house, my dears. It's lovely, and big enough for a family and guests too.'

Alice jumped up. 'Would you like me to show you around?'

'Thank you. I was hoping you would.'

Alice led the way, convinced Walter would be listening to their voices and seeking assurance that they'd spent their money well.

When they returned, Alice was beaming, and Elizabeth was full of praise. 'You've blended the old with the new very well. What about Connie Caldwell's move? Did it go according to plan too?'

'Yes, I believe so. It's in a small village, and it all sounds very nice.'

'I'm so glad. Finding out she had a sister must have come as a great shock.'

'Yes, but we get on well together, and I'm hoping to visit before too long.'

'And what are your plans? Walter still has his job, but what about you?'

'I want to prepare a home for me and Walter – and children, of course, in time.'

'Don't you want to find a job?'

'To be honest, Elizabeth, I'll be content with having my family to look after. I hope you don't mind me saying – but I want to have my family around me. I want my home to be a safe place for them because I never had one. Does that make sense?'

'Of course. I'm so sorry.'

'Don't be. It wasn't your fault. But now we can build a better future. One that Walter and I hope you'll be part of.'

Later, they tucked into their tea, and Elizabeth talked about Knutsford.

'If you don't mind, Alice, my car will arrive at seven o'clock, and I was wondering if you'd show me some places that are part of your story. I want to picture them as we talk.'

The car left Marsh Avenue and drove along High Lane, and their first stop was outside of the Haddon House Children's Hostel. The journey continued along Turnhurst Road and pulled up outside of the Haddon Workhouse. Alice then instructed the driver to travel through Packmoor, Newchapel and Whitehill to Atwood Street in Kidsgrove, and then to Napier Street, where Alice had lived, although the houses there now were new. They drove down Atwood Street and Heathcote Street and then to St John's Wood, where Elizabeth saw the outside of the house Alice had lived in before her father died. She even pointed out her bedroom window.

The journey continued along Liverpool Road and onto Goldenhill Bank, where the massive Clough Hall Colliery was situated, arriving at the High Street in Goldenhill, where she pointed out the tram depot that had featured in all of her friends' lives.

Next, they followed the main road through Tunstall, Scotia Road and then Burslem. They made a left turn and drove up Moorland Road, turning onto Dartmouth Street to show Elizabeth where Walter's family lived. Within minutes they were back at Marsh Avenue.

Both women were tearful as they said their goodbyes.

'Thank you for showing me all of that. I feel I know more about your life now.'

Elizabeth held Alice's hand for a fraction longer before the car drove away. She waited at her front door with Walter, and they both waved. She turned to Walter, smiling. 'My mother's first visit, Walter. I think that went very well.'

He smiled and gave her a slow, lingering kiss. 'It went very well, but I'm glad I have you all to myself, Mrs Latham.'

Chapter Twenty-Six

August 1922

Alice enjoyed living on Marsh Avenue. Three families now occupied the houses, and her neighbours seemed friendly enough. The only drawback was that a house on High Lane owned a dog which barked during the day and overnight. When its owners were at home, it was quiet.

On this particular day, he was barking as normal when the husband, she presumed, arrived home from work. He put the lead on the dog. Alice saw him tie the dog to a post in his garden. The man went back into the house and returned with a hammer before approaching the dog. Alice felt horrified. He wouldn't… would he?

'Stop! Stop! What're you doing?'

'People have complained, so I'm going to shut it up. What's it to you, missus?'

'Do nothing; I'll come round.'

'Be quick, I haven't got all day.'

Soon, she was standing in front of the man.

'Well, what do you want, missus?'

'He barks only when you're not there. He's wanting company.'

'Well, we've had enough. You can have him if you want, or I'll just give him a tap on the head. Your choice, lady.'

A stony-faced Alice stood, arms folded as if determined to stay there. 'I'll have him. What's his name?'

'Jock.' The man sniffed. 'You sure you want him?'

'I'm sure.'

Alice took the dog and his lead and marched off. It occurred to her later that he might have wanted payment, but consoled herself that removing the dog should've been payment enough.

Now she had to explain to Walter how they had acquired a dog!

–

'I dunner mind telling yer I'll be glad when schooling is done with, Alice. If it wasn't for upsetting Aunty Jean, I would've scarpered when they found out about me playing truant.'

Alice smiled. Luke had taken to calling round occasionally after school, before continuing home.

'Is school better these days, Luke?'

He nodded. 'When the kids ask about my folks, I talk about Mr and Mrs Adams and Mrs A. Before, I couldn't say anything about my folks cos I didn't know, and the other kids were determined to rub it in.'

'Mm. Kids can be very cruel, can't they?'

Luke said nothing.

'Do you ever think about your parents, brothers, or sisters?'

Luke shrugged. 'Never had none.'

Alice decided he was not in the mood for talking. 'I'll bet Jean and Stephen are proud of you, not missing a day's schooling this term.' Alice noticed that there was a trace of a smile on his face. 'You've not missed any, have you?'

'No, honest.'

Patty came into the kitchen. She'd taken Jock for a walk.

He trotted over to Alice and lay at her feet. She patted him. 'Good boy, Jock. Have you been rabbiting down the field?'

'We have, and thank you for asking, Alice. I'm very well. It's nice to know that Jock gets a greeting before I do.'

'Hello, Patty, sorry. Luke's not missed a day's schooling this term. What do you think of that?'

'Is that true, Luke?'

Luke grinned. 'Yes.'

Patty narrowed her eyes. 'Are you sure? I bet you've been nipping through the fence at the back after you've got your mark.'

'How'd you know?'

'It's what all the lads do, and some girls. So how many times?'

'Two or three, that's all.' Patty continued to stare at Luke, who crumbled under the pressure. 'Well, five or six times… No more than ten.'

'Oh, Luke!'

'Dunner tell Jean, Alice. I was only away for an hour each time.'

'I won't tell Jean if you promise not to do it again.'

'I promise.'

'If you do it again, I'll know.'

Alice hid a grin and thought Patty would make an excellent teacher.

'So what're you going to do now?' Alice thought it best to change to a more helpful subject.

'Uncle Stephen's got me a job at his depot in Goldenhill for the summer, just like he said he would. Cleaning, and general skivvying. He said he started at the bottom and it's as good a place as any. I like it.'

'Quite right,' Alice laughed, pleased that he had taken it so well.

'He said if I did well, the PTC might give me a proper job, with a trade, and it'd set me up for life, just like it did for him.'

Alice nodded. 'Well, you must put your heart and soul into school, my lad.' She rubbed the top of his head with her hand, making him squirm. She laughed again. 'It's all down to you now, lad. Let nothing stand in your way, and you'll make Jean and Stephen very proud.'

When Alice next spoke to Jean, she found her happier with the way things were going for Luke. He started by going into Goldenhill depot with Stephen and had forged a friendship with the mechanic, Stan Bristow, from Stoke depot, who was soon to be Walter's brother-in-law. He had been more than happy to share his knowledge with Luke.

'Show some faith in Luke. He's nearly twelve now. He needs to know you trust him, Jean. He had such a tough start in life.'

'He's talking about getting an apprenticeship when he leaves school.'

'That's good news. It'll secure his future if he can do that. You should be happy. Does Stephen agree?'

'Oh, yes.'

'Don't smother him, Jean.'

Chapter Twenty-Seven

September 1922

It was with trepidation that Luke returned to school after the summer holidays, both for him and for the Adams. At first, Jean kept Alice informed, for which she was grateful, particularly because of the connection she felt with him regarding their backgrounds. Though Luke's unannounced weekly visits to Marsh Avenue to chat were more for Patty's benefit than her own, even though he was four years younger.

It helped that Stephen had promised to get him a job at Goldenhill depot if he kept himself out of trouble. He needed to build on the qualities he already had, and who knew what might happen in the future. Stephen gave him tasks to complete so that his life outside of school was more fulfilling than it'd been. Maybe that was all it took – people to believe in him.

On the other hand, it took no time at all for the unruly Jock to settle in. Alice and Walter took him for a walk down the fields at the bottom of their road regularly, and if they were busy, then Patty would always step in. Providing he could hear people about, and there usually was someone in the house, he would sit where he could see them, and was as good as gold. He came to his name and ate everything put in front of him. Patty had been patient with him and taught him to sit, stay and to shake-a-paw just as her family had done with Rex. Even Walter warmed to him and would often be quite happy to take him for a walk when he could. In fact, Alice's only chance to be with 'her' dog was when Walter was at work.

Alice and Patty were both delighted when Luke began to call regularly, this time to tell them he was back at school again. Alice believed that having a goal to work towards had spurred him on.

'I reckon it's Jock he's come to see,' said Patty as she wiped the dishes. 'Maybe he's never had anyone show him any affection.'

Alice watched Luke each time he called. He tended to be found wherever Patty was working. He never stopped chatting, and she had some cake or biscuits set aside for him. Patty treated him the same as she would any friendly caller. Sometimes, she'd make a comment and Luke would blush, causing Alice to become more than a little concerned. Alice couldn't imagine Patty would be interested in a schoolboy. To be on the safe side, Alice had a quiet word with her before things went any further.

She didn't know how to approach the matter, not having brothers or sisters of her own – so she came straight out with it.

'Patty, have you noticed anything different in Luke recently?'

Patty was getting a large saucepan out of the cupboard, but it appeared to be stuck behind a frying pan. 'What sort of difference?' There was obvious annoyance in Patty's voice as she fought with the saucepan.

'He spends a lot of time talking to you when he comes and never takes his eyes off you. I wondered if you'd noticed.'

The saucepan came free and Patty toppled backwards, cursing under her breath. 'No, I haven't. He's got a lot to talk about at the moment. I'm a sympathetic listener.'

Alice took a breath and voiced her fears. 'I think he's taken a fancy to you.'

'Me? Why me?'

'You're an attractive young lady who can hold down a job and put a plate of food on the dinner table.'

'Dunner be daft, Alice. I'm old enough to be his big sister.'

'I'm only warning you, Patty. I don't want any trouble – from either of you. The poor lad can't help it. I just want you to be aware of the possibility. That's all.'

–

Ruth called in to see them with news about poor Thomas Walton. Since Ruth looked relaxed, Alice hoped her news would be good.

'Oh, Ruth, what is it? This news?'

Ruth held up her hand to stop Alice. 'It's good news. Wait until Walter appears and I'll tell you both.' She took her coat off and sat down to a cup of tea. 'I caught the tram to Smallthorne and walked the rest of the way. I'm having tea with Father and Jane, so can't stop long.'

The door banged.

'Hiya, Ruth. Nice to see you. Just finished work?' said Walter.

Ruth gave a broad smile. 'Yes, and I have some news for you. I arrived home on Friday evening. Dottie was still working on the allotment. She's spent a lot of time there this summer. Now I know why, and you'll never guess.' She looked from one to the other. 'She was working there with a man. Tom Walton!'

'I asked how he was keeping, and he said he still found it hard sometimes when he thought of Jimmy and Dickie, his mates from the PTC who didn't come back. But since he'd met Dottie, those times seemed to get less and less.'

Alice glanced at Walter and couldn't stop a smile forming. 'How did they meet?'

'Dottie had an accident, nothing serious. She fell through the top of a wooden box in her shed at the allotment – don't ask me what she was doing standing on a box. Anyway, she ended up on her backside. Tom happened to be passing and helped her get up. Then he took her home to make sure she was all right.'

'Interesting,' said Walter.

Ruth winked. 'That's what I thought. Over the next few weeks, Tom walked along Campbell Road regularly.'

'Perhaps he was lonely,' said Alice.

'I don't think it was that. He's got a job at the Home and Colonial Stores in Stoke and spends most of his time inside. He's grown to enjoy working on the allotment. Working in the fresh air and having somebody to talk to who knows about his past so he doesn't have to explain seems to have had the desired effect. Dottie said afterwards that it had made a difference to her too. She was coming to terms with the loss of her husband, Donald. If you ask me, they are good for each other.'

'Do you think there might be romance in the air?' asked Walter.

'There might be,' said Ruth. 'But I think at the moment they're both just happy to be in each other's company. I have to admit that I'd be pleased for Dottie if there was. I shall be leaving Dottie's when I'm married, and I'd hate for her to be left on her own.'

Chapter Twenty-Eight

November 1922

It was a cold and very wet Wednesday evening in November, when Alice had a visit from Sam White. He looked soaked to the skin, water dripping everywhere. Alice was sure he could've wrung out his cap in the sink. Most people would've been cursing, but not Sam. He was positively glowing – and Alice guessed why.

Such wonderful news. Alice put her hands up to her face, eyes wide open. 'Has she—'

'Our babby's arrived,' he said, looking around for Patty so she could receive the news too.

'Oh, Sam! How wonderful for you! Are they both…' Alice didn't want to say any more but felt the need to ask.

'Mother and babby are doing fine, but you know our Ginnie. She wanted you to know, so as you could tell Connie.'

'Of course, Sam. I'll ring her as soon as you've gone. Everything went well… did it?'

'It did. I dunner mind telling yer me heart was in me boots till I heard the little 'un cry.' His eyes were bright with unshed tears. Alice remembered how devastating it'd been when Ginnie's second pregnancy ended with a miscarriage. It must have been at the forefront of both of their thoughts.

Sam had taken off his coat and sat down hard on the settee, his face wearing a silly grin. As he didn't seem to be forthcoming with any further information, Alice pressed on. 'And is it a little boy – or a girl?'

Sam seemed to come back into the world at that point. 'Sorry, dunno whether I'm coming or going. It's a boy. We're calling him James. And Ginnie ordered me to tell you he weighed six pounds, two ounces.'

'That's fine, Sam. You must be so pleased,' said Patty, who had come in just as Sam was giving out the important information.

Alice took out some sherry left over from the wedding, and they drank a toast to the little man who had just entered the world.

'I'll ring Connie straight away. I'm sure she's desperate to know. Could you ask Ginnie if she'd write to Connie too? Just so she doesn't feel left out. I'm sure she'd love it.'

'Aye, I'll tell her, Alice. Wouldn't dare not to. She's been good to us over the years, has Connie.'

Just after Sam left, the telephone rang, and Alice hummed as she went to answer it. How pleased she was to hear that Ginnie had come through it after losing the last one so tragically. Now she had two boys to gloat over.

She picked up the telephone. 'Hello – Mrs Latham speaking.' She had not tired of saying those words.

'Is that you, Alice? It's Robert.'

'Oh, Robert – how fortunate you should call. Sam White has just been in to tell us that Ginnie had another boy, born today.'

'That is good news. And how fortuitous. I have my own news to tell you. Connie had a little girl at seven o'clock this morning. Both are doing fine.'

Alice squealed loud enough for Patty to come running.

'Connie and Robert have had a daughter,' she said.

Patty clapped her hands. 'When was she born, and how heavy is she?'

Alice turned back to the telephone and asked the questions. There was silence. 'I don't know.'

'He doesn't know, Patty.'

Patty tutted. 'There is a set of questions you always ask when someone has a baby, tell him.'

'No need, I heard her,' came Robert's voice in her ear.

'Has she got a name, Robert?'

'Yes, her name is Sylvia. Connie told me to tell you and that you would understand, Alice.'

'Oh yes, Robert, I understand perfectly, and thank you,' she said, putting down the earpiece.

Chapter Twenty-Nine

December 1922

By December 1922, Luke had earned a report to be proud of from his teacher at school. He had proved good at sport and was captain of the school football team. He could often supply useful suggestions over matters of handiwork in his woodwork classes.

Whenever Alice paid the Adams a visit, she found them more settled as a family. She might even have said – a perfect family. Luke had embraced the suggestion that he called them Uncle Stephen, Aunty Jean and Mrs A, and every time Alice met up with her, Jean's face was a picture of happiness. She may not have the longed-for baby of her own, but she had a lad that most mothers would be proud of.

The telephone rang and Alice hurried into the hall to answer it.

'Good afternoon, Mrs Latham speaking. Who's calling?'

'Is that you, Alice?'

'Yes, Jean.'

Alice heard her take a long breath above the rattle on the line. 'What is it, Jean?'

'I want to tell you my news, but don't tell anyone else yet.'

Alice became even more curious. There wasn't anything she could think of that would induce so much excitement within Jean except – no, not after all this time?

'Alice, I'm expecting!'

Alice reached out for the chair beside the hatstand. 'You mean you are… you are…' she lowered her voice dramatically, and hissed down the telephone. 'You're pregnant?'

The line went quiet. Alice could imagine Jean nodding her head before realising there was no one there to see. And the tears of happiness.

'Oh, Jean. I'm so pleased for you.'

'I can't believe it, not after all this time. It'll take me some time to get over it. I'm feeling nervous now it seems to be happening. I hope I don't have any of the problems Ginnie had. Fancy getting pregnant and then having a miscarriage. I couldn't bear it.'

'Now don't you go thinking like that. It's not good for the – you know what!' Alice couldn't have been more pleased. How hurt Jean must have been during the last three years to be childless. She thanked the Lord that it would soon be over.

Alice nodded. 'Jean, I'm going now. Walter's here. Thank you for telling me. I'll speak to you soon. Bye for now.'

She was delighted when she walked into the kitchen. Patty gawped at her. 'What's going on? I conner make up me mind if it's good news or bad.'

It was Patty's last remark that made her realise she was crying. 'Jean Adams is going to have a baby – after all this time. You can imagine what she must be feeling, Patty – she's over the moon. But don't tell anybody – she's asked me not to.'

Patty's hands went straight to her face. 'Oh, my word. She'll be that pleased. When's it due?'

'Oh, I never asked. How stupid of me.'

–

The next day, the telephone rang. Patty was busy fighting with the pastry for the meat pie, so Alice ran to answer it. It stopped ringing before she had the chance to pick it up. She wondered whether to wait in case the person rang back. She was just about ready to return to the kitchen when it rang again. Alice picked it up with the usual greeting.

'Is that… oh, it doesn't sound like you, Alice. I wonder if I've got the wrong number.'

'Jean? Jean, stop talking. It's me – Alice. You've got the right number. Whatever's the matter?'

Alice listened to Jean.

'It's Luke. He must've heard me talking to you on the telephone and he… well… he seems to have disappeared.'

'Disappeared? Why should you think that?'

'I don't know. I think he may feel threatened about our new arrival. I didn't realise he was in the house when I told you. Don't forget, he's not used to living with other kids and those he's met haven't been too good to him. I'm so worried about him, Alice.'

'You think Luke would leave because you were having a baby?'

'Yes! No! I don't know. I haven't told him yet. He might've heard me talking to you.'

'He's not at the depot, is he?'

'No, Stephen's checked everywhere and we've searched the house from top to bottom. Stella's had a go at Stephen for not bringing him home, but he says Luke left early because he wanted to do something on his way.'

Alice closed her eyes. If he had heard the news, he might well be upset they'd said nothing and wonder why he'd been left out.

'We'll have a wander around here and check a few places he goes. We'll stay in touch, Jean.'

By ten o'clock that night, Luke still hadn't got home.

–

On Saturday at teatime, there was a knock on the kitchen door at Marsh Avenue. Alice and Walter looked at each other, and they both looked at Jock, who was lying in his basket, not making a sound and his tail thumping.

'I know who this is,' said Patty, jumping out of her chair. 'Come in!'

The door opened to admit a sorry-looking Luke. Jock bounded towards him, and Luke bent over to give him a fuss so he wouldn't have to look at Alice and Patty.

Alice folded her arms. 'I thought it might be you. Where have you been? Jean's frantic. She thinks you've run away.'

'I was going to.'

'What stopped you?' asked Patty.

'Summat you said. You told me I had to stay and face my problems and that I conner just run away from everything.'

'So you listen to me sometimes then?' Patty stood, hands on hips.

'What happened, Luke?' asked Alice.

'I was coming down the stairs from my room when I heard Aunty Jean tell somebody she was pregnant.' He glanced at Patty and flushed at the word. 'It surprised me, but I was eager cos I'd never had a brother or sister. Then, Aunty Jean said the person wasn't to tell nobody yet, so I assumed it'd be bad news for me.'

'Why should you think that?'

'Stands to reason. They've always wanted a baby of their own and they were excited now Aunty Jean was going to have one. Why would they want to keep somebody like me? They dunner know me from Adam.'

'Where did you go?'

'I walked along the railway line and found my old shed, but more of the roof had fallen down and the tarpaulins had gone missing. I decided I'd best not go home that evening, as they'd be mad at me. I didn't know what to do, so I set off toward Burslem and made my way here. That was last night. When I got here, I couldn't bring myself to knock, with it being late, so I climbed in through a window in one of the new houses without glass and found a sheltered place to spend the night.'

'You were only across the road?'

'Yes, but as the night went on, I became more ashamed of what I'd done. This morning, I set off to Stoke. I was going to get a lift on a narrowboat anywhere. I was sure I could find someone who wanted summat done for some food and shelter, but there weren't many boats moving today. Anyroad, I was going to stow away on a coal barge when the captain found me and gave me a clip around the ear. That's why I'm so dirty. I had cleared a comfortable area on the coal to spend the night.'

'That was a dangerous thing to do,' said Walter. 'People do that in coal wagons, and before they know it, they tip them out into a furnace or drop twenty tons of coal on them.'

'Don't say that, Walter. You're frightening him,' said Alice.

'Yes, and he needs to know it's not safe.'

Luke seemed to enjoy the warmth of the kitchen. Alice suggested he take a warm bath, and when he finished, there'd be some tea for him.

Luke rose. 'Dunner telephone Aunty Jean. I conner go back tonight.'

'I'll get some towels and run the bath.' Patty and Luke went upstairs.

'What shall we do, Walter?'

'Well, I can't see any value in taking him home tonight. I'm on nights, so by the time he's had something to eat, you'd get back late. If Jean had told the lad as soon as she knew, then he probably wouldn't feel so bad. But not telling him made him jump to all the wrong conclusions.'

'I agree. I don't want to take him back tonight, and I want to have a word with him. He can't keep running away when things don't go according to plan.'

Patty walked into the kitchen. She had Luke's clothes in her hands. 'Don't worry, Alice, I told him to get undressed and leave his clothes outside the door. I left it a good few minutes, and the next time I checked, they were there. They're covered in coal dust, so I'll just wash and dry them on the clothes rack. Shouldn't take too long.'

'What do you make of him, Patty?'

'Well, if it was my brother, I'd box his ears. The trouble is he's been used to his own way, and if things don't go as he wants, he's always been able to move on. I don't think he's grasped what being a member of a family involves.'

'That sounds rather philosophical, Patty.'

'I don't think I was trying to be. All I meant was when I lived at home, my brothers and sisters would drive me mad. We argued, and sometimes even old Rex had to bark at us. But none of us ever ran away, that's what I meant.'

'Well, when he's finished his bath and had something to eat, we'll see if we get some sense into him. I never planned to have a dog, but I ended up with one. I'm blowed if I'm going to end up with a lad in the same way.'

The following morning, Alice popped her head around the door to Luke's bedroom. She told herself she was making sure he was all right, but she wanted to satisfy herself he was still there.

Half an hour later, he made his way downstairs, rubbing eyes that looked red and sore. Instead of having a go at him, she sat with him while he ate porridge and two slices of toast cooked on the range.

She reiterated the need for him to think about his family now he was no longer alone. He had friends, and all of them would listen if he needed someone to talk to.

Luke was quiet all the way home. Now the time had come to explain himself to Jean and Stephen, he looked nervous, his breath getting increasingly jagged.

Together, they walked up to the front door. Alice took off her gloves and thrust them into her pocket.

She looked at him. 'Ready?'

Luke nodded.

Alice knocked on the door.

Jean appeared to wrench the door open, then burst into tears when she saw them. She threw her arms around him and hugged him until he could scarcely breathe. She looked every bit the mother welcoming back her prodigal son.

'Come in, come in, Luke. Don't stand out there in the cold.'

Stephen must have heard them speaking, because he was by Jean's side in the blink of an eye.

'Luke, my boy, welcome home. Where the devil have you been?' Stephen took Luke's hand as if to shake it. Instead, he grabbed it and pulled him close.

'I'm sorry if I've worried you both. I didn't mean to.'

'Come in and sit yerself down,' Stephen insisted. He guided Luke to the table. Jean turned to Alice and mumbled the words, "Thank you."

Luke let his bag slide from his shoulder and opened it, rummaging inside. He took out a parcel and handed it to Jean.

'What is it?'

'A Christmas present. A keepsake. For you and the babe.'

Tears filled Jean's eyes. 'You didn't have to.'

'I wanted to. I've treated you both badly, and I wanted to make up.'

'Just seeing you back here, where you belong, is all the present I need. Now, have you had anything to eat, Luke?'

He nodded his head. 'Yes, Alice made some porridge and toast.'

At that moment, Stella walked in. Her face lit up when she saw Luke's tall frame standing between Jean and Stephen.

'Luke! You've come back to us.' Luke reddened. He crossed the room and fell into her open arms. 'Dear Luke. Where have you been?'

'I was meaning to come back, Mrs A. It just got more difficult as the hours passed.'

'Sit yerself down, Mother,' said Stephen.

Luke's face had lost some of the tiredness as he talked. He looked at home, relaxed, as if he'd never been away, thought Alice, smiling.

‘Thank you again for the gift, Luke. Do you mind if I put it under the Christmas tree with the other presents?’

‘It’s more of a homecoming present than a Christmas present, but it’s yours and you can open it whenever you like.’

‘Thank you. Now then, Luke. Do you feel able to tell us what’s happened since we last saw you? Take your time. You don’t have to rush.’

He nodded. ‘When I first came here, I heard you talking to Alice, saying as how much you wanted a baby of your own. Your friends had all got kids, and you, who had prayed for one so much, were probably never going to welcome your own kid into the house.’

There was a blank look on Jean’s face as she tried to make sense of Luke’s words. ‘Yes, and it was such a relief to find I was going to have one of my own. But I don’t see…’

Luke’s hands twisted together on his lap. In a small voice, he said, ‘But you’d got me, Aunty Jean. I thought that when the babe arrived, you wouldn’t need me. I mean – why would you – once your own flesh and blood arrived in the world? I decided I’d go under my own steam rather than be told to leave.’

‘How on earth could you come to that conclusion, Luke?’

‘It’s how I felt. Nobody had wanted me before.’

‘Dearest Luke, never in all this world did I, we, ever consider telling you to leave because I was expecting. You and the baby were never, ever replacements for each other.’

‘We look at you as our son, Luke,’ said Stephen, blinking. ‘We didn’t want to call you that in case it put you under too much pressure. I mean, you might have preferred to be a lodger with no strings attached. You’re doing well at the garage, and I rely on you. We would never throw you out.’

Stella gave a brief smile and then became serious. ‘It looks to me we’ve each put our own thoughts on what the situation was within this household and come up with different conclusions. For the record, I’d like to say that I should be very disappointed if you decide to leave us, Luke. You helped me in my time of need, for which I shall always be grateful.’

'I've missed you so much, Luke,' said Jean, her eyes brimming. 'I sat by the front window last night, looking out, hoping you'd come back, but fearing you wouldn't.'

'Luke, you're part of this family, our family,' smiled Mrs A, rubbing his head gently.

Alice slipped out quietly as the four made their peace. How easy it was to get the wrong impression when the right impression mattered so much. It was a lesson well learned for all of them. She wiped her eyes more than once as she made her way home.

Chapter Thirty

December 1922

Four years after the signing of the Armistice, the PTC erected a plaque at their head office to the men who lost their lives. It was an emotional moment for everyone who had worked there at the time, and no one would forget it.

It was Ruth's idea to arrange a reunion for all the women who kept the PTC going during that time. Their jobs ended when the war ended. Many would remain friends afterwards, but for some, that would not be possible. Ruth, who still worked as a cashier for the PTC, had asked Mr Taylor if it would cause any problems. After quizzing her, he agreed and even made a contribution towards the cost. Although Alice had never been a tram girl, she was roped in to help by Ruth, standing in for Connie.

The event was to take place on the evening of 23 December as a Christmas reunion. Alice, and tram girls Ruth, Jean, Molly, Madge, Pearl, Carla and Daisy spent the afternoon preparing the King's Hall for the reunion. Much as she had enjoyed working with them, Alice felt exhaustion beginning to creep in as the event drew near.

Ruth had persuaded Stan to use his van to carry everything to Stoke, and he made a quick call to collect from Marsh Avenue and from Pearl's in Corporation Street. Once everything and everyone had arrived, they began setting out the tables and chairs left out for them.

'Now then, ladies, have we thought of everything?' asked Ruth.

Each of them glanced around the large ballroom. Alice smiled. Christmas garlands, streamers and candlelight decorated the room, and a giant tree stood in one corner, decorated to within an inch of its life. She could barely contain herself. How lovely that the reunion should take place at Christmas – the best time of the year. She felt like dancing.

'It looks grand,' said Molly, arms folded. 'Are we ready to open them doors?'

Ruth glanced around the room. 'I think so. If you would like to have a seat for half an hour to get your breath back, you can open the door. You and Daisy can welcome our guests. Before we do anything else, I'd like to thank you all for your hard work for making it all happen.'

'You're very welcome, Ruth,' said Pearl. 'We make a good team – if I may say so. And many thanks to Alice for helping out too.'

Alice blushed. She couldn't convey how proud she was to be included.

When Molly opened the heavy oak doors, she found half a dozen women waiting, chattering away to each other.

'Welcome, everyone. It's good to see you. Trust you to be one of the first to arrive, Cissie.'

'Had to try, didn't I?'

They laughed together as the six women made their way into the hall.

It wasn't long before it was filled and the chattering had grown louder. Alice was eager to meet Betty again, who she hadn't seen for ages, as she was still living in Birmingham while her daughter, Hannah, continued to live in The Potteries with her grandmother.

Alice stationed herself beside the food table as the room filled until she wondered whether they would all fit in.

Betty, now used to public speaking, gave the opening address. Although she had only attended one planning meeting, she secured some additional funding and had promised to get someone to talk to the assembled women on their futures, both in and outside of the company.

Betty made her way to the front of the hall and stood on the stage, and clapped her hands for silence.

'Good afternoon, everyone, and welcome to the King's Hall. Today we're celebrating the splendid work we did for the Potteries Tramway Company during the Great War. For many of us, it was a time when we found out something new about ourselves. Four years have passed since it ended, and four years have passed since many of us had to give up our jobs to allow demobilised soldiers to return to their former positions. Some of us were lucky enough to remain.' Betty smiled and glanced around the hall. 'Take the time to meet up with old friends you may not have seen since you left – and also make new acquaintances. During this brief get-together, spare a thought for our colleagues who didn't return and to whom we owe a great deal.'

Betty stopped talking. There was silence, and then rapturous applause.

'I'd now like to introduce you to a good friend of mine. Her name is Jessie O'Neill. She lives and works in Birmingham, where she helps trades unions who are trying to support women in employment. It was down to her we had some extra funds to allow this day to take place. Ladies, my friend and colleague, Jessie O'Neill.'

There was tremendous applause as Jessie stepped forward and took Betty's place on the stage.

'Thank you, ladies, for your warm welcome. It was a pleasure to receive the invitation to come to talk to you today, and I was happy to contribute towards it. I work with trades unions based in and around the Birmingham area, and part of my job is to talk to women about joining their appropriate trade union and how it can help them get fair treatment at work. We recruit both women and men and help them sort out issues. If anyone here would like to talk to me today, then please come to find me and I'll answer any questions. Who knows, we might even recruit some of you to help your fellow workers. Thank you for listening to me. I hope you enjoy this opportunity to meet again and to celebrate happier times.'

Jessie stepped down and Ruth invited everyone to eat.

Alice was asked to compare the number of women who had agreed to come along with the number who turned up. It was more difficult than it sounded, as the women moved around the room as they found friends to talk to.

She had tried to complete the count three times, but had been interrupted. Then she spied none other than Peggy Thompson standing on her own, sipping from a glass of what looked like sherry.

Alice remembered Peggy, a mischief-maker who had caused Ruth some heartache and who the PTC sacked over a personal matter that included Ruth. Alice made her way over to Ruth, who was talking to Jessie. Her anxiety must have shown, because Ruth stopped talking.

'What is it, Alice?'

'Can I have a word with you?'

Ruth made her excuses and walked away with Alice.

'You'll never guess who's here.'

'Who do you mean, Alice?'

'I've just seen Peggy Thompson.'

Ruth drew in a sharp breath. 'She never responded to the letter, according to this list. I wonder what she wants. Leave it with me, Alice.'

Alice followed Ruth as she walked over to Peggy, who hadn't seen them approach. 'Hello, Peggy. I wasn't expecting you,' said Ruth, arms folded.

'Hello, Ruth.' Now she was close up, Alice could see the paleness in Peggy's face. 'Before you say anything, I'm not here to cause trouble.'

'So, why are you here?'

Peggy's hand went up to her hair to smooth it. A nervous reaction from someone who doesn't know what to do with their hands, thought Alice. The woman looked quite uncomfortable.

'I want to give my apologies to you, Ruth. I was a pig to you. I know that. I want to explain.'

'It wasn't just me, though, was it?' Ruth narrowed her eyes. 'You were horrible to Carla.'

'And I want to apologise to her too. I thought today would be a good day to catch both of you.'

'Alice, would you mind finding Carla Hesse for me? We'll be in the kitchen. It'll be private in there.'

'Of course.'

Alice found Carla and sent her to the kitchen. She would just have to wait to find out what Peggy wanted to say.

After around twenty minutes, the three women came out of the kitchen, and Ruth came straight over to Alice to tell her that Peggy had apologised, but Ruth was keen to inform her of some other news from Peggy.

'It was the next bit which surprised us the most. You know the PTC sacked Peggy because of an argument with me, amongst other things.'

'Yes.'

'And you know all about Dennis Laycock, who absconded with a load of money from the PTC, and that he was Peggy's uncle.'

'Yes. Dennis was the one who abandoned his wife.'

'We all thought so, but it turned out Dennis had been meticulous in his planning. He travelled to Queenstown in Ireland and caught a boat to America a few days later.'

'So he did abandon her.'

'Peggy's Aunty Kathleen made sure she told everyone that she wasn't getting any separation allowance for him being in the army. When the police interviewed her, that was her cue to leave. She played the part of a deserted wife returning to her parents in Sligo, and she fled within the day. She was carrying most of the money Dennis had taken. They had arranged to meet in Queenstown to catch a boat to America. But she never turned up.'

'So what happened to Dennis?'

'They had already agreed to travel separately. Dennis wanted to be out of the reach of the police. He was expecting a letter telling him of Kathleen's arrival, but nothing came. He was running out of money and unable to come back. Dennis is in America. Kathleen disappeared with the money. No one, not even her family, has any idea where she is. She got the last laugh. All Dennis's hard work gave him nothing. He's living in New York on the Lower East Side, where many migrants settled. But I bet there aren't many from The Potteries.'

'Well, I never!'

–

The afternoon progressed without further excitement. Alice circulated with trays of mince pies and caught snippets of conversation as she walked around. She couldn't help but chortle to herself as voices got louder as each woman tried to make herself heard. It was a pity Connie was so far away, and with a new baby and a toddler. She would've loved it. It could even become a regular event.

Many of the women remembered Alice as living with Connie and wanted to know how Connie was. Apparently, several women had had their eyes on Robert Caldwell. How lucky it'd been for Connie that she was the one who caught him! Alice wondered if Robert had been aware how sought after he was.

Among the happy, smiling faces, there were tears, as the future for some women hadn't been the happy one they were expecting. At least twelve women had left domestic service to become clippies and had had their eyes opened to what women could do with their lives.

Friends reported that when they refused to go back into service, they were told they wouldn't be eligible for financial help. So the majority of them returned to service, where most employers refused them time off to attend the reunion. What a sad state of affairs.

All too soon, it was time to pack everything away. Alice, together with Molly and Madge, took everything through to the kitchen, removing the uneaten food, and packing that which was untouched in boxes to give to people as they left.

Gradually, the women departed, waving their goodbyes and promising to keep in touch. Some were tearful and had to be guided towards the door.

What a day it'd been! Alice had enjoyed every minute. The committee members gathered together into one enormous hug, congratulating each other on their achievements throughout the day, and drew Alice and Ruth's sister-in-law-to-be, Rosie, who had also helped, into the circle. Their euphoria was so strong that there was even talk about organising something else the following year.

The three women collected together their own bags and were saying their goodbyes when Walter sauntered in, hands in his pockets.

'I came to escort you home, dearest one,' he whispered in Alice's ear, causing her to blush. 'Do you have anything for me to carry?'

Alice had put two bags to one side and pointed to them. She was ready to go home. Ruth volunteered to stay until everyone was ready to leave and she could give her key to the caretaker.

Once outside, Alice glanced up at the sky. It was a dark orange colour, something she was used to seeing above the buildings in and around Stoke. She linked her arm through Walter's and sang 'Hark! The Herald Angels Sing' under her breath.

Walter said nothing. Just listened.

'I like to hear you sing,' he murmured when she had finished.

'I enjoy singing. It's one reason I love Christmas so much. And we're celebrating in our own house. I couldn't be happier. Oh, look…'

Alice was looking up at the sky, marvelling at the snow slowly drifting down. 'It's beautiful. A perfect end to a perfect day.'

Walter coughed and cleared his throat. 'Sorry to disappoint you, my love. It's not snowing. That's the white ash from Shelton Bar steelworks.'

'Oh, Walter! You should've kept that to yourself.'

'There's always tomorrow!'

Walter took hold of Alice's arm and pulled her towards him, placing his lips on hers. 'I love you so much, darling Alice. I'll do my best to book some snow this Christmas.'

Chapter Thirty-One

Christmas 1922

A beaming Elizabeth arrived at Marsh Avenue just after dinner on Christmas Eve. The skittering of crunchy snow on the ground could have been much worse, and Alice was relieved that her mother had made the journey safely. This would be the first Christmas that she and Elizabeth had spent together, and Alice was anxious that everything went well.

Tomorrow there would be a full house at Marsh Avenue, but for now there would just be the three of them. Patty had insisted on making their tea before returning to her parents, where she'd be on Christmas morning to see her family open their presents.

Alice and Elizabeth embraced. They had grown closer together over the last few months and felt comfortable in each other's presence. Alice carried her mother's bag up to her room.

'Where is Walter?' asked Elizabeth.

'He's taken Jock for a walk; he'll be back soon.'

'I should have guessed.'

'Oh yes, I don't know who was more eager when there was a covering of snow this morning – Walter or Jock.'

Elizabeth placed presents under the Christmas tree in the corner. Alice and Patty had made all the tree decorations. They looked splendid in the early afternoon sunshine.

'Hello, Elizabeth.' It was Walter. He'd left Jock in the scullery to dry and rest. Alice was so pleased that the misgivings Walter had about her mother seemed to have disappeared. They got on well, made all the easier by her relaxed manner.

They had a light dinner, and there was time for a brief rest before Alice and Patty finished the baking. The puddings were already made, the cake decorated and the bird delivered; all that could be prepared in advance had been.

'Patty and I are going to spend the afternoon baking. Will you be all right on your own?'

'Yes, I have a book to read—'

'I bought you a pinafore, Elizabeth. It's more like a coat. It will keep your clothes clean.'

'But, my dear Patty, I have never cooked or baked anything in my life. I shall be a hindrance to you.'

'No, you won't. There are plenty of things you can do.'

Elizabeth looked at Alice, and they both looked at Patty.

'You'll enjoy it. Like my mother says, "You're never too old to learn summat new."'

They all burst into laughter.

'Who am I to say no!' said Elizabeth. Needless to say, the giggles continued all afternoon.

Time flew by. Elizabeth looked as if she had enjoyed herself. Her face had turned bright red in the heat of the kitchen.

In the evening, Walter, along with Jock, accompanied Patty to Jackfield Street. When he returned, both mother and daughter were fast asleep.

'Alice, wake up,' whispered Walter.

'Oh, I've only got my eyes closed. I wasn't asleep.'

'If you say so.'

Elizabeth woke up and smiled at Walter as if she too had been resting her eyes.

'I must remember that you both snore while you're "resting your eyes"'.

–

Patty had promised to be back by twelve on Christmas Day to help Alice with the meal, which they would eat around four o'clock, after which presents would be opened. The

Goodwin household, like many others with children, would be chaotic, with presents opened no later than eight o'clock in the morning. Hence the reasoning behind Patty's swift return to work.

Walter and Patty worked well, moving furniture and extending the dining table. By the time Alice had made breakfast, Elizabeth had joined them.

'Now, Alice. Is there anything I can do to help?' asked Elizabeth, smiling.

'I don't think so. Patty's joining us around twelve, and everything's prepared. There has been more snow overnight. Walter, can you clear a path through to the gate before dinner? I would hate for someone to have a fall.'

He nodded and slipped into his thick coat, giving her a quick salute before disappearing into the swirls of snow still falling. She needn't have worried; the snow stopped soon after he started shovelling. She got most of what she wanted to do finished by the time Patty arrived, and Alice allowed her a small glass of sherry.

'How many are we expecting, Alice?' asked Patty. 'You could feed the five thousand with all of this!'

Alice laughed. 'Remember, Patty, better to have too much than not enough.'

The two stepped up their pace, and everything was ready.

At just before three o'clock, Frank and Joan with their four were first to arrive, with Joan shouting to them all to wipe their feet before going in. They had brought with them a small toy each, and it wasn't long before the four of them plus Walter and Frank were playing football in the snow. Alice didn't blame them. Jock barked at the back door to join the fun, and Patty let him out. He was very excited, chasing everyone. Alice wondered for the first time whether the dog missed the company of children.

Next to arrive were Jean and Stephen, Stella and Luke. They had taken a taxi because of the snow, and safety for Stella and

Jean. Stephen was taking no chances. Ginnie and Sam and their two boys, Young Sam and baby James, arrived next, along with Walter's father Herbert and his wife Jane. A van pulled up outside the house, to reveal Stan and Ruth.

'I thought you would be on Gertie today,' said Walter.

'Ruth stopped at ours last night, but the snow put paid to using the motorcycle, and the van's warmer.'

Alice's house was indeed a merry place to be, with lots of singing, games, and such going on. Snowball fights in the garden produced wet little people, and clothes steamed on the rack as they dried out prior to the walk home.

She wondered what Jean was thinking about her last Christmas without a child. She had noted mothers pushing perambulators in the town. Her hand rested on her stomach for just a moment as she wondered how it would feel to have a new life growing inside her.

As she stood in the kitchen watching the excitement outside, Elizabeth walked up behind her. Her eyes followed Alice's.

'Ah, Alice dear, I recognise that look on your face. I've worn it many times myself.'

'But I thought—'

'I may not have married, Alice, but it didn't mean I never wanted another child of my own.'

'I'm so sorry.'

'Don't be. I have my child right here beside me, and I couldn't be happier.'

The adults sat around the dining table. The children would use the kitchen table, and she volunteered Patty to supervise it. Luke joined her without hesitation, so the adults had the dining room to themselves.

The meal was a success, and Alice smiled at Patty. 'I was right about the amount of food,' she said.

It was a glorious Christmas! Much had changed over the past couple of years. Never had Alice thought she would be married and living in her own house, contemplating starting a family of her own. Was that why she was so keen to find her family – and why she was so happy to have children around her?

She turned to Elizabeth, her eyes filling with tears. 'I am so thankful that I found you, Elizabeth. In searching for you, I think I've found myself.'

Elizabeth blinked twice. 'Thank you, my darling.' They threw their arms around each other.

Walter appeared and placed his arms around both of them. 'What's this crying about? It's supposed to be a happy time, isn't it?'

The two women looked at each other, each with a handkerchief at the ready.

'I believe your wife needs your company right now.'

'Are you feeling all right, Alice?'

'Never better,' she replied. 'We have all had so much to be thankful for this year. I'm thinking of all the gifts we've had. Not the presents under the tree – although they are lovely. I'm thinking of the gifts we've received in creating our families. I've found not one, but two families. Jean has adopted a son and is about to have a child of her own. Ruth and Stan are about to get married. Connie and Robert are building their family, as Frank and Joan already have. Don't you see – it's all about love and family. What better gift could you wish for?'

'I'll drink to that,' said Walter, lifting his glass. 'To families everywhere!'

Epilogue

25 December 1928

We have eaten our Christmas dinner, and Walter and Jock are fast asleep on the settee in front of the fire. I can see into the garden from where I am sitting and am pleased to say that, through Walter's hard work, and with the help of a gardener, it's turned from a building site into something I am proud of. It has been snowing since dinnertime – proper snow, not ash from Shelton Bar. Remember the comment Walter made when we were walking back from the PTC reunion?

It has been a special year for the women of this country. Following the introduction of the Equal Franchise Act this year, women may vote in next year's general election. Who would have thought it would take so long to fight for what is right and fair? Of course, Connie was ecstatic with the news. When we marched through London in 1913, neither of us expected to be voting for the first time some sixteen years later.

We have become good friends over the years, and I'm sure you would like to hear the latest news from The Potteries.

My twins, Jessica and Walter, were born in 1924 and will be five years old next June. How strange to think they will go to school next autumn. Their arrival surprised me, for there were no twins on either side of our families that I knew of. I can still remember the day they were born. How small and fragile they looked. I frightened myself with the responsibility I'd taken on. We were not planning to have a nanny, but having two babies at the same time made me realise I needed the help that Patty volunteered without a second thought. Of course, it worked out very well, and both children look on her as a big sister. It might be difficult once Patty marries, but at this stage, there does not seem to be anyone special in her life – I am sure that will not last for long. She's a very attractive young lady.

Connie telephones most weeks. She and Robert are enjoying life in Norfolk. I have travelled down to see them on two occasions, and as much as I can appreciate the fresh air, I find the countryside quite flat and isolated. Both times I was glad to return to The Potteries. She has three daughters now. Apart from Sylvia, there's Anne and Emily. I can see a theme running through the family, and if she has another daughter, I am sure she will call her Charlotte. John Robert is eight, and wants a brother. When the family came for a visit in the summer, I was surprised to see how much he had grown. He takes after Robert.

Robert is thriving in the bracing wind that often runs along the Norfolk coast. He got his own way in the end and has a lovely black Labrador called Shadow. They spend a lot of time together, walking the pathways around the marshes and up onto the farmland. He has become friendly with a widower who, along with his son, fishes along the coast. Robert enjoys helping them. The dog and the fishing give him a reason to be outside, and his chest appears to have benefited from it.

They still live in their rented house, but they will have to move in 1930 when the owner retires to England from the Indian Civil Service. Connie says she'll miss the house, but is sure they'll find something nice once they look.

Thinking of Connie brings regrets. I haven't seen Agatha Copeland since Christmas 1921. I wish I could talk to her, but Connie says to let sleeping dogs lie. I don't know if Agatha will ever forgive me for being who I am.

Jean has a little girl called Mary. She is a year older than the twins and has just completed her first term at school. Luke got his apprenticeship at the PTC and dotes on his little sister. He seems to have changed his attitude towards education and is doing very well. He still comes to visit us, but not as often as before. He has formed a firm friendship with Patty and, despite my earlier worries, they seem to act like brother and sister when together, but defer to Patty if challenged.

The last tram in The Potteries ran on 11 July this year. Much to Stan and Ruth's annoyance, the PTC is now running bus services along some routes operated by their own company, Bristow's Buses. They had borrowed money from Elizabeth and me to get the company started and had paid it all back earlier this year. Stan has also branched into haulage, where he can make use of his drivers. Ruth runs the office and helps as a clippie. They have a mix of men and women conductors and, last year, employed their first lady driver, Doris Barlow, one of the first clippies back in 1915. Luke says he'll join Bristow's once he's completed his apprenticeship and is free to leave the PTC.

Ruth's sister-in-law, Rosie, was on track to dedicate her life to education, but she mentioned to me a few days ago that she'll work for the War Office in the new year, doing something with mathematics, I think. She went to Newnham College in Cambridge, where she got a degree in mathematics and, just this year, she received her doctorate. How strange to address her as Dr Rosemary Bristow!

Ruth and Carla's school friend and former landlady, Dottie Spilling, who lost her husband during the war, surprised all of us in 1923 by marrying Thomas Walton. They moved to Canada using a scheme similar to the one Betty's brother Daniel used at the end of the war. Ruth gets occasional letters from Dottie. She enjoys the country life. Ruth always remarks that she loved her little allotment – but several hundred acres of Canadian prairies seems excessive!

Betty's friend, Martha Owen, has become a noted designer of pottery for Paradise Pottery. She married Jonas Gray in 1924, and they have two children, a boy, Joshua, and a girl, Emmeline. Mrs Owen (now Munro) and her daughter Issy own a successful business – Mrs Parker's Pies – and have seven shops in The Potteries and Newcastle and a kitchen in Shelton where they make everything. Betty's brother, Michael, also works at the company.

Carla and Bertie Hesse obtained visas for their parents to return to Britain. It took until 1926 for matters to be sorted. Unfortunately, Mr Hesse died of a heart attack only a few months after he came back. The rest of the family still live in Stoke, and Luther now has a sister, Elise, who has just turned two.

My brother-in-law Frank and his wife Joan are still working their way towards the cricket team, which continues to be his stated aim. He is funny when you get to know him, and despite getting older, his enthusiasm for the game has not diminished. They now have six children. As Walter puts it, they have the batsmen, and now they just need a wicketkeeper and four bowlers. Poor Joan, I doubt she has the same dream! Walter's father and Jane are getting on well. I like her because behind her formal façade, she has quite a sense of humour and keeps him on his toes.

Betty, what can I say about Betty? She's still single and still living in Birmingham and seems no nearer to finding a man. Her mother still looks after Hannah, who depends on her rather than Betty. Jessie and Betty were very active during the general strike in 1926. Her letters talk at length about her work and mention very little about her daughter. When I last saw Betty, she said she was going to apply for a job with the Ceramic and Allied Trades Union, or CATU for short, who are active in The Potteries, but nothing came of it as far as I know. Sadly, any chance she had with Duncan has gone – I read a wedding report in *The Sentinel*. I think that was in 1924.

Hannah, now thirteen, will leave school in the summer. She's a rather independent girl, having seen so little of her mother. I would say she has become the last child of Mr and Mrs Dean rather than Betty's kin. Hannah always appreciated that her mother had to work to support her, and she loved having brothers and sisters. In fact, it would be harder to allow Hannah to return to her mother than keep things as they are.

Ginnie and Sam White call regularly with their three. Sam is thriving and has become a valued employee in the Parks Department, especially since the borough achieved city status in 1925. Ginnie and Sam always lived from hand to mouth, but she is one of Connie's best friends, and I promised that I'd help them out if they should ever need it. It's amazing how Ginnie keeps the children so smartly dressed on her meagre resources.

Ginnie's sister, Mabel, had married for a second time after losing her first husband in the war. Everybody, including her new husband, Mr Bossons, and probably Mabel herself, was surprised when she had her second child last year. Her daughter, Florrie, from her first marriage, wants to be a nurse, but she just turned fourteen and will probably change her mind a few times yet.

Walter left the pit in 1924 and joined the staff at the technical college, where he teaches safety, mining geology, and the use of explosives. It pays less, but he only goes down a pit a few times a year. Although I would never tell him, I was so glad when he decided. And Jock, what can I say about him? He's turned out to be a pleasure to own. He loves the children, and they play with him for hours. He has boundless energy. But as I write this, he's fast asleep with Walter and neither looks capable of anything involving movement.

What can I tell you about me during the last six years? Apart from having the twins, I have somehow slipped into a similar life that Elizabeth described to me back in that December meeting in Manchester. I am on various committees, and like Mrs Copeland, I help with fundraising and am on the committee of the Stoke-on-Trent Hospital for the Poor, which is just the workhouse with a new name. I enjoy the work. It's disheartening to find that life for the poor has changed so little over the years. I often took Ginnie along on my visits, and in 1925, the hospital appointed her as a trustee.

When I started on my journey to find my family, I knew very few people. Looking at what I've written today, I see I know so many. It is a joy for me to read. I hope I shall continue to see the people who've come into my life and be thankful that I have found my family too. It hasn't turned out like I thought it would but, thanks to Elizabeth, I've no money worries and can care for the new family Walter and I are building.

Oh yes, Elizabeth. She made the move from Knutsford to The Potteries in 1923. She wanted to be closer to us, and I was surprised at how happy that made me. She lives in one of the other houses built by Mr O'Donnell and regularly pops around to see us. She was here to see the birth of her grandchildren, and they love her.

I should think of something more to do with my life. At the beginning of the Great War, everyone seemed to pull together. The Britain of 1928 seems to have returned to the class system with a vengeance. Having all this spare time on my hands gives plenty of opportunity to read, and I have become quite addicted to modern history. The occasional chat with Betty and Jessie brings an understanding that there must be something more I can do with my life, not to remain a lady of leisure, but as a valued member of the community.

But to tell you the truth, I can say that I have found my way in life over the years and have discovered what really matters. It's not a job in the true sense of the word. It's caring for my family. The family that Walter and I built – and nothing can be more important to me than that.

Alice Latham
Christmas, 1928

A letter from Lynn

Hi everyone. I would like to offer a huge thanks to you all for reading this, the final book in the Potteries Girls series. Many of you have stayed with me and got to know Ginnie, Connie, Betty, Martha, Ruth, Alice and the lovely Jean, herself a former tram girl. I have enjoyed creating these stories set in the very real world of the Staffordshire Potteries. The places referred to are real, but all the characters are friends from inside my head and I love them all.

Throughout the books, I have concentrated largely on the position of women in society and how they took on the challenge of a male-dominated world when they were called upon, only to be thrust back into the home when the war ended. I sped ahead six years at the end of the book because I wanted to show what had happened to our friends by the time the vote was open to all women on the same basis as men. Who would have thought it would take over thirty years from the setting up of the National Union of Women's Suffrage Societies in 1897 for that to happen? Unfortunately, it would take another ninety years for women to get paid equally for doing the same work as men.

It seems incredible to me that this book was written during the 50th Anniversary year of the two major pieces of legislation – the Equal Pay Act and the Sex Discrimination Act. It was due to these two Acts that equality of opportunity became a right for all disadvantaged groups. Working in human resources, as I did at the end of the twentieth century, I wrote many equal opportunities policies and procedures. I cannot believe that in my third age I am writing books on the self-same subject. It's been hard work, but I have enjoyed creating my stories. It has been a privilege.

Best wishes

Lynn xx

Historical timeline

A brief timeline showing some of the key legislation that commenced during the time of Ginnie and Connie and continued during my own time working as a personnel officer in the 1980s and 1990s:

1897: National Union of Women's Suffrage Societies (NUWSS)

1903: WSPU set up by Emmeline Pankhurst and her daughters – *Deeds not words*.

1918: Representation of the People Act and the Parliament (Qualification of Women) Act allowed women over thirty with property to vote.

1928: Equal Franchise Act – gave women the same voting rights as men.

1929: All women able to go to the polls on the same basis as men.

1948: Universal Declaration of Human Rights adopted by the United Nations set a global framework of Human Rights and freedoms.

1949: Simone de Beauvoir wrote *The Second Sex* on gender equality.

1970: Equal Pay Act was passed prohibited any less favourable treatment between men and women in terms of pay and conditions of employment, but didn't come into force until 1975.

1975: Sex Discrimination Act – setting up the Equal Opportunities Commission.

1983: The Equal Pay (Amendment) Regulations allowed women to claim equal pay for work of equal value.

2025: 50th Anniversary of the Sex Discrimination Act and the coming into force of the Equal Pay Act 1970

Acknowledgements

Over the years of writing the Potteries Girls series, I have relied on research from a number of places, and these have been mentioned in the relevant books. This book is a bringing together of all of those works, and I am pleased to give thanks to those works in completing this book.

As always, my thanks go to Keshini Naidoo at Hera Books for her unwavering support – from choosing to give me my debut contract in 2019 to guiding me through the six books in the series. I would also like to commend Miranda Ward and Lynne Walker for their editing of the book too.

My thanks go to my staunch beta readers, Jacquie Rogers, Lesley Colclough and Amy Louise Blaney, for their ongoing support over the years, not forgetting my two sisters, Carol Blood and Pat Beresford, who have urged me forward through some of the difficult times.

An added bonus this year was that publication coincided with the centenary of the creation of Stoke-on-Trent as a city in 2025. It felt an honour to raise the profile of The Potteries through books, as did so many authors before me.

My family have supported me all the way through my writing years. I only wish my parents could have been with me on the journey. My mother would have loved it. It was through her that I gained my love of reading, particularly historical sagas.

I would not have had the strength to complete the series without the support of my husband, Michael, who has been a stalwart throughout, keeping me on the straight and narrow when I would have strayed. I am indebted to him.